UNFORGOTTEN

Jessica Brody is a bestselling US author of nine novels – two for adults, the rest for teenagers. She works as a full-time author and producer and lives in both Colorado and Los Angeles.

www.jessicabrody.com

D1392294

Books by Jessica Brody

Unremembered
Unforgotten

JESSICA BRODY

UNFORGOTTEN

MACMILLAN

First published in the US 2014 by Farrar Straus Giroux Books for Young Readers

First published in the UK 2014 by Macmillan Children's Books
a division of Macmillan Publishers Limited
20 New Wharf Road, London N1 9RR
Basingstoke and Oxford
Associated companies throughout the world
www.panmacmillan.com

ISBN 978-1-4472-2114-2

1 3 5 7 9 8 6 4 2

A CIP catalogue record for this book is available from
the British Library.

Printed and bound by CPI Group (UK) Ltd, Croydon CR0 4YY

To *Alyson Noël,*
because she might just be superhuman

If time travel is possible, where are the tourists from the future?

– Stephen Hawking

CONTENTS

PART 2: THE INVASION

UNFORGOTTEN

0
ALONE

The fire is hot and relentless, rising up from a thicket of smouldering ash. Lashing at my feet. Filling my eyes with smoky tears of defeat.

The flames hungrily stare me down. Like a wolf licking its lips at the sight of an injured animal. Savouring the promise of a feast. Taking its time before moving in for the kill.

The wood crackles beneath me. One by one, branches are crushed, incinerated to black dust in the path of the merciless blaze. I am its only target. The sole destination. Everything else is a mere stepping-stone along the way. A dispensable victim to demolish and cast aside as it fights its way to me.

I search my surroundings desperately for help. But there is none to be found. Silence answers my distress. Punctuated only by the mocking *fizzle* and *crack* of the flames.

They can't let me die here. Their prized possession left to burn. To shrivel up. To turn to bitter ash. They won't. I'm sure of it.

They will be here soon. They will stop it.

And for the first time in my shallow, abridged memory, I will welcome the sight of them.

The smoke billows up, cloaking everything in a sickly haze. My vision – normally flawless and acute – is gone. My throat swells and burns. I wrench my head to the side, coughing. Choking. Gagging.

One ambitious flame forges ahead of the others. Winning the race to the top. It claws at my bare feet with long, gnarled fingers. I curl my toes under and press hard against the wood at my back. I can already feel my skin start to blister. Bubble. Scream.

And then I fight. Oh, how I fight. Thrashing against my constraints. But it's no use.

And that's when I realize . . . no one is coming.

The fire will consume me. Melt the flesh right off my bones. Turn my entire manufactured existence into nothing but grimy dust to be carried off across the countryside with the slightest breeze.

The wind shifts and the smoke clears for long enough that I can just make out a tall, hooded figure standing alone on the other side of the river. Watching silently.

The fire finally catches my skin. The pain is excruciating. Like a thousand swords slicing through me at once. The scream boils up from somewhere deep within. A place I never knew about. My mouth stretches open on its own. My stomach contracts. And I release the piercing sound upon a city of deaf ears.

PART 1

THE
DISCOVERY

1
PAST

ONE WEEK EARLIER . . .

I roll on to my stomach and clutch the side of the bed, gulping hungrily at the air. The beautiful, fresh, unpolluted oxygen fills my lungs. My blood. My brain. My thoughts come into focus. The gnarled knot in my stomach starts to unravel.

I pound my palm hard against my chest, searching for my heart. Waiting eagerly for its next beat. It feels like hours of stubborn silence pass. My rib cage, an empty chamber.

Until finally . . .

BA-BUMP

BA-BUMP

BA-BUMP

With a sigh, my head drops forward and I put forth a silent offering of gratitude.

When I look up, my vision has cleared and I can see my surroundings.

The austere wooden furnishings of our small bedroom. Cloaked in slowly vanishing darkness. And Zen. Breathing softly beside me. Lying on his stomach. A lock of dark thick hair flung over his left eye. One arm is tucked underneath him and the other is draped across the bed. Saving my place. Completely unaware that I'm no longer there. That I've been replaced by a damp silhouette of sweat.

Still sucking in frenzied breaths, I run my hand across my forehead. It comes back moist.

The light is just starting to break outside, giving the room a faint, ghostly glow.

I eye the empty space next to Zen. The thought of lying back down and closing my eyes again sends my heart into a tempest of banging and sputtering.

I gently rise and walk over to the armoire, easing open the heavy oak door. I slide my arms into Zen's linen doublet and button it over my nightdress. Zen's sweet, musky scent on the jacket immediately starts to calm me as I guide my feet into my leather mules and tiptoe towards the door. The floorboards grumble under my feet and I hear Zen stirring behind me. When I turn around, his endless brown eyes are already open, concern flashing in them. He's watching me, his forehead creased. 'Is everything OK?'

'Of course,' I whisper, certain the tremble in my voice will give me away. 'I . . .' But my throat is dry and thick. I attempt to swallow. 'I had a bad dream. That's all.'

A dream.

Not real.

I repeat it in my mind. Hoping it will sound more believable the second time around. Knowing the one I really have to convince is me.

Zen sits up. The sheets fall to his waist, revealing his bare chest. Beautifully toned from the countless hours of hard labour he's been doing since we arrived here six months ago. 'Same one?'

My lip starts to quiver. I bite it hard and nod.

'Do you want to talk about it?'

I shake my head. But then I see the frustration on his face. His constant need to fix me. And I don't have the heart to tell him that he can't.

'It's no big deal,' I say, breathing the words in an attempt to lighten them. 'It was just . . .'

Ghastly. Horrifying. Real.

I swallow again. 'Unsettling.'

I force a smile on to my face. Praying that Zen can't see my cheeks twitching from across the room. 'I'm just going to go outside and get some fresh air.'

Zen hastily kicks the covers from his legs. 'I'll go with you.'

'No!' I say. Too loudly. Too quickly. Too stupidly.

I attempt to cover with another pathetic excuse for a smile. 'It's OK. Really. I'm fine.'

He studies me for a moment. His probing eyes asking, *Are you sure?*

I'm not sure about anything right now.

But I still find the strength to say, 'Don't worry. Go back to sleep.'

I don't wait to see if he does. It's not the battle I want to fight right now – not when there are much larger ones waging in my mind. I simply turn and leave.

Once outside the house, I walk to the highest point on the property. A grassy knoll that overlooks the pasture in one direction and the wheat field in the other. I sink to the ground and sit with my legs folded awkwardly to the side. The sun is beginning its slow ascent into the sky, reminding me that my time alone out here is limited. The earthly clock is ticking. Soon the world will be awake and I will be who I'm supposed to be.

Not the trembling shell of a person I am right now.

I force myself to focus on the sky. On the sun's determined climb. It happens every day. Without fail. The same arc across the same sky. No matter the country. No matter the century.

The thought brings me a small amount of comfort.

I'll take what I can get.

The sunrise isn't as pretty here. It was one of the first things I noticed after we arrived. The pinks are less vibrant. Greyed out. The oranges are more muted. Almost faded. As though the artist was running low on paint.

Zen says it's because the air is clean. Vehicles won't be invented for nearly three centuries. Smog makes for better sunrises.

Regardless, it doesn't stop me from watching.

I wasn't lying when I told Zen it was the same dream. It's always the same dream.

They come in the night. Capture me and transport me, kicking and screaming, back to their lab. They strap me to a chair with thick steel clamps that are impossible to bend. A large intricate contraption protrudes from the ceiling. Its clawlike arm, complete with razor-sharp teeth, pries open my mouth, reaches down my throat, and pulls out my heart. Then another machine takes over, working quickly to disassemble the still-pumping organ on a cold, sterile table. Half of it is carved off, placed in a jar, ushered away, while the other half is returned to the claw and replaced in my chest cavity by way of my throat again.

The partial heart settles back into its home behind my rib cage. I can still feel it beating, compelling blood in and out of my veins, keeping me alive. But the process no longer holds meaning. A perfunctory action done out of routine, nothing more. I am now forever incomplete. Half a person. A hollow casket that will be forced to seek the other half for the rest of eternity.

A dream.

Not real.

The problem is, dreams are supposed to get fuzzier the longer you're awake. But this one only becomes clearer with each passing second. Crisper. As though I'm moving *towards* it. Getting closer.

As though *they're* getting closer.

I close my eyes, take a deep breath.

'They don't know where we are.'

'They can't find us here.'

'We are safe.'

'I am safe.'

I recite the words over and over again, hoping that today will be the day when they no longer feel strange on my tongue. When I might start to believe them.

'They don't know where we are.'

'They can't find us here.'

'We are safe.'

'I am safe.'

But then, like clockwork, the bleak reply comes from the back of my mind. The shadowy version of the truth that's much easier to believe.

I'm not safe.

I've never been safe.

They will never stop looking for me.

I reach down the collar of my still-damp nightdress and feel for my locket, rubbing my fingertips gently over the black surface of the heart-shaped medallion and the swirling loops of the silver design emblazoned on the front.

The eternal knot.

It's an ancient Sanskrit symbol that, according to Zen, represents the flowing of time and movement within all that is eternal.

To me it represents Zen.

I insisted on wearing it here even though Zen suggested I

take it off. Apparently people in seventeenth-century England don't look kindly upon unfamiliar symbols that can't be found in something called the Bible – a book everyone here seems to live by. So I agreed to keep it hidden under my clothing at all times.

But right now I need it.

I need it to soothe me. To erase the grisly images from my mind.

I hear careful footsteps behind me and I jump, scrambling to stuff the locket back under my nightdress. My head whips around to find Zen standing there, fully dressed – minus the doublet that I stole – and I let out a puff of air. He tosses his hands up in an apologetic gesture. 'Sorry. Didn't mean to scare you.'

He sits down beside me. Even though the show in the sky is over, I turn my gaze back in the direction of the sunrise. For some reason, I can't look at him right now. I am ashamed of my weakness. Every nightmare – every fear I let overtake me – is like a drop of poison in this new life that Zen and I have worked so hard to create. This paradise that we promised each other.

'Do you want to talk about it?' he asks.

I laugh. It sounds about as fake as it feels. 'I told you. I'm *fine*. It was only a bad dream.'

Zen cocks his head and raises his eyebrows. It's the look he gives me when he knows I'm lying. I cast my eyes downward and lazily pick at a patch of grass.

'They don't know where we are,' he offers. 'They have no idea.'

I nod, still refusing to meet his gaze. 'I know.'

'And if they *did*, they would be here by now.'

I nod again. His logic is sound. If they had somehow figured out that we escaped to the year 1609, they would have appeared instantly. They wouldn't delay. Which means the longer we live here without seeing one of them, the more likely it is they have no clue where we are.

The only other person who knew we were planning to come to the year 1609 was Rio. And he's . . .

I watch his helpless body writhe violently, arms flinging, eyes rolled back in his head, before he collapses to the ground with a horrific cracking sound. And then . . .

Stillness.

I shake the horrid memory away, trying to fight off the familiar guilt that comes every time I think about him.

The point is, they can't find us.

We are safe.

The last thought makes me feel like a fraud.

'You need to let it go,' Zen urges gently. 'Forget about everything that happened before. I'll never let them take you back there.'

Before. Them. There.

They've become our code words for the things we don't dare talk about.

That *other* life that Zen wants so desperately to forget.

That *other* place where I was held prisoner in a lab.

That *other* time when science has the ability to create perfect human beings out of air.

Before we came here.

I think we're both terrified that if we actually utter the word *Diotech* aloud, they might hear us. Our voices will somehow reverberate through the very fabric of time, travel five hundred years into the future, and echo off the high, security-patrolled walls of the compound, giving away our location.

'Dwelling on it won't do you any good,' he continues. 'It's in the past.'

I smile weakly. 'Well, technically, it's in the future.'

He bumps playfully against my shoulder. 'You know what I mean.'

I do. It's a past I'm supposed to have forgotten. A past that's supposed to be erased from my memory. I have no actual recollection of Diotech, the biotechnology company that created me. My final request before we escaped was that every detail of my life there be completely wiped from my mind. All I have now are Zen's accounts of the top-secret compound in the middle of the desert and a few abridged memories that he stole so that he could show me the truth about who I was.

But apparently that's enough to populate nightmares.

'Do you miss it in the slightest?' I say, surprised by my own bluntness.

I can feel Zen's body stiffen next to me and he stares straight ahead. 'No.'

I should know by now not to ask questions like this. They always put Zen in an unpleasant mood. I made this mistake several times after we first arrived, when I tried to talk to him about anything related to Diotech – Dr Rio, Dr Alixter, Dr Maxxer – and he simply shut down. Refused to speak. But now the question is already out. I can't take it back. Plus, I want to know. I feel like I have to.

'But you left behind everything,' I argue. 'Your family, your friends, your home. How can you say that you don't miss it?'

'I had nothing there,' Zen replies, and the sudden sharpness in his voice stings. 'Except a mother who cared more about her latest research project than her own family. And a father who left because of it. My friends were friends of convenience. Who else was I going to hang out with when I was never allowed to

14

leave the compound? You weren't the only one who felt like a prisoner there. So no, I don't miss that at all.'

I can tell immediately that I've gone too far. I've upset him. And that's the last thing I wanted to do. But this is also the most information I've ever gotten about Zen's parents. He never speaks of them. Ever. Which only makes me want to press further, but the rigidness of his face warns me that it would be unwise.

'Sorry,' I offer softly.

Out of the corner of my vision I see his jawline relax and he finally turns to look at me. 'No, I'm sorry.'

It's a genuine apology. I can tell by the way it reaches his eyes.

He rises to his feet, struggling slightly, as though the action requires more effort than it should. Then he brushes the damp dirt from the back of his breeches and holds out a hand for me to take. 'C'mon, Cinnamon. Everyone will be up soon. You should get dressed.'

His use of the nickname Cinnamon makes me chuckle, effectively lightening the mood. It's a popular term of endearment in this time period that we picked up from the husband and wife who own the farmhouse where we've been living.

I take his hand and he pulls me to my feet. But he doesn't let go once I'm standing. He keeps pulling me towards him until our faces are a mere fraction of an inch apart. 'It'll get easier,' he whispers, bringing the conversation back to the reason I came out here in the first place. 'Try to forget.' He places his hands on the sides of my face and softly touches his lips to mine.

The taste of him erases everything else. The way it always does. And just for that moment, there is no *there*, there is no *them*, there is no *before*. There is only us. There is only now.

But I know eventually the moment will end. Because that's what moments do. And sooner or later, I will be doubled over the side of that bed again, fighting for air. Because even though I have no real memory of the former life that haunts me, I still can't do what he wants me to do.

I can't forget.

2

FOREIGN

Living and working on a farm in the countryside of England is one of the many precautions we've taken to stay off Diotech's radar. Zen thought it would be better if money never changed hands and no official transactions were recorded. So we work here in exchange for a place to live and food to eat.

I enjoy farm life. It's not overly complicated. There is a set of tasks to undertake each day and I feel satisfaction in completing every one. Like hundreds of tiny victories. Plus, it's quiet here. Peaceful.

John Pattinson owns and runs the farm, while his wife, Elizabeth, tends to the maintenance of the home and their four children. Zen mostly works alongside Mr Pattinson, helping with the sowing, ploughing, reaping, and general upkeep of the crops. I help Mrs Pattinson with the domestic chores and the care of the animals.

The problem is, Mrs Pattinson doesn't like me. Zen says I'm being paranoid but it's something I just know. Sometimes I catch her watching me as I'm going about my work. She has a suspicious look in her eyes. Like she's waiting for me to screw up. To show who I really am.

I think she can sense that I'm different. That I don't fit in here.

I suppose neither does Zen. After all, he was born five hundred years in the future. And seventeenth-century farmwork is something we both had to learn very quickly. But somehow he's been able to assimilate a lot easier than I have.

That's one of the (many) downsides of being created by scientists in a lab. You simply stand out. Even if people don't quite know why. They can perceive there's something strange about you. Something unnatural about the way you were brought on to this earth.

That's what Mrs Pattinson senses. Whether she understands it or not is irrelevant. I understand it. Which is why I always feel like I have to tread carefully when she's around.

I remember one of the first things she said to me when I arrived. She looked right at me, her gaze darting sceptically up and down my entire body before finally landing on my eyes.

'I've never seen purple eyes before,' she said, her tone brusque and accusing.

I swallowed hard and opened my mouth to speak. Even though I hadn't the slightest idea what I would say or how I would recover.

Thankfully, Zen was prepared, as always. He stepped forward, put his hand gently on my arm, and replied, 'Her great-grandmother was from the Orient. Lots of purple eyes out there.'

'It doesn't matter that it's not true,' Zen later explained to me. 'It only matters that she believed it.'

But I wasn't even sure about that. She may never have mentioned it again, but I see the doubt on her face every time she looks at me. I hear it in her gruff tone when she addresses me.

Her children don't seem to like me either. They pretty

much avoid me as much as they can.

The only person in the house who doesn't seem bothered by my presence is Mr Pattinson. But I don't consider that any type of accomplishment. He's a sweet-tempered, jovial man who appears to love everyone. If his wife has voiced any objections to us being here, he certainly hasn't entertained them. It's fairly clear that, in this time period, the man of the house makes all the decisions.

Because it was Mr Pattinson who, six months ago on a chilly day in late March, agreed to let us work here in exchange for food and lodging. He was the one who welcomed an unknown eighteen-year-old boy and sixteen-year-old girl with open arms and offered to lend us some of his and his wife's clothing. And he was the one who enthusiastically ate up Zen's story about us being newlyweds who were both born and raised aboard merchant ships that have been sailing back and forth from the Far East for the majority of our lives, which accounts for our 'funny accents'.

I was actually quite surprised to see how prepared Zen was when we arrived. Everything had been carefully thought out ahead of time, even down to our fake period-appropriate names – Sarah and Ben. He told me that, in reality, the plan was as much mine as it was his. We'd been working on the details for months before we left the Diotech compound. Of course, I have no recollection of this.

But even if I *had* remembered planning our cover story, I was glad Zen was the one to deliver it. He's a natural storyteller. When he speaks, his voice is so calming, his face so earnest, it's hard not to invite him right into your home.

The boys, Thomas, James, and Myles, are enamoured of him. They sit around the fireplace for hours every night after dinner, listening to Zen tell made-up stories about his life on the high seas with his father, the merchant trader. Sometimes I even find myself leaning forward in my seat with anticipation, waiting to hear what comes next, desperate to find out whether or not the crew really *can* fight off a Chinese giant squid and live to tell about it. I then have to remind myself, with sinking disappointment, that none of it actually happened.

Later that morning, as soon as we're dressed and outside and the front door closes behind us, Zen pulls me towards him, capturing my mouth with his. It's a hungry kiss. Eager. It takes me by surprise. I love how he can still take me by surprise. Zen's lips gently pry mine open and his tongue starts to explore. I remark how much better the porridge we had for breakfast tastes on him than it did on my spoon five minutes ago. I feel his fingertips press into my lower back, urging me closer. Then his hands are under my cap, in my hair, massacring the tight bun that I spent the morning coaxing my hair into, but I can hardly bring myself to care. I'm too swept up in Zen's fierceness. His famine for me. It spreads over me like a wildfire.

When he breaks away, I'm breathless, gasping for air. Although I'd take his kiss over oxygen any day.

'What was that?' I ask, resting my forehead against his lips and inhaling his scent.

I feel him smirking into my skin. 'A goodbye kiss.'

This makes me laugh. I tilt my head and gaze up at him. 'Where are you going? Saturn?'

'Nah. Just the wheat field.' He reaches out, his fingertip tracing the hook of my ear and drifting off my cheek, heating my face to a boil. 'But without you, it may as well be another planet.'

I open my mouth to speak but only stammering air escapes.

He smiles, teasing me with his eyes. 'Bye, Cinnamon.'

And then he's gone. Disappearing in the direction of the wheat field. I rake my teeth over my bottom lip, attempting to savour him for another second before reluctantly starting towards the barn.

October is only a few days away, which means it's time to harvest the fruit in the orchard. Mrs Pattinson has assigned me the task of picking the apples and pears. I wouldn't mind it so much except for the fact that it requires me to work with Blackthorn, the Pattinsons' horse.

He hates me, too.

With a sigh, I grab the rope halter from the hook on the wall and let myself into the stall. Blackthorn stiffens the moment he sees me, his head jerking up and his eyes narrowing. Then, upon noticing the halter in my hand, he whinnies and stamps his foot.

'I know,' I tell him. 'I don't like it any more than you do.'

I take a step towards him and he startles and kicks his back feet against the wall.

'Come on,' I implore. 'Don't be like that.'

But my coaxing doesn't seem to be doing any good because he edges himself into the corner and stares me down, ears pinned back, nostrils flaring. I have no doubt he's planning to charge if I get any closer.

Mr Pattinson says Blackthorn only reacts this way because I'm too tense when I'm around him. I have to learn how to relax. Horses can sense fear.

Unfortunately I don't think it's my fear that he senses. Even the horse knows there's something off about me.

Before we came here, I'd never seen a horse before, or any animal, for that matter. I didn't even know what they were. When the Diotech scientists designed me, they were very particular about what I knew and what I didn't. Even down to the words in my vocabulary. Zen says that was just another way to control me. By controlling what knowledge I had access to. And apparently they didn't think horses were important enough

21

to add to my mental dictionary. I made the mistake of nearly leaping out of my shoes and letting out a piercing shriek when we arrived on the farm and I came face-to-face with Blackthorn for the first time.

Zen was quick to cover for me, stating that since I was born and raised on a merchant ship, I'd never come in contact with any farm animals before. But once again, I don't think Mrs Pattinson ever completely believed the story.

All the other tasks I can handle – cooking dinner, baking bread, working in the garden, chopping firewood, sewing clothes, washing laundry. I was designed to pick up skills quickly – after only one demonstration. And I actually enjoy the manual labour. It keeps my mind calm.

The jobs that require interaction with the animals – feeding the pigs, letting the chickens out of their coop, milking the goat – are the ones that I've come to dread every day. Because animals see right through me. Zen can't dazzle them with well-crafted stories to put their doubts to rest. They *know* something is wrong with me.

I take three slow steps towards the horse and attempt to ease the halter up over his nose. I proceed cautiously, careful not to make any sudden moves. His eyes follow me with the same distrust I see when Mrs Pattinson watches me. I flash the horse a beaming smile to show that I'm perfectly nice and not a threat, but the action seems to have the reverse effect. He flinches and whips his head up, knocking me in the chin. The force of the blow sends me flying backwards and I fall into a soft patch of mud.

The horse looks over and I *swear* I see him smirk.

Groaning, I push myself up and do my best to brush the mud off the back of my skirt. This will definitely require laundering later today.

I'm about to go in for a second try when I hear the door creak open and Jane, the Pattinsons' six-year-old daughter, slinks into the stall. She's wearing a dress with a ripped hem that will surely be added to our mending pile any day now. Her sunshine-blond curls are still matted and tangled on one side of her head from sleeping on them. She brushes them clumsily out of her face, revealing a pair of large, inquisitive blue eyes.

Dangling from her hand is the tiny doll, about the size of my hand, that she carries with her wherever she goes. She calls it Lulu. Its body was made from the stained white fabric of one of Mr Pattinson's old shirts, and its blue short-sleeved frock was crafted from one of Jane's outgrown baby dresses. It has a painted-on nose and smile and buttons for eyes.

I'm surprised to see Jane here. Since we arrived, she's never spoken to me. None of the children have, really. Maybe a few perfunctory words here and there like, *May I have some more bread, please?* but beyond that, I might as well be a ghost in this house.

There have been a few times when I've looked up from my work and caught her watching me from a distance but she always scampers away as soon as she sees me notice her. I've convinced myself that she's terrified of me. But she shows no fear now.

Without a word, she gently places the doll in the front pocket of her dress, walks towards me, removes the halter from my hand, and proceeds to approach the horse.

Blackthorn towers over her and for a minute I wonder if it's a good idea to even allow her into this stall. One little jerky move from him and she could be crushed to death. I consider dashing after her and scooping her up into my arms but I soon see that this won't be necessary because the horse actually relaxes the moment he sees her. His nostrils stop flaring, his ears bounce straight up in the air, and he lowers his head so that his eyes are level with hers.

'That's a good horsie,' she coos, rubbing the top of his nose. His eyes sink closed. She easily slips the halter around his head and ties it. Then she silently points to the harness on the wall behind me. I grab it and take one pace towards him. He tenses again but Jane is quick to soothe him with a soft clucking sound.

I manage to get close enough to toss the harness over his back and buckle the strap around his chest. Then I fetch the fruit baskets from outside his stall and secure them to the hooks on either side. He doesn't look happy about any of this, but he seems much more tolerant of my presence while Jane is here.

I'm about to say thank you to Jane when I hear an angry huffing sound behind me. We both turn to see Mrs Pattinson glaring at us. Her eyes drift down from me to her daughter.

'Jane,' she says tightly, 'go inside.'

Jane bites her lip and scuttles away. Mrs Pattinson lingers to give me one more distrustful glower before following her daughter.

She must think she's out of hearing range when she turns the corner towards the house because she whispers gruffly to Jane, 'What did I tell you about conversing with that girl?'

There's no way for her to know that my actual hearing range reaches far beyond any normal human being's. That, in reality, I can hear horse hooves *clip clopping* down the dirt road five minutes before they actually arrive at the house, a hawk flapping its wings in the next valley, or even the hushed early-morning bickering between her and Mr Pattinson in the kitchen when I'm sitting on the knoll five hundred feet away watching the sunrise.

Although I fear that even if she had known I could hear her, she wouldn't have cared.

I swallow the stinging in my throat and hook the lead rope to Blackthorn's halter, pulling him out of the barn and towards the orchard. He follows me obediently but uses the entire length of the rope to put as much distance between us as he can.

3

PRECAUTIONS

One, one thousand. Step.

Two, one thousand. Step.

Three, one thousand. Step.

I take vigilant, measured paces as I walk, counting a full second per stride, just like Zen taught me.

It's one of the numerous things I have to do on a daily basis to avoid drawing unnecessary attention to myself. To hide who I am. If I move too fast — at the speed my scientifically enhanced legs are capable of carrying me — people will notice.

When I lift heavy objects, I have to pretend to struggle with them. Carrying in the wood for the bread oven is especially frustrating because I could easily carry the entire bundle at once but that would seem unnatural for a woman to be able to do. So instead I have to take three agonizingly slow trips from the chopping block to the kitchen, timing my steps the entire way, and throwing in a few grunts and other exertion noises to make it sound realistic.

Diotech is sure to be monitoring all historical records. From all time periods. They probably have a hundred people assigned to the task, scouring the digital archives for any clue to my whereabouts. It would only take one slip-up, one sliver of unwanted attention, one mention of something unusual in a printed pamphlet or an official document and that would be enough.

They would send someone here to investigate.

And my new life – my new home – would be gone forever.

By lunchtime, I've already collected eight baskets of apples and pears from the orchard and delivered them to the house, with Blackthorn's help. Mrs Pattinson is thrilled and she claps her hands ecstatically when I report back the yield. It's actually the first time I think I've ever seen her happy. Apparently this was a 'fertile season', which means there's enough to take into town and sell.

I manage to finish my workload today with enough time to wash and hang my mud-stained skirt on the line outside before helping Mrs Pattinson with dinner. Zen and I were each given two pairs of clothes when we arrived. 'One to wash and one to wear,' we were told.

The garments definitely required getting used to. The bodice sometimes feels like it's suffocating me, I often trip over the heavy linen skirt that falls to my ankles, the cotton cap itches on my head, and the long shirtsleeves are thick and hot in the afternoon sun. But I suppose it's a small price to pay to be here with Zen.

To be safe from them.

After dinner, Mrs Pattinson and I sit down at the kitchen table to mend clothes while everyone else gathers around the fireplace with Zen to hear another one of his adventure stories before it's time for bed.

As my fingers move deftly, weaving the thread in and out, in and out, I allow the sound of Zen's soft, melodic voice and the crackling fire to silence my thoughts. Drifting away for a few peaceful moments. Revelling in the quiet end of the day. The promise of what's to come when everyone goes to sleep and Zen and I are finally alone.

It's Mrs Pattinson's nasally grating voice that eventually brings me back to the present when she asks me to pass her another spool of thread.

I smile politely, bend down to retrieve the black bobbin from the basket near my feet, and then reach across the table to place the object in front of her.

I'm just about to withdraw my arm when Mrs Pattinson lets out a horrified, deafening gasp that stops everyone short. Zen is no longer speaking. Mr Pattinson and the children are no longer listening. Even the fire seems to have been shocked to a subtle flicker.

Everyone has turned and is staring at me.

I look instinctively to Zen and his dark eyes widen in alarm. Since we arrived here, we've begun to master the art of communicating without speaking. With the Pattinsons almost always around, sometimes a glance is all we get to convey something important. It's a necessity when living with secrets. Secrets that, in this day and age, could get you killed.

He nudges his chin ever so slightly in the direction of my outstretched arm. I glance down and suddenly understand. My stomach clenches. A peculiar icy heat slithers up my legs. And for a moment, I'm completely paralysed. Staring at the sight before me that cannot be unseen. Feeling the palpable panic in the air that cannot be erased.

The sleeve of my shirt has slid up, revealing the bare skin on the inside of my left wrist.

Or more specifically, the razor-thin black line that is inked *across* my wrist.

I call it my tattoo, even though that's not an accurate term.

27

But it's what I originally thought it was. In reality, it's a tracking device that was installed by Diotech when they created me.

Zen warned me that I would have to keep it hidden under my sleeve here. That I was never to reveal it. And now I understand why.

Mrs Pattinson's mouth finally closes from her prolonged gasp and she's able to speak. 'Is that the mark of . . . of . . .'

'No,' Mr Pattinson chides her. 'Not in front of the children.'

She's flustered and breathless as she continues to stare down at my exposed wrist. I start to pull my arm away but she grabs my hand and clutches it tightly, her nails digging into my flesh.

I know I could easily yank it away. I'm about a hundred times stronger than she is, but I also know that it would be the wrong thing to do right now.

'It is!' she exclaims, studying it closer and clearly ignoring her husband's warning. 'I've heard Mary Adams describe it.' She sucks in a hissing breath through her teeth. 'That's Satan's mark!'

I don't know who Satan is but I can only surmise that he or she is not someone you want to be associated with. All four children shudder in unison and seven-year-old Myles whimpers and climbs into his father's lap, his small brown eyes narrowing accusingly in my direction.

'Mrs Pattinson,' her husband roars. 'That is enough. You are frightening the children. I've warned you before about listening to the likes of Mary Adams. She's a gossip and a meddler. I'm sure Sarah has a perfectly reasonable explanation for her −' he looks towards my wrist and clears his throat anxiously − 'for whatever that is.'

Everyone turns expectantly to me and I turn to Zen, my eyes pleading with him. I don't know how to fix this. I don't know what to say. Whatever I do will undoubtedly only make things worse.

I watch Zen's expression shift. Sliding effortlessly from one of disquiet to one of calm. He chuckles and I immediately wonder if laughing at Mrs Pattinson is really the best choice right now. But Zen appears to know what he's doing.

'Oh, that,' Zen says, casually flicking his hand towards my wrist, which is still pinned in Mrs Pattinson's mighty clutch. 'That's a great story! You're going to love it!'

His easy movements and the buoyancy of his voice calm the tension in the room almost instantly. Zen then launches into a flawless account of the time my father's merchant ship was raided and seized by pirates when I was only eight years old. The invaders took everyone captive and tattooed us with this special mark, branding us as prisoners.

Within moments everyone is completely rapt, listening to his story and the animated way in which he tells it. He stands up and swings his arms valiantly to enact the final epic battle of swords that led to our victory and daring escape.

No one is even looking at me any more. Everyone is intently focused on Zen as though they've completely forgotten about the scandal that prompted the telling of this story in the first place.

Everyone except Mrs Pattinson, that is.

When I glance up, her vicious, distrustful eyes are still drilling into me. Her mouth is clenched, slicing a rigid horizontal line across the bottom of her face. She is not in the least bit dazzled by Zen's spirited story. In fact, I doubt she believes a word of it.

I force a timid smile and ever so gently begin to pry my hand out from under hers. My arm snaps back when I finally break free. The whole time her gaze never abandons me. She never stops accusing.

I hastily finish the sock that I've been darning, place it on the table, and clean up my work space. Zen is still engrossed in the story of the great battle with the pirates, making up details with impressive ease and diligence.

I stand up without a word and head towards the stairs. Zen stops talking long enough to raise his eyebrows inquisitively at me. *Are you OK?*

I shrug and nod weakly in response, anxious to leave the room, to disappear behind a closed door. To vanish.

I hurry towards the stairs, wanting so badly to bolt up them as fast as my legs can carry me. But I force myself to take cautious, timed, human steps — one, one thousand, two, one thousand — feeling Mrs Pattinson's eyes stinging the back of my neck the entire time.

4

TELLING

As soon as the door is closed behind me, I slide out of my mules, rip the bonnet from my head, untwist my bun, and shake out my long honey-brown hair. The bed squeaks under my weight as I collapse on to my back. I rest my hand on my chest, feeling my heart pounding. My rib cage rises and falls in desperate ragged breaths.

I close my eyes and try to calm myself. Try to tell myself it's all right. By tomorrow she will have completely forgotten about it.

But I know I'm only lying again.

I wish I had access to one of Diotech's re-cognization receptors so I could dig into Mrs Pattinson's mind, find that memory, and erase it forever. I was wearing a set of them when we arrived here but Zen insisted we throw them into a nearby pond, reasoning that they would only arouse suspicion if they were ever found in our possession.

Not that they'd be of any use to us without the right equipment. Even if I was able to sneak into her bedroom while she was sleeping and secure the receptors to her head, I'd still need some kind of computer connected to them in order to find the memory within her brain and delete it.

Absent-mindedly, I run my fingertip gently over the ink-black strip of skin on the inside of my wrist.

'*Satan's mark.*'

I remember when they found me the first time. When the thin black line buzzed with electricity. When they were close enough to track me.

It was August of 2013. In the small town of Wells Creek, California. When I was living with the Carlsons, my foster family. Heather, Scott, and their thirteen-year-old son, Cody.

People believed I was the sole survivor of a deadly plane crash. That I had somehow managed to fall from the sky and live to tell about it. That I had lost my memories as a result of the accident. And that I was just a normal sixteen-year-old girl with a family, and friends, and a home somewhere.

But none of that was true.

I was never on the plane.

I was never a normal sixteen-year-old girl.

I had no family or friends.

I ended up in the year 2013 by accident. When Zen and I were attempting to escape. We were supposed to come here – to 1609 – but something went wrong.

Something neither of us has been able to figure out.

'What happened?' I asked Zen after we'd been here a week. 'How did we get separated?'

He got very quiet then, refusing to look at me. 'You let go,' he whispered.

His response startled me and I nearly choked on my next word. 'What?'

He finally brought his eyes back to mine but something had clouded them. A layer of doubt that I'd never seen before. 'You

32

let go of my hand,' he explained. 'I felt it at the very end. Like you'd changed your mind or something. When I opened my eyes and found myself here – in 1609 – you were gone.'

'It must have slipped,' I reasoned, unable to believe what he was saying.

But he shook his head. 'No.' The confidence in his tone made my throat go dry as he repeated the three words that still send chills through me whenever I think about them. 'You let go.'

Regardless of the reason, I ended up in the twenty-first century alone and scared, without an identity or a single scrap of memory. In a time period I knew nothing about.

I became an instant celebrity. The police broadcast my picture to the world, certain it would only be a matter of time before someone came looking for me.

That part they were right about.

Someone *did* come looking for me. But it wasn't my family. It wasn't my friends. It was *them*.

And they almost managed to bring me back.

Thankfully, Zen found me first. He tried to explain to me what was happening. Why I was there. Who these mysterious people chasing me were. I didn't believe him at first. I didn't recognize him.

But something inside me – some deeply buried spark – lit up whenever he was around. Somewhere beyond my vacant, spotless, overly logical brain – beyond my fear and distrust and burning need for answers that made sense – I still remembered him. Still trusted him.

Still loved him.

I'm startled by a quiet rap on the door and I push myself up to a seated position, pull my sleeve back down over my wrist, straighten my shoulders, and call, 'Come in.'

The door creaks open but I don't see anyone on the other side. At first I think a breeze from an open window might have pushed it but then my gaze slides down about three feet and I see Jane's tiny blond head poking into the room.

Just like in the barn this morning, her presence takes me by surprise.

Jane quietly pads into the room with Lulu, her doll, tucked in the crook of her elbow. She closes the door behind her without a word. Then she walks right up to the edge of the bed and stands in front of me, staring at me with a gentle but intrigued gaze. Lulu's two black button eyes watch me with matched curiosity.

I feel uncomfortable and am tempted to look away but something about Jane's innocent features keeps my eyes locked on hers. She bites her lip in concentration and her forehead crumples as she looks at me, like she's trying hard to decipher something on my face.

Then, finally, she opens her mouth and in her small, docile voice and precious accent says, 'Why do you never tell us any stories?'

The question catches me off guard. I'm not sure what I was expecting from her, but it definitely wasn't this. I don't have much experience with little children – *none*, actually. To be honest, they make me nervous. So small and fragile and unpredictable. Like they might punch you in the stomach, or burst into tears, or shatter into a million pieces at any moment.

'U-u-um,' I stammer. 'I-I-I don't know. I guess I don't have any stories to tell.'

'Then why don't you make one up?' she suggests, her voice clearly implying that this is an obvious solution.

'You don't like Ben's stories?'

She teeters her head from side to side, the straps of her little white cap bouncing on her shoulders. 'I do,' she replies, sounding almost diplomatic. 'They're for boys, though. I want to hear a *girl* story.'

She's looking at me with big, round, eager eyes and it takes me a second to realize she really is expecting me to just make up a story. Right here. Right now.

'Um,' I say again. 'OK, I guess I can make up a story for you.'

Her lips spring into an ear-to-ear grin, revealing two rows of miniature crooked teeth. One is missing from the bottom. She climbs clumsily on to the bed – hands and knees and elbows everywhere – and sits down right beside me. She places her doll in her lap, wraps one arm around its waist and the other she rests casually on my thigh, clearly thinking nothing of the gesture. As though we've sat like this a dozen times before.

I stiffen at her sudden proximity and her touch, reminding myself of the way that stupid horse reacts every time I enter his stall.

She looks up at me, chin jutted out, blue eyes blinking, mouth curved in a patient half-smile. Waiting. Anticipating. I hope she doesn't expect anything as remarkable as one of Zen's stories because if so, she'll be sorely disappointed.

'OK,' I begin awkwardly, racking my brain for something to say. 'This is a story about . . .'

About what?

Am I really expected to just *create* an entire story? An entire life? When I'm still trying to figure out my own? I rack my brain for inspiration. For a single detail I can begin with, but no response comes. My mind is blank.

Zen always makes it look so easy. Effortless. He simply starts talking and doesn't stop until an entire epic saga has been described in painstaking detail. I can't even come up with a single person, place, or thing to be the subject of one lousy story.

Did the Diotech scientists create me with absolutely no imaginative abilities whatsoever?

I suppose that shouldn't surprise me.

Creativity obviously had no function in whatever it was they planned to do with me. In fact, any creative talent at all was probably considered a liability. A threat. A skill that might facilitate an escape plan.

They obviously weren't counting on Zen.

Jane is still staring up at me, waiting for some exciting, perilous tale. Unfortunately I'll have to break it to her that it's just not going to happen. I'm simply not wired that way. She's going to have to get her source of entertainment from somewhere else tonight.

'About a princess,' she whispers beside me.

I frown back at her. 'What?'

She looks impatient for a moment before letting out a sigh and explaining, 'All good stories are about a princess.'

'Oh,' I splutter. 'Right. Yes. OK, it's about a princess.'

Jane nods contentedly, indicating her satisfaction, and then motions for me to keep going.

'It's about a princess who . . . who . . .' But once again nothing comes.

'Lives in King James's court?' she asks, raising her eyebrows hopefully.

'Oh no.' I shake my head, confident about *something* for the first time. 'She's from much further away. A very, very distant place.'

Jane's eyes light up. 'The New World?'

'Even further. Further than you could ever imagine.'

She flashes me an encouraging smile.

'So,' I continue tentatively, still unsure where I'm going with this, 'the princess was . . . she was . . .'

'Special.' Jane finishes the sentence. 'She has to be special.'

'She does?'

'Of course,' she replies with authority. 'Otherwise why would there be a story about her?'

'Good point. Yes, she was very special.'

'Why?' Jane prompts, gazing up eagerly at me again.

I peer around the room for some help. There's none to be found. 'Well, she was special because she had these . . . these . . .' I stop, press my lips together, glance down at my wrist, safely hidden behind my sleeve again. I take a deep breath.

'. . . magic powers,' I finally conclude.

'Oooh!' Jane nods her head vigorously in approval. She scoots even closer to me, our legs now touching. 'What kind of powers?'

Her excitement unexpectedly invigorates me. Makes me feel giddy. A surge of warmth runs through my body and I suddenly find myself wanting to do anything to keep the feeling alive. To please her.

'Well,' I begin. The smile on my face is automatic. Unconscious. 'She could run *really* fast. And she was *very* strong.'

'Stronger than the boys?'

'Stronger than anyone.'

Jane's eyes are wide with fascination, her mouth hanging open. Her passion fuels me. Presses me forward. 'And she could see in the dark,' I add, attempting to give my voice a mysterious lilt, the way I've heard Zen do so many times. 'And hear things from very far away. And read very quickly. And speak several languages.'

'Like French?' Jane asks.

I nod. 'Yes. Like French and Spanish and Portuguese and Russian.'

'That's *wondrous!*' Jane marvels, clearly entranced.

I can't help but laugh. 'Yes, I suppose it is.'

'She's very lucky.'

I let out a sigh. 'Actually, no. She isn't. Because you see, she was forced to run very far away from her home. To a place that she didn't know at all. She had to hide because there were bad people chasing her.'

'They wanted her magic powers,' Jane adds shrewdly.

'Exactly. They wanted to capture her and bring her back to where she came from.'

'But there was a prince?' Jane assumes, as though this solves everything.

And I suppose, when you're six years old, it does.

'Yes, there was a prince. And he was . . .' My voice trails off for a moment and I feel that subtle tingle that covers my skin every time I think of Zen. 'Well, he helped her escape from the bad people. She loved him very much.'

I can tell right away that this was the correct answer. Jane smiles triumphantly. 'So now she could be happy? Because she escaped?'

The expression on Jane's sweet little face causes a splinter to stab into my chest. She looks as though the weight of her existence – everything she knows to be true – is riding on this very answer.

'She *was*,' I say cautiously. 'However, because she was so different, she often felt . . .' I exhale, finding the truth in my breath. 'Lonely. And scared. Like she didn't belong anywhere. Like she wasn't . . .' I pause again, glancing down at Lulu, her tiny handcrafted body tucked into Jane's slender, pale arms. Her faded red lips, permanently drawn into a smile. Her blank button eyes stare back at me. Unblinking. Unfeeling.

'. . . *human*.'

The two syllables hang in the air like a puff of stale smoke, waiting for the wind to determine which way they will drift. How long they will stay.

When I look down at Jane again, her forehead is furrowed and I immediately fear that I've failed at my attempt to entertain her. 'But she wasn't an animal,' she argues, confusion soaked into her small voice.

'N-no,' I try to explain, stammering slightly, 'I meant, she didn't feel . . . real.'

Jane is pensive. She appears to be absorbing everything I said. Analysing it. Deciding whether or not this qualifies as a satisfactory story.

'If she wasn't real,' she finally says, 'then she wouldn't have been able to run away from the bad people. That was a good choice.'

My smile is strained. 'I suppose it was.'

There's a long silence in which neither one of us speaks or looks at the other. Finally, I feel a soft tug on the sleeve of my shirt. I glance down to see that Jane has ever so carefully peeled away the cuff to reveal the thin, black mark underneath.

She studies it for a moment. Then, with surprising boldness, she reaches out with one tiny finger – barely a twig – and touches it. Sweeps along the length of the line. Delicate. Like a baby mouse running across my skin. Back and forth. Back and forth.

I don't say anything. I don't try to move away. I just watch. And feel.

'She needs to hide really well.' Jane finally speaks, her voice quiet but steady. Unusually wise for her age.

She removes her hand, allowing the sleeve to fall back into place, concealing the inside of my left wrist once again. 'So they can never ever find her.'

She looks up at me, her blue eyes liquid and sparkling.

My bottom lip starts to tremble. I bite down on it hard. Small droplets of blood trickle on to my tongue. I swallow them.

'Yes,' I say, trying to ignore the bitter metallic taste in my mouth. 'She does.'

5

INSTINCTIVE

My favourite times of the day are early in the morning before everyone is awake, when I sometimes sit alone and watch the sunrise, and late at night. After dinner has been eaten, the dishes have been cleaned and put away, the children have been tucked into their beds, and Mr and Mrs Pattinson have retired to their room. That's when Zen and I slip out the front door, tiptoe across the dark field, duck under the split-rail fence, and retreat into the woods.

It's the one place where we can be alone. Where I no longer have to hide. Where I can be myself.

And where we can have total privacy.

Tonight, when we arrive in our usual clearing, Zen sets the lantern off to the side, bathing the shadowy forest in a gentle, warm light. He immediately gets to work preparing the space, pulling large armfuls of leaves, moss, and shrubbery from the surrounding area and arranging it on the cold dirt floor to create a soft surface. I wait near the trunk of a thick elm tree and watch him. Waiting for his cue.

Once he's finished, he stands in the middle of the bed he just created and stares across the opening at me. 'I want to try something new tonight,' he begins, his voice measured and careful.

'New?' I repeat, anxiety instantly creeping into my voice.

He obviously can hear it because he gives me one of his looks. His head lowers and tilts half an inch to the right. His dark eyes peer intensely into mine and his lips press together.

'It's all right,' he tells me.

I nod and stare back at him, trying to match the determination on his face with an expression of my own. But I'm feeling far less confident than he looks right now.

'This time, I want you to come to me,' he says, keeping his voice calm and even.

I immediately shake my head. Without even taking the time to think about it. There's nothing to think about. I can't do that. I simply can't.

But Zen is one step ahead of me. 'You can do this.'

I shake my head again. I can already feel my legs starting to tremble. Readying to flee. Like springs coiling in anticipation.

'Yes, you can.'

'Zen . . . I—' I start to say.

But he quickly interrupts. 'It's just like every other night. Fight against it. You are stronger than your instincts.'

I close my eyes, focusing on that sensation that's starting to blaze through my legs like fire, screaming at me to run the other way. To get as far away from here as possible.

I swallow hard and try to push it down. Deep down. Until I can't hear it any more.

'Run towards me,' Zen commands from a few yards away. 'You can do this. I am your enemy. Everything you fear. Everything you hate.'

The woods are deathly still and silent. As though all the

animals and insects and leaves are eagerly waiting to see what will happen. Holding their breath in anticipation. I can see Zen breathing deeply. Puffing himself up. Preparing for what I'm still not sure I can do.

And then he lets out a low, guttural growl. 'ATTACK ME!'

My eyes snap open. I don't give my muscles any time to think. I don't give that deep-rooted instinct any time to argue. I charge forward, running straight towards him. He widens his stance, crouching slightly to stabilize himself better.

I crash into him. He staggers but stays upright. His hand cuts through the air as he aims a left hook at my face. I duck and return with a roundhouse kick that catches Zen squarely in the shins. He yelps and goes down but is back on his feet in an instant, panting for air.

I can't! I hear a voice inside me scream. *I can't do this!*

I eye the narrow path back to the house, every muscle in my body wanting to take it. Wanting to retreat. The forest calls to me. The calm of the escape. The security of those trees.

I take a step towards them.

'No!' Zen yells. 'Don't do it. Don't listen! You're stronger than them. They don't control you any more. You don't belong to Diotech.'

I suck in a sharp breath.

He's said it. For the first time since we arrived, he's said their name. Aloud. For anyone to hear. Including *them*.

But it worked. My head whips back towards him. A bitter, furious energy swells inside me. I gaze intensely into his eyes. My teeth clenched. My muscles burning.

He throws a punch towards my stomach.

I block it with ease.

Another aimed at my chest.

Blocked.

A third flies at my face.

But it's sloppy and unformed. Desperate. I catch his fist mid-swing and twist it until he's forced to spin around and press his back into me. I've got him in a vulnerable position, which means it's time to finish him. Fast. I kick my right leg out, wrap it around his calf, and yank hard. Just as Zen taught me. His head snaps back and his body collapses against the carpeting of leaves and moss. I don't waste a second waiting to see if he's able to get up again. I'm immediately on top of him, one knee on the ground, the other crushing his chest. I jam the heel of my hand squarely against his windpipe. His chin juts up in response. With my strength, all it would take is one tiny ounce of pressure and he'd be dead.

Zen twists, trying to get away. I push my knee down harder against his rib cage until I hear him groan and he stops struggling. I stay still in my position, poised to take his life at the slightest provocation, until I hear him gasp, 'Good,' through his constricted throat.

I remove my palm and release my leg, bringing it down to the other side of his torso. Zen coughs slightly as the air returns to his lungs and then pushes himself on to his elbows and grins up at me with unabashed pride.

It takes me a moment to register what just happened. It's almost as though my mind simply vacated my body during those brief few seconds. Shut off. I blink and look down at Zen, still pinned beneath me, looking happier than I've seen him in a long time.

'You did it,' he tells me.

'I did?' I'm still somewhat dazed.

'Yes!'

I did it. I can hardly believe it. I fought my instinct to run. To flee. I was able to combat the very programming of my DNA.

I was able to fight.

When the scientists at Diotech created me, they tweaked my

genetic code to give me a flight-over-fight instinct. To make me a deer, not a lion. Which means that every time I'm presented with a perceived threat or danger, I will run away from it. Without even giving myself time to think. It was feared that if I ever decided to rebel against the people who had created me, and tried to fight against them, with my superior strength, I would surely win. So my DNA was coded this way as a precaution.

For the past six months Zen has worked with me to try to overcome it. So that I would be able to protect myself. In case they ever . . .

Well, in case I was ever in danger.

Zen was convinced that given enough time, enough practice, I could rise above it. Which is why every night, after the house has gone to sleep, we come out here and Zen teaches me how to fight. How to take down an attacker. How to render someone immobile. How to disarm an opponent. Whatever I can do to give myself time to get away.

Tonight is a major milestone. It's the first night I've been able to fight . . . and win. Not to run away. Not to flee. And more than that, tonight I was the one to initiate the confrontation. I was the one to attack.

I became the lion.

A matching grin spreads across my face as the realization of my accomplishment sinks in. I glance at Zen, who's still staring up at me with wild, gleeful eyes.

I dive down and plant my lips against his, kissing him hard. My legs kick out behind me and I reposition myself on top of him. I'm starving for him. Ravenous. Desperate to hold on to this feeling of exhilaration for as long as possible and transform it into something more. Something else.

An unfamiliar sensation that I don't recognize starts to overpower me. Take control of me.

My legs are tingling again. In fact, my whole body is tingling.

Prickling with a strange alertness. But this time, it's different. It's not because I want to run. It's because I want to stay. I want more. I want to be closer to him than I've ever been before.

I press my mouth more intensely into his, grip the sides of his face, and pull him towards me until I can feel our bodies crushing against each other.

Zen shifts beneath me and lets out a soft moan. It's not the sound of pleasure. It's the sound of pain. I recognize the difference immediately and pull back. 'Are you OK?'

He laughs, reaching up and tenderly touching the back of his head. 'Yeah. You took me down pretty hard though. I feel a splitting headache coming on.'

Panicked, I roll off him and launch to my feet. 'I'm sorry!' I cry, recognizing the familiar sense of guilt that's starting to coat my stomach like a wet rag.

He struggles to sit up, wincing. 'It's OK. I did ask for it.'

I offer him my hand and he takes it, his face twisting in discomfort as I gently pull him to his feet. He wobbles slightly before grabbing on to a nearby low-hanging branch to steady himself. He rests his head against the surface and closes his eyes for a moment that lasts a second too long.

'Are you sure you're OK?' I ask.

He forces a weak smile. 'Yes. I'll be fine after a good night's sleep.'

I nod, blinking. 'I really am sorry.'

'Don't be,' he whispers into the tree. 'You did great.'

A stiff wind rustles the leaves above us and somewhere in the distance I swear I hear a woman's voice. It's vaporous and airy. Like it's only half formed. Half spoken.

'Find me.'

My head jerks up and I glance around, searching for the source. But apart from the sleeping forest animals and creaking trees, we are alone.

'What's the matter?' Zen asks, peering at me with a concerned expression.

'Did you hear that?'

Zen lifts his head. 'Hear what?'

'A voice,' I say, tilting my ear towards the dark sky. 'I swear I heard a woman's voice.'

Zen takes a teetering step away from the tree, wincing slightly. 'I didn't hear anything,' he says through strained breath.

I'm alarmed by his weakness. I grab the lantern and hurry over to him, draping his arm around my neck. We walk ever so slowly back to the house, and I allow him to lean on me the whole way.

I admit it's a nice change.

6
LOCKED

I help Zen out of his leather boots first, then his doublet, shirt, and breeches. He collapses into the pillows and is asleep almost instantly. I take my time unlacing my corset, relishing the beautiful release when it finally liberates my waist from its clenching wooden embrace. I slide out of my long skirt, change into my linen nightdress, and braid my loose hair down my back.

I glance across the room at Zen, his chest rising and falling.

He usually looks so peaceful in his sleep but tonight his face is contorted by a subtle grimace, making me think that I should have gone easier on him out in the woods. After all, he's just a regular person. And I'm . . . well . . .

I'm me.

I blow out the lantern, tiptoe across the squeaky floorboards, and climb into bed next to Zen. He stirs slightly and rolls towards me, wrapping his arm instinctively around my body.

It's something he does every night, but this time, for some odd reason, it feels different. I feel different. His touch, which always comforts me and puts me at ease, somehow manages to do the opposite. It makes me feel anxious and uneasy. But it's not bad. It's . . . it's . . .

Amazing.

I glance down at his bare shoulder, glowing faintly from the moonlight that streams in the window. Then my gaze slides along his shirtless back, drinking in the soft lines that curve and dimple around his muscles, the velvetiness of his skin, the proximity of his lips to the top of my arm.

And suddenly I have trouble breathing. I want to reach out and touch him more than I've ever wanted anything before. I push myself closer to him but it's not enough. It will never be enough. I need to feel his bare skin against my own.

Just the thought of it makes my entire body glow with heat and my arms and legs start to prickle with that peculiar awareness again.

It's the same sensation I felt outside in the forest earlier. It's like a . . . need. A desperate, aching, burning need. Like my entire body is on fire and Zen is the only relief.

And then, I simply can't take it any more. I can't control it. It controls me.

I roll towards him, push him on to his back, and climb on top of him. My lips crush against his. I kiss him so hard, it's as though I'm trying to extract the very life out of him and unite it with mine.

He tastes like everything I've ever loved.

Zen shifts beneath me, obviously having woken up, and begins to move his mouth in rhythm with mine. Like a dance.

I feel everything in that moment. The curve of his chest, the rigidity of his hip bones, his legs between mine. It's like my nerve endings are on fire. My senses are more alive than they've ever been.

With my lips still firmly secured against his, I start to pull my nightdress up. Desperately wanting to destroy it like an enemy. Rip it to shreds.

At that moment, Zen pulls away and everything comes crashing to a halt, knocking the world off balance. I feel like I'm plummeting through space with nothing to break my fall. I open my eyes to see Zen gazing at me, a confounded expression on his face.

'What are you doing?' he asks in a measured tone.

I shake my head, feeling hot and flustered and breathless for reasons I can't explain. 'I don't know. I don't understand what's happening to me. I just feel this crazy . . . urge. Like a craving. But I don't even know what it's for.'

Zen studies me for a moment and then his mouth curves into a huge grin and he starts to laugh.

'What?' I ask, scooting off him. 'What's so funny?'

His laughter fades quickly. 'Sorry. It's not funny at all. I've just been waiting a long time for this.'

I squint at him. 'For what?'

'For you to feel . . .' He looks uncomfortable. His face even flushes. 'W-w-well,' he stammers. 'For you to feel ready, I guess.'

'Ready for what?'

He glances away, fidgeting anxiously with the hem of the sheet. Then, as though he's finally gathered the courage to look me in the eye, he meets my gaze and holds it tightly. 'Something that will bring us closer together. As close together as we can be.'

Yes! I immediately think. *That's exactly what I want.*

The internal heat starts to glow again but I'm still confused. 'I don't understand. What *is* it?'

He hesitates before answering. 'That's the thing. It's not really something I can explain. I mean, I could . . .' The red tint of his skin is back. 'But I think I'd rather just *show* you. It would be more meaningful that way.'

'If it would bring us closer together, then why haven't we done it already?'

'Well, at first you weren't ready. Mentally, emotionally . . .' He stops and averts his eyes again. 'Physically. I mean, I had to teach you what a hug was. What a kiss was. What a soul mate was. You knew absolutely nothing about love or the emotions that went with it.'

I smile. 'You're a good teacher.'

He chuckles. 'I don't know about that. It's not like I'm a professional or anything. Before I met you all I cared about was gadgets and computer hacking and food. I didn't really think about girls.' He stops, his face reddening again. 'I mean, I thought about girls, I just never . . . you know –' he clears his throat – 'anyway, let's just say I didn't know about this stuff either.'

'So who taught you?'

His entire face softens. 'You did.'

I sigh and bite my lip. 'I'm confused.'

'Sorry. I'm not being very clear. The point is, I knew you weren't ready to do what I wanted to do. And then by the time you were ready, I didn't want to do it any more.'

'Why not?'

He grazes his finger over my shoulder, sending tingles everywhere. 'Because I knew they would just take it away from you. Like they took everything away. Once we figured out that they were erasing your memories, I knew if we did this, it would be gone, too. And I couldn't bear to think about that. So I decided we should wait.' He paused, releasing a heavy breath. 'Until we came here.'

I rest my chin on his chest. His heart is pounding. 'Well, we're here now.'

He looks more nervous than I've ever seen him. 'Yes, we are.'

'So you can show it to me? Now?' The curiosity is devouring me.

'Tomorrow night,' he says softly, stroking my cheek. 'In our woods.'

'OK,' I reply, trying to hide my disappointment. I lay my head back down against the pillow. He turns to face me, the tips of our noses barely touching.

'Good night, Cinnamon,' he murmurs, and I watch his eyes droop and slowly close.

I roll on to my back and stare at the ceiling, listening to the sounds of the house. The ghostly creaking of the walls. The scurrying of mice under the floorboards. Owls calling to one another outside the window.

I reach down the front of my nightdress until I find my locket. I pull it out, pensively fingering the clasp.

It was the only thing I had with me when I woke up with no memories in that ocean full of broken aeroplane parts. The only evidence I had that someone — *somewhere* — cared about me.

I would later learn that Zen was the one who gave me the locket. He had designed it himself with my favourite symbol — the eternal knot — on the front, and a special engraving on the back.

S + Z = 1609

Forever reminding me of our promise to be together in a time without technology. Without Diotech.

But it was me who would eventually discover the locket's real secret.

The truth is, should anything happen to me, should they ever find me here, this necklace is my key to escape.

It is the device that activates my transession gene.

My ability to move through time and space.

If I want to transesse, the locket has to be open. Otherwise, my gene is dormant. Useless. And that's the *real* reason I insist on keeping it on at all times.

As I start to drift to sleep with the small black heart clutched tightly in my hand, I allow myself to think about Rio.

The man who created me.

He and Jans Alixter were the founders of Diotech. They started the company together. But somewhere along the way their opinions and priorities diverged. After I was created, it quickly became apparent that I wasn't the obedient, soulless robot they had expected me to be. Rather, I was a real person. With real emotions, real thoughts, a real ability to love. And most important, an ability to rebel.

Alixter considered that an error. A mistake that needed to be fixed.

Rio felt differently.

That's why he helped me escape. He was the one who gave Zen and me the transession gene. He was the one who installed the special mechanism inside my locket that allowed the gene to be turned on and off. Because according to him, the gene was highly unstable. And not enough tests had been done to ensure its safety. He insisted I have the ability to deactivate the gene when I wasn't using it. To protect me from any harm that it might do.

He saved my life when he gave me that gene.

And he tried to save it again in 2013 when Alixter found me. But he wasn't as lucky that time. By then, Alixter had discovered that Rio had betrayed him. And Alixter killed him. Right in front of me.

I can still see Rio's motionless body lying on the floor of that cave. His limbs tangled. His face contorted in anguish.

And me. I couldn't do anything to stop it. I simply sat there and watched it happen. After everything he'd done for me, I couldn't return the favour. I couldn't save *him*.

One more detail I'm somehow expected to just magically forget.

One more memory I'm not supposed to let haunt me.

One more way I'll surely fail.

7

STRIPPED

I run through the forest. Pine needles and sharp pebbles slice through the skin of my bare feet but the pain doesn't stop me. I need to find it. I can hear it calling to me through the trees.

But no matter how hard I search, I can't seem to locate it. No matter how far I run, the sound only gets further and further away.

I stop to catch my breath, wipe my brow, survey my surroundings. Then I hear it again. Closer this time. More desperate.

BA-BUMP!

BA-BUMP!

BA-BUMP!

I look down and finally see it. The sticky, pounding, juicy red heart lying only a few inches away. It's buried in leaves but still beating. Still alive.

That's when I notice the large gaping black hole in the centre of my chest. The skin around it is ragged and frayed. As though someone ripped me open with a tree branch.

I reach down and gently scoop up the severed organ, hugging it close to me. Protecting it.

A shadow flickers ahead and there's the snap of a twig. My head whips up and I come face-to-face with him. The man with the white-blond hair, sharp, angled features, steel-blue eyes.

'I'm sorry, Sera,' he says. 'But I'm going to have to take that now.'

'Alixter, please,' I beg him. 'Please let me keep it.'

His face remains impassive. Blank. 'It doesn't belong to you.' He pauses, extends his hand, effortlessly pries the slippery heart from my grip, leaving me with empty, red-stained fingers.

Then he smiles — that sickening slithery smile — as he lovingly strokes the still-beating heart. 'It belongs to me.'

With a gasp, I sit up. Panting, choking, battling for air. I clutch my chest, feeling the skin for a fissure. A crack. A scar. I collapse in relief when I find that it's fully intact.

It's still dark outside.

I swing my legs over the side of the bed and bury my head in my hands, attempting to catch my breath. When I open my eyes, my gaze lands directly on my left wrist. On the hideous razor-thin line that stretches across the crease. The mark that Mrs Pattinson called Satan's mark.

My brand.

An ink-black stain on my existence.

It might as well say *Property of Diotech*.

I feel anger rising up inside me. Deep, uncontrollable rage.

I rise to my feet and march across the room, not caring about the cacophony of creaks and thumps I'm making along the sensitive floorboards. I yank open the door to the bedroom and hurry down the stairs.

Once in the kitchen, I sweep my gaze left and right until I find what I'm looking for. I move hurriedly over to what's left of the two-day-old bread loaf and draw the serrated knife from its heel.

I exit the front door and head for the chopping block. I crouch down and lay my arm flat against the thick tree stump, palm up. Then I carefully place the tip of the knife against my wrist bone. Small droplets of crimson squeeze out as the blade drags across my skin. My scientifically perfected life force. I curve around the edge of the tattoo and continue up the other side, peeling my skin away in one long, gruesome strip.

The blood flows instantly. I press the hem of my nightdress to the wound, to stanch the bleeding.

I set the knife down, and with the ribbon of jagged flesh in my hand, I stride up the hill on to the knoll where I normally watch the sunrise. As hard as I can, I chuck the tainted, blackened strip into the valley, watching in the darkness as it flutters in the wind before landing by the edge of the wheat field.

Then I collapse to the ground and I wait.

The sun peeks above the horizon an hour later, just as it always does. As though nothing has changed. As though nothing will *ever* change.

The first glints of daylight illuminate the neatly ploughed rows of the wheat field, showing off Zen and Mr Pattinson's hard work from the day before.

The sky is grey and overcast this morning, a sign of storms to come. Probably later in the afternoon. Chores around the farm are always more difficult in the rain. Wagon wheels catch in the mud. Thunder puts the animals on edge. Wet clothes are heavier and harder to move in. And they take forever to dry.

For the first time since I sat down, I take a deep breath and glance at my left wrist, still covered by the cloth of my nightdress, which is now stained red all along the hem. That will have to be explained to Mrs Pattinson somehow.

I slowly peel back the fabric, cringing slightly at the way it sticks to my skin.

I let out a heavy, surrendering sigh when I see what's underneath.

Fresh pink flesh has grown back over the wound, merging with the jagged edge of the cut. It will only be a matter of time before it will blend in seamlessly.

The most disconcerting part, however, is not how fast my body healed itself – I suppose that was to be expected based on all the other 'enhancements' I've been given – but the sight of the thin, black line that looks freshly drawn across the pale new skin.

I know I shouldn't be surprised. Or disappointed. Zen already told me that the tracking device was a permanent part of my DNA. Like my skin colour, or the shape of my nose. No matter how many times I attempted to carve it out, burn it off, or scrape the skin clean, it would always grow back. Exactly the same.

But I suppose I just had to see it for myself.

I had to witness first-hand the one piece of Diotech that I will never be able to fully erase. That I will never be able to escape from.

I run my fingertip across the new tattoo. Now darker than ever.

A shiver runs through me and for the first time, I notice the brisk morning air. I hadn't even realized how cold I was. Or how little this nightdress does to stave off the chill. Despite my body's ability to protect itself from extreme weather better than any normal human being's.

I glance up at the foreboding sky, watching the greyness gather and condense. If I hope to finish my work before the downpour starts, I should probably get moving. Plus, I'm going to have to figure out what to do with my bloodstained night-dress. How will I manage to wash it without Mrs Pattinson noticing and throwing a fit?

I start to push myself to my feet but my body is suddenly slammed back down to the earth by a wave of dizziness. My head throbs. The air around me feels alive with electricity.

And then, once again from somewhere very far away, I hear it.

A woman's voice. An ethereal whisper in the incoming storm. A commandment.

'Find me.'

My gaze whips in every direction, as I try to figure out where it could be coming from. Who could be saying it. But just like last night in the forest, I see nothing. I'm alone.

I close my eyes tight and listen carefully for the voice but now I hear only the wind and the morning crows, hungrily circling the newly planted crops.

Finally, I give up. Releasing a frustrated groan, I push myself to my feet again.

This time, nothing stops me.

8

DEPARTURE

When I arrive back in our room, I'm surprised to see that Zen is still sleeping. He's usually awake with the morning light. Also, the bedroom seems warmer than usual. And there's a distinctive stale odour.

I scurry over to the window, shoving it open. The crisp dawn air immediately refreshes the room. I stick my head outside and feel the sharpness of the cold oxygen seeping into my lungs.

But when I turn around, I notice Zen is shivering. A prickle of bumps spreading over his bare arms and back. I shut the window.

I get dressed quickly, stuffing my soiled nightdress at the back of the armoire to be dealt with later. Then I walk back to the bed and sit down next to Zen.

He doesn't move.

I reach out to touch his cheek but recoil instantly when I feel how hot it is. Boiling. I pat the sheets around him. They're damp.

'Zen?' I shake him lightly.

He rouses, struggling to open his eyes. And it's not until now that I notice the heavy purple shadows beneath them. The reddish tint of the whites. His irises, which usually sparkle, have an unsettling dullness to them.

I study the rest of his body. His dark hair is matted against his forehead. His skin is pale, with a pasty yellowish hue, and there is no colour in his cheeks. His face contorts in pain as he pushes himself up and swings his legs off the bed.

'Are you OK?' I ask in alarm.

He shivers and rubs his arms. 'Yeah,' he mumbles, rising to his feet. His knees give out and for a moment he's falling forward. In a flash, I'm in front of him, breaking his fall, catching him in my arms.

'Zen?' My voice is trembling.

'I'm fine.' He brushes me off, sounding almost on the verge of annoyance. 'You know you shouldn't move that fast inside the house.'

'I . . .' I start to argue, but my throat constricts, suffocating the rest of the words.

I move back and let him walk away from me. He steps into his breeches, wobbling slightly and steadying himself with one arm on the foot of the bed. 'I'm just feeling a bit under the weather. I'll be OK.'

'Maybe you should go back to sleep,' I suggest.

But he dismisses me with a shake of his head. 'There's too much work to be done.'

'But—' I try again.

Zen cuts me off. 'It's nothing. Really. I'll have some hot porridge and I'll be good as new.'

I watch him stagger out of the bedroom and down the stairs. I follow closely behind him in case he falls again.

Mrs Pattinson is already in the kitchen working on the

bread. I've always thought the way she handles dough is telling of her personality. Kneading it with violent, forceful thrusts, as though she's attempting to murder it.

'Have either of you spotted my bread knife?' she says as soon as we appear at the base of the stairs.

I shake my head and avoid her gaze while Zen mumbles a negation, grabs a bowl from the table, and helps himself to the porridge that's heating on the fire. Mrs Pattinson takes one look at his face and her hands fall limp to her sides.

'What's the matter with you?' she asks brusquely.

I'm instantly relieved to see that I'm not the only one who noticed.

'Nothing.'

'Are you ill?' she presses.

Ill.

The word flashes before my eyes like a lightning bolt as I scramble to find a definition buried somewhere in my mind.

Ill: *being in unsound physical or mental health. Sick.*

'No,' Zen replies curtly. 'I'm not ill. I'm perfectly fine.'

Mrs Pattinson studies him, seemingly deciding whether or not to believe him. Zen ignores her, shovelling spoonfuls of steaming porridge into his mouth. I can't help but notice that his hands are shaking.

Mrs Pattinson goes back to beating the dough with the palm of her hand. 'Well, I sure hope not,' she says with a quiet grunt, 'because I'm sending the pair of you into London today to sell the surplus of apples and pears.'

'Us?' I ask in surprise, dropping my spoon of porridge. It plunks on to the table and Mrs Pattinson gives me a disapproving look. I hurry to fetch a cloth and wipe up the mess.

'Yes,' she says sternly, beating her fist into the dough. 'You'll take Blackthorn and the wagon. It's only an hour's ride. You'll leave straight after breakfast and return for dinner. That should give you enough time to sell the lot of it.'

The way Mrs Pattinson gives the order, with such finality in her tone, I know there's no use in arguing.

'We can't go to London,' I whisper hoarsely to Zen as soon as we're outside the house, heading towards the barn.

'Why not?'

'Why not?' I repeat, exasperated. 'Because it's a huge city. With people and enquiring eyes and suspicious glares. It's far too risky!'

He shakes his head to dismiss my concern and lets out a small cough. He seems to be walking better now. Perhaps he *did* just need a good breakfast.

'It'll be fun. Don't worry, we'll blend right in.'

'Maybe *you* will,' I counter. 'But I've never been good at blending right in.' We reach the post where Mrs Pattinson has tied up Blackthorn in preparation for our journey. He flinches when he sees me coming and I gesture vaguely at his reaction. 'See? Even the stupid horse knows I don't blend in!'

Zen stops and turns to me, taking both of my hands. 'Shhh,' he coos. 'It'll be fine. Besides, we can't stay cooped up here all the time. We can't let fear keep us from living our lives. An occasional trip to London now and then won't hurt. And besides, it'll be good to have a change of scenery. Get your mind off things.'

I drop my gaze to the ground. I know exactly what he's talking about. He's referring to the nightmares. The ones he wants me to forget. I choose not to tell him about my experiment with the knife this morning.

'And it'll be nice to do something together. Alone.' He tilts his head down to look into my eyes again, flashing me that irresistible half-smile that I've fallen in love with over and over again. 'Won't it?'

I admit the idea of seeing something besides the walls of

this house and that barn is tempting. Thrilling, even. But the hot itchy sensation that crawls over my skin tells me it's not a good idea.

'We'll be extra careful,' he assures me, dropping my hands. 'Just don't go bending any iron bars or lifting any oxen over your head.'

I have to giggle, despite the near-debilitating fear that's coursing through my veins. 'I can't bend iron bars,' I begrudgingly remind him as I follow.

He slaps his forehead. 'That's right. I was confusing you with Superman.'

My forehead wrinkles. 'Who?'

He chuckles. 'Never mind.'

'Well, what about you?' I ask, giving him a sharp stare. His skin still looks extremely pale. 'Are you feeling well enough to go?'

He gestures to his fully functioning arms and legs. 'I feel great now. That's some powerful porridge.'

Zen enters the barn and returns with Blackthorn's harness, throwing it over the horse's back. Blackthorn eyes me sceptically as Zen works to attach the harness to the cart.

I start loading the extra apples that Mrs Pattinson has allotted into the back and then climb on to the bench. Blackthorn snorts in disapproval and stamps his foot. But Zen is quick to put him at ease, as he does everyone who seems to distrust me. He walks up to him, pats him gently on the face, and whispers in his ear, 'Don't worry, old man. She's not that bad.'

I let out a huff. 'Well, thanks.'

Zen smiles, grabs the reins, and hops up to sit beside me. He gives Blackthorn the signal to go and suddenly we're off, trudging through the tall grass on the outskirts of the property, until we reach the dirt road that will take us into town.

I turn and watch the small farmhouse, where we've spent

the past six months of our lives, get smaller and smaller behind us. Although I know it's only my imagination, through the *clip clop* of Blackthorn's hooves on the ground, the rumble of the wheels beneath us, and the hiss of the wind whizzing past my ears, I swear I hear it whispering goodbye.

9

STORMS

Throughout the hour-long drive, I steal quick glances at Zen from the corner of my eye, taking note of his slouched posture, sagging cheeks, and general air of fatigue. I ask him repeatedly how he's feeling and every time he answers, quite snappishly, that he's fine.

But he certainly doesn't look fine. Every few minutes he has to cough and he's been consistently wiping perspiration from his brow even though the weather is actually quite cool today.

I glance up at the grey sky and wonder when it will start raining. I hope it's not while we're out. I'm certainly no expert in illnesses but I have a feeling being outside in the rain isn't the best thing for someone who looks as awful as Zen does.

When we arrive in the city, Zen steers the cart into the marketplace and pulls Blackthorn to a halt. I sit paralysed in my seat. Trying to take in the chaotic scene that is playing out in front of me.

I'm starting to feel like I left my stomach back on the farm.

Zen seems oblivious to my reaction. He's too busy marvelling.

Mumbling something about how it looks exactly like it does in the movies. I don't even know what a movie is so I don't share his admiration. All I feel is sick. And a burning desire to turn around and sprint as fast as my genetically enhanced legs can carry me back down the road that brought us here. At top speed, I could probably be back on the farm in less than ten minutes.

I'm not sure what I expected to see. The only other towns or cities I've been to are Wells Creek and Los Angeles. But this city is nothing like either of those. Instead of stores and buildings, there are hundreds of little stalls set up along the perimeter of the square. Each one selling something different. Like meat, cloth, vegetables, bread, grain, and live animals in wooden cages. People are milling about, calling out orders, and haggling over prices. One woman walks past us pulling a rope attached to a goat, while another passes in the other direction holding a dead chicken by its feet. I assume it was recently alive due to the fact that it still has its feathers and its eyes are wide open, revealing the same terrified look I saw on the faces of the bodies floating in the ocean with me after the plane crash.

There are no markings on the ground or signs on poles to direct traffic. But somehow the varieties of different-sized wheeled contraptions pulled by horses and oxen manage to weave effortlessly around one another, as though they can read the oncoming drivers' thoughts.

Zen hops down from the cart, taking a moment to steady himself before starting to unload the produce from the back, stacking the crates of apples and pears. I can tell he's struggling and I quickly jump down and walk around to help him.

As I work, I can't help but wince at the foul smell in the air. It's much worse than the odour in the Pattinsons' barn when the pig sty is due to be cleaned. I scrunch up my nose, lean in close to Zen, and whisper, 'What is that?'

Zen nods, letting me know he smells it, too. 'No indoor

plumbing. People toss their waste into the street.'

The thought makes me want to retch but I somehow manage to avoid it.

'I think we'll get used to it,' Zen says hopefully. 'Everyone here seems to have.'

After the last crate has been unloaded, Zen points to a small gap between two of the stalls on the other side of the road. 'I think we should set up there.' He turns to me and winks. 'If we sell all this stuff fast enough, maybe we can even go exploring for a little while.'

I nod, acting like the idea excites me as much as it seems to excite him, even though just standing here in the middle of all this commotion is setting my entire body on edge.

'We should really see Shakespeare performed at the Globe,' he says, then leans in conspiratorially and whispers, 'before it burns down in four years.'

'It burns down?'

He nods. 'Unfortunately. A cannon sets fire to the roof during a production of *Henry VIII*. They rebuild it a year later, though.'

'You seem to know a lot about Shakespeare,' I point out.

Zen picks up one of the crates. He seems to exert an obvious amount of effort but he still manages a crooked grin as he says, 'I researched him for you. After you read Sonnet 116, you had to know everything there was to know about him.'

Despite my frayed nerves, this makes me smile. 'Then we definitely should go see one of his plays when we're finished.'

He nods and nudges his chin towards the cart. 'It doesn't look like we can park here. Why don't you walk Blackthorn to that hitching post over there and then help me carry everything.'

I notice how he struggles to balance the crate in his arms, the unnaturally thick layer of sweat that appears on his upper lip, and the way his face seems to be losing colour by the second. I nibble nervously on the tip of my finger. 'Actually,' I say, trying to keep my voice light and helpful, 'maybe you should tie up the horse and I'll start moving the crates over.'

Zen lets out a stutter of a laugh that quickly turns into a violent cough, causing him to nearly drop the box. 'Sera,' he says sternly, 'you have to get over your fear of that horse some day.'

'I didn't mean—' I start to argue, but Zen has already swung the crate up on to his shoulder and turned away. He waits for a lull in the traffic of horse-drawn carts and riders before crossing the street.

Why does he have to be so stubborn? He's worse than the horse.

With a sigh, I trudge around the front of the cart and stomp up to Blackthorn. He jerks in response to my brusque approach and pins his ears back close against his head in his default sign of aggression. But this time I'm not tolerating it. Maybe it's Zen's foul mood rubbing off on me or my own lingering disquiet from my dream this morning, but I'm done putting up with this horse's attitude. I snatch the reins and give them a yank. Blackthorn whinnies his complaint.

'Listen,' I say firmly, looking him directly in his big black ball of an eye, 'enough is enough. Either you learn to like me or I punch you in the face. So what's it gonna be?'

I sincerely doubt the horse understood the words that were coming out of my mouth, but he seemed to comprehend the meaning just fine because suddenly it's like he's an entirely different animal.

He lets out a small snort, his ears perk back up, and his head bows slightly, as though he's submitting to me. I'm actually fairly surprised that my approach worked and I let out a snort of my own.

Maybe Mr Pattinson was right. Maybe I simply needed to stop being afraid of him first.

I pull the reins over his head and give them a gentle tug.

Obediently he picks up his feet and follows me without complaint or resistance.

'There,' I say to him as we reach the hitching post. 'That wasn't so hard, was it? Isn't it so much better now that we've dealt with our issues and can behave like civilized beings?'

He doesn't respond but I take his silence as acquiescence.

I loop the leather rein around the wooden post and pull the end through. 'Now if we can—'

A scream that turns my blood to stone rips through the air, causing both me and Blackthorn to startle.

My head whips in the direction of the sound and in an instant all my surroundings vanish. The putrid odour of the city is lifted on to an invisible breeze. The pandemonium of the bustling marketplace drips and fades into unrecognizable shapes and colours. Like someone threw a cup of water on a fresh painting. The boisterous racket of people and rumbling carts just kind of slips away into a faint hush. Like the sound of the world submerged in water.

Then all I hear is the *screech* of wooden wheels scraping against the coarse dirt, the wail of a terrified horse as it's jerked into an unnatural twist, and the rough, angry bellow of a driver as he tries unsuccessfully to steer the massive, unwieldy wagon around the young man lying unconscious in the middle of the road.

A spiral of red apples fans out around his beautiful face, the empty, inverted crate lying a few feet away. His damp dark hair is matted to his forehead and his skin is as pale and grey as the sky. I have no time to think before the wagon starts to overturn. I watch the heavy, rounded roof topple and plunge right towards Zen's head as the first drop of rain lands on the tip of my nose.

10
TORN

I must be flying. If my feet touch the ground I don't feel it. The only thing I feel is the cool air whirring past my face, knocking off my bonnet, tangling recklessly through my hair. And then . . .

Gravity.

Fighting against me as my hands cut through the closing sliver of space between the top of the descending wagon and Zen's skull. Gravity pushing back. Hard and relentless. Thrusting the massive cart towards the earth with the force of a thousand men.

It wants to win. It wants to crush him. To take him from me forever. To leave me stranded in this foreign time alone.

But I won't let it.

I fight back. Bending my knees for leverage. The wood digs into my hands, splintering off and piercing my skin. I let out a shallow grunt as I lift with all my strength, planting my feet firmly against the ground, straightening my legs, and with one final effort, I stand, shoving the wagon away.

It turns upright again but is spinning far too fast to stop there. It keeps rotating, breaking free from the slender poles that attach it to the horse that is now lying on its side, breathing heavily. The wood snaps easily and the wagon continues revolving, roof over wheels, round and round until it finally crashes into a row of merchant stalls and sputters to a halt, teetering precariously on one of its diagonal edges.

A woman screams again. I presume it's the same one but I don't look up to verify. I look only at Zen, bending down, waiting for him to open his eyes. Waiting for the confirmation that he's OK.

Did I get there fast enough?

Is he unconscious?

Is he dead?

The last thought kicks me squarely in the stomach and what little wind I have left after my efforts is gone. Crushed upon impact.

I reach out and touch his face. Gently stroking his cheek. His dark thick eyelashes flutter twice and then his eyes drag open. I exhale loudly and collapse on to him, crying softly into the dirt-soiled collar of his shirt.

'Shhh,' he soothes, moving with difficulty as he attempts to caress my hair.

'I thought . . . I thought you were . . .' I can't finish the sentence. Mild tears give way to thundering sobs that choke the last word and hold it captive in my throat.

Gone.

One second later and he would have been.

'It's OK,' Zen says to me, struggling to prop himself up on his elbows. His features contort in torment with every inch he attempts to move. Finally, he gives up and falls on to his back again.

I bury my face in the crook of his neck. It's scalding hot. So hot I have to pull away. Panicked, I glance down at him. It looks like he dunked his head in a bucket of water.

I dab at my wet cheeks with the heel of my hand. 'What's happening to you?' I ask.

'Nothing.' He attempts to reassure me. 'I'm fi—' But he never finishes the sentence. He breaks into violent coughs that cause his entire body to shudder. I watch helplessly, wincing every time another powerful convulsion rips through him.

'You keep saying that, but you're clearly *not* fine!' I shout, no longer able to hold in my exasperation.

He clears his throat and presses his fingertips against his temple, cringing. 'OK, maybe I'm a little sick,' he finally admits. 'But I'll be fine. I'm a quick healer. Always have been.'

I hear people yelling far in the distance but I ignore it, choosing instead to focus on Zen. I reach out and brush his damp hair away from his forehead, trying not to flinch as his skin scorches my fingertips.

One look at his pale face and sunken eyes and I can't handle it. I collapse into him again, wrapping my arms around him and pulling him tightly to me. He lets out a soft chuckle and continues to stroke my head. But I can tell that it's a difficult task because his hand barely grazes my hair. Like a faint breeze, hardly even strong enough to rustle the leaves of a tree.

The sound of yelling is suddenly louder. Closer. And I feel Zen's body stiffen beneath me. 'Sera,' he says cautiously. His hand falls from my head and taps me feebly on the back.

But I don't move. I don't want to go anywhere. The carts and horses and people can just go around us.

'Sera,' he says again. This time there's a severity in his tone that sends a chill through me. I jerk up. 'What's wrong?'

His eyes are dark and wild. Focused on something in the distance. Something behind me. The voices. I spin my head around and see a mass of people congregating. Speaking in frantic, fearful tones. Pointing in my direction. Sharp, angry fingers extended. Jabbing.

'She's right over there!' one of them says.

'I saw it with my own eyes!' Another chimes in. 'She lifted up the wagon as though it were made of feathers.'

'And did you see her move?' a woman asks the growing crowd. 'Like wind. Like lightning!'

I look back at Zen with panicked eyes. He's calm but alert. I open my mouth to speak but he holds one finger to his lips. He nudges his chin purposefully in the direction of my chest.

'We need to get out of here,' he whispers, holding my gaze intently, speaking to me with his eyes as well as his tongue.

I glance down at the tip of my kerchief, confused. The chaotic sounds behind me turn my attention back to the swarm of people. It's almost tripled in size. Scattered murmurings have turned into a roar of outrage. Three muscular men shove their way to the front of the group. Their angry eyes home in on me. They yell one rallying word to the crowd and start stalking towards us. Everyone follows, spreading out until they've covered the width of the road. An impenetrable wall of rage.

At last I get it.

He doesn't just want to get out of here. He wants to get out of *here*. Out of this town. Out of this time. Our sojourn in 1609 is over. I've done exactly what I wasn't supposed to do. Cause a scene. Draw attention to myself.

And judging by the size of that mob, it's a lot of attention.

He motions towards my chest again and now I understand. He's gesturing to my locket. I need to get it out. Get it open. Activate the gene. Otherwise, I'm not going anywhere.

'It's the devil's work! I'm sure of it!' comes an enraged voice behind me. They're getting closer.

I claw desperately at my clothing, scraping against my knotted kerchief and tight bodice. But my shaking hands slip and fumble. And there are just too many layers. Too much fabric.

I look anxiously back to see the mob storming towards us, shouting curse words, bellowing nonsense about Satan.

'Sera,' Zen prompts in a warning tone.

'I can't!' I cry. 'I can't get to it.'

'Rip through,' he commands me. 'You're strong enough.'

I do as I'm told, grabbing a fistful of material and yanking as hard as I can. The fabric tears with a popping sound. I dig down the front of my corset, under my shift, grappling for the chain.

I pull until the smooth, black charm is out. Zen reaches for it. Wraps his fingers around it. Slides his nail into the narrow slit that unites the two sides of the heart.

I reach out, push up his sleeve, and grasp his arm, holding on tight. We have to be touching. Skin-to-skin contact. Otherwise, we'll be separated.

I close my eyes to focus on another time. Another place. Anywhere but here. I feel my body lift from the ground. Floating upward. Tugged into the air.

It's working! I think with desperate relief.

We're safe!

But then I feel Zen's arm being ripped from my hand. The sweat causes our skin to stick together momentarily and then I don't feel him at all. There's a hard yank on the back of my neck as the chain of my necklace snaps, leaving behind a strip of searing heat at the base of my skull.

I open my eyes to find that I'm being carried by the three men who led the pack of angry townsfolk. One has his hands under my armpits, the other two have hold of my legs. We are moving swiftly away from Zen and the scene of the crashed wagon. I kick and flail, lifting my head long enough to see Zen finally manage to flick open the locket.

I squeeze my eyes shut tight and imagine myself next to him. If I can transesse back to his side, just a few feet away, I can grab on to him and we can leave. Together.

But I don't move. I stay firmly locked in the strong hold of the three men. Which means it's not working. My gene has not yet activated.

But the locket is open!

I saw him open it.

There can be only one explanation: I'm too far away. Whatever technology Rio put into that locket must only work within a short distance. Or perhaps it has to be touching me. Which would explain why Rio placed it inside my locket. Something that would always be close by, resting next to my heart.

Zen must have figured out the same thing. At the same time. Because I watch him leap shakily to his feet and run towards me. But his knees give out after a few steps and he plummets to the ground. He rolls on to his side, gasping for air, shaking, attacked by another onslaught of ragged coughs.

'ZEN!' I cry out, thrashing against my captors.

Then I watch in horror as a set of large, grubby fingers pries the locket from Zen's clenched fist. The man is tall and stocky, wearing an ornate green-and-gold-trimmed doublet, ruffled collar, and a velvet-lined cloak. His rounded middle and the gold chain around his chest mark him as a man of means.

Zen groans and tries to lift his head, tries to reach for the stolen property, but he's too weak. Whatever sickness is coursing through his veins is too strong. His body starts to convulse.

The thief stalks towards me, clutching the necklace. The broken chain dangles below his fingers. When he reaches me, he shakes it forcefully in my face, bellowing, 'Is this how you summon him? How much innocent blood did you have to spill to cast your spell on this!?'

A spray of saliva hits my cheeks.

Desperately, I reach for the locket but he pulls it away too quickly. Then he turns to the gathering throng of people, hoisting it proudly above his head, the eternal knot turned out-ward for everyone to see. 'Look at this symbol! It's a sign of the devil himself!'

Based on the revered, deferent reaction of the crowd, I infer that this man must be some kind of authority figure. A person of power.

He turns back to me and snaps the locket closed with a de-cisive click. 'Let's see how fast and strong you are without your black magic!'

He stuffs it into the pocket of his doublet and gestures to the men holding me. 'Take her to Newgate Prison. Let the central court decide what becomes of her.'

In an instant I'm being carried away. Further and further from my necklace and from Zen, who now lies trembling in the middle of the street.

'No!' I scream, thrashing forcefully. I have to get back to him. I have to get the locket. It's my escape. Our escape. With-out it, I'll be trapped here forever. Doomed to face whatever fate these outraged people have in store for me.

I hear Zen's raspy voice scream feebly from somewhere be-hind me. 'Fight, Sera! Don't let them win! You're stronger than they are!'

One giant, powerful wrench and I manage to slip from their grasp, falling to the ground. Hitting it hard. I scramble to my feet and race back towards the man in the velvet cloak.

Four men block my path. I flank left, skirting around them. One of them manages to grasp my biceps, pulling me to a stop. I twist, thrusting the heel of my hand against his nose. I hear a loud crack and warm liquid spatters my face. When I pull my hand away, it's dripping with thick blood. But still he seems undeterred, coming at me again.

I crouch low and sweep my leg around in a blur. It catches

his ankle and he tumbles feet over head and smashes into the ground.

The entire exchange took only a matter of seconds but it was still, apparently, enough time for more of them to assemble. When I look up from the man writhing on the ground, one or more of his vertebrae most likely dislocated, I see a small army converging on me.

I look left, then right, then behind me. I feel my hope plunge as I realize that I'm surrounded.

They move in, closing the circle, calling out directions to one another, encouraging everyone to stay strong. To not let me get away.

My breath comes in choppy gasps. My chest burns. My stomach knots and coils and then knots again.

One of them I can handle. Two or three, maybe. But as I spin in a slow circle, my hands up, ready to fight, my eyes wide and wild like a trapped animal's, I count twelve in the inner circle alone, with more approaching from the outside to fortify the wall.

I can't take that many. I know it's impossible.

I drop my arms to my sides. I close my eyes. I try to drown in my defeat and disappear within myself as I hear the heavy footsteps and feel the foul, angry breath of a dozen bodies descending upon me.

11

DETAINED

Everything that happens next is warped by a grey fog that clouds my vision. I hear the words spoken around me. I see the commotion that my actions have brought to this town. But it's as though it's all happening on the other side of a dirty, splintered window.

They bind my hands in front of me with rough, heavy iron chains. They load me into the back of an open-air cart, surrounded by five burly, angry-looking men. We drive. Somewhere. Anywhere. I don't know. Minutes pass. Or perhaps hours. My arms and legs feel cold. Cramped. My fingers have lost sensation. I hold up my hands and stare at them but I can't focus on them. There are ten fingers. No, eight. No, twelve. No, none.

Where did my fingers go?

My body isn't working right. I can't seem to hold a single thought in my mind. I think my brain is shutting down. Hibernating. To protect me from reality. From truth. From pain.

The wagon stops. My five escorts brace themselves, glaring

at me. I think they assume I'm going to run. How can I run when I can't feel my feet? When my brain is liquefying?

They walk me down a dark, musty hallway. I can hardly manage to put one foot in front of the other. My feet drag and slide and skid. They think I'm fighting again. They shove me and push me and yank on my chains. Shout things.

I'm not fighting.

I'm barely breathing.

I'm jostled into a filthy cell. The door is slammed with an earth-shattering, finite BANG! I collapse on to the dirt floor, my cheek pressed against the cold ground, and stare numbly at their feet through the thick metal bars.

They're walking away. They're leaving me here.

My brain struggles to send signals to my mouth. *Move. Speak. Ask.*

'Zen?' My lips form the shape but I don't know if any sound emerges.

I remember the names we've been using here as part of our attempt to blend in. I try again, summoning strength. Summoning breath. 'Where is Ben? Is he OK?'

The only response is the sound of their footsteps receding.

And then suddenly, I'm alone. In the darkness. A single torch is lit in the hallway just outside my cell. But I can still see everything around me as clear as if the sun were shining through the non-existent window. One of the many 'abilities' I was endowed with.

Or should I say *cursed* with.

I close my eyes and immediately see Zen. Lying in the street. Coughing. Shaking.

I open my eyes but the image doesn't go away. There's no escape.

And the longer I think about it, the more gruesome the scene becomes. The more my imagination takes over.

I see him gasping for his last breath. I see his body being left to rot in the road. The wheels of a merciless carriage fracturing his skull right down the middle, crushing his handsome face. I see his brains splattered on the gravel. Giant horse hooves trampling right through them. Oblivious to the fact that they once belonged to a real human being. A caring, selfless human being who never deserved any of this.

Who never deserved to fall in love with someone like me.

Someone who only invites chaos and agony and destruction wherever she goes.

Someone who should never have been created.

I roll on to my stomach and press my face into the dirt again. The smell in here is worse than it was out in the street. It's seeped into the ground. The walls. Clinging to the stale putrid air that hasn't seen daylight in probably centuries.

The guilt twists in my stomach. Swirling around, callously destroying everything in its path. Until my whole body is consumed with it. Until I am just a writhing, crying, pitiful ball of shame. Lying in filth where I belong.

Somewhere between splattered brains and falling tears, I find sleep. It comes without warning. Offering me a few hours of solace. Beautiful relief. But in the morning my head and heart are throbbing worse than before.

With no sunlight to indicate the time, I take a guess that it's around noon the next day when a guard approaches the outside of my cell. Somehow I find the strength to push myself up, to look into his eyes, to beg for information.

'Please,' I implore. 'The boy I was with. Do you know what happened to him? Do you know where he is? He's very ill. He needs help.'

He stands tall. Rigid. His face is completely impassive. 'I've come to deliver a message. From his royal majesty, King James I.'

My heart shatters when I realize he's not going to answer me.

'You will be brought to trial for the crime of witchcraft. If you are found guilty, you are to be executed.'

I only understand half of the things I'm being told. But the general meaning is clear: they don't think I'm human either. And they want me dead because of it.

Maybe it's for the best.

Maybe this is what was meant to happen.

If Zen is still alive, maybe he can leave here without me. Return to his home in the year 2115 and find a nice, normal, non-synthetically engineered girl to fall in love with. Maybe then he'll finally be able to lead a normal life.

And then one day, in the very distant future, far away from here, far away from the remnants of this shattered dream that ended too soon, he'll be able to forget me.

That is the story I tell myself.

12

BEWITCH

In the perpetual darkness I lose track of the hours, the days, how many times another faceless guard arrives to bring me stale bread and water. I sleep as much as I can. It's the only way I can shut off my thoughts, which are now crisp and focused once again.

I wish the fog would return.

By the time they come for me, my body is frail and soggy. If they were trying to wear me down, it worked. Nearly all my strength is gone. My voice is hoarse and rusty from lack of use. I remember mumbling Zen's name every time someone would appear outside my cell. There's a chance I might have called it out in my sleep, waking myself. But other than that, I have not spoken.

'How long have I been in here?' I ask as they bind my feet in chains.

'Five days,' replies one of the guards. His expression is vacant. He won't look at me.

I am led through a crowd of furious people. I am made to

stand in a daunting courtroom, surrounded by the faces of those who will be happy to see me die. I am forced to listen to the convincing accounts of the townsfolk who saw me move faster than a cannon, lift an entire wagon with my bare hands, and throw it across the street.

The gentleman who arrested me, who stole my locket, is called up to testify. He spouts angry accusations. Insists that I have arrived from a place called Hell and should be promptly returned there. That I should be tried as a heretic. Not just a criminal. That I am a special case. Unlike any other they've seen.

I don't speak. I don't argue. What is there to argue? It's all true. I may not be a witch, as they are accusing me, but I'm certainly not one of them. I certainly don't belong in this time. Or any time, for that matter. I watch the shocked faces of the jurors and spectators, their stormy eyes narrowed in accusation. Their silent thoughts scream at me. How dare I infect their town, their home, their lives with my toxin?

I am unable to meet any of their stares. So I keep my head down. My gaze low.

The next witness is called to speak. I hear heavy footsteps shuffling to the front of the large, echoing chamber. I can feel the hateful glare as the witness passes. It reaches out. Strangles me. Stabs me.

'Please state your name for the record,' the magistrate says.

'Mrs Elizabeth Pattinson.'

My head snaps up and I am suddenly face-to-face with her. The woman who has fed me, clothed me, and given me a place to sleep for the past six months. Our gazes collide. And for a moment – just a flicker of a moment – I sense that she is not here to harm me. That she has found what little compassion she has left and has brought it here today to help me.

Maybe she even knows something about Zen.

'What is your relationship to the accused?'

Mrs Pattinson breaks eye contact and turns to look at the judge. 'She has been living in my home. As a hired servant.'

Murmurs trickle across the assembly. Too muddled for me to make out anything specific, but the sentiment is palpable. Shock. Pity. Fear that it could just as easily have happened to them.

For some reason, my attention is drawn to a specific location in the back of the room. On the balcony. I squint into the crowd of spectators, trying to make out someone familiar, but I'm met only by the hateful eyes of strangers.

'And what do you have to contribute to today's proceedings?' the magistrate asks Mrs Pattinson, bringing my attention back to the woman standing only a few feet away.

She refuses to look at me, instead her gaze flicks between the twelve jurors and the magistrate, sitting on his bench, dressed in his long red gown, surrounded by clerks. I suck in a sharp breath, hoping less for a testimony of my innocence and more for some morsel of an indication that Zen is OK. Then at least I can be put to death knowing he is safe.

But a small voice in the back of my head reminds me of this impossibility. If he were safe – if he were OK – he would be here. He would be attempting to save me.

It's a painful truth that I already know.

'Sarah,' she begins, and then quickly clears her throat. 'I mean, the accused, formed a particular bond with my youngest child while she was dwelling with us. I didn't approve of the relationship. I tried to discourage it as much as possible.'

Quiet murmurs of assent emanate from the crowd.

'But it is because of this relationship that I can now stand before you and say with certainty –' she takes a deep breath, her mouth twitching – 'that this woman is, in fact, a witch.'

The quiet murmurs rapidly morph into earsplitting attacks

and cries for justice. I close my eyes and attempt to block out the noise.

'Would you care to elaborate?' the magistrate prompts.

'Of course, Your Worship,' Mrs Pattinson replies obligingly. And in that instant I know. She was never here to help me. There was never a chance in the world that she would risk her family, her reputation, her life to help me. The girl she despised and mistrusted from the very beginning.

'A few nights ago, as I was walking past the bedroom of the accused, I overheard her telling my daughter a story,' she begins.

I let out a defeated sigh as a hot ball of fire starts to burn in my stomach.

'It was the story of a princess who had run away from her home because she had *magic powers.*'

More reactions from the room and the jury. Even the magistrate – who I assume is supposed to remain impartial through this process – appears disturbed by this. Once again, I feel drawn to that location in the back of the room. As though a light is blinking on and off there, calling my attention, but when I allow my gaze to slip that way, I see nothing but unfamiliar faces.

'Yes,' Mrs Pattinson replies to the astonished crowd. 'She was actually attempting to spread her poison to my innocent young daughter!' She waits for the next wave of reactions to die down before continuing. 'I found a nightdress stained with blood at the back of the armoire in her room. Undoubtedly from one of her satanic rituals. And I assume you have already seen the black mark of the devil on her wrist?'

Confusion and agitation break out. It's evident this particular piece of information has not yet been revealed to the court or the spectators. All eyes are suddenly on me. I shrink back against the low wall of the tiny box that I'm standing in. The iron chains binding my hands in front of me feel as though they're tightening with each passing second.

In the commotion of capturing me, binding me, and leading me away, the tattoo embedded on my skin was evidently overlooked.

But it won't be overlooked for long. The magistrate turns expectantly to me, his eyebrows raised, the wrinkles on his aged face stretched with curiosity. 'Kindly show the citizens of the jury your wrists.'

I do as I'm told, raising my arms slowly, feeling the stares of those gathered in the giant hall zeroing in on my hands. Although I'm sure not everyone in the room can see the small black line from their vantage point, the gasps of repulsion still reverberate off the walls.

'She told us it was a prisoner tattoo from being held captive by pirates.'

Quiet titters of laughter gradually replace the gasps.

'But I never believed her.' Mrs Pattinson is quick to defend herself. 'I never believed it for a second.'

'Is that all?' the magistrate asks.

'No,' Mrs Pattinson replies hastily. 'There's one more thing. The matter of the young man with whom she arrived here. Her husband.'

My whole body squeezes to attention. I gnaw on the inside of my cheek and stare intensely at her, waiting for her next words with a burning, insatiable hunger that makes my skin itch.

'On the night she was arrested, he was returned to our farmhouse.'

Warmth floods through me. I shut my eyes and nearly collapse in relief.

He's safe. He's all right. The Pattinsons are taking care of him.

'At first, we thought he might be an accomplice to her immoral ways,' Mrs Pattinson continues. 'But he was very ill when he was delivered back to us, barely able to stand, almost unconscious, with sweats and chills and a fever higher than I've ever witnessed. And we quickly realized that he was not her accomplice but her victim. Clearly under the influence of her dark magic. I have no doubt that she was the one who was making him sick.'

'That's a lie!' I hear an angry voice blurt out. It takes me a moment to realize that the voice belongs to me. Until this moment I haven't uttered a word. 'I would never do anything to hurt him!' I no longer have control over my own mouth. My own body. Tears are crashing down my face. I'm finding it hard to breathe.

Chaos has ensued as a result of my outburst. Everyone in the room seems to have an opinion on the subject and they're all shouting it at once. The magistrate fights to restore order.

'And how is the young man faring?' he asks pointedly once everyone has quieted down. 'Now that she's been imprisoned and he is safely away from her.'

Mrs Pattinson looks discomfited. Her eyes dart from one end of the room to the other, as though she feels like she is the one on trial here. Not me. 'The truth is, I can't tell you.' She pauses, wringing her hands. 'He disappeared two days ago.'

Disappeared?

The magistrate echoes my confusion. 'Disappeared?'

'Probably wandered off into the woods. My guess is the witch lured him out of the house with a spell.' Mrs Pattinson spits in disgust. 'But with that sickness in his blood, he wouldn't last a mile.'

She's right.

If he tried to go anywhere in his condition on foot, he wouldn't make it far. If he attempted to transesse, looking for me, then he never arrived.

Which means . . .

'No doubt he's dead somewhere in the woods,' Mrs Pattinson concludes. 'Food for the crows.'

The floor is suddenly seized from underneath my feet. The room appears to be spinning. There is no more blood in my head, my face, my fingers, my toes.

I feel my brain start to click off again. My body quickly follows. One by one, piece by piece, cell by cell, everything shuts down.

I am floating. I am falling. The beautiful stillness of the looming darkness welcomes me. Invites me in.

I go willingly.

13

RECORDED

I awake on my feet. Hoisted up by two guards. I am outside, being hauled back into the angry mob, my feet dragging through the dirt behind me. As I come to, I try to walk, but the iron chains around my wrists and ankles make it difficult. Not to mention the numbness that has worked its way to my legs, threatening to cut off circulation to my heart.

Good.

Maybe then it will stop beating.

Maybe then I can stop breathing.

Just. Stop.

I didn't even hear what the verdict was. I passed out before it was announced. But I already know.

Although I'm not sure why there was ever a need for a trial. It seems to me I was guilty from the moment I set foot on seventeenth-century soil.

As I gaze out into the throng of people that awaits me, I'm reminded of when I left the hospital in the year 2013. After I was assumed to be the only survivor of Freedom Airlines

89

flight 121. Mr Rayunas, the social worker who was charged with the task of placing me in a foster family, had to guide me through a wall of reporters and photographers and news crews and onlookers wanting to sneak a peek at the girl who fell from the sky and lived to tell about it.

At that time, I was revered. A celebrity. A miracle.

Now I am detested. An abomination. A witch.

Regardless, I feel exactly the same. Like an outcast. Like someone who will never belong no matter where I go, no matter what I do. I will always stand out. I will always draw attention to myself. I will never be safe.

And now I've dragged a wonderful, innocent, beautiful boy down into my endless pit of destruction.

And now he's gone forever.

Perhaps the Diotech scientists had it right. They kept me locked up behind concrete walls and security clearances. They restricted access to me. They even manipulated my own memories so I would never find out what a monster I actually am.

Maybe that's the only way I'll be able to live.

As a well-kept secret.

Well, it's a little late for that now.

And besides, living just feels like an ugly, messy, thankless job I never want to do again.

Once it's evident that I can stand up on my own again, the guards release my arms and walk ahead, pulling me behind them. Most people won't meet my eye as I pass – probably afraid that I will cast some kind of spell on them and cause their livestock to die or their children to grow third arms – but some of the braver bystanders lock eyes with me. I'm surprised to see not all of their faces exhibit fear or anger. A few show flashes of pity. Some even compassion.

These are the stares that are hardest to return.

The ones I want to shut out completely.

And then suddenly, without warning, something unbelievable catches my eye. I blink to refocus my vision but there's no mistake. Far off in the distance, rising over the heads of hundreds of people, I see it.

I see . . . me.

It's not like looking into a mirror. The likeness isn't crisp and reflective. It's grainy and pixilated and not quite real. But there's no doubt in my mind that it's my face. Long hair. Small, heart-shaped mouth. A slender nose. The only detail that's missing is my purple eyes.

In fact, all the colour is missing from my face. Every feature is in black-and-white.

It takes me a moment to realize exactly what I'm staring at. And once I do, everything – what I'm feeling, what I'm afraid of, what I anticipate – completely shifts.

The rules have been rewritten.

The game is over. And a new one has begun.

Because high in the sky, secured to a tall wooden post, under big block letters spelling out the words WITCH TRIAL, is a hand-drawn sketch of my face on thick parchment. And directly below it is a date:

THE 6TH OF OCTOBER, SIXTEEN HUNDRED AND NINE.

Today's date.

An official document. A public record. Proof of where I am at this precise moment in time.

My heart hammers in my chest as I hastily peer into the crowd, this time with a new purpose, a new resolve.

They're here. They have to be here. There's no way they would miss an opportunity like this. An opportunity to pinpoint my exact location.

I admit, the timing would be perfect. Zen is gone. There is no one left to protect me. And in my current state – hungry, tired, weak, beaten down, hopeless, chained – they could take me easily. I can't see myself putting up much of a fight.

Fight.

The word punches me in the chest and I instantly think of Zen. I hear him screaming it in the street. Echoes from days ago. When the townspeople were trying to take me. When he could barely breathe. His cries reverberate through my memory.

'Fight, Sera!'

'Don't let them win!'

'You're stronger than they are!'

But how can I fight? I can't win. Not when my gene is dormant and my necklace is gone – probably destroyed. Not when the only thing I've ever had to fight for is dead.

I'm tired of fighting. Tired of running. Tired of having to.

Maybe Diotech appearing and taking me away isn't the worst thing in the world. At least then I wouldn't have to run any more. They could erase all of this from my mind. I could forget any of it happened. That I ever loved him. That he ever died to be with me.

I could just be the submissive, emotionless machine they always wanted.

It would be easy. So very easy.

I feel pressure on the chains around my wrists and realize I've stopped walking and the guard is yanking me back to the present moment.

I continue to scan the crowd, searching for evidence of them. But I soon realize that I don't even know what I'm looking for. They could be anywhere. Anyone.

Would they send the same two agents they sent last time? The frightening man with the creepy scar slicing down his face? Would Alixter himself appear to bring me back?

If they sent someone new, there's no way I would ever recognize him. Or her. Plus, they would be smart about it. Diligent. The agent would blend in completely. Disguised in seventeenth-century clothing and a seventeenth-century hair-style.

Which means the only way I'll know them is when they make their move to apprehend me.

But so far, no one has.

We're almost halfway through the crowd now, on the way back to the prison, and there has been no sign of anything unusual. Perhaps they're waiting for me to be alone. Surely that would be simpler. Create less of a commotion.

An arm juts out in front of me and I release an involuntary shriek, momentarily quieting the crowd in the near vicinity.

I glance down and see that the arm belongs to a small body, fighting its way through the swarm of larger people blocking its view. When it finally makes its way through, I breathe out a sigh. The first tingle of sensation to make its way into my limbs since I was carried from the courtroom climbs tenaciously up my arms and legs.

It's Jane.

Adorable, sweet, placid little Jane Pattinson.

She must have come to London with her mother.

Her delicate face is shining up at me and I notice there is no terror in her eyes. No fury like I see in nearly everyone else. As always, she looks serene. Contemplative. I don't have much time. I'm already being tugged forward again but I manage to hold back long enough to crouch down so that I'm at eye level with her.

I wish I could reach out and touch her soft skin, run my fingertips through the fine blond hair that's curled over the tops of her tiny ears. I wish I could embrace her. I know it would chase every other emotion I'm feeling away. If only for a fleeting moment.

But with my wrists bound in front of me, all I can do is offer her a genuine smile.

She beckons me closer, waving her minuscule hands. I lean forward and she brings her lips to my ear. 'I knew you were the princess,' she whispers.

I close my eyes and inhale her sweet scent, trying to commit it to memory. It may very well be the last good memory I have.

By the time she pulls away there are tears leaking from my eyes.

She extends her arm again and this time I see she has her little cloth doll clutched in her hand. 'Here,' she tells me. 'Take Lulu. She will look after you.'

I shake my head, unable to speak.

But Jane is adamant, thrusting the doll into my shackled hands. '*Please*,' she begs. 'Take her.'

I feel another tug on my wrist, this one much more impatient. The two guards have stalked back in my direction. They're lifting me to my feet. I wrap my fingers around Lulu's slender neck to keep her from falling.

Then I'm yanked forward, in the direction of the stone fortress rising in the distance, unable to say thank you, or even goodbye. I trip over my ankle chains, trying to put one foot in front of the other. When I finally regain my balance, I manage a single glimpse behind me. But all I see is the crowd.

14
HELP

Hours pass and no one comes. Night falls and I'm still alone.
I'm tormented by the thought of Zen's death and confused by
Diotech's absence. They should know where I am by now. They
should have seen the historical records. I have to be in them. I
was tried in the central court of London. Steps away from the
king's palace. It had to be documented.

Did they not recognize my face from the sketch?

Were the descriptions of my superhuman acts not detailed
enough?

I find it impossible to believe that they simply stopped
looking.

There has to be an explanation. They have to be planning
something. They're not going to let me die. That much I can be
certain of.

Although I'm not sure which option I find more reassuring:
death or an escape from it.

Either way, I'll soon be able to forget. And in my mind, that
makes them equal.

Somewhere deep inside of me, I feel a small shiver of release. Soon this will all be over. Soon the image of Zen's face will be permanently erased from my memory.

I lie on the floor of my cell and watch the shadows from the single torch flicker and dance across the musty wall.

At some point during the long night, I start to shiver. And soon after, I feel a pressure against my temples. Like a creature living inside is fighting, begging, scraping to get out.

Then I hear the voice again. This time, I know it's not just the wind. This time, it's clear and crisp and urgent. This time, I recognize the source.

It's coming from inside me.

Like a thought.

No.

Like a memory.

'Find me.'

I still have no idea whose voice it is. Or why it's coming to me now. I decide to take a chance. I sit up, draw in a deep breath, and speak back. Aloud.

'How?'

I'm not convinced an answer will come. In fact, I'm highly doubtful. I wait in the dark expecting nothing.

But nothing is not what comes.

The pressure in my head builds. My brain feels like it's going to explode. Like I'm going to faint. The pain is unbearable.

But eventually images flood to the surface. As though they've been long buried in the back of my mind – concealed, locked, hidden – and somehow only now I've managed to set them free.

And then suddenly I'm no longer in my cell.

I'm standing on a crowded street. People push into me from every direction. A sea of bodies trying to crush me. Drown me. Suck me under.

I fight to move through them. Shoulders bumping mine. Elbows jabbing into my rib cage. My hair is caught and my head lashes back.

Then the noise starts. A faint rolling thunder. A swelling rumble of deep booming sounds.

It gets louder, louder, louder. Faster, faster, faster. Like a parade of gigantic horses galloping through the air. Stomping on the clouds.

Until everything around me is vibrating. Pulsating with sound. Swelling. Heaving. Bursting.

I recognize this sensation. The influx of imagery. The formation of a scene.

It's a memory. I'm certain of it.

But of what? I don't recognize that street. I don't recognize that sound. Or any of the faces around me. Is it something that happened when I was living with my foster family in Wells Creek? But then why am I only remembering it now? Why don't I recognize what I'm seeing?

It can't possibly have happened *before* that. On the compound. When I was at Diotech. Those memories are supposed to be gone. Erased forever.

Perplexed, I push myself back in, trying to grasp the swirling misty images and hold them steady in my mind.

Colour starts to rain from above.

Blue. Red. Yellow. Green. White.

Tiny curling tufts of a material I can't identify float down like crisp autumn leaves.

Everyone around me turns at once. Their gazes high. Their fingers stretched upward.

I turn and lift my eyes.

High in the sky, a series of strange markings begins to appear. Scribbled among the clouds. Symbols from another world.

And then . . . a hideous red beast with black-and-gold eyes emerges into the air. Swims effortlessly over the heads of the crowd. His features are distorted in rage. His jagged white teeth are bared.

I choke down a scream and start to back away, shoving through the swarm of people. Knocking down bodies. Until I finally break free from the mob.

I stumble down a deserted street, the raucous rumbling mercifully getting further and further away with each step.

I scan the empty avenue. Every door is closed. Boarded up. Every storefront bears the same unfamiliar markings. The same foreign symbols that I saw in the sky.

I come to a stop in front of a rusted metal stairwell, leading down, under the street.

An old man stands at the bottom of the steps. In front of a dirty blue door.

His skin is deeply creased. His eyes are dark and narrow — nothing more than slender slits cut into his face. His hair is white and thin, trailing from his head down his cheeks and into a long, colourless wispy beard that drips from his chin.

For reasons I don't understand, I'm pulled to him. Forced to look. To meet his gaze.

He beckons me downward. Into his hole.

'I help you,' he says slowly.

My body wants to run. Keep running. Never stop running. But my mind tells me no. Stay. This is exactly where I'm supposed to be.

I place one shaky hand on the grimy metal banister and start down the steps.

The image shatters, breaking into a thousand pieces that spin and splinter and fade into . . .

Nothing.

The memory is over. Leaving me feeling more confused and more disoriented than before. I fight to get it back. To pick up where I left off. To continue down that stairwell. But it's no use. The harder I try to focus on the scene, the less clear it becomes. The more I try to hold the old man's face in my mind, the more it slips away. Like trying to catch water in a net.

What does it all mean?

Who am I supposed to find?

Who was that man?

And how can he help me?

I feel anger welling up inside me. Hot, blistering rage that expels from my body in the form of boiling tears that dribble down my cheeks.

Because the truth is, he can't help me. No one can. It's pointless now. It's too late. Zen is dead! I can't change that. And tomorrow I will be dead, too.

I bang my fists against the wall harder and harder until the jagged surface breaks through my skin and blood trickles down my forearms. I scream and scream until my throat is sore and raw and my lungs are empty. I kick the ground over and over again until I fall down from pure exhaustion.

Through the blur of my tears, I see Lulu, Jane's tiny doll, in the corner, where I dropped her after I was put back in the cell. I crawl over to her and stuff her cloth body down the front of my corset, pressing it close to my heart. Where my locket used to be.

Where Zen used to be.

Then I sink to the ground and wait.

15

ABSOLVED

I'm awoken the next morning by the sound of metal clanging against metal. I open my eyes to see a guard standing outside my cell, banging his sword between two of the iron bars in an attempt to rouse me.

'Last confession,' he announces with the same spite in his tone that all the guards use when they speak to me.

I push myself up and wipe at my face. 'What?'

That's when I see that the guard has not come alone. Behind him is a tall man dressed in a long black robe with a crisp white collar. A velvet hood covers his head and most of his face. I can only make out the tip of his nose and the curve of his strong chin.

'The priest has come to hear your last confession and bless your soul,' the guard explains.

I don't know what any of this means but I soon realize that the man in the black robe is expected to enter the cell. The guard points his sword through the slats and uses it to nudge me to the far back corner. I watch with great interest as the door squeaks open and the concealed man enters.

As soon as he's inside the cell, I feel a strange sensation come over me. A subtle undercurrent, pulling me towards him. I have a sudden uncontrollable desire to see his face. To peer under his hood. To look at him.

I duck and tilt my head in several directions but his features remain hidden.

'*Who* are you?' I ask. I'm gazing at him with such intensity that I instantly feel embarrassed. Foolish. I try to look away, but I just can't bring myself to. This man – this hooded figure – has a magnetism that is making me dizzy. It's unreal. Almost . . . *magical.*

'My apologies, Sarah.' His voice is deep and smooth with hardly any intonation. As though every word, every syllable, holds precise equal value in his mind. And the way that voice says my name sends a warm shiver through me. I don't only hear it. I taste it. Feel it. Smell it. It's like warm bread coming out of the oven.

'I am a member of the clergy of the Church of England.'

Clergy?

Another word I'm unfamiliar with. I want to ask what it means, but I know this will only cause the guard to scowl even deeper in my direction so I keep my mouth shut.

However, the man seems to read my thoughts. Know my limitations.

'It's a religious position,' he explains without prompting. 'I am here to offer you God's blessing and hear your confessions before you are executed this morning.'

Confessions?

Once again, my mind asks the question, but he answers.

'Is there anything you'd like to tell me before you die? Any secrets? It is believed that if you die with a clear conscience you will go to heaven.'

The guard scoffs at this from the other side of the door.

Both of our heads pivot towards him and he wipes the smirk from his face.

'So,' the priest asks in his liltless intonation. 'Is there?'

'No,' I say softly.

'Are you certain?' he prods.

I nod silently.

'Very well.' He walks towards me. The closer he gets, the hotter my blood feels inside my veins. As though it may actually start to boil.

I push myself back against the stone wall. Drawn to him and terrified of him at the same time.

'W-w-what are you doing?' I stammer, watching uneasily as he comes within a foot of me. I look up, trying to catch a glimpse of his eyes, but his oversize hood is draped low.

I could do it right now. I could reach out and rip it from his head. Gaze upon his face. My fingers itch and tremble with the anticipation of it.

'I'm blessing you,' he says simply. His voice mesmerizes me and I instantly lose my train of thought.

I follow his arm as it rises slowly and catch a glimpse of his right hand as it drifts towards my forehead. His skin is velvety. Young. Unblemished. The sleeve of his robe slips, revealing a hint of his wrist. It's wide and smooth. With soft traces of light blond hair.

He seems to hesitate for a moment, his hand trembling slightly.

Then, after regaining control, his five fingertips connect with my skin and I feel a jolt of energy. A spark. Like something wonderful – beautiful, comforting, kind – is being transferred from his flesh to mine. And then back again. I close my eyes, absorbing it. Relishing this one glimmer of happiness. The first in days. Never wanting it to end.

I feel my grief miraculously lifted from me, like a blanket of darkness that's finally been stripped away. A layer of grime that I've been struggling to see through, washed clean.

Everything before this moment feels like a long-ago dream that I've now woken up from. Refreshed. Renewed. A curtain of serenity drawn around me. As though the very source of my pain and agony and suffering has simply been blown away like dust from a neglected corner.

And then, as devastating as a stone wall crumbling around me, it's over.

His hand is gone. His touch is gone. My tranquillity and reprieve are gone. The room feels darker, colder, emptier than it ever has before.

By the time I open my eyes again, the cell door is already being opened by the guard and the man in the black robe is stepping through to the other side. A world away from this one.

'Wait!' I call, rushing towards him.

The guard shoves his sword through the bars again, staving me off. I stop just short of its sharp point.

The door is closed with a *bang*. Locked. The priest turns back to me. 'Yes, Sarah?'

There it is again. My name on his lips. His voice reaching through the bars to caress me. Comfort me. Hold me. It's almost familiar.

'I . . .' But I don't know what to say. I don't know why I told him to wait. All I know is that I don't want him to leave. Ever.

'Nothing,' I mumble, dropping my head.

Without another word, he turns and disappears down the long, dank hallway, his black robe billowing behind him. And even though I would do anything at this moment to convince him to stay, I have the disheartening feeling that he's desperate to get away from me.

16

BURNED

The time has come.

I am extracted from my cage and marched slowly down the dark corridor. No one speaks. Either out of respect for the soon-to-be dead, or because there's nothing left to say.

I am led out of the prison, through the throng of people, and finally on to a platform that rises out of a mound of chopped wood and dead brush. Extra ropes are used to bind me to the towering beam in the centre, crisscrossing my entire body.

The portly man who originally arrested me is back. He's standing next to the platform in another richly decorated silk doublet, speaking passionately to the crowd about God and the devil and a never-ending war between the two. His crooked yellow teeth snapping each word in half, spitting angry accusations in my direction.

Finally the torch is extended and a firestorm alights beneath me.

I close my eyes and think of Zen, offering up a silent apology.

Begging his forgiveness for my failure. I couldn't help him. I couldn't save him.

'I'm sorry,' I whisper.

Even though he's gone now, I am hopeful that somehow my voice will travel through the strands of time, find a place where he still lives, and whisper it softly into his ear.

I open my eyes to the inferno that blazes below me.

The fire is hot and relentless, rising up from a thicket of smouldering ash. Lashing at my feet. Filling my eyes with smoky tears of defeat.

The flames hungrily stare me down. Like a wolf licking its lips at the sight of an injured animal. Savouring the promise of a feast. Taking its time before moving in for the kill.

The wood crackles beneath me. One by one, branches are crushed, incinerated to black dust in the path of the merciless blaze. I am its only target. The sole destination. Everything else is a mere stepping-stone along the way. A dispensable victim to demolish and cast aside as it fights its way to me.

I search my surroundings desperately for help. But there is none to be found. Silence answers my distress. Punctuated only by the mocking *fizzle* and *crack* of the flames.

They can't let me die here. Their prized possession left to burn. To shrivel up. To turn to bitter ash. They won't. I'm sure of it.

They will be here soon. They will stop it.

And for the first time in my shallow, abridged memory, I will welcome the sight of them.

The smoke billows up, cloaking everything in a sickly haze. My vision – normally flawless and acute – is gone. My throat swells and burns. I wrench my head to the side, coughing. Choking. Gagging.

One ambitious flame forges ahead of the others. Winning the race to the top. It claws at my bare feet with long, gnarled fingers. I curl my toes under and press hard against the wood at my back. I can already feel my skin start to blister. Bubble. Scream.

And then I fight. Oh, how I fight. Thrashing against my constraints. But it's no use.

And that's when I realize . . . no one is coming.

The fire will consume me. Melt the flesh right off my bones. Turn my entire manufactured existence into nothing but grimy dust to be carried off across the countryside with the slightest breeze.

The wind shifts and the smoke clears for long enough that I can just make out a tall, hooded figure standing alone on the other side of the river. Watching silently.

The fire finally catches my skin. The pain is excruciating. Like a thousand swords slicing through me at once. The scream boils up from somewhere deep within. A place I never knew about. My mouth stretches open on its own. My stomach contracts. And I release the piercing sound upon a city of deaf ears.

The man who arrested me is there. He steps up to the edge of the flames. 'This is what happens when you welcome the devil into your soul!' he shouts. The spectators yell back their concurrence, raising their hands in the air.

All the while the flesh on my bare feet is rippling, turning black. The putrid smell gags me. I cry out in agony, feeling the fire devour my ankles next, travel up my shins.

When will it stop?

When will I black out?

Please let me faint.

'And this!' He draws a long silver chain out of his pocket. Through the clawing flames I can just manage to see my locket swinging from the end of it.

Not destroyed. Not broken.

'The symbol of her pact with Satan!' he's saying, raising the necklace high over his head. 'This will accompany the witch back to hell!' With one flick of his fingers the necklace is suddenly in the fire with me.

I attempt to peer down through the flames, the heat scalding my eyes, causing them to rain tears. I blink them away furiously until finally I see it. Lying next to my charred feet. Only inches away.

Determination returns to me. From somewhere I summon strength. I kick out my left foot, feeling the rope dig into my burned flesh, sending another scaring bolt of agony through me.

Blackness starts to invade my vision, withering in from the sides.

No! I silently shout back. I can't pass out now! Not when my salvation is so close. Not when I can almost touch it.

I let out a roar of anguish and I thrust my leg forward as hard as I can. The tightly bound ropes shift slightly up my leg, giving my feet a larger range of motion. I press against the wooden beam at my back, redistributing my weight so that I can slither my foot closer.

The fire continues to consume me inch by inch. The pain is excruciating. My body is begging to shut it out. Turn off. The darkness still creeps across my eyes. I blink it away furiously.

Stay here, I command myself. *Stay present.*

I wiggle my legs again, shimmying the rope further up. I stretch my toes, extending them as far as they can go until I finally feel the hard surface of the locket under my singed flesh.

My mind rejoices but I know I have a much more difficult task ahead of me. I have to get it open.

I feel for the chain and curl my toes around it, then drag it towards me.

The man in the silk doublet is still entrancing the crowd with some kind of sermon about evil. Even if anyone is looking directly at me, I'm confident my actions are shielded by the blanket of fire and smoke.

The pain has reached a peak where I almost no longer feel it. It's as if everything has gone numb. But the blackness is still threatening to consume me. Take me away. Render me useless. Leave me here to burn to death.

The smoke is so thick now, I can't see what my feet are doing. It threatens to suffocate me. I stop breathing, wondering how long I'll be able to go without air.

I hold the locket under one foot while attempting to wedge what's left of my toenail on the other into the crack of the heart. The flames have reached my waist now, relentlessly ripping through skin and muscle.

The darkness moves in quickly. From both sides. Like a curtain being drawn across a brightly lit window.

Through the growing shadow of my vision, I see a flash of movement. The towering wall of grey smoke around me billows, a sudden gash tearing it open before it quickly closes back up. As though someone has cut through it with a knife.

I just manage to unclasp the heart and open the locket clenched underneath my toes when the curtain closes completely and the night swallows me whole.

PART 2

THE INVASION

17

BOULDER

I dream of water.

Cool and clear and magnificent. It lifts me up and carries me downstream. It runs over me, washing away my past, purifying my soul, erasing my mistakes, soothing the fiery pain in my legs. I can feel it healing me. The beautiful current cleanses my rotted, charred skin, rinsing it to make way for new, healthy skin. Fresh cells filled with life and perfection.

I am whole again.

I want to float here forever. Never waking. Never knowing what will happen next. Never caring.

I hear the drip, drip, drip of water running over a steep rock, fighting to make its way up the sharp incline before trickling drop by drop over the other side. I know I am moving towards this rock. I will smash into it. It will alter the course of this blissful journey. It will change everything.

I attempt to paddle, to steer myself away, but the gravity of the massive object is too strong. All objects are helpless in its pull. Even me. I continue to float towards it, afraid of what will happen when we finally collide. When our strengths are pitted against one another. When we are forced together at last.

I don't know who will win.

I don't know if either of us can.

When I open my eyes I am in a strange, unfamiliar room. It's large with bare white walls, textured ceiling, and tall blackened windows. My eyes adjust immediately, seeing flawlessly in the near dark. But there is nothing to see. The room is empty. Apart from the bed I'm lying on, which is swathed in soft white sheets and a thick blue blanket, a small table at the foot of the bed, and a single dim lamp in the corner.

There's an inherent sadness to this room. As though it's not just vacant but somehow left behind. Abandoned. And now the loneliness breathes in and out of the walls. Like it has seeped into the paint, soaked into the plush beige carpeting, burrowed itself inside the foundation.

Drip. Drip. Drip.

I hear the sound again and I turn to see a tall metal stand next to my bed. It holds a plastic bag full of clear, unidentifiable fluid that drops into a long tube. I follow the tube to see that it leads directly into a vein just above my tattoo.

An IV. I immediately recognize it from my days in the hospital in the year 2013.

Frightened, I bolt upright, tearing the plastic needle from my arm and kicking the covers from my legs. I am poised to jump from the bed and run, but something catches my eye. My legs are covered in a thick white gauze, wrapped in perfect symmetrical layers all the way to my toes.

Someone has bandaged my wounds.

Carefully and curiously, I grasp the end of one of the

bandages, just beneath my hip, and slowly start to uncoil it. I gasp and drop the gauze when I see that my wounds are entirely healed. Where I was sure there would be mangled, burned flesh, there is now only a swirl of fresh pink-and-white skin. It's new and slightly tender. But the pain is gone.

How long have I been in this room?

And how did I get here?

I suddenly recall how fast my wrist healed when I attempted to dig out my tracking device — less than an hour — but that was a small gash. This is different. That fire devoured my skin. Ripped at me like a ravaging animal with razor-sharp teeth. I don't think there was much left when . . .

When what?

What happened after that? Before I woke up here?

I remember the witch trial. The mob of angry people. The blazing fire. And then . . .

My locket.

It was tossed into the flames with me.

I just managed to clasp it beneath my toes and unhook it, activating my transession gene before the smoke and pain and panic finally won the tugging battle with my consciousness and I passed out.

But how did I get *here*? In this bed.

And where is my locket now?

Desperately, I feel around my chest and collarbone. There is nothing but bare skin. I lift the covers up and peer towards the bottom of the bed, wiggling my bandaged toes.

I work quickly, unravelling the dressing until both of my new, healed legs are free and bare.

It's only now that I realize I'm still wearing my thick and heavy seventeenth-century clothing, minus the kerchief. Half of the skirt is gone, burned in the fire, leaving me with a jagged, blackened hem just below my knees.

I glance anxiously around the room, searching for any sign of my locket. Wherever I am, however I got here, I need to leave. I have to get back to Zen. I can still save him. I can transesse to the day they brought him back to the Pattinsons' home, after I was arrested. I can get him out of there. He doesn't have to die.

The word *die*, even in my silent thoughts, makes my stomach retch and my head spin. I lean over the side of the bed and gag, my stomach heaving. But nothing comes out.

I apparently haven't had anything to eat in the past few days.

I command myself to think. Focus. Come up with a plan.

I scan the room, noticing a door in the wall behind me. I have no idea what's on the other side of it but it doesn't matter. I can't very well stay here. I have to find my necklace. That is priority number one.

Without it, I am trapped again.

I swing my legs over the side of the bed and test them separately, putting a little weight on each foot, pausing to check for pain or discomfort or for my newly grown skin to suddenly peel right off and slip to the floor like a heap of discarded clothes.

So far, everything seems to be working as it should.

I eye the door, preparing myself for what might be on the other side. I rise warily to my feet but am suddenly stopped when I see the door start to swing open with a low creaking sound.

My heart leaps into my throat.

I ready myself to pounce. To take down the intruder by any means necessary. I don't know who brought me here, I don't know who bandaged my wounds, but if they stand in the way of me finding my necklace and getting back to Zen, then I will have no choice but to hurt them.

A foot enters the room first, housed in a shiny black shoe. A

114

modern one. Not the smooth leather boot or buckled mule of the seventeenth century. I can tell by the size and style that it belongs to a man. My gaze ascends as his leg crosses the threshold next. It's muscular and thick, cloaked in dark grey fabric. I cautiously move my eyes further up as the rest of him appears around the corner of the door. An untucked, creaseless black cotton shirt with buttons and a collar, sheathing an impressively formed muscular chest. A long, sturdy neck. And then I finally land on his face. And that's when all the sensation in my head and hands and feet and fingers and toes and lips simply evacuates my body.

I'm completely unable to move. Except to fall back on to the bed.

It's by far the most exquisite face I've ever seen.

His skin is smooth and satiny and unblemished. The colour of ripe wheat bathed in sunlight. His features – nose, chin, cheekbones – are angular and appear to be chiselled out of fine marble. His dark blond hair cascades in loose, glossy waves around his temples, tickling the tops of his ears. And his eyes are the most breathtaking shade of iridescent aquamarine.

He looks young. Possibly the same age as me. Maybe older. And he's carrying a trayful of food.

I try to hide my reaction to his stunning features but I know immediately that I've failed. He, on the other hand, is perfectly composed. His expression is as bare and emotionless as these white walls.

He walks silently into the room and sets the tray down on the table at the foot of the bed. There's something very stilted and unusual about his movements. As though his joints click into place, rather than rotate smoothly.

'You're awake,' he states in a neutral tone, making it impossible to tell if he's happy about this development or disappointed. All I know is that the sound of his voice sends a quiver up my newly healed legs. Even though it's detached and somewhat cold, there's a penetrating depth. A strange intimacy. As though he's breathing the words right into my ear.

'Who are you?' I ask, surprised by the tremble in my voice. Am I afraid of him?

Of course I'm not, my mind answers instinctively. Without even giving itself a chance to contemplate the question.

If anything, I feel the opposite. Safe. Protected. Understood.

Like I know him. Like I've never not known him.

He stands at the foot of the bed, his arms tight and rigid at his sides. 'My name is Kaelen,' he says, the syllables flat. Like he's a stone reciting definitions to another stone.

And yet a swell of emotion undulates through me, ricocheting off every surface in this room.

Kaelen.

I don't know this name but I want to. More than anything. I want to repeat it over and over again in my mind. I want to use it in place of every other word in the English language. Even if it means I will no longer speak sense.

'What are you doing here?' I bring myself to ask. I want to sound accusing. Harsh. I want to warn this stranger that I have a mission and I'm not going to let anyone stand in the way of it.

But none of that is conveyed.

And in this moment, staring into his endless blue-green eyes, I can't even remember what my mission is.

A small, almost sinister smile dances across his lips.

'Sera.' Even through his dispassionate tone, I hear an air of condescension when he says my name. As if the explanation he's about to give is pointless. Wasted breath. Wasted energy. 'I'm here because of you.'

A shudder ripples through me as I finally comprehend everything.

The figure I saw through the rising smoke. The movement just before I passed out. My missing necklace.

The truth of my realization is like ice in my veins. Fog in my head. Wood splinters in my muscles.

I knew they would never let me burn.

As the paralysing words tumble out of my lips, I know I can't take them back. I can't take anything back any more. The chase is over. 'Diotech sent you.'

18

AMBASSADOR

I'm amazed at how calm I feel as the words slide off my tongue. I've been restlessly dreaming of this moment for so long – fearing it, dreading it, waking up in a cold sweat – I guess I always assumed I would feel differently. That the rage and terror and determination to escape Diotech would all combine and coil up in my limbs, readying me to spring into action. To fight. To run.

But where am I going to go?

This man – this *boy* – clearly has my necklace. My freedom. My only way to Zen.

He nods, confirming that he is, in fact, who I think he is, and continues to stand eerily still at the foot of the bed.

'I don't understand,' I say. 'If Diotech sent you, then why am I not . . .' I glance around the large empty room, another horrifying realization settling in. 'Wait. Am I here? Am I back? Is this the compound?'

'No.' His response is unfeeling. Almost mechanical.

I'm besieged with confusion. All this time, I assumed they

were hunting me to bring me back. That's what Alixter said in the cave. I was their trillion-dollar investment. I had to be returned. I couldn't be allowed to just run loose through time.

'But I thought—' I protest.

'My orders were not to bring you back,' Kaelen explains stiffly.

'Then what *are* your orders?'

'You have information that we need. I have been assigned to acquire it.'

Information?

Despite everything – despite the fact that I'm standing in the middle of my worst nightmare – I have to laugh. Although it's more like a nervous titter. 'I'm sorry you went through the trouble but I think you were misinformed. I don't have any information. I don't even know what you're talking about.'

He appears undeterred by this news. 'It's not something you *know*,' he states in a measured tone. 'It's something you remember.'

I chuckle again, feeling satisfied that I've somehow managed to outsmart them without even trying. 'Well, obviously someone lied to you because I don't remember anything. My memories are gone. Wiped clean. There's nothing left.'

He shakes his head. The movement is so small it's almost imperceptible. 'I was not misinformed. I know with certainty that the memories we need remain intact.'

'If you're so convinced that I have them, why don't you simply put on some receptors and dig them out yourself?'

He crosses his arms, causing his black button-down shirt to crease around the chest. I can't help but be drawn to those arms. They really are quite remarkable. Muscular and yet somehow soft and inviting at the same time. I would imagine Alixter only recruits the toughest, strongest people to be his agents. And Kaelen appears to be no exception.

But I'm not worried. I managed to outrun and outmanoeuvre the last two agents he sent after me; I have no doubt I can take on this one as well. Especially after all the practice sessions I've had with Zen in the forest.

The thought of Zen almost manages to double me over again but I fight hard to keep my composure. I can't let this guy see any weakness. I'm just buying time, listening to his pointless story until I can figure out where my necklace is, and then I can stealthily make my move. When he least expects it.

'It's more complicated than that,' he replies. 'These aren't memories that you have now. They're memories that you will have. Eventually.'

My brow furrows. 'What?'

'They're called TDRs. Time-delayed recalls. Memories installed in your brain that are programmed to activate after a certain amount of time, or when introduced to a specific trigger. Similar to a series of bombs set to detonate.'

Bombs? In my brain?

'How do you even know I have these?'

'The TDRs are visible in a scan. But they're encrypted files. And they can't be decrypted unless the predetermined time period has passed or the programmed trigger is set off. We can't access the actual memories until they're activated.'

'So you scanned my brain,' I say with an unsettling realization. 'You looked at my memories.'

I suddenly feel ill. And violated.

He obviously doesn't see this as a problem. 'It was a necessary step in the successful completion of the mission.'

I want to scream but I know it won't do any good. I suppose I shouldn't even be surprised. Since when has Diotech *ever* respected the privacy of my mind?

I run my fingers along the soft cotton sheets of the bed,

wondering how long I was lying there, completely vulnerable and helpless. Long enough for my legs to heal, I know that much. But what other things did he do to me in that time? What other memories did he see?

'How long have I been here?' I ask.

He stands completely still but I swear, out of the corner of my eye, I see one finger on his left hand twitch. 'Two days,' he tells me.

'And how did you keep me unconscious?'

He reaches into his pocket and slowly withdraws the familiar black device with the dial on the side and the two metal prongs protruding from the top.

I should have known.

A Modifier.

Diotech's weapon of choice. I remember when Rio used one on me in the abandoned barn in 2013. And Maxxer in the car on the way to her storage unit. Momentarily deactivating my brain. Forcing me into an involuntary sleep. Sometimes minutes, sometimes hours. And then I remember Alixter using one on Rio. In that cave. Cranking the dial until it could go no further. Deactivating his brain for good.

I quickly shake the thought from my mind before it has a chance to debilitate me.

'And these memories,' I continue in a wobbly voice, 'you know for sure that they will be triggered. That I will be able to see them?'

Kaelen nods. 'One of them has already been activated.'

I suddenly flash back to the woman's voice I heard in the woods. And the scene that played out in my head while I was lying on the floor of my prison cell. That seemed to come out of nowhere. It pounded inside my brain like an explosion of colours and sights and sounds.

The swarm of people.

The strange symbols carved into the sky.

The ferocious beast with eyes of black and gold.

The old man beckoning me inside his dirty blue door.

'*I help you . . .*'

Is that what that was? A time-delayed recall whose clock just happened to run out? But that still doesn't explain what the memory *means.* Why the man was trying to help me.

And why did the woman's voice tell me to find her?

'*Who* put these in my brain?' I ask in a brusque, demanding tone.

Like always, his response is blank. Distant. 'I cannot divulge that information.'

I grunt. 'What exactly are you hoping to find in these memories once they're triggered?'

He seems to hesitate as he deposits the Modifier back into the pocket of his pants before resting his arms dutifully at his sides again. But as he does, his hand inadvertently snags the fabric of his shirt, causing it to shift and the collar to tug down an inch.

But an inch is enough.

I see the flash of silver peeking out from underneath before he reaches up and straightens the lapels.

Instantly my stomach clenches.

My locket. He's wearing it. He must have mended the chain while I was unconscious. It makes sense for him to keep it on him. He must think that's the safest place for it.

He's wrong.

I'm already formulating my best plan of attack, calculating the perfect time to pounce. It has to be when he least expects it. When he's, perhaps, momentarily distracted. I'll ambush him at full speed, faster than he can comprehend, and rip the chain from his neck. Then I'll stun him with a jab to the throat and a kick to the groin, giving me time to get away, open the locket, and transesse out of here. Wherever *here* is.

All I need is the right distraction.

Patience, I tell myself, even though my heart is pounding at the anticipation of my escape and the thought of seeing Zen again. Soon I'll be back at his side. Soon I'll be able to save him.

Kaelen is still answering my question, seemingly oblivious to the abrupt change in the balance of power.

'Although we don't quite know for sure what the memories reference, our intelligence suggests that they contain a map.'

My attention is instantly diverted. Did he just say *a map*?

'To what?' I can't help asking, even though it doesn't matter. I'll be gone in less than a few minutes.

'I cannot divulge that information either,' he says in the same robotic drone that's really starting to annoy me.

I attempt to bring back the memory. The old man inviting me into his blue door. Into his world.

I can't imagine how that could possibly be construed as a map.

Unless the map is somehow *inside* the door.

Well, whatever it is, I'm not waiting around here to find out. I eye the tray that Kaelen placed down on the table at the foot of the bed. 'Is that for me?' I ask.

He nods. 'I thought you might be hungry. There is much to do and you need your strength.'

I almost laugh at the irony of his statement. I have all the strength I need to take him down right here. Right now.

'Thanks,' I say, attempting to sound grateful. 'I'm *starving*.'

He nods again, a cold, perfunctory motion, and bends down to pick up the tray. This is it. My one and only chance. While his eyes are diverted and his hands are occupied.

NOW!

In less than a second, I'm behind him, one arm wrapped around his neck. I grab a fistful of his hair in my other hand and yank his head back, forcing him into a vulnerable position.

The tray goes clattering to the floor, spilling a bowl of hot soup across the pristine carpet, leaving an unsightly yellowish-brown stain.

I let go of his hair long enough to make a grab for the necklace. My fingers make contact with the chain. I close them tightly and begin to pull. But before I can break it free, I'm suddenly lifted off the ground, my feet uselessly paddling the air, gaining no purchase. In one graceful, effortless motion, I'm thrown over his shoulder, flying and flipping and rotating bottom over top until I land hard on my stomach.

He's stronger than the agents who came before him. That much I can see now. Alixter must have taken inventory of his failures and recruited a better crop of soldiers this time around.

Still, he should be no match for my speed. My manoeuvrability. My reaction time.

Not to mention the countless hours of training, preparing for this very scenario.

I leap to my feet and charge towards him, planting a powerful high kick to his rib cage, then follow it up with a solid left hook to his cheek. I'm about to continue the assault with a devastating strike to his kneecaps but I'm momentarily caught off guard by his reaction. Or rather his lack of reaction.

I should hear cracking. I should hear tearing. Bones breaking. Skin splitting. Blood dripping. And moaning. Lots and lots of moaning. These are painful blows I'm delivering.

And yet he barely moves.

His expression hardly changes. He doesn't look injured, or even faintly uncomfortable. He simply stands there, straight and tall and impervious as ever, staring at me with an almost impatient look on his face. As if to say, *Are you finished yet?*

And his cheek — which just sustained a very unfriendly encounter with my fist — doesn't show any signs of affliction. There's only a dim patch of red that is already fading. I may as well have smacked him with a sparrow feather.

Irritated, I come at him again, but apparently he's had enough because this time, he fights back. Every punch I throw is blocked. Every kick I cast is ducked. Until eventually, he bestows one of his own. A mighty strike of his hand that smacks my head, sending the room into a dizzying spin, my vision into a disconcerting sputter, and me soaring high through the air, across the room, smashing into the sole lamp in the corner, and landing, this time, on my back with a clangorous thud.

A flicker of a nanosecond passes before he's on top of me, using the weight of his dense, powerful body to crush me and render me immobile. He pushes against me, constricting my chest, thrusting the air out of me.

It takes me a moment to register how fast he just moved. Faster than he should. Faster than anyone should. But my thoughts are suddenly snagged by the intense surge of electricity that seems to be blasting through me. A hot white glow that explodes out of me like a superior sun. Ripping me apart. Rupturing me from the inside.

Everything is instantly on fire again — my skin, my hair, my bones, my muscles, my cells. Even the air around me is ablaze.

But this fire is different. It doesn't burn. It doesn't scald. It only awakens. Enlivens. Blooms luminous radiance from within.

I think he must feel it, too, because for the first time since he walked into this room, I see his face shift. I see something register. I see a *reaction*.

And it can only be described as surprise.

Pure, unexpected, unanticipated, unwelcomed surprise.

His gaze drifts slowly towards mine. It's tentative. Almost

afraid. As though he knows he shouldn't – as though he's fighting it every inch of the way – but eventually the choice is no longer his.

As soon as our eyes collide, it's like I'm transported. Everything else seems to vanish. The room, the bed, my thundering, jagged breaths. It's just me, pinned beneath him. But the weight of his crushing frame is gone. Like his body has lost gravity somehow.

I hear his heart pounding, reverberating through his chest cavity. The sound waves penetrate my skin, weave through my rib cage, find the hum of my own thudding pulse, and for a moment the entire world is nothing more than a harmonized

BA-BUMP

BA-BUMP

BA-BUMP

My brain is buzzing. I can't make sense of what is happening. But fortunately, I don't have to.

A second later, he rockets off me, launching himself into the air and on to his feet. He reaches the far side of the room before I can blink. But from the perturbed expression pulling at his features, it's evident he'd rather be on the far side of the *world*.

I struggle to my feet, catching his eye. He's glaring at me. I recognize the look. It's the same one I saw on a hundred different faces as they led me out of the court, as they marched me to the platform, as they prepared to watch me burn.

It's a look of accusation.

Although I don't, for the life of me, know what he could possibly be accusing me of. If anything, I'm the one who should be accusing *him*.

'W-w-what *are* you?' I manage to huff out, still winded from the effort and the constriction in my chest.

He hasn't stopped glowering at me from across the room, looking completely rattled. But after three difficult inhales and exhales, he collects his composure. I watch his face slip back into that irritating neutral façade, as flat and uninspiring as an unplanted crop field. I watch the robot return.

'WHAT ARE YOU?' I demand again, this time screaming it, piercing my own eardrums with my angry roar.

'Sera —' he pronounces my name with that same arrogant, condescending heaviness — 'do you really think Alixter would make the same mistake twice? Of sending a frail, ordinary human to deal with you?'

Whoosh!

My breath deserts me. Sucked out by a giant merciless vacuum placed against my lips.

'What are you talking about?' I choke out, even though I already know the answer. Even though I've already fallen to my knees and pressed my forehead against the soft carpet.

On my way down, I just manage to catch sight of it. The ultimate proof. Flashing in and out of view on his left wrist.

A black, razor-thin tattoo, slicing across his skin.

'I'm like you,' he says with chilling detachment. 'Only better.'

19

IMPROVED

Slowly I lift my head and peer into his eyes. It's suddenly like I'm seeing them for the first time.

Everything is different.

The light is different. The shadows are different. The world is different.

Because now there are two of us in it.

I should have realized it the moment I saw him. I should have seen it in his artfully chiselled face. His impeccable skin. His stunning stature.

I should have noticed it in the colour of his eyes. That incandescent blue green.

A perfect colour.

An *unnatural* colour.

Just like my own.

Except for one thing. His eyes have a disquieting quality about them. A hollowness. A deadness. They are paradoxically radiant and barren at the same time.

And his voice. So mechanical. Cold. Inflectionless. Like his lips are forming words, his tongue is forming sounds, but there's nothing behind them. No one there to form meaning. Zen once told me that when he first met me my speech was stilted and awkward. But I don't think I ever sounded like *that*.

He said he was like me, only better.

But better *how?*

Stronger? Faster? Smarter? More beautiful?

Possibly.

But there's one thing for certain that Alixter would consider an improvement over me. According to him, I had only one fault.

My ability to rebel.

To think for myself. To feel and emote and question.

To fall in love.

'How much have you been told?' My voice is shaky. Uncertain. Terrified.

He cocks his head in an inquisitive manner.

I rephrase. 'What did Alixter tell you about me?'

He appears to find frivolity in the question. 'Everything.'

'Everything?'

'I have been given high-level clearance to Diotech intelligence, including a detailed report of your defective creation as well as Dr Havin Rio's duplicity in abetting your escape.'

A reminder of Rio and his attempt to help me is like another punch in the face. And in the stomach. And in the heart. I fight back a wince.

'So you know,' I croak, 'how you were created? How *we* were created?'

He blinks. The movement is so perfunctory I swear I can hear a faint *clack* every time his eyelids touch. 'Yes. Perfected DNA sequences synthetically engineered to create a superior, enhanced specimen of human.'

'And that doesn't bother you?' I cry out, feeling cold and

weak and empty. Not anything like a superior, enhanced human.

'Why would that bother me?'

The frustration flushes my cheeks. Clenches my stomach. Heats my blood. 'That you were made against your will?! That you have no family? No friends? No life outside the one Diotech designed for you?'

'Will?' he repeats, putting a curious spin on the word, as though he doesn't understand its meaning.

'Yes! Against your will. As in, you weren't consulted in the matter. You were never given a choice. Your life is not your own.'

'My life is to serve Dr Jans Alixter and protect the Diotech agenda. That is my only purpose.'

His chilling delivery of this line is all I need to hear. I have my answer. He *does* know everything. But he's been programmed not to question it. He's been programmed not to *care*.

He wasn't lied to as I was.

He wasn't given false information, false memories, a false childhood.

For him, it was never necessary.

Alixter accomplished precisely what he wanted to accomplish. He figured out how to create the perfect soldier. One who doesn't question. Who doesn't resist. Who doesn't run away.

Kaelen is exactly what I was *supposed* to be . . .

A human machine. Someone whose brain has been so severely modified that he won't think for himself.

That he *can't* think for himself.

'How many are there?' I ask. I need to know what I'm dealing with. What I'm up against. When he doesn't respond I put the question another way. 'How many more of you – of *us* – did Alixter create?'

A lifetime passes. Seasons change outside. A hundred lunar cycles complete. And then finally, he answers. 'As of now . . . we are the only two.'

I feel something inside me release. The first good news I've heard in a long time.

However, I can't help but catch his choice of words. *As of now* . . .

The implication makes me shiver. But I try to push it aside. I can't get distracted by what Alixter has in store. I have to focus on my own plan. My own mission. I'm still determined to fulfil it.

I push myself to my feet, puff out my chest, try to command respect. Fear. Anything.

'Give me my locket back,' I say sternly, eyeing the collar of his shirt, which has been stretched to the side once again during our scuffle, revealing the slim silver chain underneath.

'No,' he says simply.

I have to admit, I didn't expect my demand to work. Especially now that it's already been proved I can't outrun him or outfight him. But I had to at least try.

I mash my teeth together and try to keep myself from charging him again. 'I have to go back,' I tell him, the anger quickly thawing from my voice. Melting into desperation. 'You can have access to any part of my brain, whatever memories you want, just please, let me save Zen first.'

'That's not how this is going to work.' The callousness in his tone brings my rage barrelling back in a heartbeat.

'Hey!' I shout from across the room. 'I'm the one with the information you need. I think that entitles *me* to decide how this is going to work.'

'That's not entirely accurate.'

I scowl. 'What's not?'

'You're not the only one with useful information.'

A lump grows heavy and sour in my stomach. 'What do you mean?'

'How exactly do you expect to save his life when you don't even know what's making him sick?'

The world is suddenly buckling and crashing in around me. Walls tumbling. Floor falling out. Sky shattering.

My throat constricts. Traps the air inside. Traps the words. But somehow I manage to speak. To proclaim the truth that suddenly changes everything.

'You know what's wrong with him.'

He nods. 'And more important, I know how to cure him.'

20
NEGOTIATION

I'm instantly sceptical. I don't know whether or not to trust him. Or if anything he's telling me is true. If he's following Alixter's orders, he'll say whatever is necessary to get me to do what he wants. But I also realize what a losing battle this is for me. I can't win. Even if he's lying, even if he has no idea why Zen is sick, I don't have any other options. If there's a minuscule fragment of a sliver of a chance that he can save Zen, I have to do what he says.

'Has Diotech been making him sick?' I ask, trying to gather as much information as I can.

'No,' Kaelen responds. 'But if you want him *not* to be sick, you'll do exactly as I say.'

'How can I believe you? How do I know you won't betray me? Let's say I do exactly what you say, and I'm able to guide you to wherever this supposed map in my head is leading, how do I know you won't just use the Modifier on me again, take me right back to the compound, and leave Zen in 1609 to die?'

He seems to contemplate the question with great serious-ness. 'You don't,' he finally admits.

I cross my arms over my chest. 'Well, I'm afraid that's not good enough.'

He takes a single step towards me. I can already feel that strange magnetism tugging at me again. He seems to feel some-thing, too, because as he takes another step, he hesitates, then rests his foot back where it was. His perfectly formed jaw pulls at the corners, like he's attempting to tolerate a bitter taste in his mouth.

'What do you want?' he asks. His static face changes ever so slightly, flashing annoyance.

'Cure him first,' I say without blinking. 'Then I'll go with you.'

He shakes his head. 'No.'

'Fine,' I say, glaring at him. 'Then let me go back and get him. I'll bring him here.'

He arches one eyebrow, clearly not believing me for a sec-ond. 'Even if I did allow that, which I won't, you wouldn't be able to go back to save him.'

My forehead crinkles. 'Why not?'

'Because you've already been there.'

'That doesn't make any sense,' I argue.

'The basic laws of transession don't allow you to occupy space in the same moment of time more than once. You are physically unable to transesse to a point in time you've already existed in. Because that would mean there would be two in-stances of you, which is a quantum impossibility.'

I've never heard this before. But then again, I'm not exactly an expert in transession. I've really only done it a handful of times. I wonder if Zen knew about this restriction. I think he would have told me if he did.

'Therefore –' he continues his haughty explanation – 'your only option would be to transesse to the moment *after* I removed you from the fire and brought you here, but by then, Zen's illness will have progressed to the point of fatality.'

I'm not sure if I should believe his explanation but it hardly matters. It's evident he's never going to let me leave. 'You go get him, then,' I counter. 'You were only there during my execution, which means you can transesse to a time earlier than that and bring him back with you.'

Kaelen falls silent, considering.

'Once he's here and I know he's still alive,' I say, 'I'll go with you.'

It's not the perfect solution. But it's better than imagining him lying dead in the woods somewhere outside the Pattinsons' farm.

Kaelen gives me a stern warning look. 'Don't move,' he says, and then, in an instant, he's gone. I watch his body disappear, melting into air.

I eye the door, contemplating my chances if I make a run for it. But it's not even an option. As long as Kaelen has my necklace, there's nowhere for me to go. And the debate immediately becomes moot because Kaelen is back in less than five seconds. This time, however, he's not alone.

I hear a deep, sickly cough. I glance down to see Kaelen's hand wrapped around Zen's biceps, holding up his limp body. It reminds me of the way Jane used to carry around her doll, clinging on to one ragged arm, the rest of the body dragging lifelessly at her side.

I gasp as I watch a dark red current flow from Zen's mouth, blossoming on the beige carpet, creating a crimson shadow around his feet. He coughs again, visibly struggling for breath.

Kaelen callously releases him. Zen's legs wilt, tugging him to the ground. The top half of his body remains upright for a long, drawn-out, painful second before he slumps over, his face resting in the amorphous splotch of his own blood.

21

REAPPEARED

'Are you crazy?!' I scream at Kaelen as I run to Zen and lift his head off the floor. I attempt to wipe away the smears of blood from his cheek. His skin is a million degrees. But I continue to stroke his face.

'Zen,' I coax. 'Zen, can you hear me?'

His eyelids flutter slightly. 'What's happening?' His voice is barely audible.

'Everything's going to be OK,' I whisper softly into his ear, pressing my lips against his jawline. 'I know how to make you better now.'

In a quick motion, I scoop him up and carry him to the bed. I lay his body gently down on the mattress and brush away the damp hair from his forehead.

'We need to make him comfortable,' I tell Kaelen in a broken voice, without taking my eyes off Zen. 'Can you do anything for him?'

When there's no reply from the other side of the room, I look up. Kaelen is studying me with a curious expression tugging at his face, as though I'm some strange, unidentified animal he's encountered in the woods and he's trying to classify me.

'Did you hear me!?' I roar. 'What can you do for him?'

'I can give him your IV,' he states plainly. 'It will keep him hydrated.'

I nod, gazing back at Zen. 'Do it.'

As Kaelen works, inserting a fresh needle into Zen's vein and attaching it to the bag of clear liquid, I hold Zen's hand and gently stroke his palm. The suffering that's etched into his beautiful face is heartbreaking. It makes my throat burn and tears sting my eyes.

Kaelen finishes administering the IV and then takes a few steps back, as though he's purposefully trying to stay as far away from us as he can.

'Where did you find him?' I ask quietly.

'At the Pattinsons' farmhouse.'

'How did you know to go there?'

'Elizabeth Pattinson said he was brought to their house after you were arrested.'

His response takes me by surprise. He's right. She did say that, but I'm struggling to remember *when* she said that. And then it hits me.

'The matter of the young man with whom she arrived here . . . On the night she was arrested, he was returned to our farmhouse.'

It was in the courtroom. She said that when she was testifying against me.

My head jerks up and I look accusingly at Kaelen. 'You were there?' I ask. 'You were at my trial?'

He nods. 'Yes. I went just now. To look for him.'

I shake my head. I remember having a strange sensation that someone or *something* was there. My focus was momentarily pulled to the far back corner of the room. Was that because Kaelen was there? In that courtroom? Was that what I sensed?

He was there because I told him to go.

And then I remember something else that Mrs Pattinson said during the trial.

'He disappeared two days ago . . . Probably wandered off into the woods. My guess is the witch lured him out of the house with a spell.'

'That's why she thought he disappeared,' I realize aloud. 'He didn't wander off into the woods. You took him from the house and brought him here.'

Kaelen looks confused by my rehashing this. 'Yes. Isn't that what you asked me to do?'

'Yeah,' I say dazedly. 'I'm just trying to get it straight.'

I turn back to Zen. 'How long does he have?'

'By my calculations, given the progression of his condition, a few days.'

'Tell me what is wrong with him.' I try again. 'What is his *condition?*'

'I did as you asked,' Kaelen says, ignoring my pleas. 'I've brought him here. Now you must hold up your end of the agreement. It's time for us to go.'

His heartless attitude towards Zen and the fact that he clearly doesn't care whether Zen lives or dies infuriates me and I feel venom welling up inside me. My fists clench. I want to scream. I want to strike him over and over again, with any object I can find, until he talks. Until he tells me what he knows. But I force myself to swallow it down. Gather my composure. Take deep breaths.

I'm no good to Zen if I can't keep my temper in check and stay calm. Right now, going with Kaelen is my best chance at saving him. My only chance.

'OK,' I agree, my voice strangled. I let Zen's fingers slowly slip through mine. His hand falls limp against the white sheet as I bid him a silent goodbye. 'Let's go.'

I have no intention of leading Kaelen to whatever it is he is looking for. Whatever it is that Diotech so desperately wants. Because I know as soon as I do, he'll take me right back to the compound. To Alixter. So that I can be fixed. So that I can be like him.

Diotech has no interest in saving Zen's life. I know this. And that's why Kaelen cannot be trusted. Under any circumstances.

But the truth is, I have to learn more about him. I have to test his strengths, uncover his weaknesses — if he has any. Find out how we are similar and, especially, how we are different. If I'm ever going to escape, these are the things I need to know.

But most of all, I need to find out everything he knows about Zen's illness. And his cure.

And as soon as I do, I'll be as far away from Kaelen and Diotech as possible.

It occurs to me that I've just discovered our first similarity: it appears I can't be trusted either.

22

NOVICE

I follow Kaelen out of the bedroom and into another empty room with floor-to-ceiling blackened windows. This one is much larger, with glossy white wooden floors instead of carpet and bright electric-blue accents painted on the white walls and ceiling. Illuminated lamps with strange rounded shades hang from the ceiling, and shelves are indented directly into the walls. I assume keepsakes or decorations once occupied the space, but the shelves are now empty and barren. There is no furniture at all, making this room, which appears to be a living room, even sadder than the last.

To my left there is a pristine, untouched kitchen. Judging from the modernity of the appliances – dishwasher, refrigerator, and a few I don't recognize – which are all a sleek metallic navy blue, it appears we're not anywhere near the seventeenth century any more.

I'm completely taken aback by the stark contrast of everything around me compared to the world I just left. While the Pattinsons' house felt warm and cosy and lived in, filled with imperfect handmade wooden furniture, a fire burning in the hearth, dust gathering in the corners, and a general atmosphere of habitation, this place feels exactly the opposite. Cold and sterile. The word *abandoned* comes to mind.

'Is this a house?' I ask, glancing around.

'An apartment.'

'Why is it so empty?'

'It was foreclosed,' Kaelen explains.

I drag a fingertip across the lustrous metal countertop of the kitchen. 'Foreclosed?'

'The people who lived here could no longer afford to pay for it so they were forced to leave. Now it's owned by the bank. Foreclosed homes are the easiest places to inhabit when you're on an assignment.'

I suppose his logic makes sense. If no one lives here, it would be simple enough to transesse directly inside and stay. Although the idea of entering someone else's home after it's been taken from them makes me feel a little ill.

I peer around in the darkness, trying to imagine what this place must have looked like with furniture in it. With people in it. When it was a home. And not an empty hole. 'What time is it?'

Kaelen glances at a watch on his wrist and I find it humorous that he even has one. Clocks aren't exactly useful when you're hopping through time. '1300 hours,' he announces officially. As though he *were* the clock, not just reading it.

I shake my head and glance towards the darkened windows. 'One in the afternoon? That's impossible. It's completely dark outside.'

Kaelen walks over to the window, swiping his fingertip along a clear glass plate affixed to one of the panes. Instantly the darkness evaporates and the view through the window magically transforms. The sunlight is bright, blinding me for a second. But when my eyes adjust and I witness what is on the other side of the glass, I'm speechless.

In awe, I take a step towards it, hardly believing what I see.

Hundreds of massive towers rise into the sky. They go on for miles. It's a forest of buildings taller than I've ever seen before. And as I inch closer, I realize that we must be inside one of them, because when I peer down, I nearly jump at the sight of the ground so far beneath us. Over a thousand feet, I estimate. On the busy street below I see tiny cars – mostly yellow – zooming around. And people. So many people. They walk in a swarm, moving as one. Expertly manoeuvring around other swarms heading in the opposite direction.

Somewhere in the distance, high in the sky, I see a flying aircraft, propelled by giant revolving spokes attached to the top of it. It soars gracefully through the air, making elegant turns and banking around buildings before coming to land on the roof across the street.

'Where *are* we?' I ask, gobsmacked. It seems unreal. Un-believable.

'New York City, New York, United States of America,' Kaelen replies.

'In what year?'

'2032.'

Now I turn away from the window. '2032? Why did you bring me to 2032?'

'It wasn't my decision,' he explains blankly. 'The memories dictate our destination.'

Find me.

I think back to the vision I saw in my prison cell but I can't, for the life of me, recall any reference to a year. I could barely figure out *where* I was, let alone *when*.

I watch as Kaelen swipes his fingertip on the glass plate and the city once again disappears behind a sheet of darkness. 'What is that?' I ask, jutting my chin towards his hand.

'Digitally enhanced windowpanes,' Kaelen explains. 'They create artificial night.'

I attempt to peer through the window at the massive metropolis outside but it's entirely concealed.

Kaelen gestures away from the window. 'It's time to go.'

I gaze down at my outdated (and charred) seventeenth-century clothes. 'I can't go out in this.'

But he doesn't seem to understand the objection. 'Why not?'

I sigh. 'Because these are old and outdated. If people see me in them it will attract too much attention. I need modern clothes.' I sniff the air. 'And a shower.'

Kaelen reaches under the collar of his shirt and flips open my locket. Then he walks towards me and extends his hand in the direction of my arm.

I move fast, darting to the far corner of the living room. 'Don't you dare touch me when that thing is open,' I warn.

As far as I know, this could all be one giant ruse to get me back to Diotech. I certainly wouldn't put it past him . . . or them.

'I am simply transporting you to a clothing store.'

'I'm not transessing *anywhere* with you,' I vow.

His jaw hardens again and I know that I'm starting to irritate him.

Good.

'Fine,' he allows, snapping the necklace shut. 'You take a shower. I will acquire some new clothes for you.'

Once he's gone I find my way to the bathroom, run the water, and peel off my scorched garments. A slight sadness settles over me as I watch each layer of my seventeenth-century ensemble tumble to a heap at my feet.

It's really over, I realize. The dream Zen and I spent so long planning and perfecting is finished. No matter what happens after this, we can never go back there.

But admittedly, it *does* feel amazing to finally be out of those binding clothes. Like I've been liberated from fabric bondage.

And the hot water is wondrous on my skin. It's been six months since I bathed in anything other than a cold tub. I turn in slow circles, letting it wash away the dirt and grime and smoky remnants of the past.

When I'm finished I turn off the faucet and step out of the stall. Kaelen is standing there holding an armful of clothing. I let out a shriek.

'What are you doing?!'

He seems confounded by the question. 'Bringing you new clothes.'

I grab them out of his hand and use them to cover my wet, naked body, as there don't appear to be any towels in this fore-closed apartment. 'I mean in *here*. You're not supposed to see me without clothes on.'

'Why?'

I remember when I, too, didn't understand everyday social rules about dress codes and manners and propriety. But you learn fairly quickly when you live in the real world. As opposed to a lab.

'Because,' I say, making zero effort to hide my impatience, 'it's not appropriate. Now turn around.'

I can tell my explanation is unsatisfactory but regardless, he turns around, suspiciously watching me out of the corner of his eye until the last possible second.

'I'm not going to run,' I tell him. 'I promise.'

Once his back is turned, I quickly survey the garments Kaelen brought me. Clamped to each item is a small metal tag with a dollar sign and a price scrolling across a transparent screen on the front.

'What did you do?' I ask, pulling an ugly brown sweater over my head. '*Steal* these?'

I could just picture him transessing into a store at night, after it was closed, grabbing random items off the rack, and then transessing out again.

He shrugs. 'It was determined to be the least complicated method of obtaining suitable garments.'

I slide my legs into the loose-fitting pants and button them. 'OK,' I announce with a sigh, 'you can turn around.'

As he does, I study my reflection in the mirror. The clothes are pretty hideous. And they're way too big. I have to roll the waist of the pants to keep them from slipping right down to my ankles.

'Nice selection,' I say, content with my appropriate use of sarcasm. My foster brother, Cody, would be so proud. He was the one who first taught me the meaning of sarcasm. And so much more. I feel a pang in my chest at the memory of Cody. When I was lost and alone in the year 2013, he was the only one I could trust. Until Zen found me.

'Thank you,' Kaelen replies, taking my compliment literally. Clearly he was never taught the meaning of sarcasm either and the thought of being somehow more experienced than him in the ways of the world makes me feel extremely smug.

And grateful that I had Cody.

I flick my finger against one of the digital price tags. 'I can't walk around with these on.'

'Then remove them.'

I think back to the time my foster mother, Heather, took me to the mall and bought me new clothes. All the items had small metal clamps, similar to these, that she explained were pro- grammed to set off an alarm if you tried to leave the store without paying for something. The cashier had to remove them with a special device.

145

'I don't think it's that simple,' I reply.

Kaelen hesitates before approaching me. I know he's fearful of the proximity, just as I am. I can feel the pull as soon as he's within a few feet of me. I grit my teeth in an attempt to endure it.

He comes close enough to study the tag fastened to my sweater. Then he grabs the two ends, one in either hand, and pulls down, bending the metal easily. I watch the tag pop off. He repeats the process with the pants before hastily retreating, as though I'm a deadly snake with bared fangs.

'We will go now.' He reaches for my locket again.

'Nuh-uh,' I say, shaking my head adamantly. 'I told you, I'm not transessing anywhere with you.'

I can tell by the look on his face that this puts some kind of damper on his plans but I really don't care. I don't trust him at all.

He thinks for a moment, glancing again at his watch. Then he finally pivots abruptly on his heels and opens the front door of the apartment. 'We'll have to hurry.'

I crane my neck to steal a peek at the long white-and-grey corridor. It's a new world on the other side of that door. A foreign world. I have no idea where we're going. I have no idea if I'll ever be back. I look longingly towards the barren room where Zen now lies, his life slipping away like the last minutes of precious daylight.

For him, I tell myself. I'm doing this for him.

I brace myself for whatever lies outside these walls. For whatever tricks Diotech might have planned. For the wretched sensation I will undoubtedly feel when I leave Zen behind. And then I take a deep breath and step into 2032.

23

IDENTIFIED

Kaelen holds the door open, gesturing for me to walk through. I edge past him, my back pressed tightly against the jamb in an attempt to keep as much distance between us as I can.

As we walk down the corridor, I stay a full five paces behind him. Kaelen stops when we reach an elevator at the end, studying it curiously, as though he's not quite sure what to do with it.

I laugh and press the Down button. 'First time out of the compound?'

His head jerks in a succinct staccato motion, like gears snapping into place. 'I've received extensive training in twenty-first-century civilization and society,' he replies, sounding, to my delight, just a tad defensive.

'What kind of training?'

He presses a finger to a spot behind his left ear, as though he has an itch there. 'Virtual-simulation downloads.'

'Clearly they forgot to include a few things,' I say with a

147

smirk. 'Like how you're not supposed to barge in on girls when they're in the shower.'

The elevator dings as the doors open and I think I see Kaelen jump, although he composes himself so quickly, I can't be sure.

'So they don't have elevators on the compound?' I prod.

But he responds gruffly, 'They work differently.'

We both eye the confined space, and I cringe, stepping in and quickly moving to the far corner while he does the same at the other side.

Seeming to have caught on to the mechanical functions of an elevator, he presses the button labelled 'Lobby.' The gears hum to life, moving us swiftly downward, and I watch Kaelen carefully. His reaction reminds me of mine during my first ride in an elevator, at the mall that Heather took me to. A little bit of fascination mixed with a lot of fear. The only difference is, he does a much better job of hiding his reaction than I did.

'Don't worry,' I tell him, a small, triumphant smile dancing on my lips. 'It won't hurt you.'

The doors open to a spacious, elegant lobby. We walk through it, towards the street. Kaelen opens the heavy, glass door. A gust of frigid wind whips across my face, blowing my hair back. It's by far the coldest air I've ever felt. But fortunately, we seem to have been built for any kind of weather. The chill doesn't appear to bother either of us. One of our many advantages, I suppose.

Kaelen walks briskly down the street and I struggle to follow him through the throngs of people.

I can feel a hundred pairs of eyes on us. Like a heavy wall closing in from all sides. Some people actually stop walking and turn to stare. The women gawk silently at Kaelen, while the men seem more interested in me, some of them actually letting out low whistles as I walk by. Kaelen is completely oblivious, but my face flushes with heat and I drop my head, attempting to avoid eye contact.

I suppose I no longer have to worry about drawing attention to myself, now that Diotech has found me, but I still don't like the feeling of people watching me. It makes me uneasy. Quickens my breath.

'Do you know where we're going?' I pick up my pace so that I'm walking alongside him.

'To the corner of Canal Street and Elizabeth Street. And we're running out of time.'

He moves fast, faster than he should in front of all these people. And when he dodges people so effortlessly, so swiftly, his body nearly blurs. Passers-by are starting to give him astonished, frightened looks.

'Stop!' I finally shout. He draws to a halt and turns to look at me. 'You can't run like that,' I whisper, barely audible, but I know he can hear me.

'Why?'

'Because it's not . . . natural. You'll cause a commotion. You have to act like everyone else. You have to act human.'

'I am human,' he says, but it's not a whisper. He speaks in his regular voice. And about ten people stop and spin to look at him.

I grit my teeth and grab him by the arm, pulling him into a small alley. But I'm taken aback by a startling electricity that suddenly zaps through me. It originates in the five fingers that are wrapped around his impressive biceps and spreads swiftly through my chest, giving my entire body a shuddering jolt.

I hastily release his arm and study my still-tingling fingertips.

I don't think I should ever do that again.

But unfortunately, just letting go doesn't completely alleviate the sensation as we are now crammed together in this small space, which I immediately realize was a mistake. His proximity is overpowering. I feel a strange energy pulsing around me, emitting waves of something I can't understand. Can't fight. Don't want to.

Suddenly I forget everything I was about to say. I'm breathing so heavily. Feeling so drawn to him. I close my eyes tight and attempt to push it away but just when I think I've succeeded, I open them again and he's there. And his brilliant shimmering eyes are setting me on fire and putting me out and setting me on fire again.

Stop that!

But I don't know who I'm sending this silent command to. Is it me? I'm certainly not the one doing it.

Is it him?

That's doubtful. He looks just as put off by our closeness as I am.

'What do you want?' he nearly growls at me. It's probably the most emotion I've heard from him since we met.

'I . . .' I search for what I was going to say. Why I pulled him in here to begin with. 'You have to try to blend in.' I finally remember. 'You're not like anyone else out there. Neither of us is.'

'I know that,' he says.

'But *they* don't,' I go on. 'They don't know anything about you or me. And unless you want us both to end up in a hospital while inquisitive doctors and specialists run tests on us, you have to be more careful. We can't draw too much attention to ourselves.'

This seems to get through to him. He silently acquiesces and takes a step back. Then another. I feel the fire fade with each speck of distance that he puts between us.

'Now,' I say, taking control of the situation, 'do you know which way it is?'

He nods sharply. 'I've received a download of a map of the city. It's about four miles south of here. And we have twenty minutes to get there.'

He starts to walk urgently again in the direction we've been heading.

'Wouldn't it be faster to drive?' I say, gesturing to the vehicles whizzing by on the street.

He stops and seems to contemplate this before finally deciding, once again, that I'm right. Another small victory for me.

'Yes. We will take a taxicab,' he resolves. 'They are the most common form of hired transportation in today's society.'

I have to fight back a groan. He sounds like he's reading from a dictionary. Did I *ever* sound that ridiculous?

Kaelen turns and walks directly into the street. There's a loud *screech* as a blue van swerves around him, its horn honking. Kaelen leaps back on to the kerb, looking frazzled.

I *almost* laugh. 'You can't just walk right into the street.'

'Then how do we get to one of the taxicabs?'

I shrug. 'I don't know. But I do know you should wait for one of them to *stop* first.'

Kaelen looks deep in thought, probably accessing one of his many brain downloads. In the meantime, I glance around and notice a woman on the other side of the street raising her hand in the air. A yellow car with TAXI written on the side slows and pulls up to the kerb.

I decide it's worth a try. I step to the edge of the sidewalk and imitate her movements, lifting my hand above my head and waving as the next cluster of cars comes barrelling down the street.

It works.

A yellow taxi manoeuvres away from the rest of the vehicles and slows in front of me. The door opens automatically and I gesture grandly. 'I guess that's how you do it.'

Kaelen, looking as embarrassed as his statuesque face will allow, avoids eye contact and ducks into the backseat, scooting to the other side. I get in after him, staying as close to the window as I can. The door closes on its own.

'Where would you like to go?' A friendly female voice emanates from somewhere above our heads. I glance up, searching for the source.

It's only then that I realize the front seat — where the driver should be — is completely empty. In fact, there's not even a seat. Or a steering wheel. There's just a divider, separating us from a complex instrument panel, and a floor.

Bewildered, I turn to Kaelen. 'Who's driving the car?'

Now it's his turn to look smug. And he does it all too well. Heat flares in my chest.

'Taxicabs have been self-operating since 2027,' he states knowledgeably. 'It was determined to be safer for the general public. And by 2050, all cars will be self-operating, reducing the number of vehicle-related deaths per year to under ten worldwide.'

'Probably just the ten idiots who walk into the middle of the street,' I mumble under my breath.

'Where would you like to go?' repeats the friendly female voice, which I now realize is not real, but rather a computer.

'The intersection of Canal Street and Elizabeth Street,' Kaelen responds.

'That intersection is located in Chinatown,' the car replies. 'Is that correct?'

Chinatown?

I look to Kaelen, who responds impassively to the car. 'Yes, that is correct.' Ironically, the car sounds more human than he does.

'Please validate your identity so that I may deduct my fare.'

I watch Kaelen as he leans back and slips his hand into his

pocket, drawing out two peculiar transparent cards. They appear to be made out of paper-thin glass. He locates a small plate with a blinking blue light attached to the divider in front of us and holds both cards up to it, eliciting a faint ding.

'What are those?' I ask as he places them back in his pocket.

'People in this time period refer to them as DIP cards,' he explains. 'Digital-Identification Pass. In the year 2025, the United States government issued a law that all legal citizens must be in possession of a valid card. It is imprinted with information pertaining to the cardholder's identification, medical records, citizenship status, and other relevant data. It also links directly to the cardholder's monetary funds. I've just used ours to pay for this taxicab fare.'

'But we don't live here,' I point out. 'How did you get them?'

'Diotech manufactured two counterfeit cards for me to use while on assignment.'

He points towards a flat screen embedded in the divider. It flickers to life, displaying a still image of my face alongside Kaelen's.

Underneath are two names I've never seen before.

And below that a single word flashes in green: Clear.

'As far as the scanners are concerned,' he replies. 'We do live here.'

'Thank you, Mr Brown and Ms Connor,' the voice says, and I feel the vehicle pull away from the kerb, gliding smoothly down the street. 'Your account has been debited. Would you like to watch TV during your journey?'

Our faces vanish from the screen and a live news report takes their place. I catch sight of the headline scrolling under a grim-looking reporter's face: Two hundred more lives claimed by white fever. CDC hopeful for a vaccine soon.

'No,' Kaelen replies to the non-existent driver, and the screen turns off, fading to black.

'What is Chinatown?' I ask him.

'It's an enclave of the city where several people of Chinese ancestry live and work.'

Is that what I saw in my memory? Was I in Chinatown?

I think back to the crowd of people. The beast floating in the sky. The deserted street. The man standing in front of the blue door at the bottom of the stairwell. Apart from having seen it all in my head, none of it feels even remotely familiar. When I remember it, it's like looking into someone else's mind.

'I don't understand,' I say. 'Are these memories real? Have I actually *experienced* them before?'

'No,' Kaelen confirms. 'For you, they are artificial memories. But we believe they are based on real events and real people. That is how you will know that you are in the right place at the right time. When we step into Chinatown, everything should look exactly the same as it does in your mind. Except this time it will be real. You will essentially be inserting yourself into the memory.'

The car stops at a red light.

'And what happens after that? After we get there?'

He glances over at me. 'That's up to you.'

'Me?'

'Something will most likely trigger another memory. You have to alert me when that happens. It will direct us to the subsequent location. We believe that each memory has been specifically set to activate the next until ultimately delivering you to the final destination.'

'Which you won't tell me.'

'I cannot divulge that information.'

'Right.' I snort. 'But I still don't understand how you know where to go. I don't remember seeing anything indicating specific street names. Or Chinatown. Or—'

'Chinatown was evident,' he interrupts, 'from the context. The street corner was deduced from visual reference points that were included in the memory and cross-referenced with historical databases of city maps.'

'OK,' I allow, 'but how did you know what date to come to? How did you know this all took place in 2032?'

'I repeat,' he says stiffly, 'it's in the memory.'

I shake my head. 'No, it isn't. I . . .' But my voice trails off as I flash back to the strange foreign symbols that were written in the sky and on the fronts of all the stores.

Chinatown.

And suddenly it makes sense.

They aren't symbols.

They're Chinese characters. And I can read them.

I take another look at the memory. At the vertical writing in the sky. And everything becomes clear.

They are numbers.

2

0

3

2

24

REALITY

My mouth falls open just as the friendly female voice comes floating back into the vehicle. 'We are approximately two minutes away from your destination.'

'Why is there a year written in the sky?' I ask Kaelen accusingly, as though he were the one who put it there.

'Technically, it's a digital projection,' he replies. 'A part of the annual Chinese New Year.'

'What is the Chinese New Year?'

Kaelen opens his mouth to answer but it's the car who speaks first; obviously my question triggered some kind of pre-programmed response.

'The Chinese New Year is a wonderful occasion,' she replies in her gracious voice. 'Honouring the start of a new cycle in the Chinese lunar calendar. There is a large-scale celebration every year. The most popular event is the parade. It begins shortly. I'm sure you will have a lovely time.'

Celebration.

Parade.

'It happens on the same day every year?' I ask. 'That's how you knew to come here today?'

'Actually, no,' Kaelen admits. 'The date varies each year as the Chinese calendar aligns with the Western calendar, but the date – February 11 – was easy to calculate once the year was revealed to us.'

I sigh, grateful to finally understand.

But still, there's a disturbing tug in my stomach. Something is not adding up.

'Wait a minute.' I think aloud, retracing everything that's happened since I awoke. 'You pulled me from that fire and brought me *here*.'

Kaelen gazes out his window but I watch the back of his head fall into a terse nod.

'Because you knew the first memory took place in the year 2032.'

Another nod.

'But that would mean,' I deduce, slowly putting the pieces together in my mind, 'you must have *seen* the memory before we got here. Otherwise you wouldn't know where to go.'

His posture stiffens, a subtle alert that I've discovered something he didn't want me to discover. He doesn't turn around.

'When did you first see this memory?' I demand of him. 'When did you first look inside my head?'

But he doesn't answer. And suddenly I feel the car pulling to a stop and this time the door on Kaelen's side swings open.

'We have arrived at the intersection of Canal and Elizabeth Streets,' the cab announces. 'Please watch your step and have a wonderful day.'

Kaelen hurriedly gets out of the cab and I scoot across the seat to follow after him.

'Kaelen—' I say, but I'm cut off the moment I step outside and we're sucked into a massive crowd of people.

I'm crushed from all four sides as the wall of bodies tightens around us. Tugged this way and that as though we're trapped inside a wave. Then the noise starts.

The giant booming.

But it's no longer safely contained in my mind, now it's real. And infinitely louder.

It echoes in my teeth.

It vibrates my bones.

'What is that?' I call out, attempting to cover my ears. No one else seems to be bothered by it.

BOOM! BOOM! BOOM!

Kaelen cringes with each strike, clearly having the same problem that I'm having.

'Drums!' he calls back over the noise.

Drums?

I rack my mind for a definition but come up short. Regardless of what they're called, they're deafening.

And they're only getting louder. Closer. Faster.

BOOMBOOMBOOMBOOMBOOM!

The people around me start to titter and point towards the sky. I look up and see it. The digital projection, as Kaelen called it. The Chinese characters. The year:

2032.

The crowd erupts in applause. I keep my gaze skyward as tiny flecks of colour start to rain down. Exactly as it was in the memory.

I catch a yellow one in my hand and study it, noticing that it's completely harmless – made out of paper.

'Confetti,' Kaelen shouts over the noise, clearly reading my confusion.

The drums get louder still and the people start to chant and yell and cheer. And that's when I see it.

The black-and-gold-eyed beast.

Rising in the distance. Floating majestically into the air. Flying towards us.

I feel the scream bubble up inside me, the fear telling me to run. But when I glance around I'm surprised by everyone else's reactions. Their faces don't show fear or trepidation. They show only delight.

Even the children.

I look to Kaelen for another explanation, grateful when he has one. 'It's a dragon,' he says over the roar. 'It's made of paper and plastic.'

Then a smirk flashes over his face. 'Don't worry,' he says, echoing my exact words from the elevator, 'it won't hurt you.'

Irritation flickers through me and I shoot him a look. But Kaelen doesn't seem to notice. He's too busy pushing his way through the mass of people and gesturing for me to follow.

'This way!' he calls.

When we finally break through the last of the bystanders, I see that we've reached the opening of a quiet street. With seemingly everyone in the city at the celebration, the street is deserted.

Just like in my memory.

I feel a chill of familiarity as we make our way down the sidewalk. I take in each storefront, mentally ticking them off as I compare them to the versions in my mind.

And suddenly I know exactly what I need to do.

Where I need to go.

The same strange pull I felt when I was remembering this place pulls me now. But once again, because the sensation is no longer filtered through my mind – because it's *real* and happening *to* me – it's so much stronger.

Kaelen falls in step behind me as I stride purposefully down the street, searching for the narrow metal staircase with the blue door at the bottom.

I find it half a block away, and just as I suspected, when I peer over the railing, down into the stairwell, I see the old man standing there. Waiting.

His wispy white beard is exactly as I remembered it.

His thin, slanted eyes are exactly the same.

When our eyes meet, as I knew they would, he opens his mouth and in a soft, gentle voice, lilting in his thick Chinese accent, he says, 'I help you . . .'

And I whisper, 'Yes.'

25

HELP

The old man leads us silently through the blue door and into a tiny cramped room that smells like trees mixed with oranges mixed with Mrs Pattinson's pigeon pie.

A gentle chime drifts through the space, repeating and reverberating in several pitches. It immediately puts me at ease.

To our right, secured to the wall, are rows and rows of shelves, each one housing hundreds of glass bottles with Chinese markings on the sides. I tilt my head to read one, translating it awkwardly as *White Wood Ear*.

The wall to our left is covered in various drawings and charts and diagrams that don't make any sense to me.

It soon becomes apparent that I *help you* is probably the only English the old Chinese man knows because once we're inside, he leads us to a table with four chairs, mumbling, 'Please sit down,' in a dialect I can't identify, but understand nonetheless.

Kaelen and I lower ourselves into the chairs and the old man sits across from us. He gestures ambiguously to me. 'I help you?'

Kaelen immediately takes control of the situation, leaning forward in his chair and addressing the man in his native tongue. 'Do you recognize this girl?' he asks.

The old man shakes his head and then adds, 'Pretty.'

I look to Kaelen as if to say, *What now?*

Because the truth is, I have no idea what to do now. The memory ended with me walking down those steps. Kaelen said I would know the trigger when I saw it. That it would immediately activate the next memory, but so far I have felt or seen nothing unusual.

'I help you,' the man repeats in English.

Confused, I look to Kaelen, who shrugs and nods.

'Yes,' I say in the man's language. 'You help me. Please.'

He extends his arms and reaches across the table to me. I glance down warily at his hands. They're chapped and wrinkled. He wiggles his fingers at me, as though he expects me to touch them.

I look to Kaelen again and he signals for me to do it.

My heart is starting to beat faster, my stomach is starting to churn. But eventually I obey, slowly pushing my own hands forward, my fingers hovering inches above his.

He reaches up and grabs both wrists, one in either hand, causing me to jump. Then he flips my hands over, revealing my black mark. I'm terrified that he's going to say something about it, ask me what it is, but he doesn't. He just places his fingers firmly against my veins and closes his eyes.

He seems to fall into a deep sleep. As though he's been deactivated. I glance over at Kaelen, whose gaze is firmly locked on the old man's hands.

The man starts to hum softly to himself.

'Your blood,' he says. 'It is strong.'

I stay silent, letting him continue.

'Very strong,' he says. 'Like warrior.'

He goes quiet again, his face twisting in concentration. The wrinkles around his eyes and forehead deepen. Stretch. A tremor seems to pass through him, beginning at his hands and working its way down, through his torso. His body is trembling and I'm not sure what to do. Is he dying?

And then, abruptly, his eyes snap open. They are wide. Full of fear.

'No,' he starts to mumble. 'No. It isn't right. It isn't right.'

He drops my hands against the table with a thud and backs away. His chair scrapes loudly against the wood floor as he scrambles to push it further and further back, until he hits the wall of the confined space and is forced to stop.

All the while, he never takes his eyes off me. 'It shouldn't be,' he says in a petrified voice. 'You shouldn't be.'

I have no idea what's going on or what he's talking about. But he's completely terrifying me. I want to get out of here. I don't want to stay in this room with this crazy man any longer.

I push my chair back as well and start to rise to my feet, but just like that early morning on the Pattinsons' farm, something forces me back down. Shoving at my shoulders. Dragging me towards the ground.

I collapse into my seat as a bolt of hot searing pain rips into my skull. Tearing at my brain. Shooting out of my eyes. I moan in agony, thrusting my body forward, sinking my head between my knees. I cradle it in my hands, squeezing my temples, trying to push out the throbbing. It's unbearable. My head is going to explode.

'Sera.' I hear Kaelen's voice but it feels like it's coming from centuries away. 'Sera, what's happening?'

Another spear slices from ear to ear, penetrating everything in between. I let out a cry of anguish. It's like something is inside my brain, desperate to get out. Pushing. Shoving. Cutting.

What is happening to me?

The room spins. I shut my eyes tight but I'm still rotating.

I hear the old Chinese man mumbling something incoherent. It sounds like a prayer.

The woman's voice is back. Echoing and ghostly in my mind. *'Find me.'*

Then a fiery flash blazes behind my eyelids, robbing my entire world of colour. Of shape. Of meaning. Mercifully, my body turns off. Shuts down.

And I fall, fall, fall.

Into the infinite white.

26

TRIGGERED

An artificial light shines from above, illuminating the confined space I'm standing in. It's rectangular with a low ceiling. Like a large box. Walls made of steel. It's full of people and strange smells. A darkened world blurs by outside a smudged window.

We are moving.

The ground rumbles beneath my feet.

I'm suddenly lurched violently to the side as the vehicle jerks left. I grab on to a smooth metal pole that protrudes from the floor. It keeps me from falling.

I glance around, confused by my surroundings.

Where am I?

What is this place?

Brightly coloured moving pictures project on to flat screens embedded in the wall. One in particular catches my attention. A beautiful woman stares out from behind the paper-thin glass. She has creamy white skin, iridescent pink lips, shimmering bright blue eyes. She looks right at me and smiles coyly, ready to tell me a secret.

From somewhere overhead, a friendly male voice speaks: 'This is a Bronx-bound 6 train. The next stop is Fifty-Ninth Street.'

Train.

I'm on a train.

But why?

Where am I going?

What is 'Bronx'?

Someone taps me on the back and I jump. I turn around to see a man covered in grime and dirt and wrinkles. He holds a piece of cardboard in his hand. The word hungry is scribbled in shaky black handwriting.

He holds out his hand, uncurls his fingers. He wants something. Food, I presume. But I have nothing to give him.

There's a loud screech and I feel the world start to slow. Pull to a stop.

Desperation stings my throat. I need to find something. Something important.

But what?

I let go of the pole and spin in slow circles, scanning the interior of the train car. My gaze falls on one of the screens on the wall. The woman's face is gone, replaced by a news report. A man is standing outside a tall, curved blue building with trees surrounding the perimeter.

He's saying something but the sound is muted. His speech is being transcribed and printed on the bottom of the screen. I catch a few sporadic words like vaccine, symptoms, fever. But it's not the transcript that snags my attention. My eyes are suddenly pulled by an unseen, unknown force. Up, up, up. Above the man's head. Until they land on small black text that reads:

February 11, 2032. 2:45 p.m.

And instantly I know this is what I've been looking for.

A date and time.

A destination.

27

STOLEN

A rush of gentle energy surges into my body, pulling me out of the memory. Warming me from the inside. Like my veins are no longer filled with blood, but with fire.

But it's not the same fire that nearly burned me at the stake. It's the good kind. The kind that warms you when you're cold. Lights up dark rooms. Brings people together around it.

The splitting pain in my head is gone. Long gone. And somehow I feel certain that it will never return. That I will never feel pain again.

Everything has gone still and beautifully quiet. This peacefulness is now a permanent part of me. As unchanging as my tattoo.

I feel light radiating from the top of my head.

And in a moment that seems to last forever, I forget all of my problems.

All of my strife.

I simply forget . . .

But then my eyes flutter open and I see Kaelen crouched over me, his hand resting delicately across my forehead, and I panic.

I roll to the side, twisting my head away from his touch.

The illusion shatters around me. The warmth running under my skin turns to ice. The glow emanating from my head is immediately snuffed out and I'm left with nothing but heartache and sadness and reminders of Zen lying unconscious in that bed. Waiting for me to return. Waiting for me to save him.

'What are you doing?' I ask, leaping to my feet and glaring fiercely at Kaelen. We're still inside the old Chinese man's shop. But he's nowhere to be found. I'm willing to guess he ran after I passed out.

'The subway,' Kaelen says authoritatively, blatantly ignoring my question and rising from his crouch. 'We need to get to the nearest subway station.'

My forehead crinkles. 'What?'

'It runs underground.' It's as though he's speaking to himself. Living on his own planet where there are only assignments and missions and where pleasing Alixter is the equivalent of breathing oxygen.

'We have to find the Bronx-bound 6 train,' he continues.

Bronx-bound 6 train.

My thoughts are hazy and dim but I know that sounds familiar.

Why do I know those words?

He glances at his watch. 'We need to pass through the Fifty-Ninth Street station in one hour.'

'The next stop is Fifty-Ninth Street . . .'

Wait.

Those words. That stop. The train. They're all from my memory. The one I just had. Only a few minutes ago.

How did he . . . ?

My hand immediately flies to my forehead. It's still warm from Kaelen's touch. My chest tightens. My teeth clench.

I know that touch.

The warmth it brings. The spark. The fire. The way it's able to lift me out of whatever grief, whatever sorrow, whatever horror I'm experiencing.

I've felt it before.

Except it wasn't here. It wasn't in this year. It was a long, long time ago. Centuries before. When I thought Zen was dead. When I thought that I was about to die, too.

I can still hear the creaking of the massive iron door being pulled open. The soft footsteps entering. The muted swish of the robe.

'*The priest has come to hear your last confession and bless your soul.*'

My eyes flash with rage as I glare at Kaelen. 'You,' I spit out.

He's already moving towards the door. 'What?'

'You were there!' I accuse him. 'You were in my prison cell in 1609.'

He stops, seemingly frozen, with his hand on the doorknob. But he doesn't turn around.

'We have to go,' is the only thing he says.

'No!' I shout back. 'Not until you tell me the truth!'

Finally, he turns, his face as hardened and callous as ever. 'Sera,' he says sternly, 'we don't have time for this. If you refuse to transesse with me, then we have to leave *now*.'

I ignore him. 'That's how you were able to see the first memory. That's how you knew the time-delayed recalls were even there. How you knew to bring me to 2032 after the fire. You came to my cell posing as a priest. You touched me and somehow read my mind.'

'Yes,' he admits. 'I did.'

I cross my arms over my chest, indicating that I won't be

cooperating any further until he explains himself.

He seems to understand. 'Your trial appeared on the historical archives. One of the researchers at Diotech found it. She recognized your face from the sketch on the poster and your abilities from the accusations brought against you. I was sent to investigate. I posed as a priest in order to perform a brain scan. I took the results back to Diotech to be analyzed. That's when they found the TDRs and the first memory pointing to this year. Consequently, I returned to 1609 to pull you from the fire and I brought you here.' He raises his eyebrows at me. 'Satisfied?'

My head is spinning.

Satisfied?!

No, I'm not satisfied.

I feel violated. Betrayed. Enraged!

Something happened to me when that priest touched me. Somehow, just for a fleeting moment, I felt like everything was going to be OK. I felt . . . happy.

Was it all fake? Was it some kind of trick to lull me into a false sense of security so I wouldn't suspect what was really happening?

'And just now –' I press on through gritted teeth – 'you read my memories the same way. By touching my head.'

Kaelen's face tightens. I can tell this is not a conversation he wants to be having. But he answers anyway. 'Yes.'

'How?' I shoot back. 'How is that even possible?'

Kaelen holds his hand to my face, palm out. 'Nanoscanners,' he explains. 'Transparent film secured to my fingertips, invisible to the naked eye. They scan memories upon contact and wirelessly transmit them to be stored here for Diotech to review later.' He reaches into his pocket and removes a familiar cube with a faint green glow around the edges.

A hard drive.

It looks similar to the one Zen stored my stolen memories on.

Kaelen points behind one of his ears. 'But I'm able to read the memories as they transmit with my receptors.'

I tilt my head to peer through his head of thick, dark blond hair, just able to make out the small clear disk fused to his skin. It's smaller than the one Zen used on me. Practically imperceptible if you don't know to look for it.

I feel sick. I think I'm going to vomit. Miraculously, I manage to swallow the bile rising in my throat. It tastes bitter all the way down.

If he can touch me and see everything – my private memories, my most cherished moments with Zen, every thought I've ever had – then nothing in my brain is safe any more.

Nothing in my life is safe.

'Can we go now?' Kaelen asks, placing his hand back on the doorknob. 'We have a train to catch.'

I feel frail. Hopeless. Like I just want to lie down on this floor and never get up. I don't have the strength to fight him any more. And even if I did, I don't know how I could ever win. He's faster. Stronger. Smarter. More capable in every way. He has every advantage over me.

How will I ever manage to outmanoeuvre him?

Any plan that I make can be stolen with a simple stroke of his hand. In fact, he probably already knows that I've been planning to double-cross him the moment I get any information about Zen's cure. He probably already knows everything.

Why does it feel like no matter what I do, Diotech is always one step ahead of me?

Why does it feel like I'm constantly running and never getting anywhere?

Kaelen opens the blue door that leads back into Chinatown.

I glance longingly at the outside world lying just beyond this tiny, cramped spaced. A world that once held so many possibilities. So many potential futures. So many promises of what could be.

Today I watched them all shrivel and die until only one remained.

This one.

The one where Diotech wins.

With a weak nod of my head, I follow Kaelen out the door.

28

TRAINED

The subway station is dark and musty and claustrophobic. Maybe it's those long lonely days and nights of being locked up in the filthy prison cell that have seeped into my subconscious, or maybe it's my flight instinct rearing up again, but the thought of being in such a confined space, so far underground, with limited escape routes is putting me on edge. Like the air has somehow lost its invisibility, turned dense and rough, scraping at my skin.

Plus, we are surrounded by people. So very many people. Ready to squeeze me to death at any minute. I can't understand how anyone lives in this crowded city where it seems as though you can never be alone.

Not to mention the stares. They follow us everywhere. Down the steps from the street, through the main level of the station, across the long dark corridors carved under the city. Kaelen still seems oblivious to the attention but I notice it. Sometimes I feel like I can't notice anything else.

The eyes – the thousands of wandering, questioning,

reproving eyes – they are all around us. They penetrate my clothes. They rip at my skin. They devour me.

I feel the constant urge to run. To hide. To huddle in a corner, shut my eyes tight, and try to disappear.

I shuffle feebly behind Kaelen as we descend another flight of stairs, bringing us deeper and deeper under the ground. We arrive on a platform full of more people.

A train is approaching. It slows and screeches to a stop. People exit. More people get on. I absent-mindedly start to lumber towards the door, cringing as I allow myself to be drawn into the current of bodies. Until Kaelen's arm juts out in front of me.

I manage to halt just before colliding with his arm.

Then I jump back, remembering the startling jolt of electricity I felt when we touched on the street earlier.

'We will not be taking this train,' he informs me, lowering his arm. 'We will take the next one.'

I blink, trying to shake this heavy fog that seems to be following me around like an oversize shadow. But I know that's probably not going to happen. Not while Diotech continues to hold all the power. Not until I can stop feeling so aggravatingly helpless.

'Why not?'

'Based on the frequency of the trains and the distance between here and the Fifty-Ninth Street station, I've calculated that we need to take the 6 train arriving here in exactly 3.2 minutes in order to pass through the correct station at exactly 2:45 p.m. The time that was indicated in your memory.'

I sigh and slouch. 'That sounds complicated.'

He arches an eyebrow. 'It would have been easier to transesse.'

I grunt and step a few paces away from him.

I'm grateful when the train departs and the platform clears

again. But my relief only lasts a few seconds before more people begin descending the stairs, slowly filling in the empty space.

Where are they coming from?

Where do they *go*?

The sheer volume and the notion of housing and containing them all contorts my mind into loops and knots.

I look up and notice a young man watching me from a few feet away. He's tall and muscular with hair cut very short. He's carrying a black bag over his shoulder. His lips are curved into an unnerving half-smile that reminds me of the foxes I used to see on the Pattinsons' farm. They would hide in the brush, watching small birds, waiting for one to fly down to pluck a seed from the earth, and then they would pounce, seizing the vulnerable little creature between their teeth and ripping its head off with one yank. The poor fluttering bird never had a chance.

When our eyes meet, the man immediately starts towards me. I wince and drop my gaze, trying to reverse whatever invitation he thought I was giving him. But it soon becomes apparent that he's not deterred because I hear his footsteps clacking across the tiled platform. The clacking rises above the other sounds clamouring around me.

And then he's standing beside me. And although I don't dare look up to see his face, I can sense that same disturbing fox-like grin.

'Where did you come from?' he asks.

I have no idea what to do. Do I answer with something dismissive so that he leaves or do I just not reply and hope he goes away?

I opt to keep my mouth shut.

But this seems to have the opposite effect of what I intended.

'What's the matter?' he says, irritation fraying the edges of his voice. 'You too good to talk to me?'

I press my lips hard together, feeling them go numb. Then I give my head a subtle shake.

'You should know I don't like girls who are rude to me.' He tugs at the strap around his shoulder. 'Wanna see what's in my bag?'

'No, thank you,' I say as politely as I can.

'She speaks,' he replies, and then, without warning, his hand is on my wrist, pulling me closer until my body is crushed against his and I'm forced to look at him, forced to breathe the same air as him.

'Let go,' I tell him, the politeness gone.

He doesn't comply. In fact, he only grips my wrist tighter. 'You know,' he breathes, 'you really should learn to be nicer to people.'

'Let go now,' I seethe.

'What if I don't want to?' I hear amusement in his voice.

'Then I will make you.'

I don't want to have to reveal my true abilities in front of all these people. I don't want to cause that kind of scene. But I realize now that I may not have a choice.

He laughs quietly in my face. 'I doubt that.'

With a firm jerk, I yank my wrist free. The man is suddenly in the air, soaring across the station and crashing into the tiled wall behind me. I glance curiously at my hand.

Did I just do that?

The answer comes a moment later when I look over to see Kaelen grabbing the man by the shirt and wrenching him up to his feet. He slams him hard against the wall again.

'What's your problem, man?' the stranger roars, squirming to get free of Kaelen's grasp. He attempts to take a swing at Kaelen's face but isn't fast enough. Kaelen ducks effortlessly and then presses his forearm against the man's throat.

'Don't touch her,' Kaelen growls.

If I thought we were drawing attention to ourselves before, it's nothing like the audience Kaelen has attracted now. The entire platform has turned to watch the spectacle, as well as the people standing across the train tracks, who are craning to see what the commotion is.

I hurry over to Kaelen, careful not to touch him. 'Kaelen, let him go.'

The man smirks. 'Yeah, do what your girlfriend says, *Kaelen*. What kind of name is that?'

Kaelen's forearm presses deeper into the man's throat, causing him to gasp.

I hear a low rumble on the tracks behind us. 'Kaelen,' I try again, 'the train is coming. We have to make that train, remember?'

I watch comprehension register on his face and in an instant the man is slumped on the floor again, gasping for air and clutching his neck, which is already starting to show the bruises from Kaelen's grip.

Without even a second thought, Kaelen turns and stalks callously through the swarm that has formed around us, people parting to make room for him.

There's another loud *screech* as the train approaches the station, and the crowd dissipates.

'You didn't have to do that,' I chide him in a huffed whisper. 'I could have handled it myself.'

He watches the bright headlights of the train grow nearer. 'It didn't look that way.'

'Your reaction was inappropriate,' I go on, frustrated.

'That's how I was designed to react.'

Evidently *he* didn't get the flight-over-fight instinct that I was given.

'I'm like you . . . Only better.'

'Well,' I hiss, 'that's exactly the kind of attention-drawing behaviour I warned you about.'

But he doesn't seem to be listening any more. His eyeballs are darting rapidly back and forth as the train barrels through the station and he carefully scans each passing car.

By the time it pulls to a stop, he seems to have found what he's looking for and starts walking briskly towards the front of the train. As we approach the door three compartments down, I finally see what he was looking for.

A man stands in the centre of the car. His skin is covered in wrinkles and caked with dirt. His aging body is rickety, hunched over. One of his hands grips the steel pole for balance while the other holds a tattered cardboard sign.

On it one word is sketched in shaky black letters:

HUNGRY.

And I immediately know that this is the right train.

A friendly male voice echoes from somewhere above our heads. 'This is a Bronx-bound 6 train. The next stop is Spring Street. Please stand clear of the closing doors.'

Kaelen and I share a quick glance before simultaneously hopping off the platform, into the train, just as the heavy slabs of steel slide shut.

29

MASKED

The train is even more suffocating than the station. I fight to keep my composure. But it certainly doesn't help that the scene on the platform is playing over and over in my mind.

Kaelen could have killed that man.

He said he was *designed* to react that way.

Well, of course he was. He was sent here for me. He said so himself. He was sent to follow the map in my head and then, without a doubt, to bring me back. So obviously he would do whatever it took to protect me. To safeguard Diotech's investment.

Kaelen is facing away from me, watching out the dirty, smudged window. We haven't spoken since we boarded the train. We ride in silence, both listening carefully to the announcement of each stop. Waiting for the one from my memory. Fifty-Ninth Street.

And then what?

What will I see?

What will happen to me?

Will that same excruciating pain erupt in my head again? Is that what happens every time a memory is triggered? Given my experience of agonizing torture in my prison cell and in the Chinese man's shop, it would certainly seem that pain is the protocol.

I cringe at the idea of having to go through it again.

Of possibly passing out here, surrounded by all these people.

The train pulls to a stop at the Fifty-First Street station – one stop away from our destination – and I feel a quick jab on my arm. The small zap of electricity that accompanies it jolts me into alertness. Kaelen is pointing alarmingly towards the doors. I peer over to see what the problem is.

The man, the one with the cardboard sign, who has been shuffling back and forth through this car, stretching his hand out to every passenger for the past nine stops, is preparing to get off.

'What do we do?' I whisper.

'He's definitely in the memory at Fifty-Ninth Street, right?' I'm grateful to hear that this time he's wise enough to speak in a hushed tone instead of announcing it for everyone on board to hear.

I nod.

'Then we follow him,' Kaelen resolves.

'OK.'

The train comes to a full stop and the doors open. Kaelen and I stay a diligent five paces behind the man as he hobbles across the platform. He stops between cars and, apparently in no hurry to go anywhere else, leans casually against one of the many thick metal beams that populate the station.

I look urgently to Kaelen, who just shrugs in return.

'This is a Bronx-bound 6 train. The next stop is Fifty-Ninth

Street,' the voice announces. 'Stand clear of the closing doors, please.'

This seems to capture the old man's attention and he quickly shuffles away from his beam and boards the nearest car. Kaelen and I leap in after him, barely managing to avoid being crushed by the closing doors.

The train rumbles off again and I immediately notice the screen on the wall, to my left.

The familiar beautiful woman is peering back at me. Her skin painted a shade of creamy smooth ivory. Her lips glinting pink. She smiles seductively.

I catch Kaelen's eye and jut my chin in her direction. He nods, understanding.

It's almost time.

I didn't notice it when the memory was invading my mind but I now see that the woman is part of an advertisement for a brand of make-up. I watch her softly caress her own face, before the image shifts and a logo appears.

After that, everything happens exactly as I remember it.

The now-familiar voice repeats the announcement: 'This is a Bronx-bound 6 train. The next stop is Fifty-Ninth Street.'

Then I feel a tap on my back. Unlike in the memory, I don't jump. I anticipate it. I turn around to see the man we followed holding up his cardboard sign:

HUNGRY.

His dirty fingers unfurl in front of me. I offer him a quick, kind smile and shake my head. I want to help – I want to give him food – but like in the memory, I don't have any to give.

I turn back to the screen and see the image shift to the newscast. Just as I remembered it, the reporter is standing in front of a building. This time, however, I take a moment to read some of the transcript of his speech below.

'The CDC has issued an official statement this morning

reporting that they are sadly no closer to creating a successful vaccine for the white fever, which has already claimed nearly one thousand lives nationwide and confined five thousand more to hospital quarantines. They have assured us that they are working hard to perfect a vaccine but have asked us to remind everyone to seek medical help immediately if you are showing any of the symptoms listed on your screen.'

My eyes narrow as I watch the list appear alongside the reporter's face.

Fever. Chills. Weakness and fatigue. Muscle soreness.

A tremor shudders through me.

Those are Zen's symptoms.

But that's impossible. He can't have whatever it is they're talking about. He got sick before we even came here. How could he have contracted a twenty-first-century disease while living in 1609?

My thoughts are distracted by the *screech* of the brakes as the train lurches to a stop and the doors open, letting more people off and on.

Kaelen shoots me a stern look, reminding me to pay attention. This is the stop from my memory. This is where the memory ended. Which means any minute now I'm going to see something that—

My gaze lands on a small child in a heavy coat, hat, and gloves entering the train. One of his hands is firmly clasped inside his mother's. And the other is holding a tiny toy sailboat.

The throbbing begins, alerting me to the incoming memory.

I struggle to keep my eyes open. I look at Kaelen. He's distracted, peering curiously around the train. He's searching for a possible trigger. He doesn't know that I've already found it.

And suddenly I realize that this is it.

My only chance to move one step ahead.

If I can somehow manage to stay conscious, to keep the pain from registering on my face, then I can hide the memory from him. I can stop Diotech from getting what they want.

The throbbing continues, growing more intense by the second. The creature inside is threatening to rip my skull open. I grip the pole tightly, attempting to channel all the pain into my hands, into this piece of metal.

You can do this, I tell myself.

Control it.

Contain it.

Conceal it.

I close my eyes, taking deep breaths, fighting back a scream of agony that's brimming in my throat, pushing against my lips, begging to be released.

When I force my eyes open, I notice that Kaelen is watching me. Studying me. He tilts his head. 'Are you OK? Did you see something?'

I force a tight smile and shake my head, keeping my lips firmly pressed together in fear that if I try to speak, the scream will escape.

'Are you sure?' he presses, taking a step towards me, his hand reaching out to my forehead.

The train jerks into motion, sending Kaelen staggering back.

I swallow hard as the memory tears at my brain with sharp claws. Slicing into the backs of my eyeballs.

I open my mouth slowly, finally managing to croak out, 'I'm sure.'

'Well, the trigger has to be here somewhere.' Kaelen continues to peer eagerly around the train.

Meanwhile, the memory has broken free, raided my mind. Preparing to show itself. I'm feeling woozy, the floor is vibrating much more than it should. The darkened walls of the subway tunnels are passing by the windows much faster than they are supposed to.

Don't pass out, I command myself.

Don't pass out!

My knees are wobbling. I press into the metal pole with my entire body, keeping myself upright. I bite the inside of my cheek, drawing blood. The pain behind my temples has reached an epic climax.

'Find me,' comes the delicate, misty voice.

And then suddenly I'm . . .

Standing in the middle of a long, empty hallway lined with doors.

Everything is clean, sparkling with artificial light cast from above.

I take a step, falling into a quiet shadow between the overhead lamps. I note the numbers on the doors.

408

409

410

I know that I'm being led somewhere. That one of these doors will call to me. Reach out and wrap a long, bony finger around my spine, sending shivers everywhere.

It's just a matter of which one.

411

412

413

The hallway is deserted. Devoid of life. Every door closed.

I pass by a window. It's dark outside. The sidewalk below is mostly empty, indicating it must be late at night. Or very early in the morning.

414

415

416

I feel my blood start to warm. I'm getting closer. I know it.

But closer to what?

Part of me is scared to find out. No . . . all of me.

A large flat screen is embedded in the wall on my right but no image is displayed. Just a blank canvas of bright blue. A flashing message says No Signal. And a date. In the bottom right-hand corner.

February 12, 2:13 a.m.

417

418

419

I freeze. This is it. This is the door. I can feel it. Every cell in my body is alerting me to it.

My hand reaches out, trembling. I can barely grasp the handle. I turn it and push.

Inside there is a long, sleek, metal countertop with various computers and scientific instruments sprawled across it.

I look up from the countertop and see a man. Alone. Hunched over a computer. His wavy blond hair sprouts in all different directions. His face is tired, covered in stubble. He is tall. Lanky. Wearing a long, crumpled white coat.

I study him for a moment, my gaze unmistakably drawn to his fingers tapping a series of numbers that I can't see into a keyboard.

For some reason, I am aware that these numbers are important, but I don't know why.

I take a step towards him to get a better look, and he startles, sensing me for the first time. His weary blue eyes dart towards the door.

Towards me.

He looks familiar. Painfully familiar. And yet I can't place him.

Not until my gaze falls to the breast pocket of his coat. Not until I see the small digital badge pinned to his lapel, illuminated with text like a tiny screen.

Not until I read his name, which appears just below the words GenZone Research Laboratory.

And then my entire world goes fuzzy.

No.

It can't be. It's not him. He can't be a part of this.

He looks me up and down. His expression matches mine perfectly. We are twins of disbelief.

Unable to accept the fact that we have found each other here. Now. In this strange, uncertain future.

I open my mouth to speak. But no sound comes out.

'You . . .' he croaks, his voice low. Too low. Too old. Too mature. It sends dizzying vibrations through my brain.

'You shouldn't be here,' he says.

I shake my head, feeling frost drift over me. I try to speak again but my voice is still lost in some deep abyss. I can't tell him what I want to tell him. I can't respond with the only thought that's running through my mind right now.

Neither should you.

30

MOTIVATIONS

'Where would you like to go?' the disembodied female voice asks us as we get into a cab outside the Pelham Bay Park subway station.

'I don't understand,' Kaelen says. 'How could there not be a trigger? We went exactly where the memory directed you.'

He hasn't stopped complaining about this since we left the train after riding it for another twenty-six stops, all the way to the end of the line, at which time we were forced to disembark. The whole time he stood there, staring at me, waiting for something to happen. And the whole time, I convincingly insisted that nothing had.

'I'm sorry, I'm not familiar with that destination,' the cab replies, referring to Kaelen's rant.

'I don't know,' I tell him, refusing to look him in the eye for fear that he'll be able to read the lie. 'Perhaps it's been triggered but will take some time to activate. You said yourself that TDRs are activated by physical triggers or after a certain amount of time has passed. Maybe this is one of the time-triggered ones.'

He ponders this, his expression neutral with just a hint of aggravation.

'I'm sorry,' the cab repeats. 'I'm not familiar with that destination either. Where would you like to go?'

I look at Kaelen. 'Maybe we should just go back to the apartment and wait.' I silently pray that he'll agree. The rest of my plan will only work if he agrees.

I hold my breath.

He sighs sharply. 'I suppose that is an acceptable proposal.'

Exhale.

Relief.

Kaelen fishes the two forged DIP cards out of his pocket and waves them in front of the scanner. '173 East Seventy-Second Street.'

A *ding* sounds from the screen in front of us, flashing our pictures side by side again.

'Thank you,' the female voice replies. 'Your account has been debited. Would you like to watch TV during your journey?'

'No,' we reply in unison.

I can't have any distractions. I need all my strength and concentration to pull this off.

The car drives away from the kerb. Out of the corner of my eye, I notice Kaelen relax against the seat, looking fatigued.

Good, I think. *That will certainly help.*

We ride in silence, watching the busy New York streets pass by out the window.

'Based on current traffic conditions, we should arrive at your destination in approximately twenty minutes,' the cab announces.

Twenty minutes, I think. *That should give me enough time.*

Kaelen is seemingly lost in thought. He's probably running back through the download of the memory he stole from my mind, trying to figure out what might have gone wrong. What we might have missed.

A flick of my gaze and I see the small lump in his left pants pocket.

The Modifier.

I remember him putting it in that pocket at the apartment before we left. If I can just get my hands on it, my plan might actually work. But since Kaelen is clearly stronger and faster than I am, the element of surprise is my only real chance.

My fingers tingle in anticipation. My legs burn with heat. I prepare my body to spring, mentally bracing myself for the current that will undoubtedly charge through my body the moment we touch.

And we will touch.

It's inevitable.

Our skin will make contact. That mysterious pulse of energy will illuminate me from the inside. The relentless magnetism will suck me in like a gravitational field.

That warmth will wash over me. Spread everywhere. Erase everything . . .

Focus, I command myself.

I think about Zen. Dying in that bed only twenty minutes from here. I have to help him. I can't trust Diotech to do it. They'll never hold up their end of the agreement. As soon as they follow this map inside my head and get their hands on whatever it is that's waiting at the end of it, all promises will be discarded.

I'll be back at the Diotech compound, strapped to a chair while they rewire my brain and turn me into someone incapable of questioning anything.

Someone like *him*.

I eye the bulge of the Modifier in his pocket again and curl my fists into tight balls, preparing to strike. I suck in a courageous breath and spring towards him, one arm outstretched, aimed for his face, while the other veers towards his pocket.

Kaelen turns his head just as I'm starting to move and I crash to a halt. I quickly settle back into the seat, pretending that I was simply shifting my weight to get more comfortable and scratch an itch on my head.

His head tilts for a moment as he studies me, seemingly deciding what to make of my strange manoeuvre. He opens his mouth to say something and I'm positive he's going to scold me for trying to attack him while his back was turned.

'Why did you run away from the Diotech compound?' he says at last.

I stare at him, completely baffled by this unexpected question. 'What?'

'The intelligence I received before I was sent to apprehend you. It informed me that you had escaped from the compound with the son of a Diotech scientist. But it didn't clarify your reason for departing. What would motivate you to do that?'

I feel myself relax. My heart eases back into a normal steady rhythm.

I hesitate, not sure how detailed I want to get about my true motivations for leaving. Especially with someone who couldn't possibly understand them. 'You've seen all my memories,' I argue sourly. 'You should know.'

'Yes,' he confirms, 'but many are incomprehensible.'

I have to laugh. 'I guess I left because I wasn't happy there. And I thought I could be happy somewhere else.'

I can tell from the crinkles in his forehead that this confuses him even more. 'Happy?' he echoes. 'Why is this obligatory?'

I shrug. 'I don't know. It just is. Apparently I was never

as accepting of my *purpose* as you are.'

Again, puzzlement flickers over his face. 'Why not?'

I throw my hands up. 'Because unlike you, I actually have the ability to think for myself.'

As soon as the words are out of my mouth, I regret them. They were rash and imprudent. I realize insulting him is not a wise course of action right now. The last thing I need is for him to get defensive, or worse, angry.

I need him calm. I need him off guard.

I quickly try to think of something to say that might reverse the effects of my mistake.

'I guess I was . . . *defective*, as you said.' I pray that this will be enough.

But I suppose I'll never know. Because Kaelen doesn't respond. He simply turns back towards the window.

It's now or never.

Without another moment's hesitation, I take a deep breath and launch my body towards him.

31
DISTURBANCE

I move faster than I've ever felt myself move. So fast my eyes can barely track my hands as they tear through the air and land on him. My left hand goes to his face, knocking his head against the window, as my right hand grapples for the device in his pocket.

I yank hard, ripping it clear through the fabric of his pants. I flick my thumb up on the switch, feeling the device hum to life, and bring the metal-pronged tip towards Kaelen's forehead.

But I'm stopped inches away from his scalp line as his hand wraps around my wrist and pushes back. I press forward, scooting on to my knees and putting my body weight into it. We struggle, but it soon becomes apparent that he's too strong. I can't beat him like this.

Kaelen leans back and wedges his leg between us, using the sole of his shoe to catapult me off him. I hit the ceiling of the cab, my head smacking hard, my neck whipping back.

As I plummet down towards the seat, I twist my body,

wrapping my arms around Kaelen's torso, dragging him on to the floor with me. A loud crash reverberates through the car as I land with Kaelen on top of me.

'Please remain in your seats.' The cordial voice of the cab is a humorous contrast to our raging battle in the backseat. 'You are disrupting the journey.'

With the Modifier still in my hand, still charged, I reach for Kaelen's face again, releasing a throaty grunt of effort as I force my hand upward. He elbows me in the lip, knocking my head against the floor. I feel blood start to trickle. I nearly drop the Modifier as I scramble to get out from underneath him.

I jump to my knees, the movement sending Kaelen crashing into the window. He looks slightly stunned from the blow. I use this to my advantage, throwing my body towards him, Modifier outstretched, ready to make contact.

'Please remain in your seats,' the pleasant cab voice advises again. 'You are disrupting the journey.'

Kaelen thrusts out his open palm, slamming it against my chest, sending me soaring on to my back across the bench seat.

He eyes the Modifier in my hand and makes a move towards it. I hold it high above my head, my knuckles smashing against the window. Glass crunches around my skin as the cold winter air streams in.

Kaelen lunges forward, landing on top of me. All the air in my lungs vanishes from the impact.

I squeeze my hand as tight as I can around the Modifier, stretching my hand outside the broken window, over the rushing street below. I can feel cars zooming past, threatening to knock the device right out of my grasp.

Kaelen reaches towards it and then seemingly changes his mind halfway there. His hand changes direction, this time descending towards my forehead.

Oh, no.

He's figured out what's happening. He knows I have the memory. He's trying to read it.

I squirm, tossing my head to avoid contact. His fingertips continue to dive towards my face. I use my free hand to block them, shoving him away.

I cannot let him see this memory!

'Please settle down,' the cab warns, 'or I will notify the police.'

I know I'm incapable of holding him off much longer. There's only one thing left to do. And I really, really don't want to do it.

Plus, I'm not even sure it will work. But I'm out of options. I'm out of everything.

I whip my head around to face him, reaching out and grabbing his cheek, forcing him to look at me. He appears confused by my action, unsure what I'm trying to accomplish.

I wrap my hand around the back of his neck and yank down with all my strength. Heaving his face towards mine. Our noses inches apart, almost touching. Closer and closer until he has nowhere else to look. Until I am the only thing he can see.

BAM!

Our gazes collide.

Our eyes lock.

The hold is more powerful than either of our individual strengths. Unyielding. Uncompromising. And utterly unbreakable.

Rendering us both motionless. Useless.

The spark ignites somewhere in the tiny crevices hidden between us. Sending electricity bouncing back and forth, back and forth. Like a bolt of lightning dancing between two trees. Growing stronger with each exchange.

I don't understand it. I certainly don't want it. But I can't fight it.

And even more important, neither can he.

I feel myself being pulled in to him. Like he's a red-hot dangerous sun, and I'm just a lonely rock hurtling through space. And somehow I know he feels the same mysterious pull.

I know it like I know my own self. Like I know my arm will reach when I tell it to reach. Like I know my fingers will clasp when I tell them to clasp.

Like I know if I move my mouth towards his, he will meet me halfway.

It's as though we're speaking some strange silent language that only the two of us can hear.

Now! I scream at myself. *Do it NOW! While he's immobile. While he's held captive by this inexplicable spell.*

Deactivate him!

I will myself to move. Pull my arm back into the cab, touch the Modifier to his temple.

But I just . . .

Can't.

I let my eyes drift down the rest of his face, taking in his beautifully shaped nose, his strong, chiselled jaw, his pale pink lips. I can see that they are drawn back in a grimace. He looks pained. Anguished. Fighting this as hard as I am.

We inch closer still.

Neither of us able to control it.

This . . . thing that imprisons us without our consent.

This . . . inevitability.

Our lips will meet. Our worlds will collide. Our lives will never be the same.

I watch his eyes drift closed as our mouths linger a whisper apart. I allow mine to close, too.

And as soon as they do, I see his face.

Not Kaelen's.

But Zen's.

And not sick and dying in a bed. Not unconscious and help-less on the pine needle carpeting of the forest. But alive. His dark eyes gleaming. His lips curved in that crooked smile. His soft, gentle voice whispering *Always yes*.

My eyes flash open, my arm catapults down. The metal tip of the Modifier jams against Kaelen's skull, behind his ear. His body slumps lifelessly against me, his head drooping over my shoulder.

I release a loud sigh, exhaling the last five minutes com-pletely from my lungs. I wiggle out from underneath him and ease his head down on to the seat, turning it so that his cheek is resting against the upholstery.

With shaking hands, I twist his wrist, getting a look at his watch. It's 3:50.

I reach into his pocket and remove the DIP card with my photo on it and the small cube hard drive. Next, I carefully peel the three receptors from his head, depositing all the items into my own oversize pocket. Pulling the collar of his shirt away, I unclasp the locket from his neck and fasten it around my own. Then I flip open the heart-shaped door and wait for the interior of the cab to fade into oblivion.

32

LAWS

Transession takes its toll on your body. It's something I learned when Zen and I first arrived in 1609. The disorientation and the queasiness were startling, lasting a few hours for me and two full days for Zen. Apparently the further you transesse, the harder it is for your system to adjust.

Even though now I'm only moving across a few miles, a few hours in time, I still brace myself for the nausea. The contortion of my organs. The pressure of my lungs banging against my sternum. The dizzying sensation of every particle in my body being flipped upside down.

I wait for it. And I wait for it. And I wait for it.

But it never comes.

I'm exactly where I was. Inside a taxicab barrelling down the streets of New York City with a deactivated Kaelen sprawled across the backseat.

I reach down the front of my shirt, making sure that my locket is open.

It is.

I take a deep breath, close my eyes, and try again. I concentrate as hard as I can on the inside of the apartment. Holding the image captive in my mind. I picture Zen sleeping in the bed, the empty white walls and lonely, barren rooms. I block out all other sounds, all other smells, all other sensations. Until I can practically *feel* myself there.

I repeat the date and time over and over again in my mind, even resorting to whispering aloud.

'February 11, 2032. 12:40 p.m.'

'February 11, 2032. 12:40 p.m.'

'February 11, 2032. 12:40 p.m.'

Ten minutes after Kaelen and I left the apartment to go to Chinatown. I figure that should give me plenty of time to do what I need to do.

But still, when I open my eyes, nothing has happened.

I haven't moved an inch. Or a second.

I let out a frustrated whimper. What's going on? Why is it not working? The locket is open. I'm doing exactly what I've always done.

Why am I not able to transesse?

The cab's friendly voice interrupts my thoughts to bring me an update. 'We will arrive at your destination in twelve minutes.'

Think, I command myself.

Did my transession gene somehow get permanently shut off? Did the necklace get damaged in the fire? No, because Kaelen managed to get me here.

Was *he* able to somehow deactivate my gene? So that I couldn't escape?

I glance at his sleeping face.

No, that's not right either. He *wanted* to transesse with me to Chinatown instead of taking a cab. He tried to do it back in the apartment. It was me who refused.

My head jerks as I'm suddenly struck with a memory. Not an artificial one. A real one. Something that Kaelen said just a few hours ago. After I woke up in that bed. In that room.

I asked him if I could go back to 1609 to get Zen and he told me it was impossible because I'd already been there.

'The basic laws of transession don't allow you to occupy space in the same moment of time more than once.'

Is that the problem? Was Kaelen telling the truth? Am I really unable to transesse back to a point in time if I've already been there?

That would explain why I can't transesse back to 12:40 p.m. Because at 12:40 p.m. I was there. I was with Kaelen heading to Chinatown. I was occupying space in that exact moment in time.

'You are physically unable to transesse to a point in time you've already existed in. Because that would mean there would be two instances of you, which is a quantum impossibility.'

Yes, that's right. If I transessed back to the apartment at 12:40 p.m today, then there would essentially be two of me. One with Zen and one with Kaelen.

Which means the only way I can get back to the apartment while Kaelen is gone is to transesse there now. At this very moment, while Kaelen is still deactivated in this cab.

OK, this puts a definite damper on my plan. Especially if the invisible driver is right and we are scheduled to arrive in twelve minutes.

The car slows to a stop at a red light and I anxiously glance over at Kaelen. His eyelids twitch, startling me.

Is he waking up?

How long will he be unconscious? I'm unfamiliar with the intricate workings of the Modifier. He could be deactivated for another hour. Or he could wake up . . . now.

I can't take any chances. I have to act fast.

I close my eyes tight and once again focus my thoughts on the inside of the apartment. This time, however, I change the time in my mind to right now.

I breathe out a giant sigh of relief when I feel the familiar swirl of the air around me. The uneasy twist of my stomach. The shifting of my cells as they prepare to disentangle me from this space and reassemble me in another.

I hear Zen's strained breathing somewhere nearby, telling me that I've returned. That I've made it back to his side.

As soon as I open my eyes and see him lying there, still unconscious, every molecule of oxygen knocks out of me and I feel like I'm going to collapse again. But I will my body to stay upright. I warn my thoughts to stay calm.

The clock is ticking. The cab carrying my enemy will be here in less than ten minutes. And in that time, I have only one goal: to get Zen out of this apartment.

33

BORROWED

Transession is out of the question. Zen is much too weak. After what happened when Kaelen brought him here, I'm afraid trying to transesse him even an inch would kill him.

I have no choice but to physically move him.

I hurry over to Zen, sliding one arm under his shoulders and the other under his knees. I test a small lift, watching his reaction. He moans slightly, the discomfort showing on his face.

'I'm sorry,' I whisper in his ear, 'but it's the only way. I think I've found someone who can help you.'

I scoop him gently into my arms, holding him close to my chest. His weight is not an issue. I could carry ten of him without straining myself. But the obvious pain he's in, just from the slightest movement, makes my knees feel like they're going to buckle.

I take deep breaths, trying to steady myself.

No time.

Go now!

I shuffle through the apartment, shifting the majority of Zen's mass into one arm so that I can open the door and then press the elevator button. I concentrate on walking smoothly, gliding across the floors, but no matter how hard I try, he still releases tiny whimpers of agony with nearly every footfall.

Hailing a cab is the hardest part. Not to mention the stares I receive from several passers-by. I manage to balance Zen unsteadily on his feet, freeing up my right hand so that I can wave it at a group of passing cars.

A yellow vehicle swerves out of the traffic, stopping at the kerb. The door flings open automatically and I gently lay Zen across the backseat, cooing soothing words into his ear.

I lift up his legs and scoot myself in, laying them down across my lap.

'Good afternoon,' the cab says, and I immediately recognize it as a different voice, this time male, making me wonder how many fake cabdrivers they created. 'Where would you like to go?'

'GenZone Research Laboratory,' I tell him. 'And please hurry.'

'I apologize, but I am only permitted to drive the speed limit.'

I try not to groan. 'Fine. Just go.'

'GenZone Research Laboratory,' the voice repeats cordially. 'I have located that destination. It is in Brooklyn. Is that correct?'

I have no idea if that's correct but as of this very second, anything is better than right here. I glance out the window, scanning the kerb for incoming yellow vehicles that might be holding Kaelen inside.

I wonder how he'll react when he wakes up and finds I'm gone.

'Yes, that's correct,' I say hastily.

'Excellent,' the cab responds. 'Please validate your identity so that I may deduct my fare.'

I lean back so I can dig the DIP card that I stole from Kaelen out of my pocket and wave it in front of the scanner as I saw Kaelen do twice. I wait for the beep and the word clear to flash on the small screen in front of me, but it remains tenaciously black.

Feeling anxiety start to rumble in my throat, I try waving the card again. But still there is no response.

'I apologize,' the cab finally says again, 'but I was only able to read one digital-identity pass. However, my sensors detect two passengers in the vehicle.'

My fists clench in frustration and I almost let out a scream.

'You're mistaken,' I say. 'It's only me.'

There's a long, confused pause before the non-existent driver replies, 'I am definitely detecting two passengers. Please scan the second pass at this time.'

'Can't you just go?' I yell back hastily, quickly losing what little patience I had.

'I apologize,' it says a third time, 'but I am not authorized to leave the kerb until both identities have been validated.'

If there was an actual driver in the front seat, this would be the point at which I would lean forward and strangle him.

With a grunt, I kick the door open and step out of the cab before gently extricating Zen's inert body and manoeuvring it over my shoulder. I glance hurriedly around the street, searching for another option.

I see another cab pulling up to the kerb, its automatic door swinging open.

'This is your destination. Please exit the vehicle,' the familiar female voice says.

I notice the tip of Kaelen's shoe dangling out the open door, twitching slightly as he starts to regain consciousness.

And that's when I really start to panic.

My gaze sweeps the street until I spot a man approaching a green vehicle that's parked nearby. He swipes his fingertip across a panel on the car's door and a faint *beep* follows, along with a voice coming from inside the car: 'Good afternoon, Mr Hall. How was your day?'

He doesn't respond, simply slides into the seat and slams the door closed. The engine hums to life.

I don't waste another second. I hurry over to the car and yank open the door.

The man looks up at me, at Zen's body flung over my shoulder, and his befuddled expression quickly morphs into anger. 'Hey!'

'Get out,' I growl, trying to sound as menacing as I can.

'No!' he yells back, reaching for the door to close it on me.

But I don't give him the chance. Before he can blink, my free hand is inside the car, grabbing him by the arm, and dragging him out. He goes skidding into the street, a look of horror twisting his face.

I peer over at Kaelen's cab. His foot is no longer there and I can see through the windshield that he's slowly starting to sit up.

The man scurries to his feet, cowering as he runs towards the sidewalk.

I mumble a hasty thank-you to him as I place my hand over Zen's head to protect it and then lower him in, positioning him in the passenger seat and resting his limp head against the window.

After getting in, I quickly survey the instrument panel. The last car I drove was back in the year 2013 and it looked completely different. First, it had a manual transmission. This car doesn't seem to have anything that even resembles a gearshift. And second, there aren't nearly as many buttons or knobs in this vehicle. The dash is almost entirely smooth.

I certainly don't have time to read through the car's manual like I did last time. Even at my reading speed. I glance in the rearview mirror and see Kaelen stepping dazedly out of his cab.

Why didn't I think to send the cab somewhere else before transessing out of it?

That would have been the smart thing to do. But apparently I was too distracted by the thought of getting to Zen to do the smart thing.

'Go!' I say to the car. But it doesn't move. I fumble my fingers along the panelling, trying to find a switch or button of any kind. All I manage to do is blow hot air on my face.

'Move!' I try again. Still nothing.

'Drive!' is my third attempt.

This seems to work. A red letter D flashes twice on one of the flat panels and the car starts to inch forward. I shove my foot down on the gas pedal and peel away from the kerb. Away from Kaelen. Away from Diotech. Towards what I can only hope will be safety.

34
VISITOR

'You have arrived at your destination,' the car tells me in a voice that sounds chillingly human. 'Would you like to activate the auto-park system?'

I learned about halfway through the journey to Brooklyn why cars in 2032 don't have any buttons or knobs on the instrument panels. Why waste energy pushing buttons when you can simply speak and the car will understand you?

'Yes,' I reply, and my hands immediately leap from the steering wheel when I feel it begin to turn on its own, easing the vehicle effortlessly back and left until we've squeezed between two other cars into a space on the kerb that I never would have imagined we could fit into.

Once we've stopped, I pull on the door handle but it won't budge. 'Open,' I tell it.

'Doors cannot be opened while the car is still in drive.'

I gesture frantically, trying to come up with the right command. 'Um . . . undrive.'

Nope, that's not it.

'Stop.'

Still nothing.

Thankfully the car seems to sense my desperation and offers me help. 'Are you trying to activate Park mode?'

I sigh. 'Yes!'

A small red P flashes on the panel and the doors unlock. I swing the door open, shoving it the rest of the way with my foot. But apparently I kick it too hard because I hear a loud ripping sound as the large slab of metal flies off the hinges and skids into the street. I'm immediately reminded of the last time I inadvertently kicked a door clear off a car. It was in the driveway of my foster family's home. I'll never forget the look on Heather's face when she saw what I had done.

I eye the piece of green metal lying idly in the middle of the street as a car swerves around it.

I really have to stop kicking doors.

I run around to the passenger side, ease Zen's door open, and pull him out. He's slightly more conscious now and appears to be trying to stand up.

'Can you walk?' I ask.

His head teeters in an ambiguous nod. I throw his arm over my shoulder and help him towards the building, his feet scraping against the pavement.

As soon as we're inside, I'm stopped by a large man standing behind a desk. 'May I help you?'

I try to act casual. As casual as I can with a nearly unconscious man sagging against my side. 'I'm going to room 419.'

The guard shoots me a very sceptical look. 'Are you an expected visitor?'

I almost laugh. If only he knew just how *unexpected* I really am. 'Yes,' I lie.

He clearly doesn't believe me. 'I'll have to call up.' He

punches at a clear screen built into his desk, then motions to a digital reader on the countertop. 'Please scan your DIP card so that I can validate your identity.'

I smile, mustering politeness. 'Sure. No problem.' After helping Zen on to a couch behind me, I slide my hand into my pocket as though I'm going to retrieve my identification. But instead, I wrap my fingers tightly around the base of the Modifier, flicking the switch with my fingertip.

I approach the desk, keeping the breezy smile plastered on to my face. The guard doesn't take his eyes off Zen. Which is a plus for me. Although I hardly need the distraction. My hand moves far faster than he could ever hope to keep up with.

Before he can blink, the metal-pronged tip is against his jaw. His body vibrates for a brief second before crumpling into his chair.

I scurry back to Zen, scoop him into my arms, and find my way on to an awaiting elevator.

As I exit on the fourth floor, I immediately spot the stark differences between the long corridor now and the one from my memory. The biggest difference, of course, being the number of people.

The hallway is bustling, alive with commotion. Nearly every door is open, and men and women in lab coats shuffle in and out of the rooms, talking, gesturing, sharing information on handheld tablets that resemble thin pieces of glass.

I receive several questioning looks as I hurry down the hallway with Zen in my arms but I ignore them all, arriving at the door marked 419.

This one, unlike the others that I've passed, is closed.

And then a disquieting thought echoes through my mind. *What if he's not here?* What if I've come too early and he won't be here until tonight? I can't wait that long.

I don't care what the memory says. I need his help *now*.

I twist the handle and shove the door open with my shoulder. The man inside is dressed head to toe in white, with a cap on his head and goggles on his face. He's delicately inserting a needle into a small dish filled with a sticky yellow gel.

He jumps at my sudden entrance, nearly spilling the viscous contents of the dish.

'What the—' he starts to spout angrily, but he stops as soon as his eyes land on me. The hand holding the syringe goes dead limp at his side. He stands paralysed for a long, long, long moment.

His mouth moves first. Falling open.

When his hands eventually unfreeze, he sets the syringe gently on the steel countertop and slowly peels the dark goggles from his face.

That's when I'm finally able to see his large, unblinking eyes.

That's when I know for sure that it's him.

That's when I know that this is real. All too real.

I'm not sure what he's doing here. In New York City. In 2032. Standing right in front of me. But I do know that I was somehow meant to find him.

The conviction pulsates through every bone in my body.

'Cody,' I say, desperation strangling my voice, 'it's me. Violet. I need your help.'

35

GROWN

'No,' the man says quietly, urgently. He takes a cautious step back, his eyes never leaving mine. 'It's not possible.'

Although it was his name tag that helped me make the identification in my memory, it was his eyes that solidified it. His hair may be darker and slightly less curly. His face may be older and fuller and lined with worry, from thirty-two years of life. But his eyes. His eyes never changed.

When I saw those eyes in my memory, I saw him.

The thirteen-year-old kid who helped me all those years ago, when I was lost and alone, and without a scrap of memory. And the thirty-two-year-old man he's become, who I pray can help me again.

Of course, now my problems have gotten significantly bigger. Significantly more complicated.

Back then, it was searching for information on the Internet and sneaking out of his parents' house to catch a bus to the city. Now it's a cure for a mysterious disease that I know absolutely nothing about and that may not even exist for another eighty-some years.

But what choice do I have? Wait for Diotech to betray me again? Wait for Kaelen to get what he's come for and then turn his back on Zen completely?

This man – this former friend – is my only hope.

'Cody,' I whisper. 'It's me. I swear.'

'No,' he repeats. I watch his gaze flicker to a screen embedded directly in the countertop. The word SECURITY glows in bright red in the top left corner.

I ease Zen into a nearby chair and stalk up to Cody. His eyes go wide as I approach. I grab his arm. 'Cody, *please*. I really need you.'

He regards me with half curiosity, half fear. 'But . . .' he argues softly. 'But . . . you're . . .' He can't get the words out. So I finish for him.

'Exactly the same, I know.'

'H-h-how?' he stammers. 'How is that possible?'

I hear a commotion behind me and a second later five guards come charging into the room, guns drawn. 'I have the intruder in sight,' one of them says into a flashing earpiece.

'Dr Carlson,' he warns Cody. 'Please move away so we can take the trespasser into custody.'

I glance anxiously from the guards to Cody, imploring him with my eyes. He looks visibly torn.

'It's OK,' he finally relents with a sigh. 'She's not a trespasser. I know her. She's my . . . visitor.'

The guards appear confused. One of them actually looks disappointed.

'Are you sure?' the head guard asks for confirmation.

Cody nods. 'I'm sure. Thank you, guys. And sorry for the trouble.'

The security team backs out of the room, grumbling

something about a false alarm into their earpieces. Cody follows them, closing the door after the final one has left.

'What is going on?' he demands. He turns and looks at Zen hanging over one of his chairs. 'Who is that?'

'That's Zen,' I tell him, recalling that all Cody's memories of him were erased. 'He's . . .' But I immediately realize that I don't know what to call him. He's not my husband, like we told everyone in 1609. Cody once taught me the word boyfriend, but it never seemed to make any sense to me. It never seemed to hold enough weight.

'He's . . . important,' I finally finish.

'Is he dead?'

The question is a punch in the chest. 'No.' I manage to huff out and keep from keeling over. 'But he needs help. Your help.'

Cody's hands fly into the air. 'Whoa, whoa, whoa. Back up. You disappear for nineteen years and then show up at my lab looking like you haven't aged a day, with a comatose boy in your arms dressed like he just got back from the Renaissance Fair, and all you can say is "he needs help"?'

'Cody, I know I owe you an explanation,' I begin softly.

He laughs. It's bitter. 'You think? You vanished from our house in the middle of the night. My parents searched for you for nearly two years. My mother blamed herself. She fell into a terrible depression.'

The guilt rips at my heart like a trapped animal.

'I'm sorry,' I offer. 'But I don't know what else to do. Or where else to go. You're my only hope.'

Cody's eyes dart towards Zen. 'How exactly do you expect me to help him?'

I nod desperately towards Cody's name tag. 'Well, you're a doctor, right?'

'I'm a scientist,' Cody corrects. 'Not a medical doctor.' He gestures around him. 'This is a science lab.'

'But you must have *some* medical knowledge. Can't you at least look at him?'

Cody sighs and starts clearing items from his work space. 'Put him on the counter.'

I hurry over and lift Zen into my arms, then rest his body delicately across the metal table. Cody presses two fingertips against Zen's throat, seemingly to check his pulse, but upon feeling the intense heat radiating from his skin, jumps back.

'Jesus,' Cody swears, 'he's burning up. What are his other symptoms?'

I take a deep breath, listing everything that I've noticed since that morning in 1609: the chills, the dizzy spells, coughing up blood.

Cody's eyes go wide and he makes a dash for the sink in the corner of the room, running the water and scrubbing his hands vigorously. 'Oh God,' he says under his breath. 'Does he have . . . is he infected with that . . .' A bead of sweat starts to form on Cody's forehead. 'Did he contract white fever?'

I shake my head. 'No.'

Cody doesn't look convinced. 'Those are the exact symptoms. Has he been in contact with sick people recently?'

'No,' I assure him. 'I swear that's not it.'

Cody fumbles around inside a desk until he comes across a blue paper mask. He scrambles to get it over his head but the string snaps in the process so he resigns himself to holding it over his nose and mouth. 'You need to get him out of here. I can't risk getting infected.'

'Cody, *please*,' I beg again. 'I know for a fact that he doesn't have white fever. It would be literally *impossible* for him to have gotten it.'

Cody is still breathing frantically into the mask. 'How can you be so sure?'

I sigh. I knew I was going to have to tell him eventually. I knew I couldn't get away with keeping it a secret any longer. I just hoped the truth would come out under better circumstances. *Calmer* circumstances. 'Because,' I begin, keeping my voice composed. Measured. 'He was sick before we got here.'

'What does that matter?' he retorts. 'There've been outbreaks of the disease reported all over the world. For the past three weeks. Not only in New York.'

'Yes,' I say softly, 'but what I'm saying is we haven't been *here* for the past three weeks.'

I watch Cody's eyes narrow above the mask. 'What do you mean you haven't been *here*?'

'I mean,' I say, taking a step towards him and holding his gaze, 'we've been living in another century.'

36

CYNIC

A peculiar noise emerges from Cody's mouth. It starts as something similar to a laugh but quickly morphs into a much more unnerving sound. Like a throat spasm. 'This is good. This is really, really good.' I recognize the sarcasm immediately, even through the blue paper mask. And my body wilts with disappointment.

'Cody—' I try to elaborate. But he doesn't even let me finish.

'Oooh!' he sings, his tone stiff with mockery as he wiggles the fingers on his free hand. 'Time travel! *Very* original.'

'Cody,' I go on, attempting to ignore his blatant chiding, 'you're a logical person. You always have been. Think about it. It makes *sense*. That's why I haven't aged. Why I look exactly the same. I've only been gone a few months. But for you, it's been nineteen years. Remember the plane crash? Remember how I wasn't on the passenger manifest? Remember how we went to LA to talk to the gate agent and she told me—'

'Of course I remember!' he snaps, his ridicule replaced with simmering rage. 'It's kind of hard to forget someone who implies that you somehow ended up in a crashed plane without ever having *boarded* the plane.'

'And she was right. I wasn't in the middle of that ocean because of a plane crash . . .'

I let the thought drift, hoping Cody can finish it on his own. And I know he can. Now it's only a matter of whether or not he can believe it.

He blinks. 'You're saying that you didn't *crash* there. That you *time travelled* there?'

I sigh, grateful that he seems to finally be coming around to the idea. 'The official term is *transession*, but yes. That's exactly what I'm saying. I came from the year 2115. Somehow I accidentally landed in 2013 surrounded by plane wreckage. I don't know why. I only know I was supposed to be going somewhere else and . . .'

I think about what Zen told me back in 1609.

'You let go.'

I quickly shake off a shudder.

'Well, something went wrong,' I continue. 'That's why I had no family, no friends, no one who came to claim me. That's why my DNA wasn't in any database. I wasn't even alive yet!'

'You honestly expect me to believe that?' he barks. 'You think just because I used to read science fiction as a kid that I'm going to go all la, la, la, oooh, time travel! Whoooooooaaaah! Hey, cool! You're from the future! Are you here to terminate the mother of the rebellion leader? Can I ride in your DeLorean?'

I don't recognize his voice. It's turned very high-pitched and almost breathy. I don't think it's sarcasm any more. It's something else. Something crazy. And I'm pretty sure he's not even speaking sense. Plus, his eyes have grown wide and a little bit scary.

I take a step back. 'Cody?'

'You're crazy!' he roars. 'Get out of my lab!'

I sigh. I should have known he wouldn't believe me. I should have known it would come to this.

'OK, fine,' I say, raising my hands in a gesture of surrender. 'I'll prove it to you. Is that what it's going to take?'

Cody doesn't respond. He crosses his arms over his chest and glares at me from across the room.

I peer at Zen out of the corner of my eye, still resting on Cody's counter. 'I'm going to transesse one minute into the future. You will see me disappear from right here and in exactly one minute, I will reappear.'

Cody's eyes narrow. I take that as a sign I have his attention. I flash him a hurried smile that he does not return.

'OK,' I say again. 'Watch carefully.'

I glance at the clock on the wall: 4:52. I close my eyes and prepare my mind, directing all my thoughts to this exact place, only one minute later.

I feel the air start to swish around me, the hum of the molecules of the space vibrating to release me. My body clenches. Pressure builds in my head.

And the last thing I hear before I completely vanish is the hushed sound of Cody's blue paper mask fluttering to the ground.

When I arrive as planned, the clock reads 4:53 and I see that Cody is still staring open-mouthed at the space where I just rematerialized. His blinking patterns have increased in velocity. And a strange gurgling sound is coming from the back of his throat. He sways slightly before finally plunking down into a nearby chair.

I kneel in front of him. 'Cody, look at me.'

But he won't. Or he can't. His eyes are lost and unfocused, wandering aimlessly. As though he's trying to follow a million dust particles travelling every which way.

I grab his hand and give it a firm tug. 'Cody.'

His gaze snaps towards me and for a brief moment I have his attention. 'Now,' I say with finality, 'will you *please* help me?'

37

TRANSPLANT

Cody packs the last of the supplies he's gathered into the van and slams the door shut. I climb in the back with Zen and sit on the floor next to a box of syringes and test tubes, and hold his head in my lap. He drifts in and out of consciousness as Cody steers the large vehicle with the name GENZONE emblazoned on the side through the streets of Brooklyn. I stare down at Zen's face, stroking his cheek and his hair, occasionally whispering into his ear, assuring him that everything will be OK.

Of course, I don't know that.

Of course, it's possible Cody won't be able to figure out what's wrong with him. But for the first time in a while, I feel safe again. I feel like I'm moving *towards* a solution, instead of away from it. I feel like I can take a deep breath without my chest caving in on me.

I was relieved when Cody suggested we bring Zen back to his house. He immediately ruled out a hospital, claiming it was too dangerous, especially since he didn't have valid identification and they'd immediately quarantine him in suspicion of having the white fever.

Not to mention the fact that I knew as soon as Kaelen realized I was gone – which was probably about an hour ago – he'd start looking for me again. And that means we have to go back to being extremely careful. No records. No documents. No hospitals.

Apart from this suggestion, Cody hasn't said much. I think he might still be in shock, processing the information slowly and methodically like any good scientist would.

The drive is short. We arrive in less than ten minutes. Cody's town house, as he calls it, is lovely and spacious. It has a warm, welcoming feel to it with rich colours and dark woods. But I don't really pay much attention. I'm too focused on moving Zen from the van to the room Cody refers to as a guest room.

At first Zen attempts to walk, sluggishly putting one foot in front of the other, but his knees give out too many times and I eventually scoop him into my arms and carry him the rest of the way.

My effortless action causes a ripple of suspicion to roll over Cody's face, but he doesn't say anything.

I lay Zen down on the bed as Cody gets to work setting up all the equipment he borrowed from the basement warehouse of the building where he works. He inserts an IV into Zen's arm and hooks him up to a variety of machines to monitor his breathing, heart rate, and blood pressure.

I feel a rush of sickness come on as I'm instantly reminded of my hospital room. After the plane crash they thought I'd survived. When they needlessly injected things into my veins, and attached me to tubes, just like Cody is doing to Zen now.

Except this time, it's not needless.

This time, it's vital.

I remember when Zen appeared in my hospital room the first night I was there. He tried to take me out. He tried to transesse with me. That was before we knew about the deactivator in my locket.

Now everything is reversed. Now he's the one hooked up to the tubes and monitors. He's the one in that bed. And I'm the one trying to get him out. In whatever way I can.

Zen is restless in this new place. He hasn't stopped twitching and squirming and whimpering since I laid him down. Like he's trying to escape his own skin. He shivers with fever and I cover him with a blanket only to have him kick it off a few moments later when the chills morph back into heat flares.

Every time I try to touch his face or smooth his hair or rub his arm, he feebly bats my hand away like he's swatting at a fly.

'Zen.' I try to talk to him, hoping the sound of my voice will calm him. 'Zen, it's me. Can you hear me? It's going to be OK. We're safe here. Remember Cody? My foster brother. We're at his house. He's trying to figure out why you're sick. He's going to make you better.'

Cody shoots me a stern look, warning me not to make promises we both know he can't keep. But I ignore it.

'Zen,' I repeat, trying once again to stroke his hand. 'Cinnamon.'

But he pulls it violently away, nearly slapping me in the face in the process. His heart monitor ratchets up as his pulse quickens. It's clear from the torment on his features and the agony in his moans that he's miserable. That whatever sickness is running through his blood is destroying him a little bit more every minute. But I don't know what to do for him. I don't know how to help him.

As he flails restlessly and lets out an agonizing cry that punctures my heart, I look to Cody. 'Do something.'

Cody bites his lip and then riffles through one of the boxes until he comes across a small vial of liquid. He draws it up into a needle and inserts it into Zen's IV. 'This should calm him down.'

I watch the drug work almost instantly. Zen's spasms slow to a stop. His features ease out of their contortions. His breathing seems to settle into a steady rhythm. He falls into a deep sleep that I pray is peaceful and dreamless.

I crumple into a chair next to the bed and scoop up Zen's hand. This time, he doesn't fight. I wipe away the few stray tears that squeezed out of my eyes during the commotion.

For the first time in a long time, when I look at his face, I see the old Zen.

The one I used to watch sleep. Who always looked so still and serene. Shielded from all the horrors of the world by the protective bubble he somehow managed to keep firmly locked around himself. No matter how chaotic things got.

It's something I always admired in him.

Something I always aspired to duplicate, but never seemed able to.

Zen just has that magical quality about him. I saw it in the way he would tell stories to the Pattinsons to ease their fears about the strange girl living in their house. The way he could wrap his arms around me after one of my many nightmares and convince me I was safe. The way he could leave his own home behind, his own friends and family, and never look back.

Seeing him this traumatized, this uncontrolled, this tormented is like seeing the very person that he is ripped apart. His identity stolen. His soul pillaged.

And I'm so completely powerless to stop it. Now it's my turn to be the strong one, the steady one, the one whose confidence can't be shaken, and I'm failing. I'm failing.

I'm failing.

Cody inserts a needle into Zen's vein and draws blood. 'This should get me started,' he says gently, screwing a cap on to the tiny vial and holding it up to the light. 'Some of the tests will take a while to run. We may not know anything until tomorrow.'

For twenty minutes I watch Cody flutter around the room. From Zen to his computer and back again. He takes more blood, checks and rechecks his temperature, inputs data into his computer. I try to stay silent, not wanting to distract him. I confine myself to my chair, keeping Zen's hand clasped tightly in mine.

As badly as I want to be optimistic, as badly as I want to have 100 per cent faith in Cody's ability to do something, I just can't help thinking the worst.

What if he can't figure out what's making Zen sick? What if Diotech is lying and even *they* don't know? I can't lose him again. I've already lost him once and I can't go through it another time.

'So is Violet even your real name?' Cody asks, interrupting my thoughts. I look up to see him peering at me over the top of his computer monitor.

I shake my head.

I remember the first time Cody learned my real name. It was outside the house party where he helped us borrow a car so that we could get away from Diotech after they discovered our location.

That was before they kidnapped Zen and held him hostage. Before I called Cody for help and he met me in the town of Bakersfield with his laptop. Before we met Maxxer and she took us back to her storage unit. Before Cody overheard Maxxer tell me about the transession gene and where I really came from.

And that's when Maxxer took away Cody's memories. She erased his entire recollection of that day and replaced it with a memory of being at a friend's house, playing video games. As far as Cody was concerned, that day never happened. He never learned my real name. He never met Zen or Maxxer. He never knew who I really was.

As far as Cody was concerned, I ran away in the middle of the night and never came back.

Until now.

For some reason, thinking about Maxxer rouses a peculiar emotion somewhere inside me. A quiet fury that stirs and festers. Like a bitterness that has been lying dormant for years only to be awoken now.

The sensation confuses me. What reason would I have for being angry at Maxxer? She *helped* me. She came to my rescue when I had no one else.

'So what is it, then?' Cody brings me back to the conversation. 'Your real name?'

'Seraphina,' I whisper.

'Seraphina,' Cody repeats with a curious ring. It's almost as though he remembers it somehow. On some level. 'It's pretty,' he says. An echo of nineteen years ago. 'I still don't understand why you didn't know who you were or couldn't remember anything when I first met you.'

I cringe inwardly. I know I won't be able to hold off Cody's questions for long. If at all. There's still so much he doesn't know. Transession is only the beginning. A small sliver of the whole story. He doesn't know about me, what I am, the memories implanted in my brain, or the ones I asked to be removed. He doesn't know about the people who created me, who now want me back. Or the young agent who is out there somewhere undoubtedly searching for me.

I owe him an explanation. A real one. A complete one. He deserves that much.

But I also know that the idea of recounting all of

that – reliving those agonizing details of my imperfect life as a perfect human being – is too much. I don't have the energy or the stamina or the stomach to go through it again.

I rise to my feet and rummage through my pockets until I come up with the tiny cube-shaped drive that I stole from Kaelen and the receptors I plucked from his head.

Then I slowly make my way around Zen's bed towards Cody, who instinctively backs away when he sees me approach.

I hold the three thin disks in my hand. 'These are called receptors,' I explain, my voice still weak and fragile. 'I'm going to place them on your head. They will give your brain access to everything that's stored on this drive.'

Cody squints, staring sceptically at the various items in my hand. 'Wait. *What?*'

'It's a technology that hasn't been invented yet. They call it re-cognization.' I repeat the exact words Zen used when he first put the receptors on me. The memory of that day slices through me like a knife.

I indicate the small cube. 'This hard drive will essentially become an extension of your mind. All you have to do is ask the right questions and the answers will come to you.'

He tenses slightly as I place the first disk behind his left ear, then the second at the base of his neck, and the third behind his right ear. I swipe my thumb across the surface of the drive, causing it to glow green. Cody jolts at the sight of it.

'I don't understand,' he says. 'What *exactly* is stored on that drive?'

I offer him a tender smile, seeing my own confusion from months ago mirrored in his anxious face. 'All of my memories.'

38
PROCESS

Cody's eyes remain closed for a long time. I observe his reaction carefully, trying to figure out which memory he's watching at any given time. When he flinches, I wonder if he's seeing the moment when Mrs Pattinson called me a witch in front of the entire courtroom. When his face twists with grief, I wonder if he's witnessing the time Zen first told me who I was and where I really came from. And when his face softens and a faint smile makes its way on to his lips, I wonder if he's remembering the way Zen always managed to make me feel safe.

I don't know how much information he receives, in what order he accesses it, or which memories he triggers with his questions. All I know is that everything is on that drive. The last six months of my life.

The truth about who I am. What I can do. Why we escaped.

The wreckage of a plane that I was never on. The family that welcomed me into their home. The boy who found me and helped me remember.

The city that discovered my secret. Called me a witch. Set me on fire.

The artificial memories that are encrypted in my mind. Leading me somewhere. A place Diotech wants to find.

The young man with the aquamarine eyes. Who is like me. Who is out there searching.

The scientist who died in front of my eyes. And the one who impatiently awaits my return.

Kaelen stole it all. Except for the last one. The one that brought me here. To Cody.

That one I keep for myself.

I don't know which memory finally causes Cody's expression to turn dark and grim, his eyes to flash open, and his hands to scratch restlessly at the receptors attached to his head, ripping them off and tossing them on to his desk.

I don't know which of the countless horrid truths finally shoved him over the edge but he abruptly rises to his feet and, without another word to me, stalks out of the room. I listen intently for the front door, praying I won't hear it open and close. I can't afford to have Cody leave. Not now. But I also know better than to follow him.

He needs time to process everything. Just as I did when I first learned the truth.

Thankfully, the front door remains closed. Which means Cody is still somewhere in the house. Dealing with the unsettling reality of my life in whatever way he needs to. It's a lot of information to learn all at once.

I will give him that time.

With a deep breath, I settle back in my chair. The rush of my own fatigue hits me like a stone wall. At first I fight it, refusing to let my eyes close even for a second. But after a while it becomes too much and I give in to the undertow of exhaustion.

I spend the next half-hour dozing in and out of sleep in the chair.

When I'm awake my eyes are glued to Zen and the monitors next to his bed. There's a soft *beep* that rings out every second, reassuring me that he's still alive. That he's still with me.

And yet every single silence that falls between is more tormenting than the last. Waiting for that next *beep*, that next sign of life, is like waiting for an eternity to pass. It's like falling off a cliff over and over again. Every empty second that goes by without a *beep* is gravity pulling me to my death.

When I'm asleep I dream of Kaelen. His ocean eyes staring at me. I gaze into them, finding beautiful relief. Finding escape from this monstrous reality that I'm living.

He slowly reaches out to touch my face. I hold my breath, anticipating his touch. The warmth I know it will bring. The serenity that I know will follow.

But I wake before it ever gets there, a thousand tiny needles stabbed into my heart. The shame I feel for wanting him to touch me – even in my dream – smothers me like a thick, itchy blanket that scratches my skin raw.

I'm suddenly irritable and angry.

Angry that I can't keep him out of my thoughts.

Angry that when I'm asleep, when his face is in my mind, I don't *want* to wake.

But I *should*. I should want to wake.

Zen is real. He's here. Now. And he needs me.

Kaelen is some kind of mistake. A confusion. An error.

Someone I shouldn't want to exist. Someone I shouldn't want to dream about. Someone I shouldn't want.

'Sera?' Zen's frail voice interrupts my thoughts and I blink down at him, forcing a carefree smile that makes me feel like a fraud.

'I'm here,' I reply, squeezing his hand.

'Where are we?' His voice is so airy, so light, it feels like it will blow away if I exhale too hard.

'We're in the year 2032. At Cody's house. Remember Cody?'

'Yeah.'

'He's trying to figure out what's wrong with you. He's going to make you better.'

'I want to be better.'

I bite my lip to keep from breaking into sobs. 'I know. I do, too.'

'Then we can run away again.'

'Exactly,' I say. 'Where do you want to go?'

His eyes remain closed, he shifts uncomfortably. 'The moon?'

I grin. 'That sounds like a good idea. Or maybe Venus?'

'Too hot,' he breathes.

I release a small giggle. 'OK, not Venus.'

There's a long silence and I think he may have fallen asleep again but then another frail whisper breaks through. 'Sera?'

'Yes?'

I feel the slightest pressure on my hand as he attempts to squeeze it. 'Did I ever tell you about the bench?' he asks.

My brow furrows. 'What bench?'

'I guess not.'

'Why don't you tell me now,' I suggest, desperate to make this rare moment of coherency last as long as possible.

'It was made of white marble,' he goes on with difficulty. 'In your front yard.'

'On the compound?'

He lets out a ragged cough, blood spattering the sheets. 'Yes.'

I pluck a tissue and wipe his lips.

'It was how I knew every time they erased your memory of me.'

'From a bench?' I clarify doubtfully, wondering if the fever is making him delusional.

He attempts a nod but his head barely moves. 'Every morning when you woke up, you were supposed to bury something under the bench.'

'Bury something? Like what?'

His smile is strained as he remembers. 'It was always different. Some days a flower. Other days a rock. One time you buried a spoon. It was your signal to me that you remembered.'

'Remembered what?' I ask.

'Me.'

I fall silent, pressing my lips together.

Zen continues. 'If I arrived and didn't find anything buried under the bench, I knew that they had erased me again. And that I'd have to start all over.'

'How did you find the strength to do it so many times?' I ask. 'Why did you keep coming back when you knew I'd look at you like you were a stranger?'

He closes his eyes and for a moment I think he's fallen back asleep. But then he whispers, 'You never looked at me like I was a stranger. That's how I knew they could never win.'

I rest my head on his chest, listening to his irregular heartbeat.

'I haven't forgotten, you know,' he says.

'Forgotten what?'

'What we promised to do. In the woods. Are you still ready?' His words come out choppy. Disjointed.

I close my eyes, remembering that unfamiliar craving I felt when I was lying on top of him. The warm desire that flooded through me. Zen's promise that whatever it was would bring us closer together. As close as we could ever be.

Remembering how we were torn apart – by sickness, by guards, by Diotech – before we could hold true to our promise.

I lift my head and lock on to his dark eyes. 'Of course. I can't wait.'

His lips curl into a weak smile and he drifts to sleep like that. His breathing falls back into an easy rhythm and his body goes still again.

I glance at the clock on the nightstand. It reads 7:05.

I don't know if Cody has had ample time to digest everything he's learned or what kind of mental state he's in but I need to get out of this room. I need to breathe different air. See different faces. Occupy a new space. I bend forward to kiss Zen's hand and then set it to rest by his side. I rise achingly to my feet and ease open the door. Completely unsure of what I'll find on the other side.

39

OFFSPRUNG

The delicious smell of food cooking wafts into my nostrils and nearly knocks me over as soon as I enter the hallway. My mouth starts watering and a gurgle emanates from my stomach. I suppose I shouldn't be surprised. I haven't eaten since . . . well, since 1609.

And the last meal I had there was stale bread and water in a dirty prison cell.

To say that I'm hungry would be a severe understatement.

The walls of the hallway that leads into the main area of the house are covered with square frames. Each one holds a small screen in the centre that plays a series of photos and videos in a constant loop.

I must not have noticed them when I first came in, too distracted by helping Zen. But now I pause long enough to watch one complete its full cycle, starting with a photo of a tiny infant wrapped in a blue blanket, transitioning to a video of a larger, pudgy baby taking wobbly steps across a carpet, then a little boy with bright red hair and a sprinkling of freckles on his face blowing emphatically towards two candles in a cake, and finally ending on a still picture of that same boy, dressed in a white collared shirt and navy-blue shorts, with a backpack on his shoulder.

'That was his first day of school last year,' Cody says as he comes up next to me. 'We couldn't put the video in the frame because the footage was too shaky. My wife was crying so hard.'

For a moment I'm speechless. I gawk open-mouthed at Cody. 'You're a father?'

He beams back at me. The previous sinister version of him that stormed out of the guest room is suddenly nowhere to be found.

He nods. 'He's my whole world.'

Now it's my turn to be completely rocked by the truth. Cody? A husband? And a father?

It's too much.

When I look at him, I still see the moody, pimple-faced thirteen-year-old boy who got grounded for helping me sneak out of the house.

'What's his name?' I ask.

'Reese.' I marvel at how bright his face becomes when he says this. It's as though someone is lighting him up from the inside. 'He's five and I'm convinced he's already smarter than I am.'

'Well, that's not hard,' I joke.

Cody raises his eyebrows. 'Hey, look who mastered sarcasm.'

'You remember.'

'I remember everything about you.' I watch his face colour with that familiar shade of red as he looks away. I'm happy to see some parts of him haven't changed. 'I guess I had a pretty bad crush on you.'

'Crush?' I ask.

He still refuses to meet my eye. 'I liked you. A lot.' He lets out a small snort. 'Don't tell my wife.'

I glance back at the frame, taking in the boy's round blue eyes and freckled face. 'He looks like you.'

'Well, let's just hope when he gets to be thirteen he'll start looking more like his mother.'

I let out a laugh that feels like it's been trapped in me for years. 'I remember your mom telling me you were at an awkward age when we first met.'

'My mother had a way of downplaying the truth. I was a complete nerd.'

'I don't even know what that is.'

He brushes a chunk of dark blond hair from his forehead. 'It's something you never have to worry about being.' He falls quiet.

'Look,' he says after a moment, his voice turning sombre. 'I want to say thank you.'

This surprises me. 'For what?'

'For trusting me with . . . well, everything. I know it took a lot of courage to show me those things. I'm sorry I walked out. It was . . .' – he pauses, struggling for the words – 'it was a lot to process. I'm still trying to sort through it all. You know, make sense of it.'

'I know,' I say softly.

I feel something warm against my hand and when I look down I see Cody has wrapped his fingers around mine. 'We'll figure out what's wrong with him,' he vows.

Gratefulness wells up inside me, threatening to overflow from my eyes. 'Thanks,' I whisper.

He gives my hand a tug. 'C'mon,' he says, his entire demeanour shifting, lightening. 'I want you to meet my family.'

I'm not sure what Cody has told his wife about the strange

teenage girl in his house – if he's even had a chance to tell her anything. I wince when I step into the kitchen and see a petite and slender attractive woman with long red hair pouring a burgundy liquid from a bottle into two stemmed glasses. I guess after the way Mrs Pattinson acted about having me in her home, I've come to expect the worst when meeting new people.

But it quickly becomes apparent that Cody's wife is nothing like Mrs Pattinson because when she looks up at me, she has a beaming smile on her face. She wipes her hands quickly on a towel that hangs from the oven and flitters over to me.

'Seraphina,' she says brightly. 'It's so lovely to meet you!'

She pulls me into a hug, a greeting that still confuses me, but I manage to return the gesture with a clumsy pat on her back. She releases me and holds me at arm's length. 'I'm Ella.'

'Nice to meet you, too.'

'Would you like something to drink? Water?'

I nod. 'Yes, please.'

Ella retrieves a glass from a cabinet and fills it with water from a thin spigot installed on the sink. When she hands it to me, the first thing I notice is how crystal clear it is. I'd grown so accustomed to the slightly brownish colour of the water we drank on the Pattinsons' farm. My first sip is glorious. It's so fresh and clean. Like I'm drinking directly from the sky. I finish the entire glass in a single gulp.

Ella laughs and takes the glass from me. 'Thirsty?'

'I guess so. It's been a long day.'

Ella gives me a pitying look from the sink as she runs the spigot again. 'I do hope your friend is better soon.'

'Me, too,' I say quietly.

'Well, you must join us for dinner,' she says, handing me the refilled glass. 'Cody is an excellent cook.'

I raise my brows at Cody. For some reason, I simply can't

picture the thirteen-year-old boy from my memory, who did nothing but read science magazines and play video games, cooking a meal. 'Really?'

Cody chuckles. 'It was a matter of necessity. Either learn how to cook or be forced to eat takeout every night.' He walks over to his wife and tenderly kisses her shoulder.

She shrugs. 'Guilty as charged. Cooking is just not in my DNA.'

Cody and I share a quick look before he clears his throat. 'Let's eat.'

'Sweets,' Ella says to Cody, 'will you call Reese down?'

Cody walks over to a staircase off the living room and yells, 'Reese! Dinner!'

'I thought you were working late tonight?' Ella asks her husband.

'I was planning to. But something more important came up.' He shrugs and gives me a wink.

Working late?

I automatically flash to the memory. The one that takes place at two in the morning tomorrow. But my thoughts are interrupted by the patter of excited, tiny footsteps as a red blur comes whizzing down the stairs. I'm fairly certain he's moving as fast as I do. He skips the last two steps and leaps energetically into Cody's arms.

Cody laughs and swings the boy back and forth. 'Hey, kiddo.'

'Daddy,' the boy says, and then he starts talking so rapidly, I can barely follow. 'You'll never guess what happened today at school.' He doesn't give Cody a chance to guess; he just keeps talking. 'This one girl, Rhi, she brought her frog to show-and-tell and Mrs Beecher doesn't like frogs. She thinks they're slimy. But Rhi's parents said she had to let her bring it anyway because Mrs Beecher can't say who can and can't bring things, unless they're dangerous things like knives and snakes. So Rhi brought the frog and this boy, Brayden, he was supposed to put the frog back into its aquarium, but he didn't close the door all the way and the frog got loose and it climbed into Mrs Beecher's hair and she was screaming and flapping her arms so crazy.' Reese is waving his hands in the air to demonstrate his story and Cody has to continually duck his head to avoid being slapped in the face. 'And everyone was laughing, except Mrs Beecher, who was screaming, and no one would help her because it was too funny.'

When the boy finishes his story, he draws a long breath. I think he used up all the oxygen in a five-mile radius.

Then he turns and seems to notice me for the first time because he lets out a small yelp and goes very quiet. 'Who's that?' he whispers to Cody.

Cody laughs and takes a step towards me. 'This is my friend Seraphina. Seraphina, this is my son, Reese.'

I paint on a bright smile. 'It's nice to meet you, Reese.'

But Reese, miraculously losing his ability to speak, turns and buries his face in his father's shoulder.

'Aw, c'mon,' Cody coaxes. 'Don't be shy. She's very nice.'

It takes a moment, but eventually Reese emerges from his hiding place in Cody's shirt and turns to look at me. He stuffs two fingers in his mouth, but Cody immediately pulls them out.

'Do you know how to play Super Suds Sub?' Reese asks.

'Uh.' I look to Cody for help.

'It's a virtual sim game,' he tells me. 'His favourite.'

'You get to drive a submarine,' Reese explains eagerly.

I look to Cody for a definition of the word submarine. He seems to understand my silent request. 'A vessel that travels deep underwater.'

'Yep,' Reese goes on, his face lighting up like a lantern as he cuts his hand through the air. 'They go really deep in the ocean. Zoom! Zoom! Really fast! And it blows soap bubbles and you look at fishes and play musical instruments!'

'Wow,' I say, widening my eyes. I'm reminded of little Jane Pattinson and the way her features illuminated when I told her the story of the magic princess. My heart pangs silently for her.

'That sounds fun,' I reply. 'But unfortunately I don't know how to play it.'

Reese looks like I've just murdered his entire family.

'But,' Cody says, coming to my rescue, 'maybe after dinner you can *teach* Seraphina how to play.'

Reese's eyebrows rise hopefully as he glances at me for confirmation.

'I . . . I would love that.'

I'm relieved to see that this has evidently erased all the harm that I may have caused. Reese bounds from his father's arms and dashes into the living room. 'I'll load it!'

'After dinner!' Cody calls.

'I'm just gonna get it ready!' Reese yells back.

Cody sticks his hands in his pockets. 'Sorry, I hope you didn't have any plans tonight. He's pretty hard to say no to.'

'He's very –' I search for the right word – 'interesting.'

Cody chuckles. 'Thanks. Coming from someone as literal as you, I'll take that as a compliment.'

A sudden panic floods through me. 'It *was* a compliment!'

'I know.' Cody bumps against my shoulder. 'I've definitely missed you.'

A smile breaks out over my face. It feels good. 'I've missed you, too, Cody.'

40

NORMALCY

Ella was right. Cody is an amazing cook. Maybe it's just because I'm so incredibly famished, or maybe it's because Mrs Pattinson's cooking was so bland and flavourless, but this chicken is the most amazing thing I've ever tasted. Even better than the grilled cheese sandwich Cody's mom, Heather, made for me on my first night at their house.

It's so rich and succulent and full of delicious spices that I can't even begin to identify.

'So,' Ella says, taking a sip of her wine, 'Cody told me you were a friend of the family back when he was a teenager?'

Cody gives me a clandestine nod, indicating that she hasn't, in fact, been told the truth about me.

I smile warmly back at her. 'That's right.' Even though the words out of my mouth might be dishonest, my smile is genuine. Cody's wife has an infectious joy about her. It's hard not to smile.

'You must have been very young then,' she calculates, 'because you don't look much older than a teenager now.'

'She's twenty-five,' Cody is quick to put in.

I nod. 'That's right.' I know exactly why he lied about my age. I can't possibly be a teenager. That would mean I wouldn't have been born in 2013.

'You look so young,' she remarks, swallowing a mouthful of chicken. 'And so incredibly beautiful. I'm sure you get that a lot.'

I feel my face warm and look down at my plate.

'I mean, truly stunning,' she goes on. 'Like a model.' She turns to Cody. 'Which reminds me, did you *see* the new bill-board that went up next to the market? I swear the women in those clothing ads are looking thinner and thinner. It makes me want to stop eating completely.'

'Babe,' Cody says, giving her a warm look. 'You know models aren't real people. They're computer generated.'

She takes another sip of her wine and sighs. 'I know. It should be illegal, though. How am I supposed to shop for clothes when the department stores are filled with digital projections of *synthetic* people who don't have a single curve or wrinkle?'

Cody and I share another glance. Thankfully, he changes the subject, asking Reese more about the incident at school today.

After dinner is over, Cody and Ella do the dishes, and Reese takes my hand and leads me into the living room, thoroughly explaining everything I need to know in order to become a master at the virtual sim game called Super Suds Sub.

The game is magnificent. It's not played on a regular TV screen, but rather in a digitally simulated world that completely surrounds you.

I stand next to Reese, with controllers strapped to each wrist, steering a giant, unwieldy vessel through an underwater universe as Reese uses his controllers to identify passing sea creatures.

The projected steering wheel in my hands has physical weight and resistance. The fish blow bubbles that float by my head, making popping sounds in my ears.

'Isn't it cool?' Reese asks.

But I can't even respond. It's beyond cool. It's the coolest thing I've ever seen.

We play again and again. Even Cody comes in and steers the submarine for a while and Ella stands in the back of the craft and plays a holographic piano, matching notes to colour-coded keys to give us more fuel and make us go faster.

After a while, I excuse myself and sit on the couch, watching the Carlson family of three moving around an invisible underwater landscape. From this angle, outside of the digital projection, it looks rather ridiculous. Cody manoeuvring a steering wheel that doesn't exist, Ella tapping her fingers rhythmically on invisible air, and Reese dancing with an imperceptible dolphin.

Cody emerges from the underground kingdom a few minutes later. 'Take over command of the ship, Captain,' he calls back to Reese, and disappears into the kitchen to refill his wine. I follow him and he asks me how I'm holding up.

'Fine,' I say. I gesture towards the living room. 'He reminds me so much of you.'

Cody smiles, sipping his wine. 'It's funny. I see myself in him more and more every day. It's strange when you have a kid. Because they pick up so many of your personality traits without even trying. It's buried in their genetic code . . .' His voice trails off and his gaze darts from me to his wine glass.

I'm suddenly curious. 'Are you saying personality gets passed down in your DNA?'

Cody glances anxiously towards his wife and son in the next room. It's the first time we've talked about who I am since I let him watch my memories. 'W-w-well . . .' he stammers, keeping his voice low, 'that's, you know, the common belief. There are many theories. It's hard to say.'

'It's OK, Cody. You can tell me.'

He takes a deep breath. 'Here's the strange thing. They've found personality genes within the human genome. But you . . .' Once again, he looks too nervous to continue.

I raise my eyebrows to encourage him.

'Well, because your DNA was manufactured by a computer, without a parental source, I don't know where your personality came from. You *should* technically behave like a robot. But you don't. Which means you must have gotten it from somewhere.'

That's exactly what Alixter told me. That it was believed I would behave like a machine. That I wouldn't have much of a personality. But I did. And that's why Rio had a change of heart about me. Why he agreed to help set me free.

So what went wrong? Where did my identity come from?

Was it possible the scientists were mistaken about where someone's personality comes from?

'Dad!' Reese calls from the next room. 'I can't steer it on my own!'

'Coming!' Cody flashes me an apologetic look and then returns to the game.

I watch as their normal Wednesday carries on innocently through the night. As though the world is not crumbling to pieces outside the window. As though a dangerous superhuman from the future is not out there somewhere searching the city for me. As though there is nothing more important in life than a five-year-old and his game.

I attempt to soak in their laughter. Let it saturate my skin. Maybe somewhere, deep within me, it will settle and stick and weather the storm that I know is far from over.

I try to capture their happiness and swaddle myself in it,

hoping it will help me create my own bubble. Like the one Zen lived in for so long. I use it to try to block out my thoughts, drain my mind, silence my fears.

So that I won't have to wonder whether or not I'll ever have this.

Whether or not I'll ever be part of a real family.

So that I'll never have to face the answer. The truth.

That, most likely, I won't.

The harrowing reality of the situation hits me without warning. Collides into me like a planet.

This idyllic, carefree Wednesday night is borrowed. Temporarily on loan. It will never be mine. Because I will never be able to sit in a room and not wonder if someone is waiting on the other side of the door to take me away. I will never be able to listen to a child's laughter without turning my other ear towards the too-silent night. I will never be able to sleep without dreaming of machines that saw your heart in half and scientists who want to surgically remove your soul.

In the end, no matter what I do, no matter where I go, no matter whether or not I save Zen's life, I will never be free of them.

Diotech will always be lingering outside my window.

Waiting for me to reveal myself.

While Cody and his family are still distracted by their game, I quietly rise from the couch and steal down the hallway to the guest room. I creak open the door and slip into the darkened room, lit only by the soft white glow of Cody's computer. I ease the door closed behind me, rest my forehead against it, and shut my eyes, listening to the reassuring sounds of Zen's breath and the pulse of the machines monitoring his life.

Then, climbing into bed next to him, pressing my body as close to him as I can, I cry into the solid, unyielding surface of his cheek.

41

ASSAULT

Water pours into my lungs. Warm and stale. Tasting of flesh and desert dust. I have no choice but to let it in. Let it spread. Replacing air with liquid. Heavy, gasping breaths with silence.

I try. I really try. Thrashing. Kicking. My arms just above the surface, punching the air. But it's useless. Nothing connects. My attacker is too quick. Too attuned to my limitations.

The fight is over now.

I open my eyes, struggling to see through the lingering ripples. The splashing has stopped. His face becomes clearer as the water settles. But still not clear enough. All I can make out is the determination in his eyes. The rage that contorts his features. The look of a madman.

His large hands continue to press against my shoulders. Pinning me to the hard surface of the bathtub floor. If I could speak I would tell him that he can let go now. I already have.

The light starts to flicker. The blackout is coming. I long for it. I welcome it with open arms. At least it will end this unbearable burning in my chest. This throbbing in my temples. That look in his eyes.

The shadows creep in, like a thick, heavy veil. I feel the pressure lift from my shoulders. His task is complete. My weightless body begins to float upward. Towards the surface. Towards the light.

As I break through, I see his radiant aquamarine eyes piercing the darkness and I know.

I've always known.

———————

I wake tangled in the sheets and drenched in sweat. It would seem my morning routine has not changed since I left the Pattinsons' farm.

Warming daylight streams through the window, illuminating the guest room of Cody's town house, reminding me of where I am, of everything that's happened.

Zen is still sleeping peacefully next to me, seemingly undisturbed by my nightmare and the thrashing that most likely occurred as a result. I wonder if Cody slipped Zen more of whatever drug he used to subdue him last night.

I climb out of the bed and tiptoe into the kitchen. The house is completely deserted. Zen and I appear to be the only ones here. In the kitchen, I find a plate of food sitting on the counter and a digital note typed next to it.

Went to the lab to run some tests.
Be back soon.
— C

I didn't notice it last night but the countertop appears to double as a giant screen. I spend a few minutes playing around with it, marvelling at its functionality. I can drag the note across the large surface with my fingertips, rotate it in any direction I want, make it bigger or smaller by pinching my thumb and forefinger together or moving them apart. I can layer it over photos and documents that are scattered throughout, creating virtual stacks.

One of the digital items catches my eye. It's an orange-and-white gradient square with a single row of black numbers running across it. On the top it reads *Magnum Ball Lotto* with a date from last week. Unable to make sense of it, I return it to the pile and scroll through a collection of photos.

After the novelty of the countertop screen wears off, I slide on to one of the stools and start to eat the breakfast Cody left out for me. Once again, it's delicious. Some kind of fluffy egg dish mixed with various vegetables and cheeses. The covered metal dish it's served on has somehow kept the meal warm. I've nearly devoured all of it when a small blue bubble appears on the screen below the plate.

It's a message from Cody.

Are you awake?

I click on the button labelled 'Reply' and a keyboard appears. I drag it to the right, away from my plate, and type out a response.

Yes.

After pressing Send, I watch the word disappear and rematerialize as a green bubble under Cody's question. A few seconds pass before Cody's next message pops up in blue.

Can you come to the lab? There's something I think you should see.

Panic floods through me.

He's found something.

Something about Zen.

I haven't even finished chewing by the time I've transessed into Cody's lab, steadying myself against the wall as the small wave of dizziness fades.

Cody jumps upon seeing me. 'Wow. I'm not sure I'll ever get used to that.'

'What is it?' I ask, my voice frantic. 'What did you find?'

'Were you able to eat the breakfast I left for you?'

He's stalling. Putting off bad news. 'Cody.' My tone is dripping with desperation. Begging him.

Please don't make me wait for this.

He seems to understand. 'OK,' he agrees, and takes a deep breath. I swear I can feel every particle of carbon dioxide that he exhales hitting my face like a million tiny drops of acid. 'Well, I finished running all the tests.'

Cloudiness starts to curtain my vision. 'And . . .'

It's the only word I can manage to get out. One syllable. Three little letters. A universe of mass riding on it. I swallow, wetting my parched throat, but it does no good. The moisture evaporates instantaneously.

Cody scratches his chin and beckons me over to his desk. He points to the large ultrathin monitor that sits atop it.

He inputs a numeric password to unlock the screen. His fingers fly rapidly over the keyboard, but my eyes catch the series of seemingly random digits as he enters them.

7123221157778

The screen flashes and then reveals a collection of data that I don't understand. Lines and lines of letters and values that make no sense to me. Cody points to one column and says, 'This is the code of a normal human genome.' Then he points to the column next to it. 'This is a breakdown of Zen's DNA.'

The discrepancy jumps out at me immediately. I point to a line in the data. 'That one is different.'

Cody nods. 'Yes.' He taps the screen, enlarging that section until only a small subset of letters is visible. 'This is the reason Zen is sick.'

My mouth falls open and I gaze up at him. 'Because of his DNA?'

'Because of this one gene in his DNA. I've never seen a gene like this in my research. It's very complex. Definitely man-made. And Zen's body is attacking it.'

I blink. 'What?'

'It would seem the gene is too powerful and his immune system is treating it like a virus. It's trying to get rid of it. Essentially his body is destroying itself.'

'But what *is* it?' I ask, panicked. 'Why would Zen have a gene that no one else has? He's just a normal . . .'

My voice trails off. I can't believe I didn't think of it before. Rio warned me. He warned me when he gave it to me. He told me this could happen. And I ignored it. I blocked it from my memory. Until now.

'If something goes wrong and you have no way to disable it, the gene could destroy you. Slowly eat you alive from the inside out. You wouldn't even know until it was too late.'

It's why he gave me the locket in the first place. So that I would have the ability to turn the gene on and off. But Zen didn't have anything. I knew I would never get him to trust Rio enough to allow him to install something similar in his genetic code. Which means his gene has been active this whole time, slowly destroying him.

'It's his transession gene,' I reply numbly, almost forgetting that Cody is in the room with me. 'It's killing him.'

'That was my conclusion, too,' Cody admits softly, and I realize that he must have seen those memories: the one where I learned about the transession gene and the one where Rio told me about my locket.

But wait, I think. *What about Kaelen?*

He doesn't have anything that activates or deactivates his gene. At least, not as far as I could tell. Why isn't the gene

248

making him sick? Was Zen's gene somehow faulty? Did something go wrong when it was implanted?

Regardless of what the problem is, there's obviously only one way to fix it.

I grab Cody's hands, squeezing them urgently. 'You have to deactivate the gene. Just take it out. I don't care if he's trapped here forever, at least he'll be alive.'

But Cody shakes his head regretfully. 'I can't. Like I said, it's complex. Tightly interwoven with the rest of his DNA. There isn't a scientist alive today who would be able to remove it. We've learned a lot more about genetics in the past few decades, but this is something else. Something I've never seen before. A human being's genetic code is like a complicated tapestry. You pull one string the wrong way and the whole thing falls apart.'

'Are you saying there's nothing you can do?' My voice is rising now, chock-full of growing despair. 'That we're supposed to stand by and watch him die?!'

Cody grimaces and reaches out to touch my hand.

'No!' I screech, brusquely pulling my hand away. 'I won't do that. There has to be a way to stop it from killing him!'

And then suddenly I feel a thin layer of ice coating my skin as I retrace Cody's words. As they chime restlessly inside my brain like bells gonging.

'There isn't a scientist alive today who would be able to remove it.'

I don't think he realizes how right he is.

'I know who can disable the gene,' I say, my voice sounding like it's coming from far away. Somewhere deep in the future. Eighty-three years to be exact.

Cody's eyebrows shoot up. 'Who?'

I draw in a long breath, feeling it energize me. Renew my hope. There's only one person in the world who knows enough about the transession gene to save Zen's life.

'The woman who created it.'

42

DEDUCTION

I pace the length of Cody's lab, memories and numbers and data streaming through my mind like rain. This discovery has suddenly turned everything on its head.

The gene is what's been making Zen sick. Not some mysterious disease.

And if Kaelen was telling the truth, and he knew all along that it was the gene, then he must also know how to turn the gene off, essentially leaving me with two options at this point. And the second one – the one that requires me to give Diotech what they want – is completely out of the question.

Which means I have to go with option one. It means there's only one person who can help me now.

'Her name is Dr Rylan—'

'Maxxer,' Cody finishes, his voice rigid and remote.

Once again, for some reason, her name sends an unexpected flare of anger blazing through me and I'm forced to stop pacing and grab on to something to steady myself.

What was that?

It was like a hot rage. As though I'd stepped across some kind of invisible battle line into enemy territory and could feel the resentment lingering in the air like smoke.

But just as soon as it came, the sensation is gone.

I study Cody's indignant expression. 'So you know.'

'That I met her and she erased the entire day from my mind and replaced it with a bogus memory of something that never happened? Yes.' His eyes are locked on a fixed point across the room. His jawline is taut.

I can tell that he's angry. And suddenly I know that this was the memory that finally pushed him over the edge. The reason he ripped off the receptors and stalked out of the room.

'She did it to protect you.'

'She had no right to make that choice for me!' he growls back. 'No right to mess with my head like that.'

'I know how you feel,' I relate. 'There was a point when I had more fake memories in my head than real ones.'

Cody grunts and crosses his arms over his chest. 'And that thing she used to knock me out. What's it called again?'

I pull the black device from my pocket and plunk it down on the countertop. 'A Modifier.'

Cody hisses out a breath as he stares at the contraption sitting in his lab. He bends down and examines it without daring to touch it.

'I don't know exactly how it works,' I offer. 'I just know that it does something to your brain waves and basically puts you to sleep.'

Cody shakes his head. 'That's messed up.'

'Yes,' I agree. 'But right now, Dr Maxx—' I stop myself from saying her name, feeling the strange fury start to bubble up again. 'That woman is the only one who can help me. Who can help Zen. I have to find her.'

'Well, do you have any idea where she could be?'

I throw my hands in the air. 'No! That's the problem. I don't have the first clue. She could be anywhere. You saw how much trouble she went through to keep her whereabouts a secret.' I gesture towards the Modifier still lying on the counter. 'That's the reason she deactivated us both in the first place. So we couldn't see where she was hiding.'

Cody suddenly goes very still. It almost looks like his body is starting to withdraw into itself.

I narrow my eyes at him. 'Cody?'

He doesn't respond. Just keeps staring at an unidentified point across the room. I take a careful step towards him, almost afraid that if I move too fast, I might startle him.

But in reality, he's the one who ends up startling me.

He suddenly soars into action, darting to the wall behind me, which I now see is a giant, virtual whiteboard. He clears away all the existing scribbles of notes and symbols with a sweep of his hand and plucks a pen-like device from a nearby magnet.

'Cody,' I begin warily. 'What are you doing?'

But again, he doesn't respond. He just starts scrawling.

At the top of the space, he writes *Invents Transession* and draws a circle around it.

Then clockwise down to the right, he writes *Cody's memories erased*. Circles it.

He continues in an arc with the phrases *Hidden Location*, *Implanted Memory Map*, and *Capable of Disabling Malfunctioning Gene*, until he's formed a complete circle.

'Don't you see?' he says, tapping the empty centre. 'This Maxxer woman is the one common factor in all of this.'

He scribbles *Maxxer* in the middle of the circle and underlines it twice.

I squint at the diagram, trying to figure out what Cody is getting at.

'You said it yourself,' Cody presses on. 'She went through so much trouble to keep her whereabouts a secret. Do you know anyone else who has reason to do that?'

'I don't think so.'

'She's on the run, like you are. She told you so. She's hiding from the same people you've been hiding from.'

'Diotech,' I say instantly.

'Yes,' Cody confirms. 'And if she was willing to expend that much effort to conceal her location from them before, it only makes sense that she would do it again.'

He points the tip of the pen at his own name. 'Just think about it. If she was capable of *removing* memories from my mind, wouldn't she also be capable of putting memories *into* yours?'

Every inch of me goes numb. Except my brain. My thoughts are spinning frantically. I stare at Cody's diagram in total disbelief. Why didn't I see it before? It makes so much sense now.

The Modifier.

She used it on him. But she also used it on *me*. When we got into her car, she turned it on both of us. She said it was to protect her. So that the memory of her location couldn't be stolen later.

I woke up on the cold concrete floor of her storage unit. I have no idea how long I was out.

She had complete and full access to my brain the entire time.

I gasp and bring my hand to my mouth.

'You're right,' I squeak. 'Maxxer is the only other person I know who has reason to hide from Diotech. But she couldn't simply *tell* me where she was. Or implant a memory of her location. That would be too easy for Diotech to steal. She had to leave clues. Clues that could only be triggered by *me*.'

The pieces are swirling around me as I eagerly pluck each one and put it in the right place.

'*Find me.*'

That voice was inserted at the beginning of every memory. Like a label. Like a heading. Tying them all together. Telling me what to do.

'She's leading me *to* her.'

The excitement of our breakthrough is so overwhelming, I have to sit down. I slide into one of the chairs.

This whole time Maxxer has been waiting for me to come to her.

It's almost as though she *knew* I wouldn't stay in 1609. That something would go wrong and I would eventually need to find her.

If she really implanted these memories when I was unconscious in her storage unit, that means she was already planning for us to meet again. She was already three steps ahead of me.

'But wait,' I wonder aloud. 'Why would *Diotech* be so interested in finding Maxxer, anyway? Why would they send someone here simply to track her through me?'

Was it because she ran away? That doesn't feel right. Why risk losing me – the trillion-dollar investment – only to bring back a rogue scientist?

'It doesn't make sense,' I say aloud. 'They have the transession gene. They don't need her any more.'

'Unless,' Cody says, tapping his pen on the circled text that reads *Capable of Disabling Malfunctioning Gene*, 'Zen isn't the only one who's sick.'

There's a creak in the floorboards and we jump and turn in unison towards the tall, statuesque figure joining us in Cody's lab. I'm not sure how long he's been standing there or how much he's heard. But I have a feeling it's too long and too much.

A disconcerting smirk dances across his perfect features as he opens his mouth and remarks in that irresistibly deep and velvety voice, 'Smart man.'

43
WAR

I can't explain what happens to me in that moment.

It's almost as though my body declares war on itself. Half of me is terrified. Angry. Wanting to transesse right back to that guest room, scoop Zen into my arms, and leap from a tenth-storey window. Regardless of whether we'll survive the fall or not.

But the other half . . .

That's the half that disgusts me. The half that feels an overwhelming rush of relief. The part of me that has been sickeningly *hoping* that he will find me. That I will see him again. It's the part that wants to run to him now. Touch him. Feel that glorious surge of energy that charges me every time our skin connects.

It's the part of me I don't understand.

That I fear I will never understand.

Back and forth they battle. Reasonable hatred and inexplicable desire. He is my sworn enemy and yet I could never bring myself to defeat him. He is despicable because he was made by the hands of the people who seek to destroy my happiness. And yet we are the same.

'Kaelen,' my lips whisper his name. It slithers out of my mouth, filled with a venomous longing. A maddening fascination. A repellent attraction.

He stands motionless just across the room from me and, despite my better judgment, I let my eyes find his. Settle in. Lock.

The exhilarating sensation that runs through me is over-powering.

What is that?

Why can't I fight it?

Why can't I hate him? The way I want to hate him. The way I *yearn* to hate him.

I feel my feet tingling. Commanding me to him. As if the path between us now – the measly ten steps – has been carved in stone. As if there is no other way. No other road.

But I won't.

I won't.

I won't.

I finally compel myself to look away, breaking the bind. Snapping the invisible wire strung between us, leaving me with the distinct sensation of falling.

I can hear his breathing. And not just because my hearing is exceptional. But because his breath is laboured. He is struggling, too. And yet I didn't need to hear it to know it.

Part of me already knows.

Part of me reads his emotions as easily as I read my own.

'Cody's right, isn't he?' I demand of him, finding my voice. 'Alixter gave himself the gene when he came to get me in 2013. He's sick, too.'

Kaelen remains stoically silent.

'That's why he sent you,' I go on, undeterred. 'That's why your orders weren't to bring me back right away. Alixter needs the cure, too. You lied,' I accuse him. 'You told me you had it.'

'I told you I knew where it was,' Kaelen corrects. He still hasn't confirmed my theory but he doesn't need to. I know it's the truth. I can *sense* it from his body language. From his energy. The same way I knew what he was feeling that first time we touched.

And it doesn't matter if I'm right or not.

If Maxxer can help Zen then I have to find her. I have to go to her. Just like she wanted me to. She's been calling to me since the beginning.

And now there's only one thing standing in my way.

Or one person, rather.

I glower at Kaelen. 'How did you find me?'

'Sera,' he says. And there it is again. My name on his lips. 'You should understand by now, I will *always* find you.'

His tone is sinister. Full of warning. It's something Alixter would say. And that makes perfect sense. He's following *his* orders. Responding to *his* programming.

And yet, in Kaelen's words, spoken by Kaelen's mouth, I hear something else. Something far less sinister. Something reassuring.

'I will *always* find you.'

And I feel that rebellious half — that half that I despise — silently rejoice.

My mind is reeling. How *did* he find me? There were no documents. No records. I left no trail. Did someone take my picture without me realizing it? But something is telling me that there's still a piece to the puzzle I don't have. That there's more to this. That it's much bigger, much more complicated, than simply scrounging through historical records.

And that's when the other part of me — the sane, rational part that knows Kaelen is an enemy who shouldn't be trusted — starts to panic.

He takes a slow purposeful step towards me and I feel it start all over again. That pull. That energy. Like the molecules in the space between us are being spun into a frenzy.

I close my eyes, attempting to fight it.

And then I feel them. His fingertips. Grazing my forehead. Pressing against me. Showering me with tingles. My whole body is alive. I never want his hands to leave. I never want him to stop.

But then he does.

It's over too soon and all I'm left with is the fading glow of his touch. Like the glorious pinks and greys that the sun leaves behind after it disappears over the horizon. And the sorrow of knowing why he really touched me, what he was really after.

The memory.

He took it. Those magic hands that somehow are able to caress my spirit also stole a piece of my mind.

And when I open my eyes, I see that he's taken something else as well.

My locket is dangling from the tip of his finger, binding my fate with his for the remainder of this journey. He swings it up and catches it deftly in his hand, bringing his clenched fist close to my face. 'I would strongly advise against trying to escape again.'

This time, the menacing quality of his voice is not lost. It's not muffled by some confusing filter and made to seem dreamy and heartening. It's a clear message. A warning from his creator. Our creator.

I can almost hear Alixter's voice crossing time and space to speak through Kaelen.

He falls still for a moment, seemingly lost in deep contemplation. When he speaks again, he looks angry. 'Do you realize what you've done?'

I look to Cody for the first time since Kaelen's surprise arrival, taking in his paralyzed expression. I imagine after everything he's seen in my memories, everything he knows about Diotech, the sight of Kaelen in his lab is terrifying.

'I was just trying to save him,' I defend, assuming he's still referring to my thwarted escape effort.

I watch Kaelen's fists ball at his sides, as though he's trying to keep from punching something. Me.

'You've destroyed our only chance of finding Dr Maxxer and the antidote.'

'What? That's preposterous.'

'You don't seem to fully comprehend the gravity of the situation or the extent of your error.'

'My *error*?' I repeat in disgust.

'The memory clearly indicated that you were to contact Mr Carlson *last* night, in his lab,' Kaelen says, and I immediately realize what he was doing during that brief moment of stillness. He was watching the memories he stole from my mind. He was catching up on everything he'd missed since I left him in that cab. I lean to the right, just able to make out a new receptor disk secured behind his ear.

'Yeah, so?'

'But you insisted on intercepting him earlier than the memory instructed,' he goes on, his gaze flashing momentarily to Cody. 'And now the opportunity to ascertain the next clue has been lost.'

I shrug. 'So why can't we just go back to last night and get it?'

Of course, as soon as the suggestion is out of my mouth, I recognize the flaw in its logic.

'The basic laws of transession don't allow you to occupy space in the same moment of time more than once.'

I've already been there. I've already occupied space in the time period of last night. I was at Cody's house, with him and his wife. Making it virtually impossible for me to go back to get the memory.

'Even if you *were* capable of transessing there,' Kaelen clarifies, 'which you are not, the memory is no longer valid. Mr Carlson would not be where he is supposed to be—'

'OK,' Cody interrupts, 'can we stop talking about me like I'm not even here? And what's this whole thing about me in your memory? Did she lead you to me? Is that how you found me?'

But I ignore him. 'Why not?' I ask Kaelen.

'Because you effectively altered his course. The memory specified that Mr Carlson was supposed to be in his lab last night. Working late. But he was not.'

Cody appears pensive. 'Actually, he's right. I *was* planning to work late last night.'

'But I showed up with Zen and we went back to your house,' I realize aloud.

'Yes,' comes Kaelen's vacant response.

It is my fault.

I did this. I went against what the memory told me to do and I messed it all up.

'You have prohibited us from obtaining the final clue, which we believe would reveal Dr Maxxer's whereabouts,' Kaelen says, solidifying my guilt.

I press my fingers to my temples. 'Wait. Final clue. Are you saying Cody was the last stop on the map?'

'Yes.'

'How do you know that?'

'Like I've already stated,' he drones, 'we were able to identify the time-delayed recalls implanted in your brain; we simply could not decode them until they were properly activated. We counted three in total.'

Three.

Chinatown.

Fifty-Ninth Street station.

Cody.

'But if there were only three,' I rationalize, 'then Cody couldn't have triggered another memory. By the time I found him there were no more memories left to trigger. So how could Maxxer's whereabouts be revealed?'

Kaelen hesitates for a moment before finally admitting, 'It would seem the final piece of information is not implanted in your brain.'

I draw in a sharp breath, feeling the weight of everything come crashing down on me.

'Hold on a second.' Cody jumps in before I have a chance to speak. He turns to me. 'Is he implying what I think he's implying?'

I feel my head fall into a stunned nod. 'I think so.'

The last clue.

Maxxer's hidden location.

The key to healing Zen.

It's buried within Cody's mind.

44

BURIED

That's why Maxxer sent me to him. That's why he's involved. She must have implanted the last piece of the map in his brain when she was erasing his memories. She must have set it to trigger when I showed up. Which was supposed to be *last* night. In his lab. But now I've ruined that. Now it might never be triggered.

'No. No, no, no, no, NO.' Cody is pacing the length of the room. 'There's been some sort of mistake. I don't know anything. I swear.'

'Cody,' I say, reaching out to him as he passes by and attempting to rest a reassuring hand on his shoulder. 'It wouldn't be something you know *now*.' I turn to Kaelen. 'Are you saying Maxxer put one of those time-delayed recalls in *Cody's* mind, too?'

'Actually, that would be impossible,' Kaelen responds.

I squint up at him, confused.

'TDRs cannot be implanted in the average brain.'

Cody stops pacing and glowers at Kaelen. 'Hey! Who are

you calling *average brained*? I'll have you know I have an IQ of 172. I went to Harvard.'

But Kaelen promptly disregards this. 'They can only be implanted in enhanced neurological systems.'

'Like you and me,' I say numbly.

'Precisely.'

Cody glances anxiously between us. 'I don't get it. So what does this mean?'

'It means,' Kaelen continues stuffily, 'that the memory has always been active. You may just not recognize it for what it is.'

'Then it doesn't matter that I didn't come here last night!' I say, a mountain of guilt lifting right off my shoulders. 'If the memory is already active, he already has the information we need.'

'No, I don't!' Cody yells. 'That's what I'm trying to tell you. I don't know ANYTHING!'

Kaelen juts his chin towards him in agreement. 'Just because it is active doesn't mean he knows how to access it. He said so himself, he doesn't know what we're looking for. Which means Dr Maxxer directed you here last night with the specific intention to draw the buried memory out of Cody's brain. But because you failed to follow her direction, the proper stimulation was never introduced. Therefore, our only option is to find the information another way.'

Kaelen takes an ominous step in Cody's direction and I watch his hand rise slowly in the air, reaching towards Cody's forehead.

'No!' I leap between them, my arms splayed out to the sides, protecting Cody. Protecting his mind. I won't let Cody become what I've become. A human database. A hard drive. I won't let Kaelen scrounge around in his brain like he's searching through a drawer.

I remember how betrayed Cody felt when he found out what Maxxer had done to him in that storage unit. I won't make him go through that again.

I won't.

'There must be another way,' I say.

'There isn't.'

I spin around and face Cody, placing my hands urgently on his arms. 'Cody, please. Try to remember. You're Zen's only hope.'

Cody shrugs my hands away. 'What do you think? I've been holding out on you? That I know where she is and have been keeping it all to myself? I don't know how many times I can tell you this. I. DON'T. KNOW. ANYTHING! You're barking up the wrong tree.'

But I'm not deterred. 'Think, Cody,' I urge. 'Think about everything that happened after the day I disappeared. Try to focus on anything unusual that sticks out in your mind. Anything that doesn't quite fit.'

Cody shakes his head and walks to his desk. 'This is pointless.'

'I agree,' Kaelen adds from somewhere behind me. I turn and shoot him a glare.

'Please,' I beg.

Cody pulls out a drawer and removes a bottle filled with light brown liquid. Unscrewing the top, he takes a long swig, then grimaces at the taste.

He sighs. 'That's nineteen years of memories. You're asking me to find a needle in a haystack. A needle that I'm still not convinced is there.'

'This is ineffective,' Kaelen determines, and walks towards Cody again. Cody flinches and backs up against his desk. Once again, I step between them. 'Give him a chance.'

'No,' Cody asserts, slamming the bottle down. 'You know

what? I don't want a chance. I'm done with this. All of this. Just . . . leave me alone, OK?' He pushes past me and doesn't stop until he's out the door.

I feel Kaelen react next to me, preparing to follow, but I stop him with a single word. 'Don't.'

He looks at me, clearly thinking I'm insane.

'Give him some time. He just needs to process this. He'll help us. I know he will.'

Kaelen crosses his arms. 'He gets one hour. Then we do it my way.'

45

SHIFT

The small park across the street from Cody's town house is cold and dreary. There's a fountain in the centre that has completely frozen over and the small brown sparrows are actually standing on its solid surface. Kaelen and I sit on a bench as far apart as we can. We are completely silent. I hear the faint sounds of children laughing on a nearby playground. I convinced him to wait until Cody came home, knowing that Cody just needed time to process.

I watch him out of the corner of my eye. Despite his handsome, chiselled features, he looks tired. A thin layer of dirt shadows his hands. His hair needs to be combed. And his clothes are rumpled. There's still a large, frayed gash in the side of his pants where I ripped the Modifier from his pocket.

He's regarding the other people in the park, completely enthralled. As though it's the first time he's ever seen humans.

After a few minutes, beautiful white flakes begin to dance out of the sky, falling around us, covering the ground at our feet in a fluffy white dust. Kaelen looks slightly startled as he stares upward.

'It's called snow,' I tell him, guessing from his reaction that he's never seen it before.

Because it's the same reaction I had when I saw it for the first time.

Six months ago. We'd just arrived on the Pattinsons' farm. It was early spring. The sky clouded over with grey, the temperature dropped, and suddenly out of the sky came this magnificent white powder. I spun in circles underneath it, loving how it covered my dress in tiny sparkling specks. I never wanted it to end.

It was so beautiful.

Kaelen stares blankly upward. If he finds any beauty in the frozen rain, he doesn't express it.

'How did you find me?' I ask. I keep my voice low, barely a whisper, but I know he can hear it.

Even so, he doesn't answer. Just keeps his gaze forward.

'Were you close enough to track me?' I guess, even though I never felt my tattoo vibrate so I know this is probably not the answer.

But again, he doesn't respond.

I glance down at his left wrist, his own black mark peeking out from under the cuff of his shirt. 'You do realize they gave you one, too.'

I see his gaze flick downward but he stays silent.

'That would imply they don't completely trust you. That it's possible you have the same tendencies as me. To disobey. To run away.'

'I would never disobey Dr Alixter.' It's the first thing he's said since we sat down and I can tell by the way his voice slips into that eerie monotonous tone that he's reciting one of his automated responses. Something he's been programmed to say. Without even knowing that he's saying it.

'Right,' I say, nodding. 'Because he's looking out for your best interests.'

His head clicks towards me. 'I sense insincerity in your tone.'

I snort. 'How observant.'

'Why are you being insincere?'

'It's called sarcasm.'

'Sarcasm,' Kaelen repeats. 'Used to convey scorn or insult.'

I have to laugh at how much he sounds like me when I first escaped the compound. Exactly like me, actually. And I immediately realize that they must have uploaded both of our brains with the same definitions.

'It means I'm ridiculing you,' I explain.

He faces me, cocking his head inquisitively. 'Why?'

'Because you have no idea what you're talking about! Because you're completely brainwashed, just as I was, regurgitating everything you've been taught to so blindly believe. Because Alixter isn't looking out for anyone's best interests but his own.' My voice is rising alarmingly fast. I have to take deep breaths to calm myself down.

Silence follows. Heavy and uncomfortable. Hanging in the air like humidity.

And then, 'Are you implying Dr Alixter is a dishonest man?'

I scold myself for getting so worked up. For letting him affect me like that. My words are just wasted breath. Wasted energy. I should know there's nothing I can do to fix him. His brainwashing is deep. Too deep. Much deeper than mine ever was. He's already proved that to me. Alixter found whatever defect in my wiring allowed me to eventually break through the programming and see the truth. And he fixed it. In Kaelen.

The thought brings a wave of sympathy crashing down on top of me.

He was never given a choice.

Despite what they led Kaelen to believe, despite how much Alixter was able to make him feel grateful for who he is and what he's able to do, he was never asked if he wanted to be special. If he wanted to be brought into this world in such an unnatural way. If he wanted to fight a battle that he doesn't even know why he's fighting.

And that's when I realize . . .

Kaelen is a victim, too.

A victim of Diotech. A victim of science. A victim of Alixter's greed.

I, at least, had someone to set me free. Kaelen has no one.

'Yes,' I say softly. This time my voice is compassionate, not bitter. Tender, not angry. Genuine, not sarcastic. 'That's what I'm implying.'

Kaelen appears to be digesting this information. I decide, knowing how his brain works, that it's better not to give him time to process.

'Kaelen,' I say as gently as I can. 'Alixter is not an ally. He's an enemy. He doesn't care about you. He only cares about his own agenda.'

If only I knew what that was.

'My agenda is Dr Alixter's agenda.' Another dispassionate reply, informing me that I'm not making any progress.

But I can't stop now. I have to at least try.

Because I believe, despite all evidence to the contrary, that somewhere inside there might be a real person. And that person deserves a chance.

'Says who?' I challenge. 'Who put that idea into your head? Where is that response coming from? Don't you see that it's just a preprogrammed reaction? It's not you who's speaking. You're nothing but a computer to him. Don't you want to be more than that? Be your own person? Think your own thoughts? Live your own life?'

'What is the purpose of that?'

I sigh, leaning back against the bench, feeling despondent. The program is strong. I'm not sure I'll ever be able to break through it.

And yet, somehow, Zen did.

For me.

So I press on, letting it all out. Maybe if I overload his system with data, I'll have a chance of breaking in. Finding a hole. A chink in the armour.

'So you don't have to be a prisoner!' I cry in a strained, hushed tone. 'Don't you see, you're no better off than I was in that cell in 1609! He is controlling everything you do. Everything you think. Everything you say. Any thought that enters your brain is designed to benefit him. Any desire you feel is something *he* devised. It's all to serve *him* and that company. But it doesn't have to be like that. You can get out. You can break free. You have a *choice*. You want to know why I ran away from the Diotech compound? Because I didn't want to be *his*. I wanted to be *mine*. I wanted to be *me*.' I pause and take a breath before adding sombrely, 'I wanted to figure out who that even is.'

I see his eye twitch ever so slightly. Then his face goes rigid. He looks frustrated. He pounds the bench so hard, the wood splinters, causing a few curious stares from passers-by in the park. But for the first time, I don't care about making a scene or attracting attention. The anger – the imbalance – means it's working. I'm getting somewhere.

'You're only saying this to distract me so that you can try to run again,' he argues, and I hear it. The smallest, faintest crack in his otherwise stable voice.

I gaze at him with pity in my eyes. I feel sorry for him. So very sorry. I remember what it was like to be told that my entire existence was a lie. I remember that feeling of useless-ness. Pointlessness. Betrayal.

'I'm saying it to help you.'

There's a long, drawn-out silence. Kaelen stares at the ground. But I watch his face intently. Searching for signs of a transformation.

After almost a full minute, I finally see something. His jaw hardens. He grits his teeth together. His fists clench like he's going to pound the bench again. A feeling of victory starts to shiver across me. I've done it. I've broken through. He looks as livid as I felt when I finally learned the truth. And I can't blame him for being enraged, disgusted, fuming. His entire world, everything he thinks he knows, has just crumbled around him.

He opens his mouth to speak and I give him my full atten-tion, wanting to be there for him. To support him as he goes through this difficult discovery.

'Dr Alixter warned me that you would do this,' he seethes. 'He told me you would use whatever means possible to sway me from my mission. I won't let that happen.'

He turns towards me and at once I realize that I must have set off some kind of trap. A minefield. His anger is not directed at Diotech. It's directed at me. Alixter was prepared for this. Prepared for my attempts to influence him. And he evidently built in reassurances.

Another preprogrammed response.

This one, however, is not benign.

It's a monster.

Kaelen's eyes are wide with rage. His face scarier and more crazed than I've ever seen it. The calm, collected, steady Kaelen is gone. And something far more frightening has taken its place.

'If you try to do that again,' he growls, 'I will kill Zen myself.'

46

LUCKY

The conversation is over. I refuse to say anything else for fear that whatever has triggered Kaelen's sudden transformation will only get worse. And Kaelen seems too angry to speak.

We sit in the cold, bleary silence, with snow gathering at our feet, until the sun goes down. A few minutes later I spot Cody shuffling along the sidewalk across the street, evidently on his way home. He looks haggard, tired, drained, like the weight of a planet has fallen on to his shoulders. He disappears into his house.

Kaelen must spot him, too, because he starts to rise to his feet. I put my hand up to stop him. 'Wait.'

To my surprise he actually breaks focus and looks at me expectantly.

'Let me go in alone. Let me try.'

I can tell by the look on his face that this is not his favourite idea. But he also hasn't said no. So I go on. 'He's overwhelmed. And you busting in there is not going to help. I think I can get it out of him.'

'You don't even know what you're looking for,' Kaelen argues.

'Neither do you,' I point out.

This seems to stump him. He lowers himself back on to the bench. 'You have fifteen minutes,' he says.

'Twenty,' I retort.

Kaelen gives me a sharp look.

'Fifteen,' I yield quietly, and then exit the park, jogging across the street to Cody's house. I bound up the five steps and press my finger against the buzzer and wait.

There's no answer.

I press it again, holding it longer.

Finally, I hear a voice come through the small box attached to the brick wall. 'Go away.'

I look straight into the camera. 'Cody,' I say as gently as possible, 'can I please talk to you?'

'Why don't you just magically appear? With your stupid transession gene or whatever?'

I break into a small smile. 'I don't want to do it that way. I want you to let me in.'

'I don't know anything!' he screams. It echoes into the street below.

'I know,' I say quietly. 'I believe you.'

There's a long pause and then finally I hear a chime and the door clicks open. I enter the hallway. Cody is waiting for me.

I brush the snow from my shoulders and hair and walk further inside, eyeing the hallway that leads to the guest room. The thought of Zen back there, sick, sends a shard of glass through my heart.

'Still no change,' Cody informs me, as though reading my thoughts.

'Where's Ella?' I ask, glancing around at the empty rooms. 'And Reese?'

'I convinced her to take him to her parents' house. I thought it would be safer that way.'

I bite my lip and nod.

Safer.

From Kaelen.

From me.

'Can I sit down?'

Cody beckons half-heartedly towards the couch. I take a seat and exhale. He turns on the wall screen and pulls a small white video game controller from a cabinet. He plops down next to me. 'I was just going to play a game.'

'OK.'

He flicks a small knob on the controller and the screen illuminates with the image of a destroyed battle zone. Cody carefully manoeuvres an animated warrior through it.

'Why isn't this like the one we played last night?' I ask, remembering how the underwater kingdom surrounded us on all sides, blocking out the real world, protecting us from its horrors. This game appears to be limited to the wall screen.

Cody doesn't avert his eyes. His tongue hangs out in concentration as he attempts to move his man around a series of barrels that have the word EXPLOSIVE written on the side in big red letters.

'This is an older game. From when I was a teenager. I like to bring it out when I'm having a bad day.'

A bad day.

I guess that would be me. I'm the cause of his bad day. It seems like no matter where I go, no matter what year it is, no matter how old or mature Cody gets, I always manage to swoop in and ruin his life.

I lean back and watch the action for a moment, noticing how easily the man on the screen is able to battle his way through the torn city. Fighting off enemies at an impressive rate. It reminds me of my time in the woods with Zen. When he tried to teach me to fight. When we thought that was all I needed to protect us. A few combat moves.

Oh, how much more complicated everything has gotten.

'Where's your friend?' he asks, his focus still on the game.

The term catches me off guard. *Friend?* I definitely wouldn't call Kaelen a *friend*. From the moment we met, I've considered him my enemy. Because Alixter was my enemy. And he works for Alixter.

I look at one of the fictional enemies Cody just killed in the game, lying dead in the middle of the animated street.

Could I actually kill Kaelen? Even the thought of it makes me feel nauseated.

'I left him outside.' I peer at Cody's fast-moving fingers. 'Can I try?'

He pauses the game and looks at me for the first time since we sat down. 'You want to play?'

'Yeah.'

Cody considers this for a moment and then shrugs. 'Sure. We can team up.'

He walks over to the cabinet and removes a second controller, identical to his own. He presses a button and a blue light illuminates on it. Then he hands it to me.

'What are we doing?' I ask, glancing curiously at the controller.

'Winning World War II.'

'OK.'

'Shoot anything that has a swastika on it.'

'What's a swastika?'

He points towards a strange red symbol on the screen. 'That thing.' He shows me his controller and begins pointing at the various knobs and buttons. 'The joystick moves you back and forth. This button makes you shoot. This one makes you jump. These two together make you duck. And these two together make you swivel.'

I blink, memorizing his directions. 'Got it.'

Cody regards me for a moment. 'The girl who proved Goldbach's conjecture? Yeah, I'm sure you do.'

He restarts the game and we're off. I pick it up easily. My fingers moving swiftly across the controls. It's enjoyable. It occupies my otherwise swimming mind. I can see why Cody turns to it when he's having a bad day.

We survive a surprise attack on the bridge and make it to a sleeping enemy camp. I manage to annihilate everyone within a matter of seconds. Before Cody has even made it off the bridge. He whistles, impressed.

'You got a secret vendetta against Nazis?' he asks.

I laugh but don't respond otherwise. I just keep going. Keep shooting. Keep ducking punches. Diving away from bombs. Keep fighting.

Never. Stop. Fighting.

What Cody doesn't know is that when I look at the screen, when I stare those computer-generated soldiers in the eye, I don't see their flat, two-dimensional faces. I see Alixter.

In every single one of them.

I see his chilling blue eyes. His white-blond hair. His handsome, smug features. His soulless grin.

And I destroy it.

If only it were that easy.

But then I remember Kaelen waiting outside, counting down the seconds until my fifteen minutes are up, and I know I can't hide in here all day. Neither of us can. Any minute now, Kaelen will be transessing through that door, ready to use whatever means necessary to get the information he's looking for out of Cody's head.

'Cody?' I say cautiously, keeping my eyes glued to the enormous screen.

'Yeah?'

'Why do you think the memories in my head would lead me to you?'

I can hear him sigh next to me. I can tell I've broken the rule. Brought up the subject I wasn't supposed to bring up. But what choice do I have?

If I want to protect Cody from the wrath of Alixter via Kaelen, and save Zen's life, I have to get the information myself.

'I told you,' he says, sounding irritated. 'I don't know.'

I open my mouth to argue but I'm interrupted by a bright beeping sound. A notification box has popped up on the upper left side of the screen: *The lotto announcement will air in two minutes. Would you like to change the input?*

'Yes,' Cody says to the screen, pausing the game and dropping his controller next to him. He taps the surface of the coffee table, causing it to shift into another giant flat-panel screen. Like the one embedded in his kitchen counter. He manoeuvres through various digital contents until he comes across a small orange-and-white square with a row of numbers displayed across the middle. I recognize it. I saw something similar on Cody's countertop just this morning. Except that one was almost a week old. This one has today's date.

The wall screen has changed. I'm now staring at a three-dimensional projection of a life-size woman who appears to be standing in the middle of the room. Next to her is a large clear container filled with tiny white balls that have numbers printed on the side.

'What is this?' I ask.

'It's the Magnum Ball Lotto.'

I watch as the balls in the container start to jumble and hop and dance until one of them is blown into a tube at the top and rolls all the way down to the base. The woman standing in the living room picks it up and reads the number aloud. She continues to do this until seven numbers have been read.

Cody, who has been standing directly in front of her, slouches and swipes his fingertip across the glass coffee table, causing the small white-and-orange square to minimize into the corner.

'What happened?'

'I didn't win,' he says dejectedly.

I lean forward and drag the digital lotto ticket back into the centre of the coffee table. 'How does it work?'

'Switch to game mode,' he commands the wall screen. Then he sinks back into the couch and scoops up his controller again. 'Twice a week they pick seven random numbers. If your numbers match, you win the jackpot. It was up to $1.1 billion this week.'

'How many numbers are there in total?'

'Eighty-five.'

'But,' I protest, 'the chance that you would have the same seven numbers as the ones randomly selected from eighty-five options is one in 200 million.'

Cody rolls his eyes. 'That's right. I forgot, you're a walking calculator.'

I stare down at the numbers on his ticket.

$$7 \quad 12 \quad 15 \quad 21 \quad 32 \quad 77 \quad 78$$

They seem familiar somehow. But I can't remember why.

'Why did you select these numbers?' I ask.

Cody sighs and unpauses the game. But I don't pick up my

controller. He continues playing without me. 'They just feel lucky to me. Some day I'm convinced they'll win.'

And suddenly I know where I've seen them before. These are the *exact* numbers that were displayed on the lotto ticket I found this morning. With last week's date on it.

'Do you play the same combination of numbers every time?'

His gaze is still intently locked on an aircraft carrier that his avatar just boarded. 'Yeah.'

'How long have you been doing that?'

He shrugs. 'I don't know. Probably since I was old enough to play.'

'And when was that?'

He sounds irritated by my constant questioning. 'Eighteen. Now will you please get back in the game? I can't defeat these guys on my own.'

But I don't touch my controller. 'You've been playing these exact numbers for fourteen years?'

'Yeah,' he repeats, distractedly.

This jump-starts my heart. 'Why *these* numbers?'

'Like I said, they just feel lucky. Call it a hunch.'

A hunch.

'Cody,' I say, grabbing the controller from his hand.

'Hey!' he protests, but I ignore him and drop it on to the couch.

'Where did you get these numbers?'

He leans back with a scowl. 'I don't know. They've always just been in my head.'

Out of the corner of my eye, I see Kaelen materialize in the dining room. My time is up. But I raise my hand in the air, signalling him to give me a second.

I'm on to something. I know it. 'For how long?' I press Cody.

He opens his mouth to answer but suddenly nothing comes out except a strange, mouse-like squeak.

'Cody?' I prompt.

'I . . .' He stumbles, jumping slightly when he, too, notices that Kaelen has arrived. I snap my fingers in front of his face, keeping him focused.

'How long have these numbers *just been in your head?*'

Cody rubs his hands on his pants, leaving behind a sweaty streak. 'I . . . don't know.'

I nod. 'You *do* know.'

His eyes drift upward and to the left as he struggles to remember. 'I . . .' He tries a third time.

'Think,' I command him. 'Think *hard.*'

'I . . . guess since –' his eyes close – 'I was about thirteen.'

47

SUBMERGED

I'm out of my seat, running into the kitchen before Cody even opens his eyes again. I tap on the glass countertop, bringing it out of its hibernation.

'Numbers,' I tell Kaelen, who is by my side in a flash. 'She left the final clue in a sequence of numbers.'

With a swoop of his hand, Kaelen clears the clutter of virtual pictures, documents, and videos in front of us and opens a blank white tableau. I grab a pen device, just like the one in Cody's lab, from a holster on the refrigerator door and scribble down the numbers Cody plays twice a week in the lottery.

7 12 15 21 32 77 78

'Are you sure about this?' Kaelen asks, tilting his head to read what I've written.

'Maxxer knows my brain is designed to pick up patterns. It

only makes sense that she would try to speak to me in numbers.'

I study the sequence, immediately noticing they are listed in ascending order. 'Cody!' I call back towards the living room. 'Is this the order you remember them in?'

Silence follows and I lean around the corner of the kitchen wall to see that Cody is still sitting on the couch staring into space, looking dazed.

'Cody?' I repeat.

'No.' I hear his quiet mumble. And then, 'The lotto machine puts them in that order when it prints the ticket.'

'So what order do you remember them in?'

He doesn't reply for a minute. I think he's gone into shock. Nineteen years of his life he's been carrying this around. Never knowing what it was. Never understanding why. Never expecting that eventually a girl would appear out of thin air, claiming to be from another century, asking him about a series of seemingly insignificant numbers in his mind, telling him that they mean something. That they *lead* to something.

I guess I can't fault him for feeling just the slightest bit stupefied.

But finally, he speaks. His voice faint. Trance-like. He lists the numbers one by one, pausing for long stretches of time between them. As though reciting each digit robs him of every ounce of energy he has left and he has to wait until he can replenish before starting again.

I erase the original string and transcribe each one as he announces it, until I have a new sequence staring back at me.

7 12 32 21 15 77 78

I let out a small gasp and cover my mouth.

'What?' Kaelen asks, his eyes scouring the digits.

'The password. On Cody's computer. It's the same sequence. I watched him input it earlier today. And in the memory . . .'

'He was inputting an unseen password into a computer,' Kaelen finishes the thought as we arrive at the same conclusion simultaneously.

'That was supposed to be the trigger,' I deduce, feeling more confident than ever. 'The password. It's why I felt drawn to it in the memory. The sequence is telling me where and when to go next.'

Kaelen and I both stare at it, our eyes focused, our lips pressed together. Concentrating. Searching for an indication of time and place.

I circle the 32. 'This has to be the year.'

'You don't know that,' Kaelen disagrees. 'Any of those numbers could indicate a year.'

I shake my head. 'Why suddenly send me to a whole different year? She wanted me here. Every clue has been in this year.'

'Maybe because he's here,' Kaelen suggests, glancing back at Cody, who still hasn't moved.

But I refute him again. 'He's in a lot of years. There's a reason she sent me to 2032. I just don't know what it is.'

'OK,' Kaelen concedes. 'What about the other numbers?'

I study the sequence. 'If 32 is the year,' I say, pointing to it, 'then it's only logical the two numbers before it are also part of the date.'

'7 12 32,' Kaelen reads aloud.

'July 12, 2032.' Excitement is boiling up inside me. And even though I know we have different motivations — even though I know once he acquires what he's been sent for he won't hesitate to rip me away from Zen — I feel a kind of bond forming between us. The connection of a shared goal. A common ground.

I glance at Kaelen out of the corner of my eye and for a split second our gazes connect. That energy exchange starts. That pull. He flashes me the smallest of smiles.

But the expression itself isn't what surprises me. It's the emotion behind it.

It feels genuine.

Real.

Not programmed.

I blink and focus back on the countertop.

'If that's the date,' Kaelen speculates, 'then the next two figures must be the time.'

With a flick of his fingers, he pulls the 21 and the 15 out of the sequence and places them above the original string.

21:15.

'9:15 in the evening.'

We both study the last two numbers: 77 and 78.

'When I was with Maxxer I received a message from Alixter,' I point out. 'It was a pair of two-digit numbers, like this.'

'GPS coordinates?' Kaelen suggests.

I nod. 'That's what I'm thinking. She knows I would recognize them because I followed them once before. And if that's the case, then she's telling me to go to this location –' I point to the last two numbers – 'on this date –' I indicate the first two numbers – 'at this exact time.' I point to the middle sequence.

Kaelen is one step ahead of me, tapping an icon at the bottom of the counter. A huge map of New York spreads across the glass, taking up every inch of the surface.

He drags the coordinates into a search box above the map.

Immediately the map morphs and we're flying over terrain, heading east, through the streets of New York City, off the edge of a bridge, and into the sea. We travel over miles and miles of ocean, veering up. We cross more land. I catch sight of labels on the map.

Ireland.

Norway.

Sweden.

Russia.

The terrain has turned snowy white. And still we travel upward. Into a swatch of crystal-blue water teeming with massive chunks of ice. The map identifies it as the Kara Sea.

And then suddenly it stops. A small, blinking orange dot indicates that we've arrived at the location of the coordinates.

Near the top of the world.

In the middle of nowhere.

'Where is that?' I ask, tilting my head to try to find a landmass nearby. An island. Even, perhaps, something floating in the water. But there doesn't seem to be anything around for miles.

Of course, I think. Where would you go if you never wanted to be found? What location would ensure that anyone who tried to transesse there without an exact date and time would die?

'She's on the water?' Kaelen says, squinting at the map.

I shake my head, remembering the lesson I learned the last time I followed GPS coordinates: they're two-dimensional. They only track left and right. Not up and down.

'No,' I say with certainty, tapping the blinking orange dot. 'She's *under* it.'

48

UNSHAKEN

The lamps have all been turned off in the guest room. The only light emanates from Cody's computer and the various monitors surrounding Zen's bed. I've asked for five minutes alone and, surprisingly, Kaelen has granted it.

He and Cody wait in the living room. When I left, Cody had gone back to playing a game – a different one this time. Clearly something more modern because for the past five minutes, life-size three-dimensional street fighters have been battling each other in the middle of the living room. They look so real, I don't know how you can tell the difference between the game and reality.

Maybe you can't.

Maybe this is all a game.

A game about a sixteen-year-old girl with golden-brown hair and purple eyes who can lift heavy objects, run like the wind, speak every language, mentally calculate like a computer. Who is beautiful and strong. Who was created by science to be perfect but whose life is far from it.

In this level, she is forced to find a cure to save the boy she loves while being tormented by the company who made her. If she is to survive and move on, she must find the missing scientist, the only one who knows how to save her soul mate, all the while trying to fight the strange, inexplicable, and completely unfounded attraction she feels for the agent who was sent to apprehend her.

And then, when it's over, regardless of whether I succeed or fail, I'll simply switch off the console and go back to my real life. Whatever that may be.

If only . . .

I close the door quietly behind me. I can still hear the sounds of death and avatars falling in the next room from Cody's game. I try to block it out. To focus everything I have left on the boy in front of me.

The one who found me brainwashed and helpless on the other side of that concrete wall. The one who convinced me that everything I knew, everything I *ever* knew, was a lie. The one who risked everything to take me away from it all.

The one who saved me.

And now it's my turn to save him.

I pull a chair up to the side of the bed and sit down. Zen's eyes are closed. His chest rises and falls in an uneven rhythm.

'Zen,' I begin. But it quickly occurs to me that I don't know what to say. I'll be leaving in a few minutes. With Kaelen. I'll be going to find Maxxer. Going to find the cure.

But I don't really want to explain all that to him. For one, I'm not sure he can even hear me. But mostly because, if I somehow can't return, I don't want that to be the last thing I ever said to him.

The truth of the matter is, I can't be sure that I'll ever come back here.

Although he's never said it outright, I'm confident that

Kaelen's mission wasn't just to get the cure from Maxxer and then leave me to go on my way and live out my life with Zen. He has his own motives. His own plan outside the one we've created together.

And I can't guarantee that I'll be able to outsmart him. Outmanoeuvre him.

'I'm like you . . . Only better.'

So what do I say to Zen now? How can I possibly describe what I'm feeling?

I'm *scared* isn't enough.

I'm *sorry* isn't enough.

Even *I love you* doesn't seem like enough.

And *goodbye* will only make me lose my nerve to go.

My time alone with him is running out and I fear that I may have to leave him with only silence.

But somehow, from somewhere inside me, the answer comes. I know what I have to say. The only thing I can say.

Although they are borrowed words and stolen letters, the meaning – the soul – belongs to me.

I press my lips together to keep myself from shuddering as I slowly reach out and press two fingers to the centre of his forehead, just above the bridge of his nose. My throat is constricting. Tears are burning my eyes. But I manage to recite the entire poem – our poem – in a clear, unbroken voice.

> 'Let me not to the marriage of true minds
> Admit impediments. Love is not love
> Which alters when it alteration finds,
> Or bends with the remover to remove:
> O, no! it is an ever-fixèd mark,
> That looks on tempests and is never shaken;
> It is the star to every wandering bark,
> Whose worth's unknown, although his height be taken.

Love's not Time's fool, though rosy lips and cheeks
Within his bending sickle's compass come;
Love alters not with his brief hours and weeks,
But bears it out even to the edge of doom.
If this be error and upon me proved,
I never writ, nor no man ever loved.'

I hear the creak of a footstep on the other side of the door. Kaelen coming to tell me that my time is up. I expect the door to open but, surprisingly, it remains closed, allowing me a few more private seconds with Zen.

I bend down close to his ear and whisper, 'I am not shaken.'

Then I place my lips to his, feeling the fire of his fever burning me. Feeling the lingering threads of his life reach out to me. Entangle me. Weave together with mine. Creating something that can never be duplicated.

I invite it in, finding solace in the heat. The energy. Letting it spread through me. I commit it to memory. Not knowing how long his lips will stay warm. Not knowing how far away I will be if they cool forever.

Miles?

Months?

Years?

Decades?

Regardless of what happens next, this is what I want to take with me. This is what I want to remember. And even if they win, even if I never return, even if they bring me back and destroy my identity and wipe my mind completely clean, this is what I will always have.

This is what will remain unforgotten.

49

MEANING

I step out into the hallway and close the door behind me.
When I reach the living room, Cody looks up from his game.
'How is he?'

I shrug. 'The same.'

He pauses the game. 'I'll go check on his fluids and get a
download of his vitals.'

Cody passes me on the way to the guest room. I stop him
right as he's about to disappear behind the door. 'Cody?'

Cody looks at me. 'Yeah?'

'If I don't come back,' I say, my gaze flickering momentarily
to Kaelen. 'If something happens,' I amend, 'take care of him.
However you can.'

Cody holds my gaze for a moment, offering me silent agreement, before slipping behind the door. '*Good luck*' is the last
thing he says to me.

'What did you tell him?' Kaelen asks, and I see his expression
shift from his usual blank, detached look to one of curiosity
and intrigue.

I turn back. 'Who? Cody?'

'No,' Kaelen corrects. 'Zen. I heard words. I understood each one. But together they are nonsensical.'

The poem. He's talking about the Shakespeare sonnet.

'You heard me?' I think of the creak I heard outside the door and my voice turns accusing. 'Were you listening?'

He raises a single eyebrow and I feel stupid. Of course he heard me. I was only one room away and his hearing is as good as mine. If not better.

'It was a poem,' I admit begrudgingly. I hate that I have to share my last private moment with Zen with Kaelen. That he intruded in it without invitation.

'What's a poem?' he asks.

'It's . . .' I struggle to describe it, wondering what words Zen once used to explain it to me. Because just like Kaelen, in the beginning, I didn't know what a poem was either. And at one point, it was probably nonsensical to me, too. 'It's like a story,' I try, 'but more beautiful. And cryptic. Almost like it's written in code. You have to really feel the words to understand the meaning.'

'What is the meaning?' he asks.

I bite my lip and look to the floor. 'That specific poem is about love. The kind that never goes away.'

'Is that what you feel for Zen?' The bluntness of his question catches me by surprise. But I suppose it's simply a testament to his nature. His programming. The way he was made. If there's one thing Alixter hated about me it was the fact that I fell in love. And that means it's pretty safe to say that Kaelen was created without that ability. Alixter would have made sure not to make the same mistake twice.

So I guess I can't really expect him to understand anything I say about Zen. But I answer regardless. 'Yes.'

'What does it feel like?'

I stop and think. I've never actually had to describe it before. I'm not even sure I can. And even if I could, I know for a fact it wouldn't have any impact on Kaelen. He's clearly so intricately conditioned, whatever I say is going to sound like gibberish to him.

But I decide to make an attempt anyway. For Zen.

'It feels like . . .' I begin hesitantly, '. . . falling from the sky.'

As I suspected, confusion registers on Kaelen's face.

'Thrilling and terrifying at the same time,' I add.

Kaelen ponders for a while. 'Falling from the sky equals death.'

I bite my lip to keep from laughing. 'Only if there's a ground underneath you,' I counter.

'There is.'

I shrug. 'But what if there wasn't? What if you simply fell forever? Never knowing if there was a ground beneath you or not.'

'It's not possible,' Kaelen rationalizes. 'Unless you were falling in a vacuum.'

I smile. 'So maybe that's what love is. Falling in a vacuum.'

I sneak a peek at Kaelen out of the corner of my eye. His face is very serious and intense. 'That does not sound enjoyable,' he finally concludes.

I nod, imagining that I probably felt that way once, too.

'Why did you choose to do it?'

His question startles me. 'Fall in love?'

'Yes.'

'I didn't.'

Three lines appear between his eyebrows. 'I don't understand.'

'It's not something you choose. It's something that simply happens to you.'

'Against your *will*?' Kaelen clarifies, and I definitely don't miss the fact that he's chosen to use the exact same words I used with him. When we first met and I asked if it bothered him that he was created without his permission.

'I suppose so.' I bite my lower lip, which has begun to tremble.

'I would refuse it,' Kaelen puts in confidently.

I shake my head. 'I don't think you can. Because once it's happened, once you even *realize* it's happened, it's too late. It's already changed you. And I don't think you can go back.'

Kaelen turns to face me. I can feel his eyes on me. Burning my cheeks. I keep my gaze forward. 'In our world,' he states defiantly, 'you can always go back. You can unlove.'

A shiver runs through me as my mind dissects the variety of meanings that are so cleverly hidden in that sentence. I'm anxious to get off this topic and move on to the important one.

Finding Maxxer. Getting Zen's cure.

I clear my throat. 'So have you thought about how you want to do this?'

He stands rigidly next to the kitchen counter. 'Dr Maxxer is most likely in a submarine or other submerged vessel. We will transesse to the GPS coordinates together. And there we will wait until we receive further instruction or indication of subsequent steps.'

'In the middle of the ocean?' I ask. 'That's probably freezing?'

Kaelen doesn't appear to be bothered by this detail. 'Should it become clear that we are not in the right place, we will transesse back here and reevaluate our options.'

I wince and feel my body stiffen. The thought of transessing with him, letting him control my destination, makes my insides curl and twist. I've avoided it this long and I still have a nagging suspicion that this has all been one giant trick. A ploy to get me back to Diotech. That as soon as my locket is open and he touches me, I'll be inside my prison cell with a scientist hovering above, ready to dissect my brain and make me 'agreeable'.

Make me more like Kaelen.

But I quickly reassure myself that if Kaelen wanted to bring me back there, he would have done it already. He had countless opportunities while I was unconscious. While my wounds were healing. In fact, he didn't have to take me to 2032 at all. He could have brought me to the compound straight from the fire.

Even still, as Kaelen stalks menacingly towards me, fishing the locket out from under his shirt, my breathing quickens. My heart races. I feel an itchy anxiety trickle down my back.

'Wait,' I say, holding out my hand. He stops. 'I'm not sure we've thought this through properly.'

Kaelen's head clicks ever so slightly to the side, indicating that he's willing to hear me out.

'Maxxer left these clues for me. She's expecting me to show up. Probably alone. What if we get there and she refuses to give us any further instruction because she sees I'm with you? I don't think she's going to like the fact that I showed up with a Diotech agent.'

'You're not going alone,' Kaelen states blankly.

I had a feeling that was going to be his response.

'Well, what if that's the only option?'

'It's not.'

'You don't know that for sure,' I point out.

'I was given specific instructions to follow you until Dr Maxxer's location was disclosed and the antidote was obtained,' Kaelen argues, sounding slightly exasperated.

This is the first time he's admitted any details of his mission. We both seem to realize it at the same time. Kaelen's eye twitches faintly.

'Fine,' I say.

He eyes the space between us. I estimate it's about seven steps. I can tell he's calculating the same thing. But approaching me means getting close to me. Letting that peculiar magnetism draw us together. Touching me means electricity. Heat waves. Strange things that neither one of us seem to be able to explain or understand.

Intentionally getting this close, making skin-to-skin contact goes against all the unspoken rules we've established over the past two days.

But it's the only way.

And we both know it.

He takes one step. Then another. I notice how his paces seem to slow, get smaller, as he nears me. But he keeps coming. The hum of energy begins. The dizzying spirals of air. I feel it heaving me towards it. Like a vortex. Like an unavoidable fall.

Like gravity.

He reaches up and opens the necklace. I know he won't let me wear it. That's too risky. Which means he has to hold it up to my skin to activate the gene.

He pulls on the chain, drawing the heart-shaped amulet out from under the collar of his shirt. I can't help but notice how wrong it is to see it around his neck. My gift from Zen. The symbol of everything we have. Held hostage by this tall, handsome Diotech agent.

And yet, it's appropriate as well.

Diotech has always come between Zen and me.

Kaelen takes another step. The pull becomes more intense. I attempt to anchor my feet to the ground to keep from being yanked towards him. To keep from launching myself into him, my arms around him, my lips against his. And never letting go.

He towers over me. I look up to meet his gaze. I know it won't help anything. I know it will only make this worse. But there's nothing I can do to stop it.

I see the strain on his face. The struggle. We are both fighting.

He extends the locket out, towards my chest. The chain doesn't reach. I can see the annoyance on his face as he's forced to come even closer to me. His feet step between mine. I feel his pant legs brushing against my own. His heavy breath hits my skin like an intoxicating wind. My brain turns to pulp. My limbs turn to liquid. I'm dizzy. So dizzy.

I swallow and attempt to breathe through my mouth.

Finally the chain reaches, the cold, hard surface of the back of the locket chills my body as he presses it against my chest, below my collarbone.

I can almost feel the engraving digging into my skin.

$S + Z = 1609$

How obsolete it's become, knowing we can never go back there. Not even if I succeed today. That promise is long lost. That dream is over.

Kaelen's hand rises up. I'm instantly drawn to it. It takes every ounce of strength I have not to press my cheek into his palm.

He looks at his hand, seemingly trying to decide where to place it. Where to make contact. What body part will yield the smallest effect?

I don't think it matters.

Wherever he touches me, I will feel it everywhere. In my feet. In my toes. In my legs. In my chest. In my heart.

Completely, utterly, undeniably against my will.

Against both of our wills.

I lift my hand up, too, silently offering it as a neutral meeting point. He understands. His hand drifts towards mine, our palms about to meet, our fingers about to collide. I close my eyes, anticipating his touch. Anticipating the delicious sting.

All the while still fearing what will happen when it comes and where I'll be when I open my eyes again.

I can feel the heat of his skin just before it makes contact. And then suddenly I am surrounded by white. A warm light. I am floating. My feet are off the ground. And I don't know if it's because we've left or because we're still here.

Every emptiness I've ever felt is suddenly full.

Every silence I've ever heard is suddenly singing.

Every sadness that's ever come over me is lost beyond discovery.

Our bodies converge. Melt. Combine. As though we are two people, made out of the same foreign substance. Separated for centuries. Waiting to come back together.

Waiting for right now.

And then I feel the piercing, cold rush of the icy water slamming against me from all sides, knocking me back and forth. Splashing into my nose and mouth. I instinctively kick and flail with my arms to stay afloat. Hold my breath.

After a few seconds, I break through the surface. And when I open my eyes, I see that I am exactly where I started.

Floating in the middle of an endless, dark ocean.

PART 3

THE
CHOICE

50

BEHOLDER

Unlike the last time I found myself in the middle of an ocean, I don't have any broken aeroplane parts to keep me afloat. Kaelen and I are forced to flap our hands and feet to keep our heads above the surface. Not to mention keep ourselves warm. Despite our being built to withstand extreme temperatures, this water is something else. Like daggers of ice stabbing every inch of my body.

It takes us both a few seconds to get the hang of paddling in place and learn how to exert the least amount of energy, but after that it becomes easy. Like running. I could do it for hours and never tire. Despite the choppy current of the water and the occasional larger wave that slaps us both in the face.

Once we've managed to stabilize, Kaelen reaches down and snaps the locket shut. 'I'm going to swim down a ways. Perhaps I can see something.'

'I'll go with you,' I reply immediately, knowing that from here on I cannot let him out of my sight for an instant.

We both suck in a large breath and dive under. As soon as I

open my eyes, I'm surprised by how well I can see. I knew my enhanced vision allowed me to see across long distances, and through the dark, but I expected everything underwater to be blurry and distorted. It's not.

The world below is crisp and clear and sparkling. Kaelen seems to be pausing to reflect on this discovery as well.

I watch him carefully, waiting for a cue. He makes his way down deeper. I still can't see the bottom. Even with my enhanced vision. Which means we must not even be close to it. I don't know much about submarines, apart from the limited knowledge I received via Reese's video game, but I have a feeling it's not all that accurate. I sincerely doubt most submarines blow soap bubbles or have magical instruments that make you travel faster. But I do know that if there's any kind of underwater vessel passing below us, I certainly can't see it. And judging by the expression on Kaelen's face, neither can he.

He dives a little deeper and I follow. This is my first time swimming. That I can remember, at least, but I already know that I like it. And I'm good at it. The feeling of manoeuvring through the water is soothing.

It's also very quiet under here. Peaceful.

I'm not sure I've ever heard such silence before. With my superior hearing, there's always noise somewhere. Even if it's far off in the distance. A fox howling five miles away, people arguing in the apartment across the street, a bus approaching a kerb three blocks away.

But down here the world seems to have finally gone to sleep. Apart from the gentle *shhh* sound of the water against my ears, and the occasional ripple-splash of Kaelen's stroke, my ears pick up nothing.

It's wonderful.

For a second, I'm almost able to forget how cold it is and

everything that's happening above the surface. I'm almost able to feel OK again.

Kaelen and I make a small circle below the spot where we landed. There is still no sign of anything apart from a few schools of fish that pass.

I'm not sure how long an average person can hold their breath, but I estimate we've been down here at least three minutes and I don't feel the need to surface anytime soon. However, I do notice that the deeper we go, the more pressure I feel between my temples. And in my chest.

Kaelen must feel it, too, because after attempting to paddle even further into the depths, he suddenly stops and starts to float back upward.

We break the surface a few moments later and I wipe the water from my face and eyes. We're both shivering.

'Did you see anything?' Kaelen enquires, his teeth chattering slightly.

I shake my head. 'You?'

'Nothing.'

We tread water in silence but I keep my gaze tightly on Kaelen. His wet hair is slicked back against his head, revealing more of his smooth, arched forehead than I've ever seen before. I can't help noticing the way the moonlight reflects off the moisture in his hair. Like his loose waves are woven with tiny diamonds.

He senses me looking at him and turns, the light momentarily catching one of his brilliant blue-green eyes.

It would be ridiculous for me to deny how beautiful those eyes are. Breathtaking. Even more so against the deep blue sea and darkened sky behind him.

Then I think about Zen's soulful brown eyes. When I look into them I see everything. I see love. I see light. I see home.

And yet, somehow, sadly, they seem so mild in comparison to Kaelen's.

It's like regardless of what nature can do, regardless of how hard it works, how hard it tries, how magnificent the results, science always manages to find a way to surmount it. To make things not just magnificent . . . but perfect. And I find myself thinking how unfair that is. How devious.

Like science is somehow cheating at the game.

And nature simply doesn't stand a chance.

How do you compete with eyes like that? With skin that flawless? With hair that glitters in the moonlight?

The answer is obvious to me: you can't.

But still, it doesn't stop me from wondering what Kaelen sees when he looks at the world. Does he even have the ability to perceive with subjectivity? To look at something and think it's beautiful? Or has Alixter removed that, too?

And somehow, *that* is the saddest idea of all.

What does Kaelen see when he looks at the sunrise? Is it just a sequence of atmospheric pigments and light patterns? Or can he recognize that it's masterful? What about when he looks at the stars? The ocean? The snow falling from the sky? Does he only see frozen water? Or does he notice the exquisiteness of each unique snowflake?

What about when he looks at *me*? Does he see another genetically enhanced, scientifically created, Diotech-manufactured superhuman? One whose programming has gone awry? Or . . .

Does he think I'm beautiful?

The thought makes my stomach turn and for a moment I stop paddling and begin to sink. Kaelen is quick to grab me and pull me back up, and once again the touch of his skin is like nothing I've ever felt before. It's like the world comes alive. I come alive.

The sharp cold of the water is gone. I am suddenly swimming in liquid fire.

And then, just as he lets go, taking all of that energy and warmth with him, his thumb brushes curiously against my forehead. Reading my thoughts. Stealing my memories.

But suddenly it doesn't feel like stealing any more.

I *want* to give them to him.

I want him to see things the way I see them. Know what I know. Feel what I feel.

'I do,' he says quietly, answering my unspoken question as his fingertips slip from my skin.

I *do*.

Those two little words feel like buoys drifting up from somewhere unknown to rest beneath my feet, to keep me afloat. Making me weightless.

But which question was he answering? The one about seeing the sunrise? Or the snow? Or the one about me? About what he thinks when he looks at me?

It has to be the first. Or the second. The sunrise. Or the snow.

Except I know it's not.

I know like I know which way is up. Like I know that if I stop swimming I will drown.

I know which question he was answering. Regardless of what he makes of the snow and sunrise and stars, he thinks I'm beautiful.

And somehow that changes things.

I don't know how. I don't know why. I don't even know what is different, but I know that it is.

We've managed to drift a few feet apart and I start to swim towards him. But my foot seems to be caught on something below. I attempt to yank it free but I'm unable to.

And then suddenly I'm being pulled downward. With incredible force. My head drops below the surface of the water. Through the ripples of the current I hear Kaelen call out my name.

I fight to pull myself up, managing to break through. But once again, I feel a tug on my leg, dragging me downward.

Kaelen swims towards me, grasps my hand. But our fingers are wet and slippery, they slide right through.

'Kaelen!' I yell, reaching for him. The hold around my ankle is firm and I'm suddenly back under.

It's just like my nightmare. Except everything is upside down. Everything is reversed.

It's not Kaelen attempting to hold me under. It's him attempting to keep me afloat.

The water floods into my open mouth, threatening to suffocate me. I try to cough it out but it just won't expel. I kick and thrash in vain. My hand reaches up, grappling for something to hold on to.

I feel the cold metal of my locket chain around his neck. I clench my fingers around it and pull. It snaps and plummets into the water with me. I clutch it tight, struggling with slick fingers to open the clasp.

I manage to pry apart the tiny door just as the water streams into my lungs. Arctic and salty. Tasting of loss. Just like in my dream, I have no choice but to let it in as I'm dragged further and further into the unknown depths of the sea.

I don't resurface.

51

VIAL

The next thing I know, I'm coughing up water on a cold concrete floor. The salt burns my throat and my lungs but I finally get it all out. I blink and look around me, shuddering from the cold wet clothes clinging to my body. I'm in the middle of a long, narrow room with a domed ceiling that appears to be made of glass. Above it is dark swirling water. Either it's moving or we are.

The locket lies by my hands. The chain is broken. Yet again. I scoop it up and place it in the pocket of my drenched pants.

Next to me stands a man in a rubber suit with a mask. He has a metal tank strapped to his back. A thin cord winds around to a device in his mouth. I presume it's some kind of contraption for breathing underwater.

'You nearly drowned me!' I accuse him, my voice still raw from the coughing and the scratchy water.

He pulls the device from his mouth and exhales. 'Sorry about that. I had to get you away from your friend.'

With effort I push myself to my feet and attempt to stand.

I'm still wobbly and soaking wet. A puddle forms at my feet. 'Why does everyone keep calling him that? He's not my . . .' But I stop talking. It's not even worth trying to explain what Kaelen is to me. Especially when I'm not quite sure myself.

'Whatever he is,' the man goes on, 'Dr Maxxer gave me strict instructions to bring you alone.'

'Maxxer,' I say softly, glancing at my surroundings with new eyes, feeling the same peculiar animosity course through me at the mention of her name. 'She's here, isn't she?'

He nods and pulls the mask from his face. I immediately recognize his small eyes, round nose, and pinched mouth. But I can't think of where I might have met him before.

He smiles. 'I'll take you to see her now.'

He gestures towards the end of the narrow room and I start to walk but eventually drag to a halt. 'But wait. What about my . . . what about him?' I point upward at the domed glass ceiling, into the swirling sea.

I'm surprised to hear myself ask the question. I shouldn't be worried about Kaelen or where he is or whether or not he drowns out there. Without even trying, I somehow managed to accomplish my goal. I found Maxxer and at the same time was able to evade him. Plus, I have the locket. Which means everything is going to be OK. I can get the cure, transesse back to Zen, and, hopefully, this will all be over in a matter of hours.

But then why do I feel so awful?

Why do I feel so hollow?

I can't possibly *want* him to be here. He would only cause complications. He would only get in my way. He was sent here to get the cure for Alixter – my enemy. And then most likely, he was planning to bring me back with him.

So why on earth would I care that he's not here?

I don't.

I won't.

'Maxxer only trusts you,' the vaguely familiar man explains. 'She won't allow anyone else admittance on this vessel.'

I try to respond. But even a simple word like OK has trouble making it past my lips. It gets lodged somewhere in the middle, choking me.

I cough, expelling another few drops of seawater.

'Right this way,' the man says. He opens a door at the end of the domed-top room and we walk through it, down a dark corridor. When he leads me through the second doorway, at the end, I have to stop. A small gasp escapes my lips as I gaze upon the miraculous giant chamber that lies before me.

It's two storeys high with floor-to-ceiling windows that look out upon miles and miles of black ocean. An artificial fire roars in a clear cube-shaped fireplace in the centre of the room. A curved sateen sofa sits atop plush white carpet, forming an S shape around a glass coffee table with a single white flower in a vase in the centre. A winding spiral staircase coils up to a second-floor loft that overlooks the entire room.

On either side of the staircase stands a very large, very burly man. They are dressed in matching white uniforms from head to toe. I find their imposing placement odd, but I refrain from remarking on it.

'I can't believe we're under*water*,' I say instead. To no one in particular.

But it's a familiar woman's voice that answers me. 'Pretty spectacular, isn't it?'

I look up in the direction of the sound. Dr Rylan Maxxer stands on the balcony of the loft gazing down at me. She looks exactly the same as I remember her. Silvery-grey hair cut bluntly across her forehead and along her shoulders. Black-rimmed glasses hugging her slender face. A short frame so slender it makes her look slightly emaciated.

I'm not sure why, but somehow I knew I would some day see her again. That the day we said goodbye was not the end.

But what I didn't expect was the way I would feel when I did.

That unusual hotness starts to gurgle in my stomach. It bubbles up, stinging my chest. I suddenly feel furious. Outraged. Which is ridiculous because I clearly have no reason to be angry. Maxxer has only proved to be an asset.

She helped me when I needed it.

She answered all my questions about Diotech and transession and my past.

In fact, she brought me *back* to Zen.

And now she's led me here.

Maxxer is an escapee. Just like me. She fled Diotech after she discovered how corrupt they had become. How immoral Alixter really was. We are the same in that way.

But that doesn't stop me from feeling this strange, unfounded rage when I look upon her. It's not powerful. Almost subtle. Like it's brewing below the surface, heating behind my eyeballs, simmering in my chest.

I attempt to push the feeling away.

Maxxer descends the stairs, looking somewhat elegant despite her plain black pants and red sweater.

When she reaches the bottom, she walks towards me and takes my hands. 'Sera,' she says with a bright, beaming smile. 'Welcome to my command centre. So nice of you to come.'

I have to laugh. 'You didn't give me much of a choice.'

She chuckles at my comment. 'Sorry about all the theatrics. You see, I simply had to do it that way. I couldn't risk you getting caught and your memories being scanned. This was the only way I knew how to get you safely to me. And to protect my location.'

'Actually,' I begin, 'about that . . .'

She tilts her head and gives me a sceptical look. 'What is it?'

'Diotech did scan my brain. And somehow they knew that you left me those memories.'

She nods. 'I was afraid of that. They must have seen the imprint.'

'Imprint?'

'There are only a handful of computers capable of creating time-delayed recalls and I have one of them. Each one imprints the memory with a special code, like a brand, signifying which computer created it. That's how they would have immediately known it was me who implanted them. But as long as they weren't able to access them, we should be safe.'

'Yes, but,' I continue, a dull pain starting in my chest, 'they sent someone to follow me here. An agent. Except he's different from all the others. He's . . . like me.'

'Only better.'

I leave this part out.

She inhales sharply, clearly not expecting this. 'And where is he now?'

The dull pain starts to stab as I nod towards the windows. 'Out there somewhere. I don't know. I was pulled under and he was left behind.'

Maxxer flashes a satisfied smile in the direction of the man who led me here. 'Well done, Trestin.'

He nods tightly in response.

'Don't worry,' Maxxer replies gently. 'He's long gone now. We're a good three miles from the coordinates I directed you to. Another precaution I took. Trestin was instructed to transesse there and back with you. So it seems as though we've outsmarted them.' She beams again.

I smile, too. Because it feels appropriate. A minor triumph over Diotech. But the subtle celebration distresses me. Makes

311

my stomach flip. It feels so . . . so . . .

Wrong.

I don't speak, however. I reassure myself that Kaelen can't drown. He's a strong swimmer. Like me. Plus, he can transesse out of the water whenever he wants. He won't stay there.

This eases my discomfort.

He can't find us. But he won't perish either.

For just a moment, I allow myself to hold his face in my mind, focusing on his bright aquamarine eyes and creamy white skin. I wish him a silent goodbye. I've won. And that means I won't be seeing Kaelen ever again.

Exactly as it should be.

And yet, somehow, I always thought victory would feel . . . I don't know . . .

Better.

Dr Maxxer strolls over to a counter indented in the far wall. It is backlit with a soft blue light and stocked with numerous bottles of liquid. 'Would you like something to drink?' she asks. 'We have a fully stocked bar.'

I shrug. 'Sure.'

I watch as she removes two glasses from a shelf, drops a few ice cubes into each, and pours a fluorescent green liquid over them.

'Trestin,' she says sweetly to the man who brought me in here, 'give us a few minutes to catch up, would you?'

The man eyes me and I swear I see doubt flash over his face. 'You'll be OK?'

She smiles and gestures towards the two men in white still standing motionless on either side of the staircase. 'I'll be fine.'

'Of course, Doctor,' Trestin replies, and then disappears through the door, closing it behind him.

Dr Maxxer invites me to sit on the S-shaped couch and I oblige. She takes a seat next to me and hands me one of the glasses. I stare down at the strange green drink with trepidation.

'It's an energy drink,' she tells me with pride. 'My own creation. I modified the molecular structure of caffeine to make it ten times more potent without the jitters or the crash.'

I'm not sure what most of those words mean but I smile politely regardless.

'Who are they?' I ask, glancing at the men in white.

'Bodyguards,' she says bluntly.

'To protect you against *me?*'

She laughs and takes a sip of her drink. 'Heavens, no.' But I notice that her voice rises a few octaves when she says it and she doesn't make eye contact with me. Instead she hides her face behind her glass. She swallows and presses the bottom of it into her palm. 'To protect me against the unknown. It's a crazy world we live in.' She gestures to me and herself. 'Full of so many surprises. Don't you agree?'

'Yes.' I sniff the drink. It smells rancid and bitter. I place it down on the table.

'But don't worry,' Maxxer assures me, 'we can speak freely in front of them.' She leans in close and whispers, 'I adjust their memories at the end of each day.'

I shoot a wary look towards the men in white, feeling sorry for them. Then I eye the door through which the man who brought me here just disappeared. 'Why did he look so familiar to me?' I ask.

Maxxer's gaze shifts uneasily towards the door. 'Trestin?' She swats her hand in the air. 'Oh, he has one of those faces.'

'One of those faces?'

'Meaning he looks familiar to everyone regardless of whether you've met him or not.' Her knee starts to bounce.

Why does she seem so nervous?

'But I *have* met him,' I argue. 'I'm almost certain of it.'

313

'I'm sure you have many questions,' Maxxer says dismissively, 'but first I believe we have some business to settle.'

I raise my eyebrows. 'We do?'

She takes another sip of her drink. 'Of course. It's the reason you came, isn't it?'

'The cure,' I say automatically.

She exhales, seemingly in relief. 'Yes. I imagine Zen is very sick.' She sighs apologetically. 'An unexpected side effect of DZ227, I'm afraid.'

'DZ227?'

'Sorry. It's the official nomenclature of the transession gene. It would seem the way it was designed was simply too powerful for the human body to take in. It causes the natural immune system to attack itself, thinking it's being infested by a virus. Anyone who has had the transplant, depending on their own chemical make-up and how often they transesse, would be dead within a year.'

'Including Alixter,' I verify, eager to finally have the confirmation that Kaelen would never give me.

Maxxer smiles. 'Yes. I imagine that's why he sent the agent to follow you. And why I had to take such precautions when I brought you here. He's probably fairly ill. And fairly desperate. Which, of course, only makes you that much more valuable.'

'Me?' I repeat sceptically.

She cocks her head. 'You *have* noticed that you are not affected by the gene?'

I quickly make a move for my pocket. Out of the corner of my eye, I swear I see Maxxer flinch at my sudden motion. I withdraw the locket on the broken chain. 'That's because Rio made me this. It activates my gene when it's open. He was worried about what the gene would do if I couldn't turn it off.'

'Wise man,' Maxxer commends. 'But in reality, he had nothing to worry about. You're not like the rest of us, Sera. I'm sure you've figured that out by now.'

I look away. I think about the horrified look on the old Chinese man's face when he held my wrists and declared my blood to be too strong. I think about Blackthorn, the horse on the Pattinsons' farm, and the distrust I saw in his eyes every time I entered his stall. I think about the screams of rage directed at me as I was led through the streets of London. I think about my legs and how the fire ripped through them, shredded my skin, and gnawed at my muscle, and yet there's not a single scar of evidence.

So yes, I've figured it out. But I've spent the last six months wishing it wasn't true. Wishing I *was* like the rest of them.

'Your body, your mind, your genes, everything about you was perfected by science. I could transplant this gene into you a thousand times and it wouldn't affect you.'

She may as well just say it. She may as well just tell me what I am. Or rather, what I'm not.

I'm not human.

'Which is probably why Alixter had to create another synthetic being,' she adds. 'Because neither he nor his other goons can transesse any more. Without that new agent he created, they'd have no hope of ever finding me. Or you.'

Once again, Kaelen's face flits into my mind and my stomach wrenches with guilt.

That's why he wasn't sick.

Because he's like me. He might very well be the *only* one ever to be like me. And yet I left him. I abandoned him.

'But Zen,' Maxxer goes on, oblivious to the torment in my mind, 'Zen's body didn't stand a chance. It was too fragile. Like the rest of us.'

Fragile. It's the exact right word to describe the way he looked when I left. Ready to crumble. Ready to shatter into a million pieces. On the brink of death.

He never deserved it.

He never deserved this atrocity.

He never deserved me.

Maxxer places her glass on the table with a clink and rises to her feet. 'Which brings us to the reason you're here.'

As I watch her walk across the room, I can feel my heartbeat accelerate. And that mysterious anger begins to resurface at the thought of what will happen next. My palms feel greasy and wet. I rub them anxiously against my wet pants and stand up, following her with my eyes. She ascends the stairs gracefully, disappearing into the loft only to reappear a moment later holding a small, clear vial filled with an electric-blue liquid. She pauses at the top of the stairs, seeming to study my expression.

'This,' she begins, 'is a repressor for gene DZ227. When injected directly into the bloodstream it will permanently disable the transession gene. The immune system will cease its attacks against the body and the recipient will experience a full recovery, essentially reversing all negative effects of the gene transplant.'

My legs are aching with anticipation. My fists curl and uncurl involuntarily. I feel my muscles tightening. Like they're preparing to pounce. Attack.

The inexplicable wrath is boiling up, threatening to spill out of my mouth, my ears, my eye sockets. My whole body is hot. Searing hot. On fire. Like lava is running through my veins.

Just the sight of Dr Maxxer holding that vial suddenly sends a thunderbolt of fury through my body.

What is happening to me?

She descends the stairs slowly, never taking her eyes off me for a second. My mouth has suddenly gone dry. Bone dry. I rub my tongue around it, practically hearing the scratching sound it makes against the inside of my dehydrated cheek.

Maxxer seems to be moving in slow motion and when I look closely at her hand, the one holding the vial, I see that it's trembling.

Why? Why would it do that? Why would she possibly be afraid of me?

She glides towards the table and ever so carefully places the vial down on the glass surface.

I attempt to swallow but there's nothing to push down.

I glare at the tiny bottle in front of me. I take a step towards it, feeling fear rush over me. An inexplicable, paralysing fear.

I can't take it. I can't.

Something inside is fighting against me. A warning bell is ringing in my head.

Don't! it cries. *Don't take it!*

But I have to! This is what will save Zen! Why wouldn't I take it?

I press forward, ignoring the clamouring in my brain, the resistance in my muscles. I take another step. I'm within arm's length of the tiny bottle. I lean forward, my hand shaking violently as I reach for it.

The tips of my fingers graze the cool exterior of the vial and then . . .

CRASH!

I let out a shriek and leap back. Dr Maxxer rapidly withdraws five stairs up. Her bodyguards spring into action, surrounding the dark, wet figure that has seemingly dropped from the sky into the room, shattering the glass table in front of me, sending the vial flying across the room only to land with a soft thud against the carpet.

The figure – which I now see is a person – lies huddled on the ground, facedown, shaking. Shards of glass protrude from his skin.

The guards launch themselves on top of him, restraining him, pinning down his legs and arms. I hear the familiar sizzle of the Modifier and his body goes limp. The guard on the left pockets the device and together they flip him over so I can finally see his unconscious face.

I gasp for the second time in the past twenty minutes, breathing his name softly. Urgently.

'Kaelen.'

52

COMPELLED

Maxxer's usual calm and collected demeanour is suddenly shattered like the pieces of table now lying on her carpet. 'Who is this? Is this him? The Diotech agent they sent?'

I nod, fighting every inclination I have to bend down and touch his face.

'How did he find you!?' Maxxer roars.

'I don't know. I swear I don't know!'

'Your tracker.' She nods towards my left wrist. 'Did you feel it set off?'

I shake my head, realizing this is now the second time Kaelen has somehow managed to find me without the help of a tracking device.

Maxxer bites her lip in thought and sits down on the stairs. Without even looking over at Kaelen, she waves her hand and orders, 'Take him to the holding cell. Keep him deactivated.'

'Wait,' I say, watching helplessly as the two guards hoist Kaelen up by the armpits and drag him out of the room. 'I don't understand what's happening. How could he possibly—'

My thoughts and words come to a crashing halt when my eyes land on the tiny glass vial lying only a few feet away, shimmering blue against the soft white rug.

Zen.

I can fix him.

I can fix all of this.

Once again, I'm drawn towards the small bottle. I move towards it. My hand extending in the direction of its salvation. I kneel down before it, reach out, and . . .

'No! Wait!' Maxxer calls, launching to her feet.

But it's too late. The vial is already in my hands, clutched tightly. And then, suddenly, it's as though the world has turned a shade of red.

My mind empties.

My thoughts vanish.

A rolling storm of blackness seeps into my head, hiding everything from view – who I am, what I want, who I love. I am no longer me. I am someone else.

An entity fuelled by rage.

A brain capable of only one concept. One idea. One goal.

The hot ball of ferocity that had once been dancing around the edges of my consciousness is now all I can see. All I can feel. All I am.

It explodes inside me, the blast pushing me forward.

I rise obediently to my feet, storing the vial safely in my pocket.

For him.

For Alixter.

He needs it. And he needs me. My mission is only half complete.

I glance up. Maxxer's face is contorted in fear. The sight of her sends another frenzy of wrath bursting through me. It consumes me. It spreads to the very tips of my toes and fingers. My hands spasm with the anticipation of feeling her throat crush. My ears await the sound of her heart sputtering to a stop. My existence will not be complete until I watch the light fade from her eyes.

'Sera,' Maxxer tries, her voice cracking, laced with panic. But the sound of my name on her lips only fuels my fever.

I feel my legs instinctively bend into a crouch. My muscles coil. I spring forward, reaching her in a single, lightning-fast bound. I clobber her and we tumble down the last few stairs on to the floor below. Her head hits the final metal step, breaking open her skin. Blood flows, blooming red on the pristine white carpet.

She attempts to fight but her measly stature and human strength are no match for me. In an instant, I have flipped her on to her back. I sit astride her chest, one hand pressed against her windpipe.

Do it! a raspy voice from far in the back of my mind commands.

'Don't do it,' Maxxer pleads through her constricted throat. 'Sera, listen to me.'

Do it now!

I press harder. Maxxer squeaks. The air trapped in her lungs, desperate to get out. She opens her mouth again. 'This isn't you,' she manages to croak out. 'It's *them.*'

Them.

The word tumbles around in my abandoned brain. Like a leaf caught in the wind. I shake my head, trying to brush it away, but it won't stop echoing.

Them.

There.

Before.

The words Zen and I once used to talk about Diotech. To

talk about my former life. When I was held captive in a lab. When I was a prisoner.

Do it! the voice commands, sounding angry at my hesitance. *KILL HER!*

I let up ever so slightly, only enough to allow her to speak. 'What are you talking about?' I yell, the rage still piloting my body, still radiating out of my eyes and dripping into my voice.

'Diotech,' she chokes out. 'They're controlling you.'

No. That's not possible.

My brain is aching. Splitting in half. One side is still being controlled by that unyielding wrath. The other is trying to make sense of everything. Trying to hold on.

'How?' I scream. 'How are they doing it?'

'The . . . boy.' She's barely able to form the sounds. They come out choppy and hoarse.

Kaelen?

But how could he possibly—

I'm not given the opportunity to complete the thought. I feel myself being yanked into the air, thrown across the room. I land hard on the sofa, my legs tossed over my head. My neck makes a sickening cracking noise.

I hear Maxxer coughing violently. The air flowing hungrily back into her lungs. The sound of her life forces me to stand again, determined to put an end to it. But one of Maxxer's guards is already there beside me, shoving me down again. The black steel of his Modifier flashes into view.

And that's the last thing I see.

53

DISEASED

Music is what I wake to. Soft. Melodic. Soothing.

My eyelids feel like they've been sewn shut. I have to work hard to open them. Even more to focus my vision once I've succeeded. My pupils feel lazy. Not wanting to do what my brain is telling them to do. Because it would require too much effort.

Effort I can't muster.

When I'm finally able to stare at one thing long enough to make sense of it, I realize that I'm looking at the ceiling. Or rather through it, at dark swells of flowing water.

I am still on Maxxer's submarine.

We are still moving. To where? I don't know. I doubt she ever has a destination in mind. If she were wise, her only goal would be to never stop.

I try to push myself up but my arms don't work. And apparently neither do my legs. Or seemingly any other part.

Fortunately my lips seem able to form words. Although not very well.

'Whaa happened?'

'We gave you a sedative,' I hear Maxxer's voice respond. 'It should subdue the impulses.'

I see her face. She's hovering over me. I notice one of the guards attempting to pull her away but she brushes him off. 'I'll be fine. She has enough Cv9 running through her bloodstream to placate a killer whale,' Maxxer says.

I attempt to roll on to my side but that's a lost cause as well.

'Help her up,' Maxxer commands the guard, and suddenly I'm being hoisted into a seated position. My head is propped up by a pillow. My legs are adjusted in front of me. I can't move my head to look at her but thankfully Maxxer squats down in front of me so I don't have to.

She takes a deep breath, speaking almost to herself. 'I should have known they would send you.'

I'm able to blink, but that's about the extent of my mobility. I feel sleepy. I want to go to bed. But I also want answers. I command myself to stay awake and ask, 'Whaa?'

'While you were out, I did a quick scan of your brain. It appears they implanted a stimulated-response system. It's a kind of mental programming that will only activate when certain requirements are met. Similar to a TDR. In this case, it was set to go off as soon as you acquired the antidote from me. Basically it's computerized brainwashing.'

I think back to what I saw on the park bench. When I tried to convince Kaelen that there was more to life than being a machine. Something snapped inside him. He turned into an entirely different person. I surmised that I must have set off some kind of automated reaction that was built in to protect him from the truth.

I never even imagined I might have the same thing buried somewhere in me.

'Buh,' I try to argue. 'How? Wheh did they puh ih in?'

Maxxer presses her lips together. 'I have no idea. The agent they sent most likely installed it. Probably after he pulled you from the fire and you were unconscious.'

Yes, I think immediately.

The entire time I was recovering from the burns, he was keeping me sedated with the Modifier. He could have done it at any point during that time.

'Well, anyway,' Maxxer goes on, 'my guess is once they figured out I had left you the memory map, they knew I would only allow *you* access to me. So they created a back-up plan. They essentially turned you into an assassin without your knowledge.'

I feel ill. Like I might vomit.

This whole time, I've been carrying around a disease. An infestation in my mind. Like a bomb ready to explode. Except I was the bomb.

I thought I had finally escaped them. I thought I'd finally broken free. But no, it was just an illusion of freedom. They've been manipulating me from the moment I woke up in that room. From the moment I first laid eyes on Kaelen. And he knew.

He knew it all along.

And yet, even though I want to feel angry at him, I can't. All I feel is guilt. I judged him for being Alixter's personal robot. For being a brainless avatar in Alixter's real-life video game. But in reality, I was no better than him.

I was an avatar, too.

A puppet. Just waiting for Alixter to pull the right string to make me kill someone.

It turns out Zen and I both had the disease of Diotech running through us. Destroying us from the inside. Taking away our life. Our humanity. Our ability to choose our own destiny.

I feel tears welling in my eyes but my cheeks are so numb, I have no idea if they ever fall. My head slumps forward and I can't get it up again. Although to be perfectly honest, I don't really try all that hard.

Maxxer places a hand under my chin and props it back up.

Then she reaches out and gently brushes my cheeks. Her hands come back wet. So apparently I *am* crying.

'It's OK,' she soothes, her voice melodic and sweet.

'I doh unda-stah,' I say. Now the words are garbled by tears as well as my droopy lips. 'Why do they wah to kill yoo?'

But somehow Maxxer understands what I'm trying to ask. 'They've wanted me dead ever since I left the compound.'

I allow my eyes to close for a moment and immediately regret the decision because I can't seem to open them again.

'Get me a 50 ml of Zellex. The sedative is too strong. I need her conscious.'

I can feel sleep tugging at my mind. Inviting me into its warm, comfortable bed. Then I feel a sharp stab in my arm and a few moments later, my appendages start to awaken. There's sensation in my legs again. I try to lift my arm. It rises slowly and then falls again. I open my eyes. Focusing is decidedly easier.

'Thank you.' I breathe out, grateful to be able to form complete words again.

'You're welcome.'

Maxxer is still kneeling in front of me. I notice the splinters of glass have been cleared away. She stands and walks back to the bar, pouring herself another serving of her weird green energy drink.

'Why do they want you dead?' I ask, watching her pace, the glass clutched tightly in her hands. I get the sense things have not exactly been going her way thus far.

'Essentially because ever since I left the compound I've been trying to destroy them.'

'Destroy Diotech?' The feat seems nearly impossible.

She shakes her head. 'Not just Diotech. But the people controlling Diotech.'

I think back to the first conversation I had with Maxxer. In her storage unit. She mentioned she had a suspicion someone else was funding the company and pulling the strings. But she had indicated she didn't know who it was.

'You figured out who Alixter is working for,' I realize aloud.

She stops pacing long enough to flash me a cunning smile. 'Actually, I already knew.'

'You did?'

She nods. 'There's a group of very influential individuals, some of the wealthiest, most important people in the world. They call themselves the Providence. No one knows much about them because they stay almost completely under the radar. But it's rumoured that they've had their hands in every war, every political election, every economic crisis for decades. Some people believe they control everything. Most of these people are labelled crazy conspiracy theorists and quickly discounted. Which is a shame, because it's the truth.'

'I don't understand,' I say. 'Why didn't you tell me all of this the last time?'

'For many reasons,' Maxxer explains. 'The most important being I knew you weren't ready to hear it. I had to bring you into this gradually. Otherwise, I knew you'd become overwhelmed and possibly reject it completely. And I couldn't afford for that to happen.'

Bring me into this?

I draw a heavy hand to my forehead and press my temple. 'Wait,' I say, trying to process the flood of new information. 'Why exactly did you lead me here?'

She kneels back down in front of me. 'Because, Sera, I *need* you on my team. You are special. One of a kind. You can do things no one else can do. I've been *waiting* for you.' Her voice is quiet. Tentative. Desperate.

'You can help me defeat them.'

54

ORIGINS

What I really want to do is rise to my feet and stomp right out of this place. But first, although whatever Maxxer just injected into my bloodstream has allowed me to finally speak correctly, I still don't have full capacity of my legs. And second, obviously there's the problem of the fact that we're currently hundreds of feet underwater.

'That's why you brought me here?' I ask. 'Because you want me to help you defeat Diotech?'

Maxxer looks taken aback. 'I would think, after everything you've gone through, this would be top on your list of priorities.'

'Zen is my only priority,' I argue. 'I came here to save his life.'

Maxxer stands up and backs away a few paces. I can't help but notice the shift in her body language. Her shoulders sagging, her face registering what I can only interpret as remorse.

My hand immediately goes to my pocket. I'm horrified when I realize the vial I placed there is gone.

'Where is it?' I demand.

'Sera.' Maxxer tries to calm me. 'There are some things I need to explain.'

'Where's the gene repressor?!' I yell, causing the guards to step menacingly towards me. Maxxer calls them off with a subtle shake of her head.

'I had a hunch that Diotech might have gotten to you first. That a stimulated-response system might have been installed without your knowledge. I couldn't take any risks. I had to—'

'GIVE ME THE CURE!'

Maxxer sighs. 'Sera, I don't have the cure.'

Ice. Suddenly every inch of my body is covered in ice. Tiny pricks of unbearable chill stab me over and over and over. I feel like I'm falling. Hurtling. Not in a vacuum. Not in the sea. But plummeting headfirst towards the hard, unforgiving ground.

The impact is inevitable.

I will hit.

It will crush me.

And yet, somehow I'll survive. I'll go on. And be forever haunted by the memory of my plunge. A permanent dent in my brain. A scar that cannot be healed. Regardless of what my DNA says.

'What was in the vial?' I say, my lips barely moving, the sound barely travelling.

Maxxer shakes her head, refusing to look at me. 'Coloured water,' she admits softly. 'It was a decoy. I had to test you. To see if you had been manipulated.'

'You tricked me?' I shout, struggling to stand up but eventually collapsing back into the couch after much failed effort.

'Please calm down and listen to me,' Maxxer coaxes.

'Zen will die and it's because of YOU! The gene will kill him!'

'Sera,' she says again. Each instance of my name on her lips reignites my rage. 'You need to trust me.'

'TRUST YOU?!' I shriek so loudly my voice bounces off the thick glass and echoes back to me. 'After you lied to me? Tricked me? Lured me here under false pretences?'

'Now,' she replies in a sharp tone, 'I didn't give any indication in the memories that I was leading you here to give you the repressor.'

I open my mouth to reply but quickly shut it, my teeth snapping together, when I realize that she's right. The memories just said, 'Find me.' I made the assumption that Zen was the reason I needed to find her. Even so, her defence does nothing to quell my anger.

'That's irrelevant,' I spit. 'You knew he was going to get sick. You knew I'd be looking for a cure. And you knew I would blame Diotech for his illness. That's probably why you didn't tell me that he was going to get sick when we first met, even though you had to have known. You thought that if I was given enough time and enough motivation, I would come to despise them and that would only make it easier to recruit me.'

'That's not true.' But she licks her lips and doesn't meet my gaze when she says it, giving her away. 'I care about you, Sera. And Zen.'

I scoff, 'I don't believe you.'

The door creaks open, interrupting our argument. The man identified as Trestin pokes his head inside. 'Is everything OK?' he asks, his curious eyes darting from me to Maxxer.

I'm still plagued by the unyielding sensation that I know him. That I've met him before.

'We've been tracking the news of the outbreak in the nav deck,' he informs Maxxer. 'It's turning into quite the media circus. It shouldn't be long now.'

He turns and offers me a friendly wink.

Media circus.

I know that phrase. I've heard it before. When I was leaving the hospital in 2013. When everyone thought I'd survived a plane crash.

The first time I heard it said was by the man who was trying to locate my family. Mr Rayunas was his name. He said he worked for Social Services. He's the one who placed me with the Carlson family.

I study the man who just came into the room and I feel my stomach tighten.

No.

It can't be.

Mr Rayunas was much rounder. Older. His hair was thinning. He had wrinkles around his eyes. An extra layer of skin under his chin.

This man is young and slender with a full head of thick brown hair.

But the eyes. And the voice. And the smile. They're the same.

How though? How is that possible? Why would an older, heavier version of this man be in 2013 with me?

'Thanks, Trestin,' Maxxer replies with a tight smile. 'I'll deal with that later.'

He nods and ducks out again.

Something is going on here. Maxxer is hiding something. A lot of things.

I narrow my gaze at her. 'Why did you lie to me about Trestin?'

Her eyebrows rise. 'I didn't.

Another lie.

'He works with you.'

She nods. 'He's a crucial part of the alliance I've formed to bring down the Providence.'

'Why did he also work for Social Services in 2013?'

Maxxer freezes. I see the panic on her face. Apparently I

wasn't supposed to remember that. Or I wasn't supposed to piece it together. Either way, she's caught. 'I don't know what you're talking about. Like I said, he has one of those faces.'

'Oh, STOP!' I cry. 'I'm not stupid. I remember him. He called himself Mr Rayunas. He placed me with Cody's family. I want to know why!'

Maxxer's eyes close just for a moment, seemingly in surrender. She pulls a chair out from under the bar and places it across from me. Then she lowers herself into the seat.

'The first thing you need to understand,' she begins tentatively, 'is that the Providence is bad news. Very bad news.'

'Answer my question,' I seethe.

She raises her hand in the air. 'I will. But you have to know my motivations. You have to understand why I did what I did. I've learned a lot about this organization. I've been transessing all around the world, through hundreds of time periods gathering data on them. They are insufferable. Pure evil.'

She motions out the window at the endless sea. 'There's an outbreak going on right now, in July of 2032.'

'The white fever,' I say, remembering the news footage I saw in the subway.

'Yes. It's a virus that if left unchecked could destroy the entire population.' She pauses and takes a breath. 'They released that virus.'

I try not to let my astonishment show. I don't want Maxxer to know that I'm in any way sympathetic to her.

'But of course, they won't let the human race perish. That's not part of the plan. In two weeks they will release the vaccine for it. A vaccine they've been holding on to for months.'

'But the news footage I saw said the Centers for Disease Control was working on a vaccine,' I counter.

'Sure, the CDC was working on it. But the Providence already has it. They created it at the same time they created the virus.

They wanted people to think the situation was dire. They wanted it to get to a point where panic started to spread. That way, when the vaccine *was* released, people would be lined up around the block to get their hands on it. And they will. I've seen it.'

I shrug. 'So what?'

'So,' Maxxer says gravely, 'the problem is, it's not just a vaccine. It contains untraceable technology that will forever alter the genetic make-up of everyone who is injected with it.'

Despite myself, I lean forward, rapt.

'This genetic modification will make people more susceptible to other, less-extreme ailments. Allergies, flu, common cold, headaches. It will remove the body's natural ability to fight off regular, everyday illnesses and make people completely dependent on drugs. Drugs manufactured by companies owned solely by members of the Providence.'

I cross my arms over my chest. 'How does this explain why Trestin was in 2013?'

Maxxer nods anxiously. 'I'm getting there.' She takes another breath. 'This kind of manipulation has been happening since the early twenty-first century and it will go on for decades to come. But in about seventy-five years, there will be a small uprising among US citizens. A naturalist movement, if you will. People who will, more or less, recognize what's going on and will blame the government for it. Of course the government is a mere pawn in the Providence's game. In reality, it's powerless. The plot to use vaccines and the pharmaceutical companies as a way to keep tabs on people will be, for the most part, exposed and therefore no longer effective. And that's when the Providence will turn to an even scarier method of grasping control. A method they've actually been planning for decades. In fact, the origins of it are being developed right now.' She jabs her finger towards the window three times, in syncopation with each of her next three words: 'Right. Out. There.'

She shifts in her chair. 'But the plan will not actually be put into effect until the year 2109. And that's when the Providence will buy into a very small but very promising biotechnology start-up company.'

'Diotech,' I whisper.

'Exactly,' she replies. 'Diotech will receive an insane amount of funding, be moved to a remote desert location, clearance and security measures will be maximized, and the most important research project in the Providence's history will be initiated.' She looks pointedly at me.

A cold and hopeless gust of invisible wind blows over me.

'The one that created me.'

'Yes,' she states. 'It will be called the Genesis Project. And it will be used to create the most perfect sequence of human DNA in existence.'

'But *why*?' I ask. 'What do they hope to gain from creating me?'

'Aha,' Maxxer says. 'That's what I set out to discover. And fortunately, or unfortunately, I finally figured it out.'

I bite my lip in anticipation. This is what I've been waiting for. For I don't know how long. The reason I'm here. The reason they made me.

'*You*,' Maxxer says, 'and I imagine Kaelen as well, were intended to be used as promotional material.'

My brow furrows. '*Promotional material?*'

She nods. 'For a series of genetic modifications that will be sold over-the-counter at virtually any store in the world. Perfection in a bottle. Do you want to be as beautiful or as handsome as this? We have a solution for that. Do you want to run fast, heal quickly, never wrinkle, outsmart everyone you know? We can do that, too.'

She watches my reaction carefully. 'It's a product line that plays to every human desire, every fear, every fragile ego. And *everyone* —' she pauses, allowing her next three words time to sink in — 'will want it.'

'But just like the vaccine,' I deduce, 'there will be something else in it.'

She smiles warmly at me. '*Exactly*.'

I shudder. 'What?'

'Essentially the same thing they did to you when you unknowingly attempted to kill me. Highly complex stimulated-response systems. Nanotechnology that will nest inside your brain, remain completely dormant, completely undetectable, until it's ready to be activated.'

'But what will they use it to do?'

Maxxer's face goes rigid. 'Anything. They. Want.'

I swallow hard, imagining the implications. The horror of having billions of bombs walking around, unaware that any moment they could explode. Just like I did.

'Wars, mass suicides, assassinations, comatose states, purchases of new products, runs on the bank. The possibilities are endless. All they have to do is broadcast a signal and people will do the rest.' She dramatically mimes pressing something with her finger. 'The entire human race controlled by the touch of a button.'

Then she leans forward, meets my gaze, and holds it tightly. 'And it all starts . . . with you.'

55

CONTENDERS

Suddenly it's as though the sedative is back in my bloodstream and every molecule of me is useless again. Lips won't move. Tongue won't speak. Eyes won't close. Forcing me to stare, unblinkingly, at the woman sitting before me.

'The most brilliant part of the Providence's plan,' Maxxer goes on, 'is that they're going to successfully make people *want* it. They won't have to force the product on anyone. Once consumers see you, they'll be lined up around the block, willing to *pay* for it. That's why Alixter has been fighting so hard to get you back. You are a key ingredient to pulling off this plan.'

I shake my head. 'Why doesn't he just create another synthetic being? He did it with Kaelen. If it's that easy, then I should be replaceable.'

'My theory is that Kaelen was actually part of the original plan. They always intended to create him. A male counterpart. It makes sense. It was called the Genesis Project, referring to the first chapter of the Bible, which tells the story of the creation of Eve *and* Adam. Alixter always loved mocking anything to do with religion. It's the reason he pushed to name the company Diotech, meaning *God's science*.

'But making you was expensive,' Maxxer continues. 'And I'm sure Kaelen was as well. If Alixter hasn't told the Providence that you went missing – which, if he values his life and his kneecaps, I can't imagine he would – then he'd have to pull another trillion dollars out of the budget to replace you. That kind of money doesn't disappear without being noticed. He'd never be able to cover it up. No, he needs *you* back.'

'But he sent me *here*,' I argue. 'Kaelen could have taken me back to Diotech at any time.'

'That's where the little hiccup in his plan happened. He got sick. He needed the repressor. He knew you were the only one I would let near me. Then I'm sure he intended on having Kaelen deliver you back to the compound. Preferably before the Providence notices that you're gone.'

'OK,' I allow, trying to steady my thoughts in this spinning room. 'But that doesn't answer my original question. About Trestin appearing in 2013.'

Maxxer stands and walks to the bar. This time, she doesn't reach for the strange green beverage. Instead she pours from a flask full of a light brown liquid. It looks like the same thing Cody was drinking at his lab.

'You realize how awful they are, don't you?' Maxxer prods. 'You see how they have to be stopped? How this plan can't be allowed to continue?'

'Answer my question.'

'I just need to know that you understand what I'm fighting against.'

'Fine,' I say, losing my patience. If I even had any to start with. 'I understand.'

'The truth is, it wasn't an accident that you landed in 2013.'

Maxxer takes a gulp and exhales loudly. 'I sent you there.'

Whether my legs are working now or not is irrelevant. I launch to my feet, wobbling slightly on the way up. 'Y-y-you did WHAT?'

'After I fled the compound, I used to return from time to time to –' she hesitates, looking anxious – 'visit. In secret, obviously.'

'Visit?' I repeat. 'Who?'

Her hands get fidgety. 'Mostly Dr Rio. He and I were . . . close. He was the only person on the compound who I shared my research with.'

Close?

'Anyway, during one of my . . . *visits*,' Maxxer says, 'Rio told me about your request for the transession gene so that you could run away with Zen. He also told me that you'd asked him to wipe your memories before you left. I didn't think anything of it at the time. But then later, as I started to gather information about the Providence and their developments, I transessed back to the compound the night before you left. I implanted a trigger in your mind. A trigger that would send you to 2013 instead of 1609.'

'*You let go.*'

Zen was right. I did let go. I was *programmed* to let go. That's what went wrong. That's how we got separated. And all this time Maxxer knew.

'I'm sorry,' she offers, and somehow her apology feels genuine. Heartfelt. But it doesn't matter. Everything is beyond apologies now.

'Why?' I ask, my voice breaking. My body dissolving. I sink back into the couch. 'Why would you do that?'

'Because I needed you,' Maxxer says, her voice dripping with desperation. 'I needed you to join the alliance. To fight the fight.'

'I didn't ask to fight your fight!' I scream. 'I didn't ask for any of this!'

'I know,' Maxxer admits, looking distraught. 'I just . . . someone had to get to Cody Carlson.'

'Cody?' I repeat. 'What does he have to do with it?'

'More than you know,' she responds. 'We have reason to believe that the Providence is funding his research. That the breakthrough he is about to make will pave the way to everything that's coming. The problem is, we still can't identify even *one* member of the organization. They are that secret. Cody was our only lead. But adults are hard to crack. They're not very trusting. We couldn't just show up today and demand he provide us with information. But if there was someone he trusted. Someone he'd known for a while . . .'

Her voice trails off and I already see where she's going. My brain may be one step ahead but my stomach has been left a hundred miles behind us, somewhere in the darkness of the ocean. 'So you sent me back to 2013 to gain his trust.'

She nods. 'Trestin just facilitated the introduction by placing you in the Carlsons' home.'

'But he looked different,' I say, remembering Mr Rayunas's aged features and thinning hair. 'Older somehow.'

'Just a disguise. I temporarily altered his genetic make-up to advance his age and add more weight to his body. The effects wear off in a few days.'

'And the plane crash?' I ask. 'Was it your idea to plant me in the middle of all that wreckage? To make it seem like I was a survivor?'

Maxxer cringes. 'The crash was an unfortunate side effect.'

'Wait. *What?*'

She breathes out. 'Transession is complicated. Sometimes entries can cause small riffs in the surrounding energy. Especially if perhaps half of your brain was fighting against the trigger and the other half was obeying it. I didn't intend for it to happen. But it was just a wrong-place-at-the-wrong-time kind of thing.'

My eyes widen with horror. 'You mean, I *caused* the plane crash!?'

'Collateral damage, I'm afraid,' Maxxer says, looking remorseful.

I flash back to the moment I awoke in that ocean. To the bodies floating lifelessly around me. Their faces forever frozen in fear. In horrible, terrifying death.

'All those people died because of me,' I say numbly. 'And because of you.'

'This is war, Sera,' Maxxer says, the remorse instantly gone. 'There will be casualties.'

I let out a choked sob. Everything I've ever known is crumbling around me.

This whole time I've been fought over. Torn in half. Yanked in two different directions. Manipulated to the point of murder. From *both* sides. And I never had a clue. I never knew about any of it.

'I never even had a choice.' I don't realize that I've said this last part aloud until Maxxer responds.

'You have a choice now,' she says emphatically. 'You can help me bring them down. The evil people who did this to you.'

I squint at her and then shake my head. 'Don't you understand?' I say, my voice trembling but intensifying. 'You are just as bad as *them*! You manipulated this whole thing. You were controlling me from the very beginning! How can you stand there and lecture me about *them*? You *are* them!'

'Sera,' Maxxer tries, 'that's ridiculous. You can't possibly compare me to those monsters.'

'I can!' I shout back. 'And you want to know why? Because you are *exactly* like them. You use people to get what you want. You manipulate innocent minds to achieve your own goals. You steal people's humanity, just as you've stolen mine!'

On shaky legs, I stalk towards the door. Out of the corner of my eye I see the guards make a move to intercept me but Maxxer stops them. 'Let her go.'

'Oh, really!?' I spit back at her. 'I can go? Thank you *very* much for your *permission!*'

The sarcasm is bitter and hot on my tongue. Cody would be proud.

I slam the door behind me.

56

PLACE

Once I'm on the other side of the door I fall to pieces. It took the last ounce of emotional strength I had not to break down in front of Maxxer, but now all of that is gone. I slide against the wall, allowing gravity, and the weight of everything I lost today, to drag me down.

The world is underwater. I view it through my relentless ocean of tears. My body is involuntarily convulsed by the sobs. My chest screams in pain. I let go. No longer trying to gather myself. No longer attempting to take deep breaths. What is the point? Breath. Air. Living.

They're all illusions.

Deceptions created to make me think that I'm alive. That I matter. That I'm a human being.

I may have blood running through my veins. I may need oxygen and water and food to survive. But beyond that I'm merely a machine. A toy. A weapon of wars. And the victory will go to the side who can best figure out how to exploit me to their advantage.

I reach into my pocket and find my locket.

It feels worthless now. I am so undeserving of such a precious gift. Unworthy of anything that it once represented.

I flick open the door. A robot activating. I close my eyes.

I could go anywhere. I could escape. The possibilities are endless. I could live out the rest of my days — however long that might be — on a remote island somewhere. Where I can't hurt anyone. Where no one cares who I am or what I've done.

Or I could transesse right into the mouth of a volcano.

That would certainly be faster. A more efficient way to end my own suffering. And the suffering of everyone who I've hurt — and even killed.

But strangely, in that moment, there's only one place I want to go.

There's only one face I want to see. Only one person who could possibly understand what I'm feeling.

The problem is, I don't know where he is.

But for some reason I have this perplexing nagging feeling that it doesn't matter. That I don't *need* to know. I've never actually tried transessing to a *person* before. It's always been to a place or time.

However, right now I feel him calling to me. Not his voice. Not with words. But just . . . him.

I gently twist the broken chain three times around my wrist, securing the open heart-shaped charm under the wrap. Then I close my eyes and focus my attention on his face.

The tiniest drop of warmth spreads through my icy-cold body.

But right now, it's enough.

When I open my eyes, I find myself in a cramped, dimly lit room. It's a stark contrast to the massive command centre I just left. There are no windows here. No sleek glass or crisp white furniture. No warm, blazing fireplace or glossy countertops.

All the extravagance is replaced with dirty metal and rusted pipes and paint peeling from a cold floor.

But one thing brightens the room more than any window. More than any fireplace. One piece of incomparable beauty sits alone in the dreariness, slumped on a hard metal bench.

Kaelen opens his eyes when he hears me approach. He smiles, somewhat dazedly, the effects of the Modifier starting to wear off.

I don't allow myself to think. I don't allow myself to feel or doubt or analyse or argue.

I bound forward.

In one step, I reach him.

In one breath, my lips are crushed against his.

In one stuttered, confused heartbeat, he's kissing me back.

It's impossible to know how he learned what to do. I have no doubt this was not one of the many instructional downloads he received before setting off on his mission. Perhaps it's just something we're born knowing. Or in our case, *created* knowing.

Because he does.

His mouth moves perfectly in sync with mine. Anticipating me, completing me. His hands find their way up my back, his fingertips urging me closer. I collapse into him. Press against him. Disappear inside him.

The intensity of the energy that passes between us is unlike anything I've ever known. Now. Or before. Or ever.

It's the highest voltage. The strongest current. The brightest light. The fastest wind. The highest mountain. The deepest breath.

It's raw and powerful and untamed.

And right now, it's the only thing keeping me alive. It's the electricity that fuels me. Like being plugged directly into the sun.

Kaelen breaks from my mouth long enough to gasp for breath and ask, 'What is that?'

'You feel it, too?' I ask.

He nods earnestly.

'I don't know,' I admit.

But I do know I want more.

We dive for each other again. Our mouths aching for each other. I reach for his shirt, yanking it up over his head. I have no idea why I'm doing it, I just know I have to touch his skin. And he has to touch mine.

We have to be closer. Closer than I've ever been to anything.

My sweater comes off next and in a blurred instant, we're pressed back together. The feel of his bare chest against mine is indescribable. The previous sensation times a trillion.

My whole body is tingling. I want something. But I don't know what.

It's like my whole body is alert, waiting for it. Expecting it. Knowing it will not be satisfied until it gets it.

I haven't felt this way since . . .

Since . . .

In a sickening flash, I see it. I remember.

That night in the woods. Our last night together. I was taken over by an unfamiliar urge. An unfamiliar *need*. When I asked Zen about it later, he tried to explain.

'*Something that will bring us closer together. As close together as we can be.*'

I pull back, disentangling myself from Kaelen, sitting up. He pants beside me, his face registering confusion.

'Why did you stop?' he asks.

I clutch my sweater in my hand and quickly slide it over my head. 'I can't do this.'

He doesn't understand. I know that. 'I'm sorry,' I tell him.

He sits up, reaches out, and touches my face. Tenderly.

Kindly. There's no trace of the boy I met in that bedroom two days ago.

The one powered by Alixter.

The one driven by a program.

This is someone else. Someone new. Someone buried deep inside. Who never knew how to get out.

Who never knew he could.

'Don't be sorry,' he says softly.

I shake my head, willing the tears to stop. They don't listen. He catches one on his fingertip and studies it carefully. As though he's never seen one before.

And chances are . . . he hasn't.

I push my arms through the sleeves of the sweater, still damp from our swim, and pull it down. 'I don't understand what is happening between us.'

'Neither do I.'

I believe him.

'I found you without knowing where you were,' I tell him. 'I transessed to you. Like you were a place in my mind. A physical location.'

He nods. 'I know.'

I tilt my head and study this new Kaelen. Still perfect, but made even more beautiful by the shift in his eyes. The realness I see there now. I don't know what changed him. What flipped the switch. But if I had to guess, I would say it was the exact same thing that changed me.

'That's how you found me,' I realize aloud. 'Today in Cody's lab. And here in the submarine. You transessed to me.'

'I don't know how it works,' Kaelen admits. 'Alixter never said anything about that. The scientists taught me how to transesse to places and times. Not people. I just somehow knew I could do it with you. Like if I tried hard enough, I could *feel* where you were.'

'Does it work with other people?' I ask.

He shakes his head. 'Only you.'

'Alixter sent you to get the cure,' I confirm for the final time, needing to hear it from him. To hear it said aloud.

'Yes.'

'And to bring me back.'

This answer takes more time. More strength. 'Yes,' he says at last.

I swallow, allowing myself to sink into him. I lay my head against his bare chest, feeling the electricity of our contact sizzle pleasantly against my cheek. I close my eyes. I listen to his thundering heartbeat. Like a horse galloping. Like a prisoner held against his will.

'You were right,' he says quietly into my damp hair.

'About what?' I whisper, keeping my eyes closed.

I think about my own heart. The one held tight against my wrist. Still open. Still active. If he decides to obey the second half of his orders and bring me back, I can't stop him. I am defenceless. My future is his to take. If he wants it.

But it doesn't matter. Right now I know I would go anywhere with him.

'About this,' he replies. Then he lets out a stale sigh that feels like it's been trapped inside him for ages. 'It's not a choice.'

57

REMAINED

I drift in and out of sleep for what feels like days. When I wake, Kaelen's face is the first thing I see. He didn't leave. Although he certainly could have. His transession gene doesn't have an Off switch.

But he stayed.

Right here. His chest solidly under my head. Supporting me while I slept.

I push myself up and stretch my arms over my head. As I do, something falls off my lap and tumbles on to the floor. Curiously, I glance down and see Lulu, Jane's fabric doll, lying on the grimy floor. Half of her left arm has been burned clear off, leaving behind a charred, black stump.

I scoop her up and look curiously at Kaelen. 'Where did this come from?'

He shrugs sheepishly. 'I took it from you.'

I frown. 'You did? When?'

'After I removed you from the fire. You were unconscious. I was ordered to empty your pockets and confiscate everything.

I didn't know which items were functional – like the locket – and which ones weren't.'

I bring Lulu up to my nose, inhaling the fabric, hoping to catch a brief scent of Jane or the farm or my life before everything fell apart. But all I smell is the smoke that seeped into her cloth body during my failed execution.

'Well, thank you for giving her back to me.'

'I don't understand.' Kaelen frowns at the doll. 'What does it do?'

I laugh for the first time in what feels like weeks. 'It doesn't *do* anything. She's just . . . I don't know . . . a comfort, I guess. She reminds me of someone I used to know.' I tuck the doll in my pocket, keeping her safe there. 'Any idea what time it is?'

He glances at his watch. 'By my calculations, 7:22 a.m.'

For a moment I feel invigorated. Refreshed. Then the moment passes and the previous night rushes back to me. Maxxer's betrayal. Diotech's manipulation. Zen's lost cure. And the anger seeps back into my thoughts.

'What do we do now?' Kaelen asks.

But I don't have the slightest idea. I can't simply desert Zen and let him die alone in Cody's house. And yet, what hope do I have of saving him?

No matter what I do, no matter where I go, someone will always be following me. Someone will always be chasing me. Someone will always be trying to use me.

But what about *me*?

What do I want?

At one point, this was an easy question to answer. An automated response. Now, the answer is not so clear any more.

'Sera.' Kaelen's voice interrupts my thoughts and I peer over at him.

'Yes?'

'What happened last night?' he asks. 'After they used the Modifier on me.'

The fact that he asked the question means he didn't take my memories while I was sleeping. He left them alone. The thought comforts me.

I shake my head. 'Everything went wrong. Maxxer gave me the cure and I tried to kill her.'

'I'm sorry,' he admits. 'I didn't know what I was doing. I was just—'

'Following orders, I know. I don't blame you.'

'So you have the antidote, then?' he asks.

I feel tears start to well up again. 'No. It was a fake. Maxxer was testing me. She had a suspicion that you – I mean, that Diotech would try to manipulate me. And she was right.'

'So she can't save Zen?'

The sound of Zen's name in Kaelen's deep, smooth voice sends a series of flutters through my stomach. Like a flock of birds scared out of a tree. It's all wrong now. As though he shouldn't be allowed to say it. As though I shouldn't be allowed to hear it on his lips.

Lips I touched last night. With my own.

'I don't know,' I say in a broken voice. 'She said only *we* –' I drag my finger through the small crevice of space between us – 'have bodies that can sustain the gene. It's why Alixter made you. Any normal human who receives the transplant will inevitably . . .'

My voice quivers to a halt as last night plays back through my mind. I fast forward, I rewind, I pause, I replay, I search for signs. Symptoms. A shiver. A bead of sweat. A hint of weakness. Anything.

But there's none.

Maxxer appeared to be perfectly healthy.

And she's had the transession gene in her system for the

longest. After all, she was her own first test subject.

'Come on.' I spring to my feet and tug Kaelen's arm.

'Where are we going?'

'To figure out why Maxxer is still alive.'

Kaelen hesitates, pulling back. 'She won't divulge any information in my presence. She knows I work for Alixter. You'll never get her to talk.'

I nod in agreement. 'Which is why I don't plan on *talking* to her.'

58

PURSUED

The warm dry air slams against Dr Maxxer's pale, sunken face as she opens the door of the lab and gazes into the desert night. Her heart thuds against her ribs. Sweat trickles down her face as a shiver tremors through her body.

Clutched desperately in her palm are three capped vials.

She peers into the darkness, listening.

She is alone.

But it won't last.

A loud, earth-shattering cough rises up in her throat, thrashing to get out. She cements her lips together and pushes it down, tears stinging her eyes. Blood trickling down the back of her throat.

She shudders. Gauging the distance. Wishing she had the stamina to transesse there. Knowing she has to conserve enough energy to get back. Otherwise she'll be stuck here forever.

She shoves the vials of clear liquid into her pocket and slips out the door. Her legs scream with pain as she forces them to run. Her heart sputters helplessly trying to keep up. Her body threatens to give out. To collapse. To finally let itself be destroyed by the very process that was designed to protect it.

She is too weak to do this.

She waited too long to return.

But she knows she has to reach the house. She has to get there.

If he dies, it will be her fault.

She takes the long way, knowing there will be fewer sensors to dodge. But she knows that means more time on her feet. More opportunities for everything to fail and for her to become food for the foxes.

She stumbles along the rough dirt terrain. One particularly large divot sends her smashing to her knees. The impact of the fall crushing her like a thousand horses galloping across her organs. She gasps for breath. Her stomach convulses, attempting to vomit up empty air. She gags and expels more blood on to the desert floor.

She wills herself back on to her feet.

GET UP!

Another chill rocks her ailing body but finally she's able to push herself up and stagger forward.

She reaches the concrete wall that separates the house from the rest of the compound. Knowing her fingerprint will never open the gate, she has no choice but to go over it.

Her feet scrape ineffectually against the façade as she fights to get traction up the side. The rough concrete rips at her palms, shredding her skin.

She crashes on to the other side, biting her lip to keep from screaming in agony.

A light shines down from above, blinding her. She squints into the sky, barely managing to make out the sharp silent blades of the hovercopter circling above.

'Stop,' booms an emotionless voice. Not human. 'Don't move.'

With the vials tucked safely in her pocket, she struggles to her feet and runs. Her legs threatening to give out with every painful step.

She reaches the front door of the house and yanks it open, tumbling inside.

He's asleep when she reaches him. Looking peaceful. His soft red beard rippling with each breath. She digs into her pocket and pulls out two of the three vials, thrusting them into his palm and tightening his fingers around them.

He wakes at her touch, his eyes heaving open. A smile appearing.

'You're here,' he says, his voice thick with sleep.

But the joy fades as soon as he's able to focus on her haggard, diseased face.

'What's wrong? What happened?'

'The gene,' she manages to squeak, the oxygen barely able to fuel the words.

The light from the hovercopter blasts through the window, lowering steadily as the craft comes in for a landing. Her time is coming to an end.

'You have to find him,' she whimpers as she squeezes his fingers tighter around the two vials. 'You have to find him.'

She gathers whatever energy she has left and focuses it all on her final destination. Knowing this is the last time she will ever see him.

The front door of the house bursts open just as the feel of his touch dissolves against her skin and the first tear treks down her face.

She lands huddled on the floor of the submarine's command centre, trembling. She drifts in and out of consciousness as Trestin covers her with a blanket, tugs on her pants to remove the vial from her pocket. He works quickly, inserting the needle and drawing out the fluid.

She feels the prick in her arm as he locates the vein.

The heavy, clear, cleansing liquid chugs through her bloodstream. Reversing the past. Healing the pain.

Trapping her in time forever.

59
BATTLE

Maxxer's memory fades to an end and I open my eyes and take in the mess that we've created.

Furniture has been overturned. Framed artwork has fallen from the walls and shattered. Breakfast food and broken dishes are scattered across the white rug. Maxxer's two guards lie in a heap at the base of the stairs, looking like a lumpy pile of snow in their crisp white uniforms. One's nose bleeds from where it came into contact with the heel of my hand. The other sports a swollen lip from Kaelen's elbow.

And Maxxer. She is unconscious on the couch. Sitting upright with her head slumped forward. Kaelen's fingertips are still resting against her forehead. Sending her memories directly to the receptors he removed from his own head and placed on mine.

I blink and study my surroundings. Recognizing the room from the memory. I eye the section of carpet at the base of the dining table where Trestin injected Maxxer with the clear liquid from the vial.

The repressor.

The cure.

Disabling her gene permanently. Reversing the effects of the illness. Keeping her here forever. She will never transesse again.

'What did you see?' Kaelen asks, interrupting my thoughts.

I blink up at him. 'There were three doses,' I explain.

Kaelen nods, as though he already knew this. 'When it was believed that Dr Maxxer returned to the compound, Dr Alixter confirmed that the molecule accelerator in Maxxer's lab had been used to manufacture three doses of a serum. But they could never be found. He assumed she came back to produce an antidote to reverse the effects of the gene. But when he attempted to re-create it, he was unsuccessful. Dr Maxxer made sure no one could replicate her process.'

I nod. 'I didn't see how the antidote was manufactured. The memory started after the vials were already created.'

'She most likely erased it.'

I gaze at Maxxer's sleeping face. She's been so careful to guard so many secrets. And yet I feel like there are still some that have yet to be uncovered.

What did she mean when she said — 'You have to find him'?

'Did you see what happened to the three doses?' Kaelen asks.

I bite my lip. 'Maxxer used one of them on herself.'

'What about the other two?'

Maxxer's memories may have been fuzzier and harder to decipher than my own, but I recognized the man she gave them to. I know exactly who it is.

And this is where the road seems to come to a dead end. Yet again. Just further evidence proving that the forces of the universe have banded together to fight against me. To keep me from Zen.

'She gave them to Rio,' I tell Kaelen with a crestfallen sigh, feeling the stab of another hope disintegrating into nothing. 'And he's dead.'

Kaelen falls eerily quiet and I glance over to see his bottom lip is twitching. As though his body is having an epic battle with his brain. The outcome of which will determine whether or not his mouth moves and words emerge.

It's the old Kaelen — the brainwashed, programmed, order-abiding version of himself — declaring war against this new, unfamiliar rebellious one. Attempting to regain control.

I stare in stunned silence as the internal battle wages on. As his eyes squeeze tightly shut. As his face contorts into what I can only describe as torment.

'Kaelen,' I finally say, gently placing my hand on his. He jumps at the contact and his eyes flicker open. 'Are you all right?'

With visible effort, his mouth moves. His fingers curl into a tight ball underneath my hand. And for a minute I think he's going to let out a scream.

'It's OK,' I assure him, rubbing his tense, white knuckles. 'You're safe. You're with me.'

For some reason, my comforting seems to work. After minutes of brutal combat, a victor emerges. The old Kaelen is shoved back down into the dark corners of his mind. And the new Kaelen speaks. His voice breathless and weary. His words choppy and clipped.

'Dr . . . Rio . . .'

'What about him?' I ask, my eyebrows pinched together.

'He's . . . not . . . dead.'

60

INCISED

I saw him.

I saw him fall. I saw him shake and shake and shake until he was deathly still. I saw the life fade from his eyes. Right in front of me. In that cave.

I saw him die.

The memory has haunted me since that day.

'But the Modifier.' I stumble through the words. 'Alixter turned it all the way up.'

'It's a destructive setting, yes,' Kaelen admits. 'But it's not fatal on its own.'

'What does it do, then?' I ask, my voice trembling as I remember Alixter describing the setting as something he called *scramble*.

'His brain has been severely damaged,' Kaelen explains. 'Dr Alixter brought him back to the compound after your escape. The lack of brain activity will eventually cause his body to shut down permanently. But Dr Alixter has been keeping him alive.

Artificially. He's in a guarded room at the compound's medical facility.'

Bombs are exploding in my head. Tiny detonations of joy. Of relief. Of hope.

'How do you know this?' I ask, a small shadow of my former distrust resurfacing.

'It was part of my intelligence briefing before I was sent on this mission. And —' Kaelen hesitates, his eyes shifting — 'I've seen him.'

'We have to go there,' I say immediately, surprising myself with my own eagerness.

This is Diotech I'm referring to.

The place where I was made. Where I was imprisoned. The place Zen fought so hard to help me escape from.

But if that's where Rio is, if that's the only clue to finding Zen's cure, then there is no hesitation.

'You have to take me there,' I tell Kaelen. 'Rio knows where the other two doses of the repressor are.'

Kaelen's head is already swinging back and forth before I've even finished speaking. 'His brain is in an indecipherable state. He's not even conscious. He'll never be able to tell you where it is. He won't even know you're there.'

But I'm not deterred. Not when this is my last chance. 'We have to try,' I vow. 'I have to try. For him.'

Kaelen looks away, refusing to meet my eye. 'Are you sure you want to go back there? If you're caught—'

'I know the risks,' I say quickly, before he can finish the thought. I fear that if I hear the consequences aloud, I'll lose my nerve.

I don't have to guess what Alixter will do if he finds me there. If I'm apprehended. He's already made his intentions for me perfectly clear.

I won't lie. The thought of returning to the Diotech

compound nearly paralyses me. But there's only one thing I'm sure of. And that is my desire to save Zen. Even if someone told me I had to go to the moon to do it, I would say yes.

Always yes.

'You said Rio's room was guarded,' I say.

'From the *outside*,' Kaelen clarifies.

'Can you get us directly *inside* then?'

He nods. 'Yes.'

Then there's nothing else to debate. The decision is made.

I reach for the locket that's still dangling from my wrist and ease open its door. Then I slide my hand into Kaelen's and he closes his eyes, focusing.

I wait, staring down at our intertwined fingers. And that's when I see it.

Peeking out from underneath the sleeve of his shirt.

His tattoo. His black scar. His tracking device.

I quickly fling his hand away. 'Wait!'

Kaelen's eyes snap open. 'What?'

I flip over my own wrist and show him my matching mark. I can see the comprehension flashing over his face.

'They'll know the moment we arrive,' I tell him.

He nods. 'What do we do?'

I think about that morning on the Pattinsons' farm. When I slashed it out with a knife in a fit of rage. How fast it grew back.

'We can cut them out,' I say, my voice stern and decisive.

'They will grow back,' he replies immediately.

'Not right away. We'll have less than an hour to figure out where the two doses are and get out before they're scannable again.'

I'm already glancing around the dishevelled room for a tool. Anything with a sharp edge. My eye falls on a broken shard of glass from one of the fallen pieces of artwork. I dart over to retrieve it. Kaelen scurries behind me.

Feeling my heart race and my throat go dry, I look up at him, our gazes colliding. Sparks flying. 'I'll remove yours if you'll remove mine.'

He holds his arm out, wrist up. 'Go deep,' he whispers. 'It'll give us more time.'

I nod, wincing, and take a shuddering breath before pressing the sharp edge of the glass to his flawless skin.

61

RETURN

I bite my lip and wince against the pain as Kaelen makes the last cut along my wrist, completing the rectangular gash where my tattoo once was. The blood is dripping down the side of my arm, staining the pristine white carpet beneath me, next to the small crimson splotch that Kaelen's wound already created.

I press the palm of my hand against the cut, trying to stanch the blood.

'Don't,' Kaelen says, pulling my hand away.

'It's bleeding everywhere.'

'You'll heal faster if the blood clots.'

Warily, I remove my hand and cringe at the feeling of the warm, sticky liquid oozing into my palm.

'Just keep it elevated,' Kaelen tells me, raising his own hand above his head. I do the same.

'Remember,' I tell him, 'since we don't know exactly when Alixter created you, we have to transesse to a time *after* you left.'

'I know.'

'Do you know when you were sent to 1609 to apprehend me?'

Kaelen nods.

'So a week later, to be safe?'

He agrees and grips my raised hand with his. I immediately feel our exposed blood blending. Our scientifically perfected life forces combining.

'Are you ready?' he asks.

I take a deep breath, glancing around the room. My gaze lands on Maxxer, still lying unconscious on the couch. She told me I could decide. I could join her alliance, or say no.

I guess this is me . . . saying no.

But I never thought this would be the alternate option.

For as long as I can remember, I've been running from Diotcch and all the things they represent. For as long as I can remember, I've been doing whatever I could to evade them. Deceive them. Stay as far away from them as I can. And now I'm about to go back there. *With* one of them.

But Kaelen is different, isn't he? He's changed. He's proved that he's changed. He's proved that he no longer holds allegiance to Alixter. That he's no longer being controlled by his programming. He's broken free. And made his own choice.

Just as I have.

But a nagging thought creeps its way into the front of my mind.

What if it's been an act?

The cure. The kiss. Kaelen's seeming change of heart.

What if this whole thing has been one giant trap designed to take me back there? To get me to come willingly?

No, I tell myself.

I refuse to believe that. I *know* Kaelen. We are one and the same. I can read him almost as well as I can read myself. We are linked somehow. We've both proved that already.

He wouldn't deceive me. Not after everything that's happened. Not after everything we've been through.

And even if it is a trap, even if he has been conning me this whole time, what other solution do I have? Rio knows where the last two doses of the repressor are. And that makes him the only option.

I look up, meeting his intense gaze, and whisper, 'Yes,' with what little conviction I have left. 'I'm ready.'

I close my eyes. Even though I'm not the one directing this transession. Even though my concentration is not needed. I can't watch. I can't look.

After everything Zen did to break me out, I'm about to step right back into the middle of my prison.

I'm about to willingly return to the one place I vowed I would never return to. Where I was created. Where I was manufactured. Where my life began.

I'm finally going home.

62

MESSY

The hospital room is white and sterile and filled with sleek, sophisticated machines unlike anything I've ever seen before. There are no wires anywhere. Every piece of equipment seems to be powered by an invisible source. The screens of the various computers and monitors are paper-thin, making me think they could be snapped in half with the slightest pressure.

When my vision focuses, I see the bed on the other side of the room. There are no legs or other support mechanisms holding it up. It simply hovers above the ground.

It isn't until I see Rio's face resting on the crisp white pillowcase that I know we've made it.

His rough red beard is fuller, scragglier. His hair is longer, falling into his eyes. And his skin is worn and tattered. Like it's been left out in the rain one too many times.

But other than that, he looks the same.

Seeing him in this comatose state, his eyes open and unnervingly staring into space, I realize how robbed I feel. He was the closest thing I'll ever have to a family and he's gone.

Our time together was too short. As soon as I realized how important he was, what he meant to me, it was over. Alixter turned him into this.

I will never have another conversation with him.

I will never be able to ask him questions about my past. Or his relationship with Maxxer.

I will never be able to see the gentleness – the life – in his soft green-grey eyes.

I have this irresistible urge to run to him, to place my palm against his check, to rest my head on his chest. But something stops me.

A noise.

A kind of grinding sound. And that's when I see the woman. At least, from the waist up, she *looks* like a woman. But instead of legs, she has wheels attached to the bottom of her torso.

The sight of her makes me shriek. But Kaelen is one step ahead of me. His hand covers my mouth, muffling the sound, and he yanks me back. We scuttle under a table, scooting as far away as we can until we hit a wall.

'What is it?' I ask in that inaudible voice I know only he can hear.

'A med bot.'

'A what?'

But apparently I was a bit too loud because he presses his finger to his lips. 'Robotic intelligence. They're assigned to do various tasks around the compound.'

I watch the strange lifelike creature in wonderment as she wheels around the room, going about her duties, checking the machines and computers monitoring Rio.

'Does she know we're here?' I ask in my hoarse whisper.

'If she did, we would know.'

She rolls over to the table that we're hiding beneath and Kaelen and I both suck in a simultaneous breath, pushing ourselves as far back against the wall as we can. I watch her bottom half glide efficiently across the length of the table. The spherical wheels turning effortlessly front to back, side to side, even diagonally.

My heart is pounding so loud right now, I'm convinced that it will only be a matter of time before she hears it and sounds the alarm.

After what feels like hours, I watch her wheel up to the wall opposite us and swipe her eerily human-like hand across a clear panel. A door appears where there once was just a seamless white wall, and it slides open. She exits and the door closes behind her, blending back into the façade as though it never existed in the first place.

Kaelen moves fast. Crawling out from under the table and then reaching down to help me. 'We have to be quick. She's probably on a rotation.'

'How long?' I ask.

'Twenty minutes,' he guesses. 'Maybe less.'

I check that the receptors are still securely attached to my head and hurry towards Rio's bedside. On a nearby table is a thin plastic screen. Information is flying across it at dizzying speed. Lines and lines of what appears to be code.

'What is that?' I ask.

'Looks like a search,' Kaelen responds, picking up the screen and studying the data. 'It's probably connected to his brain. Alixter is looking for something.'

'What?' I ask, feeling nauseated.

He squints, absorbing the numbers as they soar past. 'I can't tell,' he says. 'The search is encoded.'

'Can you link me to his brain?'

Kaelen nods, tapping the piece of plastic. 'Initiating link,' he reports back. 'You'll be connected in five, four, three, two . . .'

SCREECH!

I'm suddenly bombarded by a swirling, dizzying array of images and rapidly moving scenes. None of them are complete or clear. They're all choppy and faded, some even distorted, like they've been wrung out by extremely strong hands, causing the picture to look twisted and alien and terrifying.

They spin frantically. But there's no order to any of them. I'm getting woozy from the influx of data.

And the noise. It's the loudest, most distressing sound I've ever heard. Like a million people screaming into my ear at the same time. Demanding to be heard.

I press my hand to my head, trying to steady myself. Trying to block out the sound and concentrate on just one picture. One face. One voice. But it's impossible. There is no logic. No sense. No way to sort through anything.

'I can't,' I whisper hoarsely, trying not to throw up from the dizziness. 'I can't do it.'

And suddenly I understand what Alixter meant when he said *scramble*. Kaelen warned me his mind would be incomprehensible but I never expected this. It's pure chaos. I'll never be able to find anything in here. And certainly not before our tracking devices grow back, or the med bot returns.

'Sera,' Kaelen urges. 'You have to try.'

I cringe and dive back into the disorder, allowing myself to be swept up in the churning of faces and landscapes and mathematical equations. As the imagery whirls by, I try to catch a single memory and hold on to it long enough to see it and possibly classify it.

But no matter how hard I try, nothing works.

I glance down at my wrist. The bleeding has stopped. A thin scab has already started to form.

I want to cry in frustration. I have to find it! I have to figure out what Rio did with those other two doses.

But that's like trying to find one droplet of water in a stormy ocean. I'm sorting through a lifetime of memories here. Memories that have been completely muddled by Alixter's Modifier.

I reach out and grab Rio's hand, holding it tightly. 'Rio,' I plead. 'Can you hear me? Does any part of you know that I'm even here? It's me, Sera. Please. I need your help. I need to find the two doses of the repressor that Maxxer left you. You have to remember what you did with them.'

I stare at his lifeless face, frozen in time. His unblinking eyes. His slightly agape mouth.

I get no response.

I think back to the memory of the night Rio gave me the transession gene. The night I asked him to erase all my memories and give me a fresh start.

I remember the way he looked at me. With such sadness in his eyes. Such remorse.

'*I'm sorry about everything. Everything I did to you,*' he said to me.

And then I called him something. Something I've never been able to call anyone. And I never will.

'Dad,' I whisper aloud now, tears streaming down my cheeks. 'He's going to die. I can't let that happen. I love him. Please help me.'

Something happens then. For just a moment, the briefest flit of a moment, the disorderly bustle of memories slows to a stop. As though someone turned off the power that was fuelling them. The earsplitting noise mutes into a hushed garble.

'Look!' Kaelen whispers.

I lift my gaze to see Rio's eyes flutter closed and then open again. Just once.

'I think he can hear you!' Kaelen adds.

A single moving picture rises to the surface. Floats upward, through the chaos, through the wreckage of his mind, and lingers in front of me.

It's a picture of a girl. A young girl. She looks to be about the same age as Jane. Maybe five or six.

She jumps up and down giddily on a springy bed. Laughing and kicking the air between each bounce.

A deep voice booms out, frightening her. I recognize it immediately as Rio's. 'I hope you're not jumping on the bed again,' it warns.

The little girl immediately falls to her knees and clambers under the covers. Giggling quietly to herself. She looks innocently at the open doorway. At Rio. Her big brown eyes shining.

'No more monkeys jumping on the bed.' She sings the familiar tune. The one he taught her. It's her favourite.

His heart melts. And despite his earlier warning tone, he can't stay mad.

'It's way past your bedtime,' Rio says. Softly. Tenderly.

'One story,' the girl bargains.

Rio relents with a sigh. He can't say no to her. He never could.

'Fine,' he says. 'Which one?'

She flashes him a look that he knows all too well. He translates it as Don't be silly.

'Of course,' he answers, and he pulls a worn, tattered green book from a table near the bed.

As he brings it over to her, the title flashes into view.

The Giving Tree.

He sits down on the bed and the little girl snuggles up close to him, entwining her little body in his arm. He flips open the book and begins to read aloud.

'Once there was a tree . . .' He turns the page.

'Can I turn?' she asks hopefully.

'OK,' he allows. 'But remember, you have to be very careful. This book is older than I am.'

'That's old,' she says wisely.

He tickles her, pretending to be angry.

Her giggles echo around the pink bedroom, louder than they should. Until everything fades into white and her joyful high-pitched laughter is all I can hear.

The raucous, deafening noise returns an instant later, banging into my head. Followed quickly by the chaotic swirl of images.

I open my eyes and stare at Rio, wondering who that girl was. Wondering how much about this man I don't know. Probably everything.

There's a tugging familiarity about her.

Not as though I knew her, but as though I knew of her. One level removed from my recognition. Like a memory of a memory. A dream of a dream.

'What?' Kaelen asks, breaking into my thoughts. 'What did you see?'

But his voice is muffled through all the noise in my head. I pull my gaze away from Rio and look at Kaelen. His face is swimming. I can't seem to focus on it. I blink again and again but reality is no match for the anarchy that's playing in my mind, echoing off Rio's ruined brain.

'Disconnect me,' I tell him, cringing against the bombardment.

'But . . .' he argues.

'Just do it,' I tell him.

Reluctantly he taps the plastic screen and gradually the noise fades into nothing. I breathe a sigh of relief, relishing the silence. It takes me a moment to steady myself. I feel like I've been rotating in circles at two hundred miles per hour.

I hold my head in my hands and take deep breaths. When the room finally stops spinning and my surroundings start to make sense, I release my hands and look up again. Kaelen's bright aquamarine eyes settle into focus.

'I know,' I tell him quietly.

'You know what?'

I rise to my feet. 'I know where he hid the last two doses.'

63

HOME

The house feels different in person. In the memories that Zen stole for me, it felt larger somehow. More spacious. It's actually quite small and somewhat cramped.

It has a warm energy about it, though.

Somehow I always thought that it would feel cold and isolated. Like the prison cell where I spent too many long nights in 1609. As prison cells go, I suppose this one isn't terrible.

I appreciate that Rio attempted to make it nice for me. Homey.

I guess he felt it was the least he could do.

I know we're running out of time. The scab on my arm is already healing. I stare down at a small speck of black peeking through the corner of the wound. My skin is growing back. My DNA is doing its job. Re-creating the tracking device.

In a matter of minutes, the satellites will scan me.

An *alert* message will appear on someone's screen. In someone's head. On someone's radar. And it will all be over. Alixter will know that I'm here.

But I need to do this.

I walk slowly from room to room, grazing my fingertips over the walls, the wood panelling, every square inch of the furniture. Committing it to memory all over again.

I need them to be real. The memories I have of this place where I lived. Where I slept. Where I fell in love.

I need them to be mine.

Not stolen. Not triggered. Not transferred from a glowing green cube. But mine. Made in the moment. And stored directly in my head.

'Sera,' Kaelen warns from somewhere behind me, 'we don't have time for this. My tracker is already 25 per cent healed.'

I ignore him and keep walking. Down the hallway, turning the knob on the first door.

A bedroom. My bedroom.

I don't know how I know but I do. It just *feels* like mine.

The furnishings are sparse, reminding me of our quarters at the Pattinsons' house. There's a bed, a nightstand, a desk, a chair, and two lamps. A picture frame hangs above the bed, the image cycling through several different landscapes. Sunrises. Meadows. Seashores.

There's a window in one of the other walls. It looks into the yard. Green grass surrounded by the high concrete wall that Zen used to climb when he would come see me.

The comforter on the bed is a light lavender. I wonder if I picked it out. Or requested it. Was it my favourite colour? Because of my eyes?

Or was I not given a choice in that either?

'Sera!' Kaelen calls from the doorway. 'We need to move. NOW. Where is the antidote?'

With a sigh, I stand up and walk out of the bedroom, glancing back longingly. Part of me doesn't want to leave. Part of me wants to curl up on that bed and wait. Wait until Zen comes back. Wait until he climbs over that wall again. Wait until my life becomes simple once more.

But I know that can never happen.

I close the door and continue back up the hallway until I reach the living room. Kaelen stands in the middle, looking terribly out of place. He doesn't belong in this house. He doesn't belong in these memories.

This house is mine. Mine and Zen's. Mine and Rio's.

But he's here anyway. Reminding me of why we came. Why we risked everything to be here.

I snap to attention and make my way to the bookshelf on the far back wall of the room. I scan the titles rapidly, running my finger along the spines.

'Why are there so many?' Kaelen asks.

'Rio used to collect them.'

'Are you looking for one in particular?'

'Yes. *The Giving Tree*.' I don't look up. 'I remember seeing it in one of my memories of this place. It was on the bookshelf behind me when I was sitting on that couch.'

'Why do you think that it has anything to do with this?'

I decide not to tell Kaelen about the little girl in the memory. For some reason, it feels like a betrayal of Rio's trust. Like he shared that memory with me and only me. And I have a feeling if that one memory was capable of rising above all that messy chaos, then it was significant to him.

She was significant to him.

And if he wants to keep it a secret, then I will help him do that.

So instead, I just reply vaguely, 'It was important to Rio.'

Kaelen appears next to me and starts scanning the collection. There are over two hundred books on this shelf. My finger grazes past *A Wrinkle in Time*, the book I was reading when I first met Zen, and my heart flip-flops.

I glance down at my wrist. The thin black line is 50 per cent complete.

I force my eyes to move faster, whizzing past the titles until finally they flicker upon the familiar faded green spine. The white letters.

The Giving Tree, by Shel Silverstein.

I carefully pull it out and flip it open. I fan through every single page, taking in the text in a matter of seconds. Absorbing the story. Realizing instantly how very meaningful it is.

A tree who gave everything she had to the boy she loved.

Her apples, her branches, her leaves, her trunk, her shade.

Until there was almost nothing left for her to give.

I turn the final page, and there, in shallow compartments carved into the thick board of the book's back cover, are two tiny vials of sparkling, clear liquid.

Without speaking a word, I carefully remove each one and close the book, placing it back on the shelf.

Kaelen hurries over and stares in amazement at the two bottles of salvation in my hand.

'I can't believe how much trouble we've gone through just to find *that*,' he remarks.

I nod, releasing a small chuckle.

It is amazing how much power these two vials hold. Zen is sick. Dying. And this, this tiny thing in my hand, no more than few drops, is the only thing that will save him.

'What are you going to do with the other one?' Kaelen asks, leaning over and gazing into my hands.

'I don't know,' I admit. I guess I hadn't really thought that far ahead. 'Save it in case of emergencies, I suppose.'

'I'm rather insulted that you wouldn't think to give it to *me*.'

The voice comes from behind me, causing me to jump. The vials slip from my fingers and plummet towards the ground.

Kaelen moves fast. Faster than I've ever seen him move before. His hands are extended in front of him, cradling the tiny bottles before they even hit.

When I turn around I already know who I'll see.

His voice is ingrained in my memory. Burned into my skin. The fire may not have been able to leave a lasting scar, but his voice? His voice will stay with me forever.

He greets me with a cold, snake-like smile. 'Welcome home, Sera.'

64

PAIRED

Dr Jans Alixter sits in a chair that, similar to Rio's hospital bed, hovers just above the floor. Like it's floating magically in the air. I immediately notice how frail he looks. His skin is yellow and sallow. His eyes are sunken in. The same dark purple hues I saw on Zen's face shadow his as well.

And that's when I realize what the chair is for. He can't stand on his own. He's too ill.

'Alixter,' I breathe out his name, feeling the pure hatred on my tongue as it passes.

He's flanked on either side by two burly-looking guards. I don't recognize any of them as the men who came to find me in 2013. But then again, if they had the transession gene in them, they're probably sick, too. Maybe even dead.

'I see you've located what we've been looking for,' Alixter says, grinning at me and gesturing towards the two vials, which are still protectively cradled in Kaelen's hands.

I look at Kaelen, who is back on his feet. But for some reason, he won't meet my gaze.

'Kaelen.' Alixter turns his attention towards him. 'Thank you for bringing back our little lost merchandise here.'

He remains silent but his head bows in the slightest of nods.

'He didn't bring me back,' I argue. 'I came here willingly.'

'Are you quite *sure* about that?' Alixter counters, breaking into a ragged cough. One of his guards hands him a handkerchief. He wipes his mouth and the white cloth comes back speckled with blood.

'After all,' Alixter continues, clearing his throat, 'you're here. With the antidote. Just as I commanded.'

The truth is, I'm not sure. Not about anything.

How did Alixter know we were here? Our tracking devices haven't completely re-formed. Did Kaelen somehow get a message to him?

I turn to Kaelen and stretch out my hand. 'Kaelen,' I say gently, 'please give me the vials.'

But he doesn't move. He seems to be frozen. As though his body has stopped working completely.

'Of course I'm sure,' I lie, glaring spitefully at Alixter. 'He docsn't follow your orders any more. He follows his own.' I peer back at Kaelen, standing inches from me. 'Right?'

But again, he doesn't answer.

Alixter feigns pity. 'Awww . . . that's cute. Did you really think your charms would work on him like they did on poor Zen? You don't actually think I would let that happen, do you? That I wouldn't protect against that sort of thing when I had him created? Do you really think I'm *that* stupid, Sera?' Alixter makes a clicking sound with his tongue. 'Well, that's just offensive.'

'Kaelen,' I urge one more time, pronouncing his name gently, compassionately. I take a slow, cautious step towards him. He flinches and instinctively retreats. Like I'm some kind of dangerous criminal. Like he's actually *afraid* of me. I freeze. My heart is pounding.

This can't be happening.

I refuse to believe that this was just another manipulation. I refuse to believe that he tricked me.

I know him. I *felt* him. We felt each other. We shared something.

He *changed*.

I saw it in his eyes. I saw the shift. I simply can't bring myself to accept that it was all a lie. All part of an act. Part of his programming.

Alixter lets out a throaty, sinister laugh that sends a thousand tiny ripples down my back. 'See, that's just priceless,' he says, wheezing.

He pushes a flat button on the arm of his chair and it starts to glide smoothly towards us. I retreat, my back hitting the bookshelf.

'Kaelen,' Alixter says in an authoritative tone, 'congratulations. You've successfully completed your mission. I knew I could count on you. Now hand over the antidote.'

He reaches out, palm up, and waits.

I wait, too, my breath caught in my chest.

I watch Kaelen. His face twitches ever so subtly. The sign of that same internal battle being waged.

'Kaelen.' I repeat his name. 'Remember the submarine. Remember the kiss. Remember how that felt. Hold on to that. That is real. Whatever sensation you're experiencing right now, whatever power he holds over you, it's fake. Please, Kaelen. Just give me the vials.'

His face flinches again but he still won't look at me. His gaze is locked on Alixter, who's smirking smugly.

'Come on,' Alixter coaxes. 'Hand them over. This is an essential part of your mission.'

'Don't listen to him, Kaelen. Give them to me.'

Kaelen's foot rises, taking an indecisive step. I can't tell which way he's headed. Which side is going to win.

But as soon as his foot lands, I know I've lost.

He's headed directly towards Alixter. Away from me.

'NO!' I scream. I launch myself towards Kaelen, letting my legs carry me as fast as they were built to go. I land on top of his shoulder, but he easily shoves me off with a flick of his arm, sending me flying across the room. I hit the bookshelf hard, feeling it slam into my back. Several of Rio's precious antiques come pouring off the shelf, piling on top of me on the floor.

I look up to see Kaelen gently placing the vials in Alixter's outstretched hand.

But I can't let that happen. I can't let him have them. I rise to my feet again and sprint towards him. But his guards step forward, forming a protective circle around him.

Meanwhile, Kaelen handles me, thrusting an arm out. The heel of his hand connects with my face. I feel something crack. Blood splatters.

'Restrain her,' Alixter commands, coughing into his hand-kerchief.

Kaelen doesn't hesitate. He grabs me, pinning my hands behind my back. I manage to turn my head, meeting his gaze. I search for the other Kaelen. The one I know I saw once.

But he's gone.

A pair of cold, lifeless blue-green eyes stare back at me. As though that other version – the one I kissed, the one I slept against, the one I trusted – only existed in my imagination.

Maybe Alixter is right. Maybe I was naïve to think he was ever on my side. That I was ever able to break through to him. Maybe it really *was* a ploy to get me here. To get the cure.

I melt to the ground, blood trickling from my nose, into my

mouth. Kaelen's hands stay pinned around mine. I can feel that heat passing between us. That energy. I wonder if he feels it, too. I wonder if he ever did.

'It's a shame,' Alixter says, shaking one of the vials. 'I have no doubt Dr Maxxer did intend for these remaining two doses to be given to her lover and her son. But Rio clearly has no use for it now. And Zen . . . well, I'm afraid he's just unlucky.'

Zen?

Son?

Alixter's words drift through my mind as I struggle to find a place where they make sense. Where they fit.

Zen is Maxxer's son?

Maxxer is Zen's mother?

Is that what she meant when she told Rio to find him? Was she talking about Zen?

No. That can't be.

Why wouldn't he tell me?

Every time I tried to bring up Maxxer or anything relating to Diotech Zen would shut down, switch off, close me out. He refused to talk about the past, wanted me to forget it, wanted to pretend it didn't exist.

I remember something he said to me on the morning before he got sick, when he came to find me outside. I asked him if he missed his former life.

'I had nothing there,' he replied. 'Except a mother who cared more about her latest research project than her own family.'

Was he really talking about Maxxer?

Was that how he got the idea for us to run away into the past? Was that how he even knew about the transession gene? Because his mother invented it?

If all of this is true, then Maxxer honestly did think she was protecting him by leaving Rio those doses. That's what she was trying to explain to me last night, when I was hysterical. She told me to trust her.

She thought Rio was going to find him and save him.

She had no idea Rio was nearly dead.

And what about Rio? Why *didn't* he come find Zen earlier? Why didn't he heed Maxxer's request?

The answer comes to me before the question has even had time to fully sink in to my brain.

He did.

He came to 2013. He was looking for me. He found me in that dilapidated barn. He was trying to warn me. And then Zen showed up with the gun and took me away. And Rio never got the chance to accomplish what he'd set out to accomplish.

'Zen didn't tell you, did he?' Alixter says, clearly reading the bewilderment on my face.

I don't reply. Although I'm sure my expression gives it away.

Alixter sighs. 'Ah, well, I can't say I blame him. I would be pretty upset, too, if my mother disappeared from my life without a trace. I guess it's no surprise that he found his solace in something . . . *else.*' His gaze drips down my entire body as that nauseatingly creepy smile returns to his lips.

I think about the boy climbing over that concrete wall outside the window, searching for a distraction, for consolation. And finding me.

Apparently he needed me as much as I needed him.

Now more than ever.

But I can't see how I can help him now.

'So,' Alixter says, gliding his chair past the guards and glancing between me and Kaelen. 'You *kissed,* huh?'

I refuse to look at him. I just sit there, my breath coming out in heavy, angry rasps.

'While your true love lay dying, you kissed another man?'

I bite my lip, breaking the skin. Blood trickles out, joining the flood from my nose. It'll only be a matter of time before both wounds heal, making my face whole again. But doing nothing to mend this gaping gash in my heart.

He claps his hands together and lets out another one of his sadistic laughs, which quickly morphs into a cough. 'You have no *idea* how happy that makes me!'

I close my eyes tight, trying to block out the sound of his grating voice.

'This calls for a celebration!' he announces jubilantly.

When I don't respond, he touches another button and his hovering chair moves closer. He leans forward and lifts my chin with his fingertip. His icy-cold hand sends a shiver through me.

'Don't you see what this means, dear Sera?'

I remain silent. And despite the angle of my head, I still refuse to meet his eye. I focus, instead, on a distant corner of the room.

'It means,' he goes on, unfazed by my lack of enthusiasm, 'that my latest experiment was a grand success!'

'What experiment?' This is the first time Kaelen has spoken since Alixter appeared in the room.

Alixter glances up at him. 'I'm so glad you asked!' He releases my chin and glides a few feet backwards. 'You see,' he begins pompously, 'you, Kaelen, are very special, as you know. But more important, you are very special to *Sera*.'

Reluctantly, I drag my gaze up to look at Alixter.

'I was quite moved by your devotion to Zen,' Alixter goes on. 'Well, *moved* is the wrong word. Let's say, *impressed*. And I thought to myself, how many people would simply die for that kind of connection with someone? Or rather, how many people would *pay* for that kind of connection. And a light bulb went off in my head. I thought, what if we could package it?'

I'm pretty sure I'm going to throw up.

'We'd always had plans to create Kaelen at some point.' He grins down at me. 'An Adam to your Eve, so to speak. But after that whole debacle in the cave and seeing how far you would go in the name of *love* –' he pronounces the word with the same degree of disgust that I remember from that night – 'I knew that I had to go one step further. I had to truly make him an Adam to your Eve. Because I realized the only way I was going to overcome that unyielding devotion you have to Zen – that power he has over you – was to manufacture an even stronger force to counteract it.'

My eyes go wide with horror as I think about that spark. That magic electricity that passes between Kaelen and me every time we touch. That's passing between us right now.

Alixter smiles down at me, appreciating my response. 'That's right. I created Kaelen to be your scientifically perfected match. Essentially the same blueprint we used to create you, we used to create Kaelen. Making a few crucial adjustments, of course.' He winks.

'I'm like you . . . *Only better.*'

'But at the very core,' he goes on, 'you two are the same. You are literally soul mates. Created from the same source.'

He folds his hands in his lap, looking pleased with himself. 'And judging by how fast you moved on from Zen to Kaelen, I'd say it was a success.'

I glare up at him. But Alixter is undaunted. 'So you see, no matter what you do, no matter how hard you try, you will *never* be able to resist him. And he will never be able to resist you. It's in your DNA.'

He sighs, like he's just completed a hard day's work. 'I imagine we can have this fully tested and ready to go to market in less than a year. What a popular product that will be. Soul Mate in a Box!' He cocks his head, thinking. 'The name might need some work.'

The guards snicker.

I'm furious. Fuming. Livid. Although I'm not sure why I should be surprised. I've been manipulated this whole time. So why should this be any different.

In a strange way, it is like my love for Zen.

I wasn't given a choice in that either.

But I'm momentarily distracted from my anger when I feel Kaelen's hands start to slip against my wrists. I can't be sure, but I think his grasp is actually loosening.

Is it because he's simply so shocked by this news that he's losing focus? Or is it because he, too, feels angry for being manipulated? Could he possibly be remembering all the other truths I told him about Alixter? Or is he doing it on purpose? Offering me a chance to escape.

I decide it's not worth waiting around to find out the reason, what matters is that I take advantage of the situation.

I eye the two vials in Alixter's hands. About five feet away from me. Without giving myself much time to think or debate, I duck and roll to the ground, slipping right through Kaelen's grasp. Then in a lightning-fast blur, before the guards have had even a second to react, I jump to my feet, land in a crouch, and snatch the doses from Alixter's hand. In another streak of motion, I've arrived in the far corner of the living room, holding them both over my head, one in each hand, pinched between my fingers.

Kaelen, who has been suspiciously slow to react, takes a step towards me. The guards are also ready to pounce.

I squeeze the vials tighter. 'Don't,' I tell them all. 'One squeeze and there will be no more antidote.' I look pointedly at Alixter. 'For anyone.'

Alixter gives a nod to Kaelen and he backs off, retreating that one step he took.

'Now,' I say, my voice coming out nasal and stuffy due to

my rapidly healing nose, 'we're going to do things my way.'

Alixter grits his teeth together. 'What do you want, Sera?'

I sigh. It's a good question. A question I haven't yet figured out how to answer. What *do* I want? At one point, I thought that all I wanted was to escape with Zen. Leave this world behind and forget everything that happened inside the walls of this house.

But now that I've done that – and failed – I realize how impossible that is.

No matter how far we run, no matter how many years back we go, Alixter will never stop looking for me. He'll never stop sending better, faster, stronger, more advanced agents to find me. And I'll never be able to stop looking over my shoulder. I'll never be able to fight the nightmares and fears that one wrong move will destroy everything.

How many more people have to die or become brain-dead or fall terminally ill for me? How many more people have to suffer so that I can live outside of this cage?

I thought that was the answer. I thought that running away, continually outmanoeuvring them, was how I could prove that they didn't own me. That I was not just one of their scientific miracles. That I was my *own* creation.

Me.

But I was wrong.

I feel Lulu, Jane's doll, bulging in my pocket, reminding me of the words Jane said to me so many centuries ago.

'*If she wasn't real, then she wouldn't have been able to run away from the bad people. That was a good choice.*'

If that's true, if humanity really is just our ability to choose, then this is finally the chance to prove mine.

This is the last thing I have to give.

'I want to stop running,' I tell Alixter. The truth feels amazing. 'And I want Zen to live a long, happy life.'

He cocks an eyebrow. 'You can't have both. I will always find you, Seraphina. No matter where you go.'

'Yes, I can.'

And with that, I transfer both antidotes to one hand and slowly unravel the long silver chain of my locket from around my wrist. Holding it in the other hand, I hoist the necklace high over my head, letting it drip down my now fully healed wrist. Then I elevate the two vials as well, dangling them precariously in the air.

Zen will never be safe as long as I am near him. As long as I love him.

And that makes my choice easy.

With an exhale, I release one hand, allowing the contents to fall to the floor. Then I raise my foot and with all my strength, thrust it downward. There's a horrible crunching sound as the object crushes and breaks and shatters, becoming useless.

I lift my shoe, revealing the destroyed locket underneath. The key to my escape.

The heart that will forever remain broken. For as long as I live.

65

DECEIVED

'Save Zen,' I tell Alixter. 'Take one of these doses, send Kaelen back, and cure him. Then you can have the other and I will stay here. I won't run any more. I won't try to escape. I am yours.'

Alixter narrows his cold blue eyes, clearly not trusting me. Clearly thinking this is another trick. Like the one I pulled on him last time we were in this position. In the cave.

But this time I'm not bluffing. I'm not playing games.

This is the only place I will ever fit in. The only place where I can't hurt anyone.

'I'll go,' Kaelen says, stepping forward again. 'I'll administer the antidote.'

He holds his hand out to me.

I lock on to his gaze, feeling my face warm from the connection. And although his eyes have turned back to that cold, lifeless bluish green – a sparkle with no soul – when he stares at me, I see a flash of life. I see a hint of the other Kaelen. That same glint that I saw on the submarine. When he became some-one else. Someone not controlled by a mad scientist.

But someone real.

And yet, once again, there's a nagging voice in my head questioning everything. Wondering if now I'm the one who's being tricked. Kaelen has already shown his allegiance to Alixter and Diotech. He's already chosen Alixter over me. So again, how can I be sure that he's not deceiving me? That he was ever the person I thought he was?

How can I know that if I hand these vials over, Kaelen will actually do as he says? How can I know he won't just turn around and give them both right to Alixter?

The reality is, I can't.

I never will.

Kaelen holds my gaze tightly and offers me the slightest of nods. His lips barely move as he speaks to me in that low whis-per that only I can hear. 'Trust me,' he says.

And I realize that I have to.

I nod and slowly slip the two vials into his outstretched fin-gers. He backs away, out of my reach. There's nothing I can do now.

Out of the corner of my eye, I see Alixter smile, looking triumphant.

'Very good,' he says. 'Now, Kaelen, hand them over to me.'

But Kaelen doesn't move. Once again, he's trapped between us, his face twitching as the debate is waged under his skin.

'Kaelen,' Alixter repeats, his voice full of warning and bal-ancing on the edge of rage. 'Hand them over NOW.'

I don't speak. I know my words won't do anything. Either Kaelen has it in him to defy Alixter or he doesn't. My voice won't change that. He looks to me, his eyes searching for help. Searching for guidance.

All I can offer him at this point is a quiet smile. Then I close my eyes and wait.

Alixter is getting angrier and angrier. He's on the verge of screaming. 'Agent, this is a direct order. Hand over the antidote or there will be consequences.'

I keep my eyes shut tight. If Kaelen betrays me, I don't want to see it. I just hope that they'll deactivate me quickly and I'll wake up with no memory of this moment. Then at least I won't have to live with the betrayal for long.

I can hear my heart pounding in my ears. I can feel the sweat dripping cold down my back.

There's a loud commotion. A crash. My eyes snap open and I see another pile of books on the ground and an empty shelf above it.

I assume they must have already been hanging off the edge from my earlier scuffle and that gravity has just now completed its task, but for some reason, I don't remember crashing into that particular shelf.

My confusion, however, comes screeching to a halt when I see Kaelen slowly approaching Alixter's hovering chair. The two full vials of liquid salvation resting in his outstretched palm.

And all my hopes for Zen's future come tumbling to the ground as suddenly and helplessly as Rio's treasured collection of books.

66

AMITY

I collapse in a heap next to my crushed necklace, the weight of Kaelen's ultimate betrayal so heavy on me, I fear I may never be able to stand up straight again. I will be doomed to walk the earth crooked. Hunched over. Forever.

I took a chance. I handed over my faith. And it was destroyed.

Now all I can do is wait.

Wait until it's over.

Until they erase everything. And I won't have to imagine Zen's dying face again.

I can start new. I can start fresh.

Alixter is cackling, speaking words that I can't hear. Or won't hear.

I glance up and allow myself one final look at Kaelen, the man who betrayed me. I want to see if there's even an ounce of remorse in his eyes. He catches my gaze and I see his lips move ever so slightly again. Whispering one secret syllable that could never be heard by anyone else but me.

'Watch.'

He runs his fingertip across his own forehead. And that's when I feel it. The pressure in my head. The influx of a memory. The energy pulsing through my receptors. I allow my eyes to drift closed. Alixter's gloating laughter fades into the background as I float into Kaelen's world. Merging my consciousness with his. Seeing through his eyes. Remembering through his mind.

He appears in a dark, quiet room. The soft beeping of machines is the only sound.

Cody, who sits next to the bed looking hopeless and forlorn, startles when he hears Kaelen's gentle footfall. He looks up.

'Where is Sera?' Cody asks accusingly.

Kaelen doesn't reply. Instead, he steps forward and uncurls his hand, revealing the tiny vial with the clear liquid inside.

'Is that it?' Cody stares wide-eyed at it.

Kaelen nods. 'Please administer it immediately.' His voice is distant. Cold. A shuddering reminder of his old self.

Cody stares somewhat distrustfully at him, unsure whether to do as he says. Unsure whether to trust him without me.

Kaelen reads his distrust well. 'There is no other option. Administer it or he will die.'

Cody considers, and then finally rises from his chair, takes the vial, and walks to Zen's bedside. He opens the cap, stabs a long needle into the liquid, drawing it out. Then he inserts it into Zen's IV.

'Now,' Kaelen says, 'give me something clear.'

Cody's forehead furrows. 'What?'

'A clear liquid,' Kaelen demands impatiently. 'Anything.'

Cody riffles through one of the nearby boxes, removing an unmarked bottle. He proffers it to Kaelen, who quickly goes to work refilling the empty vial with its contents and securing the cap.

And then . . .

A subtle beeping sound snags their attention. They turn. Watching the screen in silence. Expecting nothing and everything at the same time.

Slowly but surely, the numbers begin to rise. Zen's heart rate begins to stabilize.

Cody's face lights up. He looks from Kaelen to Zen, beaming. 'What did it do?'

'It is a genetic repressor.'

The light on Cody's face immediately dims. He understands. 'You mean . . .'

'He will never be able to leave this time,' Kaelen verifies.

Cody's shoulders slouch as he gazes back sorrowfully at Zen. 'He's stuck here.'

'That is correct.'

'And Sera?' Cody asks hopefully.

Kaelen's gaze flickers momentarily to Zen and his thoughts turn fuzzy. Indecipherable. His emotions are jumbled. The memory becomes cloudy and vague. Despite how fresh it is.

'Sera will never be returning.' There's an almost imperceptible crack in his voice.

The sound of fabric rustling snags Kaelen's attention and he and Cody both turn towards the bed.

Zen's face twists and pulls. The first sign of movement in days. His leg twitches slightly under the sheet. And then, miraculously, he opens his eyes.

The memory drizzles to an end. As soon as my gaze lands on the fallen books on the floor, I understand. They were a diversion. Kaelen knocked them over on purpose. He had to distract Alixter and the guards long enough to slip into the past and return less than a second later without anyone noticing.

He had to make sure Alixter still believed he was on his side.

That he was incorruptible.

The joy I feel in this moment is like nothing I've ever felt before. Zen is alive. He will be OK. He will live long and, hopefully, find happiness.

I whisper a quiet thank-you to Kaelen.

Then I take three purposeful strides towards one of Alixter's guards and lift my chin high in the air. Exposing my neck. Offering myself freely.

I don't speak. There is nothing left to say. I've made my choice.

My life belongs to him now.

It takes Alixter a few stunned moments to react. But then he snaps his fingers and points towards me. The guard closest to me responds, wielding his Modifier as he approaches.

I don't run. I don't move. I breathe in. I breathe out. The air comes easily. Without a fight.

It feels good not to fight.

The cold metal prongs jab against my skin, just at the base of my ear. And I welcome the darkness.

67

GREYED

The table is cold and hard against my bare back, causing me to shiver in the chilly room. I open my eyes and gaze into the blinding white light above my head.

I try to move, but it is pointless. My wrists and ankles are cuffed to the table with large, steel clamps. My head is restrained by a strip of metal stretching across my forehead, keeping me from struggling.

A man in a lab coat appears above me. His eyes are grey and emotionless. Like a robot's. I wonder if he is one.

My throat is parched and scratchy, making it impossible for me to speak. But it doesn't matter. I don't need to ask what is happening.

I knew when I agreed to stay that this was what my future held.

They will rebuild my brain.

They will make me docile. Compliant. Agreeable.

And they will take everything.

But I know it's the only way I will be able to survive. The only way I will be able to live with my decision.

When Zen is completely erased from my memories. When there is nothing left to remind me.

He is safe. And that's all I need to know before he is stolen forever.

'Don't worry,' the man reassures me in a completely un-reassuring voice. 'This won't hurt. And you won't remember a thing.'

That's what I'm hoping for.

I watch him prepare a long, sharp needle. Drawing up an unknown substance.

I feel the sharp prick as the needle settles into my arm. The mysterious fluid works fast. Clouding over everything in my vision. Turning my world to a dreary, colourless grey.

I focus my thoughts on Zen's face. His vibrant, deep brown eyes. His perfect crooked smile. The soft urgency of his lips against mine. The way one strand of his hair would curl down his forehead when it got wet.

The gentle warmth of his touch on my forehead as he whispers in my ear.

'Yes. Always yes.'

I hold on to all of that. Clenching it tightly as my mind is infiltrated. Gripping it desperately as my thoughts are seized. Keeping him alive in my memory for as long as I humanly can.

ACKNOWLEDGMENTS

Well, well, here we are again. Another book finished. Another chance to offer my UNdying gratitude to all the amazing people who help me navigate this crazy journey called book publishing.

Author Disclaimer: If there's anyone I did not include herein, I take no responsibility. Diotech has been erasing my memories for years.

Anyway . . .

As always, thanks to the bubbly, energetic, supersavvy crew at Macmillan Children's, who put together some pretty darn spectacular-looking books and who shout about them tirelessly from the rooftops. Janine O'Malley, the editor of my words, calmer of my fears, and champion of my work. The ever-elegant and impressively efficient prom queens of publicity: Mary Van Akin (the better half of Jessary!), Molly Brouillette (we'll always have Boston!), Kate Lied (I miss you tons!), Court-ney Griffin (ain't no party like a Tampa party!), and Allison Verost (proud new mama!). Thanks to my BFF, Caitlin Sweeny, to whom I will be forever indebted for introducing me to *New Girl* and whose name I finally learned how to spell. (I triple-checked it this time!) The *fierce* and fantastic Stephanie McKinley, Elizabeth Fithian, Ksenia Winnicki, and Kathryn Little, who market my books like it's their job (oh . . . wait). Seriously though, you guys are the best! Thanks to Lauren Burniac, who manages to make the paperbacks even more exciting than the hardcovers! Also thanks to the extraordinary Angus Killick, who always makes me laugh; the dynamic Jean Feiwel, whose publishing prowess makes me *swoon*; Joy Peskin, whom I adore beyond words; and Simon Boughton, who always has my back. This book would be a sloppy mess if it weren't for the copy-editing talents of Chandra Wohleber. Thank you! The biggest, squishiest hugs and gratitude to Elizabeth Clark for another amazing, eye-catching, heart-melting cover! And thanks to Mark Von Bargen and the awesome sales team, who work so incredibly hard to get my books on the shelves.

Also thanks to the foreign publishers who bring my work to life worldwide, especially Polly Nolan, Catherine Alport, Katharine Smales, Amy Lines, and Claire Creek in the UK.

Bill Contardi, my agent, deserves heaps and heaps of gratitude for guiding me through the makings of a trilogy, as well as Marianne Merola, who makes selling foreign rights look easy (even though I know it isn't).

Thanks to all the teachers, librarians, and booksellers who have invited me in with open arms and supported my books around the country, especially Courtney Saldana, Allison Tran, Damon Larson, Crystal Perkins, Dalene Kolb, Cathy Berner, Maryelizabeth Hart, Mel Barnes, Shane Pangburn, Stephanie Squicciarini, Amy Oelkers, Julie Poling, Jade Corn, Cori Ashley, and Michael Johnson.

The BLOGGERS! Oh, the bloggers. How you rock my world. How you rock it hard! Thank you for accepting me as a sci-fi author and for your endless enthusiasm about Sera and Zen and the Unremembered universe. I couldn't do this without you guys constantly cheering me on and begging for more. THANK YOU!

My author tribe: Jennifer Bosworth, Jessica Khoury, Marie

Lu, JR Johansson, Brodi Ashton, Morgan Matson, Gennifer Albin, Ann Aguirre, Alyson Noël, Anna Banks, Emmy Laybourne, Leigh Bardugo, Brad Gottfred, Carolina Munhóz, Raphael Draccon, Carol Tanzman, Debra Driza, Elizabeth Fama, Marissa Meyer, Lauren Kate, Gretchen McNeil, Lish McBride, Claudia Grey, Victoria Scott, Mary Pearson, and Robin Reul. You are each more important to me than you know! Thank you for being sounding boards, listeners, beta readers, collaborators, promoters, tour mates, and friends.

And a special thanks goes to Michelle Levy. Only she knows why . . . for now.

Keith Wrightson of Yale University, thank you for the crash course in seventeenth-century society, criminal proceedings, and family life. And, Dan Starer, thanks for your invaluable research assistance.

Brittany Carlson, I'm proud to call you a companion. Nicki Hart, you continue to impress and amaze.

Thanks to Honey Pants, my adorable puppy. It's impossible to have a bad day when you're around.

And of course, thanks to my wonderful, if at times quirky, family: Terra Brody, Laura Brody, and Michael Brody. I'm so proud to come from such a talented gene pool.

Charlie Fink, there are no words. There is only love. And gratitude. And forever.

Hmm. Is that it? I swear there's someone I'm forgetting . . .

Just kidding. I could never, *ever* forget you. The reader of books and the holder of this one in particular. Ask me if I'm grateful for you. Go ahead, ask. I have only one answer: 'Yes. Always yes.'